The Wheel Trilogy

Includes the following books:
The Big Wheel
Take the Helm
Battle for the Cure

Susan Larned Womble

The Wheel Trilogy

Susan Larned Womble

Published by Page Pond Press

DEDICATION

For all readers everywhere who would like to read a trilogy to its conclusion—Here you are.

Also

For my children, Thomas and Amanda
Yes, their names were used for characters in the book
I figure that's one of the perks of writing ☺

ACKNOWLEDGMENTS

I would like to acknowledge my family, my husband, Gregg , my daily helper and supporter, my children Thomas and Amanda, my reason for living (see dedication), my father, Tommy Larned, my tireless cheerleader, and my sister, Judi Taylor, my other self. I would also like to thank my writing critique group: Hannah Mahler, Rhett DeVane, Peggy Kassess, and Donna Meredith. They help with every aspect of the writing process and keep me on track. I would also like to thank my St. George retreat-writing buddies, especially our fearless leader, Adrian Fogelin and our organizer, Perky Granger for all of their guidance and fun times every year. I would also like to thank the teachers of Hohenfels, Germany along with the people of Bavaria and Europe for the wonderful experience of learning about their culture as I travelled throughout Europe.

Chapter 1

I'm an "Uncounted." Two people, my mother and sister, are all I have communicated with since forever. Can't even talk to the Mercs. Not that I'd want to. They collect our harvest once a year, but all I see is a glimpse of an ankle or an arm. It's hard to get a good look when you're hiding.

This moonlit evening, the giant Ferris wheel casts an ominous shadow beckoning to me as I gaze out my cracked window. Been waiting all year for this. No, longer than that.

Left over from a long forgotten carnival that blew through town many years ago, the rusty, dilapidated wheel remains workable, albeit tarnished and sluggish. It operates twice a year. On tally day, it's full of Mercs, but the night before, it runs empty. It's a free ride and I want it.

Anticipating this ride has kept me going. A couple of minutes to pretend I'm free. I've climbed the massive wheel before just to sit, something I'll never forget. That spectacular view and the exhilaration that came with it are what drive me to want more. This year, I can ride if I hurry. Tomorrow will be too late.

Tonight, I'll take the gamble, knowing the wheel could start up any time. It's dangerous, but that's the best part. I'm the good girl, always doing exactly what I'm told. I follow all the rules. Not by choice, but to please my mother and sister. And to survive, there's always that. Thinking about the ride makes it hard for me to catch my breath.

Sneaking out of the house is not going to be easy; my older sister, Gretel, is a light sleeper. Assigning herself the role of my protector, Gretel is a creature of habit. She hangs her coat and places her shoes in exactly the same spot every night. Everything my sister does is accurate and perfect. Not a hair out of place, the complete opposite of me. It isn't fair to have such a flawless sibling.

Gretel moves on the raggedy blanket-covered pad on the floor, but quickly settles. One of her medical books cradled under her arm shifts for a moment and almost slips out before it finally rests. Relief! I may succeed with the plan, after all. Good idea that I pretended to doze off in the chair tonight or this adventure would be over before it started. Tiptoeing across the room in stocking feet, I manage to get out without waking Gretel. I creep by my slumbering mother in the outer room of our two-chambered shack, winding my way around the shabby sofa and the scraped table toward the exit.

I open the door to the outside just enough to slip through and cautiously close it behind. The first wave of brisk Bavarian air pricks my face like a hundred needles, but that initial feeling quickly subsides and the excitement of the impending quest returns. I make a quick mental note to remember to put a hat, gloves, coat, and shoes outside if I ever try this again. It's freezing, but I can't risk going back in. I'm committed now.

The Ferris wheel has been on our farm as long as I can remember. I love it, even though it's rusty, tattered, and the color of a rotten banana peel. Its uniqueness makes it special.

No way of knowing how many times it will go around tonight. It's different every year. Once it only twirled twice, but last year the count was ten revolutions. Tonight, I hope for another ten. Shivering with anticipation, I allow myself to dream of even more. Dashing quickly through the grass covered by the melting snow, I arrive at the cracked concrete below the wheel. My toes are numb, so I bare hand the lowest spoke.

"Ouch!" I jerk my fingers away, reacting to its ice-cold touch. Maneuvering rapidly, I grasp the next rung and strategically position my feet along the way. Maybe the cold won't hurt as much if I climb it as fast as I can.

Feverishly, I navigate the frosted rickety metal of the long abandoned Ferris wheel to claim the highest seat in the land. Good fortune is smiling; the wheel doesn't start mid-climb. Maybe it's meant to be. Sighing with relief, I slump into the top chair, causing it to sway. Now, I wait.

From my perch, I see hints of grass peeking out of the shimmering snow and watch the hills roll into the evening darkness. I'm overcome by a tranquil sense of freedom. My thrilled heart beats and my face flushes. It's the most control I've ever felt.

Surveying the moonlit land, I spy the familiar: the horse corral two kilometers northeast of our farm, home of Hershey, the chocolate-colored steed I feed illegally. Sometimes, you just want to have something that belongs to only you. That's what Hershey is to me, although in reality the animal is not really mine. But it's nice to pretend.

The workable solar panel farm that is controlled by the Mercs sits on the southeast quadrant. Every year on the day before tally day, they use the solar energy to remote test the wheel, passenger free.

Creaking movement interrupts my thoughts as the Ferris wheel slowly begins its descent. Just made it! Ecstasy surges through me! Complete joy as I soar through the air. I spread my arms and imagine myself fledging my way out of this world. In my new reality, I am a person and not an Uncounted. In my world, I matter.

"Paisley!" Gretel's voice jolts me back into reality.

Gretel stands at the foot of the enormous rotating machine. Should have been quieter. Now, Miss Perfect will say over and over again how unsafe, how dangerous, how immature I am. For once, why can't Gretel be spontaneous and have some fun?

Although shabbily dressed, Gretel is perfectly coiffed. Doesn't make sense. How does she do that with her clothes in such disrepair?

Patiently standing by the wheel's passing cars and clutching my tattered coat and boots, Gretel is outfitted warmly. Of course, Miss Perfect wore the right clothes for the weather. Wouldn't expect anything less.

Gretel cups her hand around her mouth and yells, "What are you doing? Get off now. Jump out when you hit bottom, it'll be slow enough."

Not this time. I'm not following the rules. This time, I am taking the ride.

"No, you climb in. It'll be fun." As the wheel passes at the bottom, decelerating for a slight moment, I open the rusty, creaking carriage door. "Hurry, before you miss it."

With a groan, Gretel reluctantly complies and I snag her arm with the crook of my elbow, dragging her in.

"Paisley, what were you think—" Gretel falls back hard in the chair, the door clangs shut, and we ascend.

No choice now. I give my sister a tight hug, drawing out my plea. "Pl—ea—se. Just this once. Besides, we can't get off now. We have to ride."

I try to appease her by shoving my arms into the threadbare coat and then pulling on the worn out boots to warm my numb toes. Hopefully this will make my sister happy or, at the very least, less oppositional.

It works for the moment. Gretel quiets and the wheel whisks us higher and higher. Singing softly a song I remember from long ago, I breathe in the world and count: one, two, three, four, five—Five times around before the wheel stops, leaving us dangling at the highest point. Five trips of freedom. I smile. Five trips are more than most people get.

Immediately, I am drawn back into reality by Gretel's snapping fingers and scolding. "What were you thinking? Mom is going to be mad at you." She sighs. "Both of us now. You're lucky you weren't killed. You're supposed to be getting ready to hide. You know tomorrow's tally day." Taking a breath, she asks, "What was that song you were singing?"

I nod slightly and smile again. "It's from when we were kids. ' Circle up, Circle down.'"

"I've never heard that tune or heard those words."

No songs left in Gretel's head, just rules. So sad. "You just forgot." I point to the sky. "Look how high we are."

"*I know,*" Gretel shifts in the chair. "We're at the top. How do we get down?" Peering over the edge, she shakes her head. "Why did I listen to you?"

I guess I showed her, I'm in charge now. I relax and recline back in the chair enjoying the moment. "Don't worry. I'll show you how in a minute." I want to feel the freedom just a bit longer so I spread my arms wide. "Isn't this great? You can see everything from up here." The moon and stars illuminate the hills glistening with snow. It's beautiful.

Gretel grabs at me. "Quit making the chair swing! We're going to fall."

By gripping the handrail of the car and leaning up, Gretel causes the chair to move even more.

"You better sit still." I giggle, shift, and the chair rocks again. "It swings when we move."

Both of us fall back in the corroded passenger car and it rocks back and forth like the pendulum on the black forest cuckoo clock that keeps time in our living room. The night fills with rusty creaking sounds; then after a moment or two, nothing but serene silence is left.

Finally, Gretel whispers, "Be serious. The Mercs might come early. We *need* to get off and you *need* to hide."

Always a killjoy. Somber to a fault. "If you say so." I succumb, stand, and grip the rusty beam. My eyes scan the field one last time. Is that movement? I point to a figure thrashing about, approximately four hundred meters away in the northeast corner of our farm. "What's that? Do you see it? Something's moving over there. It's large. It might be a deer or—" I dangle by both hands on the bar like a monkey swinging loose. "—a horse."

"Quit hanging like that. You're going to fall. Besides, it's probably the Mercs. We need to get off before we get caught."

I challenge. "*You first.*"

"Okay." Gretel lets out a broken sigh. "It really is a long way to the bottom."

Gretel scared? Never knew Gretel to be afraid of anything. But, what was there to be afraid of on the farm? We work all day long. No fun. Gretel is going to try to get down without my help though; it's her nature. She is the one who gives orders, not the one who takes them.

I watch as Gretel swings herself out, grasping the metal tightly with her hands, balancing tiptoed on the rusty prong of the wheel below and on the outside of the wobbly passenger chair. Shaking at first, and then steadying herself, Gretel barks, "We need to hurry!"

Never seen Gretel this out of sorts. It's nice to see the imperfect human side of her.

More movement from the field below. "Look!" I reach out, steadying my sister's arm with mine on the steel cross bar. "I think it's an animal, maybe caught in a trap."

"We can't—" Gretel starts.

Not this time, Miss Bossy. I'm controlling this now. "I'll go first. Watch me." I descend halfway gracefully, weaving in and out of the metal spokes with exact precision like an experienced spider dancing down its web, spinning one last strand to complete its lair. I love this. It's fun. Wish my sister could enjoy it with me.

I stop and yell to my sibling, "Take your time, Gretel. The wheel won't go around again tonight." I pause a moment, remembering to add, "Or at least it never has before."

"Sure, the wheel starting up again. What's one more thing to worry about?" The sarcasm drips out of my sister's mouth. She holds onto a corroded prong with one hand and grasps at air with the other a few times before hitting her mark.

"Careful, Gretel." I scramble back up beside her to help her snag another rusty spine and take the next step.

She seems hesitant so I tap her shoulder. "You can do it."

"I wouldn't have to, if you hadn't got on this wheel in the middle of the night. It's reckless. If I fall, it's your fault."

A guilt trip? Now? What would happen if I weren't here? Gretel might not ever get down. I could leave her. But sisters, they help each other. It's probably a law somewhere.

I give step-by-step verbal commands. "Hand to the left, grab the rail above. Now drop your hand to the beam on the right and scrunch up so you can make the next step. Make sure your foot is steady before moving." I watch her progress. "You're doing it! Take your time."

Gretel white-knuckles each rung of the rusty apparatus and tiptoes, mimicking my movements. "I'm doing it, but I still don't like it."

"Afraid of heights. Didn't know that about you, Sis." She ignores my comment.

As I wait for Gretel to catch up, I look toward the forest again. "We should help that animal."

Out of breath, Gretel stops for a brief moment and pleads, "Paisley, what can we do? It could be a trap. We don't have time for this."

She's wrong. We have time. Life isn't always lining up everything perfectly and working dawn to dusk for a harvest we can't keep. At least I hope that's not what life's all about.

This animal deserves a chance. I shimmy the rest of the way down the antiquated giant, jump to the ground, and run toward the ensnared animal.

Turning around for a glimpse, I see Gretel flailing the rest of the way, hitting the ground hard, and yelling. "Paisley, stop!"

Not listening this time. I run to the edge of the forest with Gretel close behind. The animal whimpers. How can she ignore the cry for help?

"Don't you hear that?" I turn, and face my sister. "C'mon. The Mercs won't be here for hours. We can save this creature. It's in pain." I don't wait to hear if she agrees, I take off running again.

"I don't like this. I guess we could use the meat though." Gretel sprints after me. "If it dies, we're going to eat it."

"What?" I stop immediately. "Eat it?"

Gretel says, "We need the food."

I one-arm hug my sister. She's right. Fresh meat is a great prize for us. I need to make sure she understands. "We'll eat it, but only if it's dead, and only if it's not—well, I'm not going to eat Hershey. Greverstand."

"Of course not. Greverstand!" Gretel repeats. "But let's hurry."

I like it when we use our own language.

Although we try to be quiet, our feet rustle in the leaves and Gretel says, "We're making too much noise."

I'm not familiar with this particular area. It's dark and even though I don't want to admit it, it might be dangerous being out here on the eve of tally day. Too late to be cautious now.

Gretel finally concedes, "We might as well hurry and get this over with."

We sprint together, reaching a clearing in the forest with an embankment of yellow canola flowers. The bright field shines like a jar of captured lightning bugs, illuminating with a pulse of canary gold. What a beautiful meadow. Love the way the blossoms shine like a blanket of stars. It would be so nice if we could relax and enjoy it. But tonight is not that night.

As we clomp through the flowers, yellow dust colors the night sky and rains flecks of gold. Slowing down, Gretel cautions, "It's too bright. The Mercs could see us now even if they're not looking for us. We *really* should go back."

We're too close to turn back now. "We're right at it. We can't leave it suffering." I squat, hiding behind the embankment and pull Gretel beside me. I put my finger to my lips signaling for her to be quiet.

We both sit, silent for a moment. The animal whimpers again. I can't wait any longer so I lay flat on my belly and crawl to edge of the flowers, dragging Gretel as I go since she has a death grip hold of my leg.

"I just want to see it." I plead. "Please, let go for a minute! We might be able to save it."

I yank away from Gretel hard just as she releases her grip. I fall forward, rolling down the hill, head over feet, yelping the entire way. At the bottom, I abruptly stop when I clang into the trap. A muffled moan rings into the night and I spin my head around to face the captured one.

"Paisley!" I hear Gretel hiss from above. "Are you hurt?"

"Hush!" I whisper back over my shoulder, keeping my eyes trained on the struggling captive. "I was wrong. It's not an animal!"

Chapter 2

Moonlight shards speckle the terrain like a crystal prism breaking through the cloaked darkness. It's a person. No mistaking it now. Writhing in agony, the filthy teenage boy struggles, pulling at his bloodied foot, and begging with his eyes full of pain for me to help free him.

A real life boy. Don't remember the last time I saw one this close up. Memories of my dad long ago have faded. No glimpses of bits and pieces of a person, this is the whole human. He doesn't look real. He looks different than I imagined he would. Maybe it's the mud or the fact that he is crouching and in pain. Not scary looking at all. I freeze momentarily and then take a step toward him.

Gretel scrambles down the hill. "Stop! We don't know who he is!"

Isn't she the one who has been studying medicine for as long as I can remember? Here's a real live person who can use some of that knowledge. He's hurt and needs help. He's caught in a trap, how dangerous could he be? "Don't be silly. We have to help him. You're the wannabe doctor. Don't you have to help him? Isn't it an oath or something?"

"That's true. I guess I have to try." Gretel creeps up beside the grimy teenager and steps in front of me. "Let me." Gretel tugs a little on the trap. "You're not a Merc, are you?" The captured one shakes his head violently and yanks harder to free his imprisoned limb.

"Maybe he doesn't understand us." I squat down beside him. "What if we pull it apart together?"

Gretel analyzes his confinement. "Stop squirming and we'll try to free you. Maybe there's a release."

"I understand you." The boy studies Gretel's face. "I remember you. Careful!" He winces as Gretel shifts the metal claw around his foot, looking for a release. "You live on the Ferris Wheel farm, right?" His face softens and he touches Gretel's hand. "You're Gretel. I remember your smile."

"What?" Gretel grins quickly. Her face reddens as she concentrates on the snare. "Paisley, get some pieces of wood. We need to hold this apart."

Someone who remembers Gretel from before the virus. He can tell me what Gretel was like then. Did she always line up her shoes? Did she always want to be a doctor? She's acting strange, not at all like herself.

Wonder why? Stories, there have to be stories. I barely remember before the quarantine. Just a few flashes here and there that mostly make no sense.

I locate three small branches nearby and give one to each of us. Tree limbs in hand, we move our pieces back and forth until the trap is stretched wide enough for him to pull free.

Gretel scrutinizes his bloodied ankle. "We need something to wrap around it, to stop the bleeding."

He tears the sleeve off his shirt and hands it to Gretel. "Will this do?"

Gretel gently wraps the material around his ankle. "It'll do for now. We'll have to clean it out and change the dressing soon."

He shoves on his ripped sneaker. "We gotta get out of here. The Mercs are close. I've heard them. I know a cave. It's this way." He pushes to his feet and limps a few steps.

"Just a minute." Gretel holds her hand up. "You're free now. Remember to change the bandage. We need to get back to our farm."

The boy almost falls. "I appreciate the help. Don't worry. I can get there on my own. Be careful going back, you two."

The stories, I have to hear the stories. I shove my shoulder underneath his arm holding him up. "He's not going to make it there without help. Are we really just going to leave him to crawl?"

Gretel lets out an exasperated sigh. "Just far enough to get him to cover then we go back to the farm. Greverstand."

"Greverstand. And by the way, you're not my mother."

Gretel shoves her shoulder under his other arm. "Since when are you so into helping other people?"

I ask, "Since when do we have a chance to help other people?"

Colt stiffens. "Quiet!" He motions to the ground and says in a low voice. "Wipe up our footprints and hide!" He whispers, "Mercs are coming."

I quickly brush our footprints with my boot and we stumble to middle of the canola field and lay flat.

A voice shouts, "Thought I heard something."

The sound of clanging metal breaks though the silence of the night. "Nothing here, but a broken trap." Another voice yells. "No footsteps anywhere. You probably heard an animal."

The first voice again. "Yeah, you're right. Let's get back to doing our jobs. Boss won't wait forever."

The voices trail off, but we don't move.

Chapter 3

In a few moments, Gretel pipes in. "Told you the Mercs were out here, but you *had* to come." We stand and pull Colt to his feet.

I challenge, "You were the one being loud. You know we should help him."

The boy leans on us. "Can you two stop arguing? We need to move. We *all* need to hide. Be quiet. The Mercs are going to hear you."

He's right. We nod and even though he stands a head above us, we help him hobble quickly across the empty field. The moon, so beautiful and bright, is now the enemy, threatening to give away our location. The forest is eerily silent with the painfully obvious exception of our gasping breaths and the snap of leaves crushing under our every step. Periodically, we stop and listen for any enemy movement, and hearing none, we venture a little farther.

I'm tired, probably because I trekked up and down the Ferris wheel, ran through the forest, and now am lugging this full-grown boy. It's an adventure, but not quite what I imagined. I am relieved when he finally signals the arrival of our destination by motioning toward some brush. He directs us to pull the overgrown greenery to reveal a shrub covered door, which we open and quickly enter.

Discovering a new place is exciting, anything different is better. I only remember our farm and its surroundings. Although at night, Mother would regale us with stories of times before that were vividly descriptive with excitement intertwined, but this is different, I'm living the adventure not just hearing about it.

The boy picks up matches by the door, easily lights a kerosene lantern located at the entrance and illuminates the contents of our new haven. Boxes, some closed and some half opened are scattered about, full of canned and jarred foods. Huge water jugs rest on the dirt floor. It smells musty like the barn back on the farm when it's been closed up for the winter. This place must have a history associated with it.

The boy hobbles toward the center and we three plop down on the cavern floor. For a few minutes, all is quiet.

Hesitantly, the boy extends a hand towards Gretel. "Your mother taught me English before the quarantine. Remember, I'm Colt. I came to your house many times."

What was Gretel like before this quarantine and all the work sucked the life out of her? Was she fun?

Gretel places a small box under Colt's bloodied foot, pauses to shake his hand quickly before returning to her task. "We need to keep this elevated." She cocks her head and looks him up and down. "Colt? Yes, I *do* remember you from the classes Mom had after school. You've grown." She pauses. "It's been a long time. How old are you now?"

"Seventeen. I'll be eighteen in two months, I think. Sometimes it's hard to keep up. Remember when we used to hide out back and play princess. I was always your prince."

Gretel flushes. "I remember how much Mom loved teaching those classes. I'm eighteen now so we were around six or seven then." Gretel twists her hair, sighs, and stares blankly toward the top of the cave. "Seems like a lifetime ago."

Gretel at seven. No way. It seems like she was born grown.

My feet are in need of some breathing so I take off my boots and empty the dirt and debris on the floor. "I just turned fifteen, we had a party. Well, it was just Gretel, mom, and me but we had a party just the same. Had bread and everything. It wasn't perfect though." I frown. "No meat. Meat would have been nice."

Gretel kicks at my shoes. "Put your shoes back on! There's food in here, Paisley. Quit trashing up the place."

Acting like my mother again. Has she looked around? I glare at her. "Trash! The floor is dirt!"

Colt drags a box over beside him, reaches into it, pulls out a dusty jar, and breaks the sealed metal lid. Pulling out the goods, he eats rapidly. "Pears! Never know what to expect. Want some?" He passes the jar to me. "Paisley, right? How do you know Gretel?"

I greedily take the jar and slurp the pears, losing one to the floor. I quickly pick it up, brush it off a little, and gobble it down. "I'm Gretel's sister."

Colt turns to Gretel. "I didn't even know you had a sister. I don't remember her coming to the classes."

"Too young." Gretel shifts uncomfortably and picks up another jar, studying it. "Where did these come from, and more importantly, how old are they?"

The fruit is delicious. Is she really going to say not to eat it?

"They're collected to help the Uncounted or anyone who needs food." Colt turns one of the boxes around to reveal a circle with a line through it. "See the mark."

"I'm an Uncounted. So they're collected for me." I run my finger over the mark, a capital "U" with a circle around it and a line drawn diagonally through the center. "I've never seen that mark."

Gretel glares at me. "I'm sure that's not what he meant. He probably means the people who have no one else. You have us. You have someone."

What's she so mad about? Why all the hiding if I'm not an Uncounted? Sometimes Gretel makes no sense. I don't care who the food is for, I'm going to eat it until I can't eat anymore.

Gretel opens another jar and tastes the contents. "Apples! Mmmm delicious." She waves her arm around the cave. "What is this place?"

Colt finishes his jar and opens another. "Part of a series of caves—an underground system—where the Uncounted or anyone else who needs it can hide." He surveys the area. "I am supposed to supply this one soon. Thought it would have less in it. From the boxes still here, looks like no one has been here lately."

I sniff the stale air. It smells like my boots do when I've run in them without socks and my feet get all sweaty before I take them off. "It stinks!"

Gretel rolls her eyes.

Colt chuckles at my last comment, which seems to bother Gretel. He says, "I'm guessing you've been hiding for a while."

Gretel replies quickly, "When Dad died, we were supposed to send her with the Mercs, but we just hid her and told them she ran away. We didn't want to send her to the camps. It just didn't feel right. She belonged with us."

"Marked?" Colt asks.

I lift my sleeve to reveal bare arms. "No, and quit talking about me like I'm not here."

Gretel exposes a burned mark on her forearm, close to her wrist, of a crude outline of a local plant, edelweiss, with the number 22. "Marked forever, showing I've been counted and where I'm from. Did you get the edelweiss brand too?"

Colt turns his arm backwards. Above his elbow on the back of his upper arm, he uncovers a distorted edelweiss with what looks like the number 15. "Needless to say, I didn't want to be branded. When I saw that red-hot piece of iron coming toward me, I jerked and this is what happened. I didn't get away completely. They let me pass every year since our farm is number 15. They just tallied our farm yesterday, so we have a group of Uncounted that showed up last night who will be hiding with us for a few days. I'll remember to tell them this cave is fully stocked."

Gretel shoots up. "Gosh, we need to get back. We tally today. I have to be there to be counted. Paisley has to hide, and I need to help Mom get the harvest ready." She glances at Colt. "I promise to come back after the Mercs are gone and help you home. I won't leave you here."

Colt smiles, touching Gretel's arm again. "I know you won't. I want to see you again. Maybe your mom could sneak us some lessons." He grins and Gretel makes a high noise I've never heard. She is acting weird. Maybe she's sick or something.

I open another jar of fruit, stuff my mouth with its contents, and mumble, "Why can't I stay here while you're gone? When you get back, we'll both help Colt. It'll save me from having to find a place to hide. What better hiding place than this?"

Colt puts his latest jar down. "That's a good idea. Gretel, if you're caught, they'll just take you back to your farm. You have a mark and you are supposed to be in this area. You can say you were doing something and lost track of time. With the brand, you'd be safe, but if Paisley gets caught?" He smiles at Gretel again. "Besides, I know if Paisley is with me, I'll see you again."

Staying out in a cave for a whole night, now that would be an adventure. The cave is quiet for a few moments.

Finally, Gretel looks at Colt and then back to me. "You might be right, besides it's so late now. I guess we have no choice, but I don't like it. I'm supposed to look out for Paisley." With that, she hugs me and taps Colt's shoulder lightly. "I'll be back as soon as I can. Don't let her eat them all. She'll get sick. You probably wouldn't like her getting sick in this cave."

Mothering again, will it ever stop?

"Don't worry. I'll watch her. I'll take care of her for you." Colt nods and throws an arm around me, interrupting my slurping of my latest discovery. "We'll be here. See you when you get back."

"I don't know what time they'll come. If it's late, I probably won't make it back today. But if I'm not back in two days, then come looking for me because I couldn't get away." She raps his head. "If that happens, you're in charge of making sure Paisley gets home."

"No problem. We'll talk more then."

Gretel hugs me tight and says, "Be careful. You *must* stay hidden."

It's just one night. What's the big deal?

Gretel squeezes Colt's arm. "I'm serious. Take care of her."

He nods and she disappears out of the hidden cave door, into the dark night. What a drama queen!

Food, there is an unlimited supply of food in here. Yum!

"Slow down, Paisley." Colt takes a jar out of my hand. "You heard

15

your sister, and if you throw up in here, it'll stink worse, and we can't go outside until the Mercs are gone."

Ut-oh! Is he taking up where Gretel left off? What's he supposed to be now, my big brother? I quickly finish the piece of apple hanging halfway out of my mouth. Of course he did have a point; if I vomited, it would stink and smell worse than it does now. Don't think I could handle that. "I guess you're right. It's just I can't remember the last time I could eat and eat." I lick the last of the syrup off my lips with my tongue. "We have to portion eat at home."

"Us, too." Colt hobbles over to another box, drags out a couple of blankets, and places them on different sides of the cave. "Let's set up a place to sleep."

"Fine." I unfold the blanket. "What'll we do after that?"

"What do you mean?" Colt smiles. "We don't have to do anything."

"I can't remember a time when I didn't have a chore to do. It's one thing after another at the farm. It's hard to make harvest." I flatten out the quilt and sit on top of it. "Tell me a story. What do you remember about the quarantine? I don't remember it at all."

Colt sits on his quilt. "Nobody knew what was going on for a while. The first time we realized something was wrong was when the military base called all of its troops back."

I interrupt him. "Troops? There's a military base? Is it close?"

I saw a book once about the military. It looked like a rulebook. I wish I had paid more attention. My mother told me about the army and uniforms so I know a little about them. Mother said they are the "good guys." Guess that makes the Mercs the "bad guys." They seem bad to me, especially since I have to hide from them every year.

"Yeah, it was close." Colt waves his hand toward one side of the cave. "About twenty or so kilometers to the east. I can't believe that Gretel or your mother didn't tell you about the base. I'm pretty sure your mother worked on the base."

"They don't tell me much about before. Maybe they think it'll scare me. I think they're glad I don't remember much." I cross my legs.

"Maybe so. I guess I shouldn't be the one to tell you then. It should be your mom."

"They're never going to tell me anything. I'm fifteen and they still treat me like a baby. Like a little doll that might break. Do you know what that's like? I can handle hearing the stories. It might help me to understand. Tell me. I promise I won't tell them you did."

"Okay." He lets out a long sigh. "You have a right to know any way. We first heard about the virus from the soldiers." He faces me. "We knew

16

about it because of all the people dying. That's when we were ordered to stay on our farms to prevent more contamination."

"Is the military still here?"

"The military hasn't used the base in a long time. The Mercs have taken it over."

"Where did the military people go?"

"Not sure. I can't remember exactly when the troops pulled out. Helicopters flew in and out for days. The Mercs came soon after, taking control of the power grid and forcing us to give up pretty much all of our harvest."

I point to Colt's arm. "Is that when everyone was branded?"

Colt shakes his head. "No, that happened later. I can't believe they haven't told you any of this."

"They tell me little bits. I know about the brands. Just didn't know when they started. And the Counted and Uncounted, is that when that started?"

Colt takes off his shoe. "Soon after, some kind of population control to distribute people evenly. The Mercs brought fliers when they collected harvest to let us know. They took a lot that year. Only one child per adult. You can only replace yourself at your farm. You're lucky your dad was still alive during the first census or you would have been taken before we set up the hiding. Did you become an Uncounted when your Dad died?"

"I guess so, I'm not sure?" I squirm on the quilt, first sitting up, and then rolling over on my stomach. "Do you know where they take the Uncounted?"

Colt unwraps his ankle. "Not really. I've heard they take everyone to a big farm near Passau. You might have visited the town before the virus, but I doubt you remember it. It's a beautiful town with three big rivers. At least it used to be beautiful. Rumor is they put the Uncounted to work or send them on big ships."

I prop up on the quilt, cupping my face in my hands. "To where?"

Colt pours water over his ankle. "Don't know. One time I heard they sent them to America. I think my foot stopped bleeding."

"Good." I tap my fingers on my face. "Is America a good place or a bad place?"

Colt rolls over on his back stretching his legs out. "Who knows? It probably used to be a good place, just like Bavaria used to be. Now, we all just try to survive. Maybe no good places are left."

"That's sad."

Colt scoots to the side of the cave, leaning against it as he rests on his quilt bunching up part of it to elevate his ankle. "Maybe the virus is contained now. How would we know?"

Not really the stories I had hoped to hear. I like the stories Mother tells me at night. Good stories about fun, amusement parks, cotton candy, big heart cookies with writing on them, candied apples, and Oktoberfest. She told great stories about Oktoberfest. What fun that must have been! These stories of Colt's are just depressing. I could have lived my whole life without hearing these tales.

Colt puts his arms behind his head. "It's nice to talk to someone different." He lowers his voice, and he takes a breath.

Not having too much fun now. It's boring on the farm, but I always felt safe. Just had to stay hidden every once in a while. Gretel was right to want to get home, what a little spoiled brat I had been not to listen. I am going to make it up to her tomorrow.

"Look Paisley, I'm just frustrated from having been caught in the trap. I need to be home to help and here I am doing nothing. I feel bad, so I'm venting. Don't worry."

Tomorrow, on the farm, I'll try to forget about all of this. I didn't realize how happy I was. I roll over with my back to him. "I think I'll go to sleep now."

"Sure." Colt puts out the light.

Before long, calm steady breathing lulls me to sleep.

The next morning, I wake up squirming and shake Colt awake. "Where do we go pee?"

Colt laughs a little. "I'll show you. There's a pot in the back behind some boxes next to a hole. When you finish, throw it out the hole, and it'll trickle down and out into the river that runs next to this cave. Not too sanitary, but it's better than it being in here with us."

"It sure is!" What an understatement! I locate the pot. "Don't look!"

After I take care of my business, I think of a question as I straighten my outfit. "This is embarrassing, but what if I have to go?" I can feel my face turn a deep shade of red.

He says, "Don't be embarrassed. We all have to do that. We'll have to go out for that. I'll scout first. You have to do that now?"

There are advantages to a family of all females living in the same place. It is uncomfortable here.

"Not—*Now*." I need to take my mind off it so I run around in a small circle. "But with all of this eating, I'll have to go sometime."

I wish it were time to go home. This adventure is not fun at all now. I should have gone with Gretel, hope it's not long now.

Colt wraps his ankle again. It looks better now. "Let's find

18

something to do. Want to see what I do when I come to the cave?"

I nod. He pulls a pad of paper and a pencil off a box.

"I take inventory, so we know what's used down here and when we need to restock it." He points to the paper. "See? How about if we take inventory of what is in the cave, get organized, and clean it up?"

"I actually like to write." It is the truth. "I guess that'll be okay. I have nothing else better to do."

We work together, Colt unpacking and repacking boxes, calling out the contents as I record.

"Your mother was a good teacher. Did she teach you to read and write?"

"Yes, we have class all the time."

Seems silly how much I used to gripe about those classes and whine to Mother. I'll pay attention more in class from now on. All I want now is to get back home as soon as possible.

At lunch, we stop, eat, and discuss the crops that grow on our respective farms. I decide to ask more questions. I probably won't ever see him again. I might as well find out as much as I can. The stories are not easy to hear, but Mother always said that knowing our history is important to plan for the future.

"What else do you remember about V-day?" I prod and slurp the rest of the apples left in a jar.

Colt picks up a water jug. "V-day?"

I turn up the jar, letting the dollops of syrup dribble in my mouth. "Mom called it V-day for virus day. I don't know what you call it."

Colt swallows a gulp of water out of the jug. "We didn't call it anything. We just called it *before* and *after*."

"Interesting." I wrap my arms around my legs. "I don't remember anything about that day."

Colt sits the jug down. "I was young too, but I do recollect everyone being scared and losing an uncle to the virus. It was horrible. There was a rash on his face and in his mouth, and he couldn't eat. He died after two days. We thought we would all catch it, but we were lucky."

Can't do another round of these kinds of stories. I pick up the water jug. "New rule: Nice stories." I take a swig. "Nice stories make me happy."

"Nice stories." Colt chuckles. "I'll try to think of some."

Guess he couldn't because he is quiet. So sad. I wish Mom were here to tell Colt some of her Oktoberfest stories. That would cheer him up, it would cheer me up.

I decide to tell him a good story. "I rode the Ferris wheel last night." I smile as I think about it.

19

"Really, it's been forever since I thought about that Ferris wheel. I remember riding it a long time ago. It was fun." His face lights up as he talks.

I entertain him with the story of the ride blow-by-blow. He smiles the whole time. Happy stories are better.

I'm in a better mood now. We work diligently for the rest of the day, stopping once for Colt to scout out an area to go to the bathroom. When night comes, we have a complete list of supplies.

"I'm turning the lantern off now." Colt reaches for the lamp. "Paisley, it's good to know exactly what's in this cave. It could help the Uncounted if we have to send them here."

"I like good things."

"Me, too." He pats me on the head.

"Quit patting me like I'm a dog."

He stops. "Gretel should be here tomorrow. It'll be two days. I'm glad I got to meet you and to spend this time together. You tell a good story."

"Yeah, it's been just Gretel and Mom for as long as I can remember. I forget there are other people in the world. I'll kind of miss you. We should name this cave."

Colt laughs. "What should we name it?"

I know exactly what to name it. I don't hesitate. "Orlando."

Colt turns off the light. "Why?"

"My mom has a special box where she keeps important papers. One day when she was looking for something, one of the papers fell out. It was a picture of a castle and all of the people in the picture looked so happy. Written across the bottom of the picture, it said, 'Visit Orlando Where Dreams Come True.' This cave is like a dream. This has been an adventure. Something outside the farm, so my dream came true."

"Orlando, I like it." He settles on his quilt. "Good night Paisley."

The next morning there is still no word from Gretel. We try to convince each other at different times that Gretel will come any minute with an adventurous story, but as the afternoon sun peaks straight up in the sky, we realize that something unplanned has happened.

That afternoon, Colt gathers two bags of divided jarred goods. "This is for you and your family. I'm going to take you home today. We need to leave now so we can make it before dark. My foot is healed enough to walk."

I tie the bag onto my shoulder. "Yes, it's time to go home. It won't be hard to find, it's the one with the big Ferris wheel." I force a smile. "You can see it from a long way off."

It's a little over an hour's walk to my farm. No sign of the Mercs and the forest is deserted. We pass by Hershey grazing in the pasture and I stop for a moment to give him a bite of the jarred apples. "This is my horse, Hershey. He's not really my horse, but I claim him and sneak food to him. I rode him once. It was wonderful." As we travel, I regale Colt with my story of the ride; compare it to riding the Ferris wheel and how free I felt doing both. Closer to our farm, my steps quicken.

Finally, I spy home and run full throttle throwing open my front door with Colt trotting close behind.

"Mom!" I sprint from room to room yelling. "Mom! Gretel! Where are you?"

No answer. I finally make my way back to the front door. "They aren't here. Must be outside. Maybe you can look out back, and I'll run out to the fields. Don't leave until I find them. Okay?" There is an eerie silence and a mood that hangs. I stop and look at him. He hasn't moved and his face is flushed.

"Are you okay, Colt?"

"Paisley, you better sit down." Colt holds a wadded up letter and envelope in his hand; I notice the scribbling on the envelope. I recognize the writing. The number 22 is scrawled across the bottom.

"That's Gretel's handwriting."

"It's for you. The Mercs were here. Your family's been taken."

Chapter 4

"**T**aken?" What is he talking about? I grab at the letter and the envelope falls. "What does it say?"

How could something this bad happen in a couple of nights?

Colt picks the envelope off the floor. "It's a message for you. Paisley, calm down. I'll read it to you."

The nerve. This is not Colt's house.

"It's mine! Why did you read it? It's not yours!" I fall angrily onto the shabby cushioned sofa, if you could still call it a sofa, as a few tufts of cotton fly in the air. Jutting my chin out defiantly, I shout, "I can't believe you read my message!" I stubbornly cross my arms and grunt, hugging the lumpy, fabric-covered sofa pillow. Long devoid of its design, the raveling seams barely hold its contents. I'm too upset to read it anyway. Might as well hear it now, what does it matter if he's read it. "What does it say?"

He reads: *Paisley—Mercs took us- Be back as soon as we can —Stay with Colt—Be safe —G*

Heaving the pillow across the room, I stand, snatch the letter out of Colt's hands, and proceed to read it aloud again. There has to be more, another clue. Come on paper, more. Closing my eyes tight, I attempt to coax additional information by flipping it back and forth, repeatedly. Giving up, I ask, "What are we going to do now?"

"Paisley, I have to go back to my farm. I don't want to leave you here so you need to come with me." He takes a breath. "Paisley, did you hear me?" He snaps his fingers in front of my face, I don't move. He yells. "We need to go now, there's nothing for you here."

They're gone. What if they never make it back? I can't think that way. I have to stop thinking that way.

The room we're standing in houses three mismatched chests of drawers, two have chipped white and pink paint in various levels of disrepair and the third in decent shape is made of ornate wood. Colt rummages through a few of the drawers and opens the rest, tossing the contents on the floor and pilfering through them. "Paisley! Do you have any food or weapons stashed anywhere?"

Who is this person? Is he going to rob my house now? My family has been taken and all he can think about is to steal something?

"Weapons? Do you plan on shooting someone?" I face him, stone-faced.

"Of course not. Help me, we need to go." He dumps out another drawer. "Paisley, if we're going to find your mom and sister, we need to get to my farm. My dad will help us. Do you hear me?"

I mumble. "Get them back? Could we get them back?"

"Of course!" Colt screams.

I rock back and forth like a rag-doll and then Colt shakes me. "Get a grip! Help me!"

I want Gretel or Mother here. I blankly nod. "Yes. We'll get them back."

After all, I am fifteen now. A flash of a story mother told me about rites of passage alights in my mind. The girl in that story was fifteen. I'm fifteen and my quest is to save my family. Calmness and a sense of determination take over.

I purse my lips and look defiantly at him. "I know what we need."

Leading him to the back room, I point to a closet. He opens it, pulls back clothes to uncover a chest occupied by two knives and three crudely made shanks.

"This is a start." He squats, grabs them all, and looks at me. "Backpacks?"

In my house, I know where everything is. I rummage through the closet and emerge with two packs; he stuffs the weapons in his and stands. "What about stashed food or clean clothes? You need to change. Do you have any warmer clothes? Better shoes? You're wearing pajamas! We might be gone for a while."

What's he talking about? I gaze down at my filthy pajama top. "You're right. I'll show you some things Mom has stashed in her room behind the dresser as soon as I change." I disappear into the back room to change into clean jeans, t-shirt, jacket, and sneakers.

When I return, he follows me down a corridor full of pictures with smiling faces adorning the walls of a past far removed. "What great pictures. Bavaria was a wonderful place to live before the virus. I remember that time." He points to a smiling Gretel. "Look how happy she is." His fingers move to a tall man. "This is your dad, right? I vaguely remember him. He was always gone when I came over."

It hurts to think about my family, but I nod. "Yes, see he is standing in front of our car." A smiling man, clothed in a suit, is pictured in front of a small blue automobile, scraping snow off the windshield. "That same car is out in the front yard. It hasn't moved in years. No gas." I pause for a minute to gaze at the picture before I start down the hall again. "We have to hurry. We can't let them get too far ahead of us."

23

Colt runs his finger over three of the framed memories. "You're not in any of the pictures, Paisley. Is that because you're an Uncounted?"

"Probably. There's another album hidden back here with some other stuff we might be able to use." I open the door. The room is filled with a small bed full of pink and green ragged pillows decades old. "Over here." I carefully pull back the trifold-mirrored dresser to reveal a hidden cubbyhole and reach in. "I was forbidden to look in this secret place. I saw my mom looking at the pictures one time." I hand him a photo book. The album's front is cracked and the pages very delicate. "Be careful. It's about to tear apart."

"We'll look for a few seconds, but then we need to go." Colt quickly and carefully looks at a couple of pages of the album. "Still, no pictures of you."

"Really? I thought they'd be there. Mom said they lost most of our pictures and these were the only ones they could save. I want to see a picture from when I was little."

"I'm sure they're in here, but we don't have time to look right now. We'll do it later. Put the album in your pack." Colt reaches in the cubbyhole and pulls out a box, along with a few trinkets including a watch. "There's a knife and a cigar box. We'll take them both."

I cradle the box. "Mom's treasures. I'll take them to her. That'll make her happy." I slide the box, knife, and a watch into my pack and stand. "Let me get something for Gretel." I search Gretel's and my area in the room to retrieve her pink and black polka-dotted ribbon. "It's for her hair, it's her favorite." I unzip my pack and put the ribbon in.

Colt waves his hands in a circular motion, signaling for me to hurry. "Food? As quick as possible, we don't know how much of a head start they have on us."

"In here." I lead him into the kitchen part of the shack. The non-working appliances, chipped with missing handles and burner lids, serve as storage now. I yank the stove out, to uncover a similar hidden cubbyhole, and pull out bread, dried meat, fruits, and vegetables. "We're in luck. We just put the extras up from the harvest. Everything's fresh. The bread won't last long, but the other stuff will be good for as long as we can keep it, and here's a couple of canteens. We'll keep them full of water from the streams." I twirl around. "Oh." I stop right in front of him. "I just remembered we also have a stash in a storage area hidden under a hay bale in the back yard by the barn at the foot of the hill. We'll stop and pick up some more things, and you can put that place on the list for the Uncounted to hide. We might use that hiding place once we find Gretel and Mom. That's where I hide on tally day."

I realize that if I had been hiding there when the Mercs came, I would be here all by myself. I'm happy that I'm not alone and I smile at Colt. It is nice to have someone.

"Good idea. Planning ahead." He taps me on the back with his hand. "Don't worry. I plan on protecting you. I'll be your big brother."

Great! Another protector. "Protecting me? I'm protecting you. Who saved you from the trap?" The nerve.

"Of course, you're right." He nods. "And I thank you for that."

Besides, he's the hurt one or did he forget? I point to his ankle to remind him. "By the way, how's your ankle?"

"Fine." He picks up his foot and twirls it around. "It's still a little tender, but nothing I can't handle."

"Guess it's time to go then." I follow him out, shut the front door, walk to the Ferris wheel, and sigh. "I've never been without my family." I'm afraid. I look back at the house, and kick the bottom passenger car of the Ferris wheel, causing it to rock. "Ferris wheel, I'll be back and so will Gretel and Mom." I catch a glimpse of Colt, widening his eyes. "Don't worry, I'm not crazy, I just need to say good-bye and nobody's here, so the Ferris wheel will have to do."

Colt walks beside me. "I didn't say anything." He points to the hill by the barn. "Is that where the food is hidden?"

"Yes." I guide him through a couple of bundles of old, rusty, rolled up fence wire and a few workable plows. We continue around one sedentary plow and the aforementioned-pictured blue car covered with years of vegetation. We pass a rusty combine and tractor with flat tires arriving at the corner of my farm. I lift a few bales of hay close to the river, uncovering an underground supply cave full of harvest food. "Mom saves this food for the hidden people who come in the middle of the night. I've never seen them, but I guess they are probably other Uncounteds." I smile at him. "Guess we were all looking out for the Uncounted. Sad, we didn't know about each other, we could have worked together."

He nods. "True. I think that is why the Mercs kept us separated."

"That's over, we're working together now." I open my bulging knapsack, full of the mementos, food, and libations from home, and add the newfound treasures. I close it and heave the sack on my shoulder. "My family had no clue that they were to be taken. We need to find them quickly."

"Definitely. We also need to find out what's going on." Colt fills his knapsack already half-full of bread and food from the pantry with a few more jars of food and some boxed milk. "I didn't even know there were any more of these in existence. I won't ask where you got this milk."

25

"Mom said the others brought it, and she didn't ask either."

Closing his sack, Colt remarks, "Mine's full, Can't carry anymore. Let's go."

I stop for a moment. "Wait." I turn toward the Ferris wheel, gallantly guarding my family's farm and sigh. I wipe a tear from my cheek with the back of my hand. "I'm ready to go now."

Colt walks silently beside me, not saying a word.

The trek to farm 15 takes a lot longer than we anticipate as we navigate rivers, steep inclines, and stomp through left over snow banks. Branches and brush hinder our pace on the less traveled trail choice. The untouched path is eerily quiet with only animal tracks peppering the area. Fortunately, there is no evidence of Mercs. It is an unexpected surprise to see a flock of sheep wandering aimlessly.

"We're here." Reaching the outskirts of farm 15, Colt spies a couple of untethered horses, grazing on the sprouts of green grass breaking through the thawed ground. "Slow down a minute." He looks toward the farmhouse. "These horses shouldn't be here. Something's not right."

How could he tell something isn't right? The whole day, in fact the last few days have been off—not right. There stand three horses and one I know.

"Hershey!" My horse. I cannot hide my excitement. "How did you escape?" The horse nudges its way over to me, and I obligingly offer a dried apple from my sack.

Colt leads the horses and me to a forest cover. "You stay here with the horses. I'll go scout it out, just to make sure. Be back in a few minutes."

I hug Hershey quickly, and then release the horse's neck. "What should I do if you don't come back?"

Colt holds both of my shoulders. "I promise I'll be back." He turns and leaves.

As I plop down beside Hershey, I'm a little afraid and I call after him. "That's exactly what Gretel said."

At least I have my horse with me. I guess if the worse happens, I can ride out of here. Hershey nuzzles me, as I stretch out on the soft grass. "Hershey, why can't you be my horse for real?"

Limbs break and the sounds of crunching movement alert me. "Back so soon?" I mumble before turning around. I gasp as I come face to face with a dirt-faced boy outfitted in muddied clothes. He is taller than I am, wiry, but muscular, with an angular chin. His clothing is a uniform of sorts, an opened jacket, navy colored with brass buttons decorating the front and the sleeves. His belt holds up striped trousers with a worn stained white gauze shirt tucked in. A billed hat covers his head except for a few strands of curly dark hair that peek through at the sides and the back. Is he part of Colt's family? Could be a Merc, could be an Uncounted, or could be something else entirely. He is so muddied, I can't tell.

Startled, I ask, "Who are you? Are you from farm 15?"

"No, I'm guarding the place. I have orders to gather runaway horses?" Despite the fact that he looks about Colt's age, he sounds younger.

"Orders?"

"Yes, I'm part of the Merc regiment of Bavaria. See?" He pulls up his sleeve to reveal a burned mark on his forearm; it's an "M," the identifying stamp of the Mercs. "I need to see your mark."

Mark? I freeze as he grabs my arm and yanks back my sleeve exposing my bare upper limb.

"An Uncounted!" He yelps with delight. "My lucky day! I'm going to get a big reward for finding you, girl."

Chapter 5

The Merc holds tightly onto me with one arm and releases the rope that is clasped to his belt loop with his unfettered hand.

"Let me go!" I vehemently struggle like a saddled unbroken stallion to free myself.

Forcing me to the ground with his arm planted powerfully at my throat, he wraps the freed rope around my wrists one time before his body is hit hard and thrust two or three meters away, liberating me.

I immediately stop screaming and unbind my hands, looking up at the giant hovering creature. "Hershey!" I know why I love that horse now.

The horse shifts to tower over the downed Merc in a menacing manner using its hoof to pin him down by the tails of his shirt.

"Get that horse off of me! Call him off!"

Why would I do that? One minute, he has me imprisoned and the next minute I'm just going to let him go? I guess Mercs are not very smart. Let's see how he likes being tied up. I grab the rope and rush to Hershey, allowing the animal to nuzzle me for a few seconds before binding the boy's hands and feet.

I'm not helpless; I can take care of myself. I just proved it. I smile at Hershey. Of course, my steed gave me a little help. "That ought to hold him."

I hear a rustling of the leaves as Colt bolts beside me out of breath. "I heard you screaming!"

"A Merc! I caught a Merc!" I smile so wide it encompasses my whole face and I proudly point to my roped captive. "I got him! Actually, Hershey and I got him." I stroke Hershey's mane.

"Who is he?"

"An enemy. A Merc, he showed me his 'M.'" I point to his forearm with the M. "See?"

Colt pats me on the back. "That's impressive." He studies my handiwork on the boy. "But what's a Merc doing here?"

That is the big question. Didn't Colt's family see him or the horses? I point up toward the farmhouse. "What did your family tell you?"

"Everyone's gone. No note."

Everyone's gone. What does that mean? Where did they go? I lean down and tug on the Merc's rope. "What about him? He must know something. He told me he was here on orders. Maybe he can tell us what happened."

"Maybe he can." Colt lifts up the boy's head giving him a good look over. "You look familiar. What's your name?"

"Riley." Riley stares at Colt.

Colt shifts for a moment. "Riley?"

Colt cocks his head. "Are you Mr. Lutter's son from the farm over to the west of us? I remember a boy a bit younger than I was. Is that you?"

The boy squirms. "Yeah. I'm sixteen or as close as I can remember, I'm sixteen."

Colt relaxes, and squats on his toes beside Riley. "Riley, yeah I remember you. I'm Colt. This is my farm. I remember you used to trade feed corn with us." He looks over at the boy. "You remember that?" Getting no reaction he continues, "You were one of us, a Bavarian farm boy. How'd you become a Merc?"

The boy rolls over, both hands tied in front of him, sits up, and they talk as if they were chatting in their living room back home. "Yes, I do remember you. That was a lifetime ago. I became a Merc a long time ago. I had to forget about the farm. This is the first chance I've had to stay any time in this area. I don't think they remembered I was from here."

Was he telling the truth? Better to be careful, after all, he planned to turn me in as an Uncounted just a few minutes ago.

"They gave me a choice: Become a Merc or get deported to America—I wanted to stay in Germany. I guess I always hoped to see my family again. I knew I wouldn't see them in America. When you are an Uncounted, you don't have many choices."

I blurt out. "Do you know their plans?"

The boy shifts uneasily in his restraints.

Colt begins to untie Riley and I jerk Colt's arm away. "Colt, what are you doing? He's the enemy!"

Colt releases him, slapping at my hand as I try to stop him. "No he's not. He's a boy from a farm in Germany. He's my neighbor and he did what he had to. Am I right, Riley?"

Riley rubs his wrists. "I really want to help, but the truth is that I am a Merc. She's right."

"See?" I fling my arms in Riley's direction. "This boy isn't going to help us, he's going to turn us in, and then I'll never see Mother or Gretel. He needs to be tied up." Why couldn't Colt understand that?

Colt pulls Riley to his feet. "You plan to turn us in, is that right?"

Riley pauses, "Well, no. I'm not going to turn you in now, but I'm no longer a farm boy. I'm a Merc. It's like she said. I'm the enemy."

Colt puts his hand on Riley's shoulder. "Paisley is an Uncounted and you're not planning on turning her in now. How does that make you the enemy?"

I start. "He *was* going to turn me in."

"But he's not going to do that now, right Riley?"

Riley drops to the ground and buries his head in his hands. "Right, but I am a Merc. I deserve to be hated. I should have stopped them from—"

Colt whispers, "From what? From taking you at a young age? From being an Uncounted? From taking everyone from the farms? You couldn't have stopped them and you know it." Colt glares at me. "She knows it too."

Is Colt right? Is Riley a prisoner? If he is, he's been one for a long time. No matter. Bottom line, Riley is the only one who has the information about my family. Like it or not, we have to trust him. It's our only choice.

I soften. "You may be a Merc, but it doesn't sound like you're our enemy." I help Riley stand up. "Help us. Don't you want to be free?"

Riley slumps back to the ground. "I don't know what free is."

I scrunch down beside him. "Me neither, but I went on a Ferris wheel ride a couple of days ago with the wind blowing through my hair and for a few seconds I didn't think about having to give my harvest to the Collectors or watch out for the Mercs or hide or anything. I was free and it was great. I want that all of the time. Bet you want that too. Why don't you help us and maybe we can help you?"

"I remember that Ferris wheel." Riley is silent for a minute, eyes closed. Maybe he is trying to conjure up the image of the Ferris wheel or his farm or simply trying to digest what I just said.

Finally, Riley sighs, "It could work. There are more farm people than Mercs right now. But only for a few days."

"Why for a few days?" Colt asks.

"That's how they control. Some of us train for the Mercs, some help with the harvest, counting or distributing. But since there is the big political push for control, they decided it was time to take over the farms. That's why they emptied all of the farms of the owners. It was coordinated to happen all on one day, the last tally day."

Colt nods. "They didn't want us to know. If we had known, we could have gotten together and stopped them. But now, it's too late. Everybody's gone. The Mercs have them all. Why now?"

"It's the political thing. There is a push to lift the quarantine. That will change everything." Riley hangs his head down, takes a stick off the ground, and begins stabbing the grass with it. "The Mercs want to own

Bavaria."

Own Bavaria? All of Bavaria? Something has to be done. We can't give them Bavaria. We have to try to stop them. I shout, "That can't happen!"

Colt shifts his foot and anxiously asks, "Where are they taking everyone? Passau?"

"Yes, that's the division point. They will trade and sell some people right there or transfer them to a ship to be bartered for later. Some will be recruited for the Merc Army or to help with the harvest or I guess now they'll need people to work the farms, like me."

I feel the color drain from my face. "Sell?"

Colt drops to Riley's level. "How much time do we have?"

Is he going to stay and be a Merc or help? Before Riley can answer, I stop pulling Hershey's mane. "Decide! Are you going to help us? Are you a farm boy or a Merc?"

Riley holds his arms up palms out as if he is a prisoner. "I don't have a choice, right?"

Colt and I look at each other.

Colt answers, "You have a choice. You're free to choose. Of course, you understand that we won't be able to let you go if you decide to side with the Mercs. We'll tie you up and leave you here so they can find you or fix it so you can escape on your own in a few days. We just need a head start. Your choice?"

How can Colt be so gullible? Something must be done. I grab Colt's arm. "Are you crazy? What if he turns us in?"

Chapter 6

Colt isn't thinking straight or maybe he doesn't hear me. I repeat, "He's a Merc. He said he was. We can't trust him; he'll turn us in first chance he gets. I just know it." I nuzzle Hershey and shoot my most defiant stare at Riley.

Colt frowns. "He just gave us information. Why would he do that then turn us in? You're not making any sense."

It's true that Riley gave us information, but how do we know if what he said is true or not? It could be a lie. A clever trap to get us caught. I don't know Riley, but then again, I didn't know Colt before yesterday. Could I really trust either one of them?

Colt shakes his head, glares at me, and then turns his attention to Riley who locks eyes with Colt for a few seconds. "I don't believe he'll betray us. I can see it in his eyes. I don't think he'll turn us in." Colt turns again to me and then back to Riley. "He started out as one of us. He *is* one of us. We probably would have made the same choice if we'd been put in that situation."

Riley interrupts. "I'll tell you what I know. I won't turn you in. I promise."

Of course, he would say that. He certainly wouldn't own up to the fact there was a clever trap ahead. I turn my back to Riley and stand in front of Colt. "He said before he would get a reward for me. He's a Merc. He'll say anything to get free." Colt has to listen to me. I flip my attention back to Riley. "Then he'll take off and find his Merc friends and then we'll be captured too. Everything he tells us is probably a lie. One that will get us caught." I spin back to Colt again. "What good will that do? What will happen to Gretel, Mom, and all of your family then? Think about what it could cost us if you're wrong about him."

"Paisley, I haven't been off this farm in twelve years and neither have you. We don't know where they've taken our people. We have no way of finding them. It's been twelve years since I've been anywhere. I don't remember much. I understand what you're saying, but we have no choice. We have to trust him. We need his help."

Riley humbly bends his head. "It's been so long since I've had a choice about anything. Let me help you find your family. I won't betray you. I want to remember what it was like to be one of you."

At this point, Hershey ambles over to Riley and nuzzles him. Talk about entanglements, this is a no-win scenario, if we don't listen to Riley we don't know where to go, but if we do trust Riley and he turns us in, then we will be in a worse predicament. A hard choice, but the thought of not trying and never seeing my family again makes it a little easier to take the leap of faith and hope for the best.

Finally, I relent. "I guess it's the only choice, but I don't have to like it. It does help that Hershey likes you." I can't help but let Riley know what I'm thinking so I glare at him. "I still don't trust you, people have to earn trust. Everyone knows that."

"Thanks, Hershey. I like you, too." Riley smiles and strokes Hershey's mane. "None of this will matter if we don't leave soon. Your family will be gone or the Mercs will get reinforcements, then we'll be outnumbered. If we are going to catch up with them, we need to go now."

Colt agrees. "Let's stop by my house first."

"Fine." Riley takes the reins of one of the horses. "It's on the way."

We mount the horses, including Hershey, and travel through Colt's pasture which is scattered with several farm machines in various stages of disrepair.

Sun is setting behind the hills illuminating the sky with a magnificent hue of soft tones playing a song just for us. The orange ball of fire descends slowly signaling the end of another day. The rolling hills are quietly lulled to sleep in the transcendent beauty of the Bavarian countryside.

Riley stops and sighs for a moment gazing towards the house as the sun disappears. "I forgot about the beautiful sunsets."

Everywhere around us is despair. Families taken in shackles. People forced to be Mercs or worse. The beautiful sunset, the only pureness in this marred reality.

We arrive at Colt's farmhouse. The outside door hangs open, with the broken hinge dangling. Inside, pieces of oversized wood furniture crafted from the local forest trees are upturned and strewn about the large entrance room.

Suddenly, I realize how tired I am. I yawn, righting a hollowed out tree trunk chair, and plop down hard in it. "What's the plan?" I may only have a second to rest, but I'm going to take it.

Colts searches through the cupboards. "They have a big head start so we need to travel tonight." He opens empty cabinets. "Did they take everything?"

Riley lifts his backpack off his shoulder. "They left me supplies."

Colt slams the door of the cabinet. "You keep those. You might need them." He retrieves a paper and pencil. "Draw a map. It might be quicker if you stay here with Paisley. I'll go alone and then come back for you."

I jump out of my chair. "You're not leaving me here! I'm coming with you!"

Riley stands beside me. "Sorry, but I agree with her. We need to stay together. We can come back here after we get your family. Maybe we can find my family too."

It never crossed my mind that Riley might be thinking about his family. How selfish of me! Traitor or no, at least he is on my side for this argument. I like that.

"We have the horses. We'll be quicker than they will. They'll have to walk with that many. They'll be slower. You need me and—" Riley looks over at me. "We can't leave her here by herself. The Mercs might come back. It wouldn't be right."

Maybe he isn't completely on my side. I snap my fingers at Colt. "Two against one. We win."

Colt shakes his head in defeat. "Democracy in action. I guess I'm outvoted. Our first act as free people." Colt slaps Riley on the back. "I hope you don't regret this, but there is no time to argue. Let's get going."

As we exit, Colt leans over close to me and whispers, "This is not a democracy. You need to vote with me." He taps my forehead.

"I won't ever vote with you if you try to leave me." I glare defiantly.

Riley pulls a piece of paper out of his knapsack. "I have a map." He unfolds it. "It'll help us. It shows the short cuts and hidden trails we can take the horses. We should be able to make up a lot of time." He holds the map up in the moonlight. "They won't travel at night. Too much of a chance of escape."

Colt squints his eyes. "Let's get started and if you're right it'll definitely give us the edge."

At the pasture gates, we mount our horses to begin our trek.

Colt trots ahead. "Follow me, we'll take the shortcut through my farm."

Riding beside us, Riley says, "They'll be heading to Passau."

I gallop beside Riley. "What can you tell us about the Mercs?"

He brushes me off. "In a minute."

We race together through the open field as night sets in with nothing impeding our dash to the other side. I like the wind blowing through my hair and the small taste of freedom. Any flicker of freedom is wonderful, no matter how fleeting.

After the long gallop, we slow down and Riley speaks. "My Mercs are hooked up with a network of Mercs from other countries. They use the harvest like money to barter for weapons, power, whatever they can. Money is no longer used, but food is gold. We collect the harvest, bring it back, keep the peace, and control the people by whatever means necessary." With the last statement, he pulls a gun out of his inside pocket.

Colt immediately pulls back on his reins. "Whoa!"

We all stop.

Chapter 7

A gun! I knew it. He is going to betray us. That didn't take long. Colt is so trusting. Maybe I can wrestle it away. Probably can't do it without getting one of us killed. Think! Think! Why do I always have to be right? Well, I'm not always right, but why did I have to be right this time?

Colt calmly stares at the weapon and says, "Did you have that all along?"

What kind of question is that? At least Riley isn't pointing the gun *at* us. No choice, but to let this play out, for better or for worse. I sure hope it's not the latter.

"Yes, all of the Mercs are armed." Riley slows down and we pace him. "I knew I wouldn't use it. I've never used it. The bullets are in my knapsack and the revolver is in a hidden pocket."

Wait, it's empty. An empty gun. No threat after all. Who would pull an empty pistol out and wave it around?

"You scared me for a minute." I pet Hershey. "Full of surprises aren't you?"

"We might need it later." Colt sits up straight on his horse bopping up and down as the steed quickens his pace. "Good to know that we do have some fire power, but really glad the bullets and gun aren't together because you might have gone crazy and used it on us."

"He said he's never used it, why would he use it on us?" I gently nudge my mount into Riley's horse.

I plan to be nice to the person with the weapon. Later on, I'll make a plan to get the gun away from Riley. Right now, all that matters is it's not loaded.

"Of course not." Riley smiles. "Have you and Colt known each other long?"

"What do you mean? We just met."

"That explains why you're giving him such a hard time."

I stop for a moment. "A hard time? Nobody's giving Colt a hard time. If anyone is giving anyone a hard time, it's you." I calm myself. We still need as much information as we can get so we can save the farm families and I can go home.

"How did the Mercs get all of this power? What do they do besides take the harvest?" I yell as we resume a faster gallop.

"I'll tell you what I know, but let's make it to this trail. We'll have to

36

slow for the terrain and then we can talk as we ride. No wasted time." Riley pulls his horse farther south.

Better keep a look out. This would be a great place for the other Mercs to be hiding. Unfortunately, can't carry on a conversation while you're galloping. Riding a sprinting horse gives me that free feeling that I so love. Not going to worry about a betrayal right now.

"Stop!" Riley abruptly pulls his steed into some brush. "Hide!"

We follow mounted shoulder to shoulder with him hiding in the brush. A minute later we see three Mercs gallop down the trail going the opposite way. A bound man is being dragged behind them. One of the Mercs orders, "Stop, this is the place." They both get off their horses and one of the men pulls a gun and shoots the tied man in the head hitting him between the eyes at point blank range. It sounds like a balloon popping. Blood gushes and splatters all over the dirt and the men. The explosion of red causes the men to take a step back.

My stomach roils as I gasp at the horrific scene and Riley holds his hand tightly over my mouth. "Shush!" he whispers.

"I can't believe the blood sprayed like that." The man who shot the gun laughs and yells, "Throw him down the ravine with the others. The animals will finish him off." The two men toss the crumpled body over a cliff, mount back up, and trot off.

A tear runs down my cheek. Riley releases me and I whisper, "How could you just let that happen?"

Colt squeezes Riley's shoulder. "I'm sure you had your reasons. I'm also sure you've seen a lot worse. Paisley, he did what he had to do to save us. We were out gunned. Nothing could be done to save that man."

I see Riley's dejected look and realize that is true. "I know you're right, but it's so horrible." I gasp in uneven breaths. "Can we at least bury him?'

"No point." Riley points down the ravine as we pass by. It's full of skeletons in varying stages of decay. "We can't make it down to the bottom. Believe me, I've tried."

I choke up and say, "Riley, how long—"

"That was my old life." He pulls out a piece of metal and twirls it in his hand. "I made a four leaf clover out of a bullet once. It has been lucky for me. I probably would have been at the bottom of that ravine many times if it wasn't for my lucky four leaf clover."

"What happened?" I ride alongside him.

He holds up his hand. "Please I don't want to talk about it."

I don't ask anything else. Now I realize I have been sheltered from the ugliness of the world. I've been lucky. We trot together until we arrive at a rough trail. Hindered by low branches and an uneven path, we line up single file to wind up and down a large hill, still snow-covered and slippery.

Riley takes the first spot, ducks his head to avoid the branches and we two mimic his movements. "It's slow going for a while. Now I can talk. At Passau, the Mercs split up the captured Uncounted. They are assigned to train as a Merc like me or transferred to other locations in Europe or to America."

Maneuvering through the forested terrain, we come upon a wider pathway. Orlando, could that be in America? Maybe America was close. Better yet, maybe Orlando was close. I ride beside Riley and his horse. "How do you get to America?"

He doesn't answer. Does he not know or does he just not want to tell me?

The sound of flowing water echoes in the night and Colt spies the stream. "Let the horses get water here before we go on and we can rest them too."

"Water sounds good. I'm parched." I notice the cloudless night sky filled with dancing stars that twinkle as our horses slurp from the waterway and graze on the green sprouts at river's edge.

I unpack my knapsack, fill my water canteen, scarf down an apple, and pass the jar to Riley. "How do they get to those places?"

Riley doesn't answer again. I'm not giving up so I inquire again, "How do people travel to other places?"

Riley sits on the ground in the makeshift circle we three have formed and swallows two pieces of apple whole. "Mostly trains, but sometimes by ferry boat. I've seen some walking, or riding on horses, or in wagons. There are some working cars and a major ration on gas. If you're going by ship, they take you to Hamburg on the train. Then you get on a huge ship that sails to lots of places including America."

"How long to Passau?" Colt drinks the rest of his water and fills it again.

Riley stands up and stretches. "At this pace we should reach it by morning. We should be there before they divide up so at least we'll know where they are going, but we have to be careful when we get there."

I sigh. "I hope Mom and Gretel are okay and they haven't hurt them."

"We'll find Gretel." Colt knocks into me. "I'm worried about my dad. He is the kind of person who would get hurt trying to be a hero."

Riley shrugs. "I was at your farm when they took it over. Your father is fine and from what I saw of the rest of the people walking and that would include your mom and sister, Paisley, they were okay too. The Mercs don't want to hurt anyone; it would lower their worth. They want to use them to barter. Remember how I told you food was like gold. People are worth even more. They have to keep them healthy."

I can't believe my ears. "What do you mean people are worth even more? Do they sell people? How can people sell people?"

Riley shakes his head. "Do you think when I became a Merc that the person who trained me didn't have to pay," he puts his hands in air quotes, "a reward for getting me? Let me just tell you like it is. The Uncounted are sold like cattle to the highest bidder. There are no rules, except the rules the Mercs make up."

Colt mounts his horse. "Let's get going. We don't want them to sell any of our people. Riley, you still have family don't you?"

"I really don't know. Some were still alive when I left, but it's been so long."

Colt looks down from his horse. "I'm sorry Riley, I don't know either. We were quarantined from everyone else."

Riley pulls his horse over by the reins. "I know."

I hug Riley's arm. "Let's get going. We'll find out when we get there. I'm sorry Riley, for questioning you. I really didn't understand." I let him go and mount Hershey. "Let's get them all back. Do we have far to go?"

Riley shakes his head and mounts his horse. "Not too much longer now."

Realizing the nearness to our families, quietness takes over and we travel in silence for the rest of the trip.

We arrive at our destination, as a glimmer of light peaks on the horizon, bathing the world with a soft pinkness filtered by a wispy morning fog. Dawn is coming. I remark, "We don't have much time."

At the foot of the last hill before the city, Riley dismounts his horse. "We'll leave the horses here and go the rest of the way on foot."

We tie up the horses, hide them as best we can, and scale the last rise peering over the city. We survey the area and spy a big group people sleeping haphazardly in a large clearing below us.

I whisper excitedly. "It's our people. They're here."

Quiet now, the camp is guarded by two armed Merc guards situated on each side serving as sentries marching in timed intervals around the sleeping captives.

Riley whispers. "Only two guards. The rest of the Mercs must be inside. The captives will be tied up. We'll have to free them." There is no movement except the sentry guards, pacing back and forth.

I murmur to the boys, "I've never seen this many people in one place." I strain my eyes in an attempt to make out forms. "I can't see mom or Gretel, it's still too dark."

Riley points to the fenced area. "We have to take out the guards and free the people before the rest of the camp wakes up. We shouldn't have any resistance. They don't expect us since there are only two people guarding." He pulls out the unbulleted gun. "Do you think we need this?"

"No!" Colt pushes the gun back toward Riley. "Put it up. No use giving them a reason to shoot us." Colt turns around and faces me. "It'll be easier to do with a distraction. Can you be a distraction?"

"What should I do?" I jump up and down softly waving my hands. "This?"

Colt pulls me down. "Be careful. They'll see you. Besides, I was thinking of something a little simpler." Colt pushes my head toward the sentry. "Make some noise, like you're a captive who got loose, get his attention, but not enough to alert the other guard. He's not expecting it. Maybe it will startle him enough for me to subdue him."

"I'll go on the other side and secure the other guard at the same time." Riley motions to the other guard. "Let's do this."

Colt creeps silently with me close behind and as we reach the guard, I quietly circle in front of the sentry and ask, "Can we go back to the farm now?"

Surprised, the lookout shifts his gun up and into the firing position. "Back!" Colt yells from behind him and pushes the gun butt hard causing the guard to juggle the weapon allowing Colt a couple of seconds to wriggle the rifle out of his hand. "Hands up!" Colt yells, pointing the firearm at the guard and motioning to me. "Tie him up and gag him."

At the same time, Riley jumps on the other guard and he falls to the ground unable to cock or even reach his pistol in time. With both guards subdued, we circulate through the crowd untying and waking people up.

"Be quiet!" I whisper. "Once we untie you, help the others. We need to leave quietly and quickly. Hurry!"

Working together, everyone is freed in a few minutes.

"This way!" Riley motions for the crowd to follow him. "We've got to get out of here and hide before the rest wake up. We're going over this hill to the outskirts of town."

A group of about thirty newly freed men, women, and children walk single file over the rise to the clearing on the other side and gather.

"Dad!" Colt reunites with his father. "We need to get these people out of here and to safety before it gets too light outside."

I realize that Mom and Gretel are not here. I need to find out where

40

they are. "Does anyone know what happened to my sister and my mom, Gretel and Frieda Mueller?"

Colt's dad hugs his son and glances over at me, "Yes. I know them. They were with the group that went to Hamburg by train. They left a couple of hours ago and from what I overheard they are slated to leave tomorrow on the big ship docked there."

"A big ship?" My shoulders slump. "Sorry, I'm really thankful for the information." Someone must have a schedule—the guards. I sprint off, turning for a moment. "I'll be back in a minute."

Colt throws hands up as he watches me flee the area. "Where are you going? We need to get out of here. Your family's not there."

"I know. I'm not leaving. Go ahead, I promise I'll be just a minute. I'll catch up with you."

"Paisley, come back soon. I can't help them and chase you too." Colt shakes his head. "Be careful and quick, we don't have much time."

"I'll catch up. I promise." I push back through the single file of people walking toward their freedom. I smile, at least these people are free.

The guards are still tied up and out cold. I quickly rummage through one of the captive guard's pockets. I was right, I find schedules. After removing all of the papers in his pockets, I hurry back to join the others.

"Glad you made it back." Colt pushes and pulls the recently freed along. "Hurry! We need to go now!" Colt bellows as loud as he can to the group without alerting the Mercs to the disappearing prisoners.

Just enough darkness hangs on for us to get all of the free ones to the outskirts of town.

Along with the others, the three of us arrive at the hiding place on the other side of the hill and Riley says, "We've freed all of these people, now what can we do? Do we hide them? Where? For how long?"

Colt hands one of the sentry's rifles to his Dad. "Dad, this is Riley. We can trust him. He's one of us, a farm boy. He was a Merc, but now he's helping us. Riley this is my dad, Granger." Granger and Riley shake hands.

Colt motions toward the horses. "We have horses to help with travel, but we need to move everyone into the underground caves to hide out until we figure out what is going on. There is plenty of food and water to last you for a while."

Colt pulls out a leather pouch full of paper. "Dad, these are maps to the caves. Hide there. It's time. We need to keep these people safe until we can figure out what to do."

Granger leans the rifle against his leg and takes the pouch. "You can show me. We'd better get going, son." He motions for everyone to gather.

Colt hugs his dad hard. "I can't go, Dad."

His father's arms drop. "Why not?" He takes a couple of steps back away from his son.

Colt drops his head and slowly shakes it. "I have to find Gretel. I can't explain it."

Granger cocks his head to one side and frowns. "Gretel?"

"She's important, Dad." Colt shoulder bumps into me. "This is her sister, Paisley. I made a promise. I have to rescue Paisley's mom and sister." Colt grabs his dad's shoulder and squeezes it. "I made a promise that I plan to keep. I'll catch up with you."

I pull out a piece of paper. "I found this in the guard's pocket. I know where they're taking Mom and Gretel. I'm going with you."

Colt shakes his head. "No, you're not. I also promised Gretel I'd take care of you. Leaving you in the safe hands of my dad is fulfilling that promise."

This is *my* quest. More than Colt or anyone's quest—this is mine, *my* rite of passage. I'm brave. I rode the Ferris wheel. I know what I am capable of doing. I know I can help and no one, not even Colt, is going to tell me any different. Mom and Gretel have been there for me all of my life and now it's my turn to save them. With or without the help of Colt.

I take Hershey's reins and hand them to Riley. "We'll catch up with you later. Riley, take care of my horse." I glare at Colt. "Don't try to talk me out of it. I'm going and that's that."

Colt shakes his head. "No, you can't go. That's crazy."

I unfold the paper. "I took this from the guard. It's the train schedule. We have to hurry." I have the goods and he knows it. And the best part is that it's time-sensitive. There is just no time to talk about it. If we are going to save my family, we need to leave immediately.

I run my finger over the paper. "The train to Hamburg leaves in fifteen minutes and if we run we can make it. No time to argue. You can come with me or stay. It's your choice, but I'm going. We need to leave now before they discover people are missing. If we don't, it'll be too late."

"No choice, Dad. Take care of everyone. Riley will help. He's one of us, now. " Colt clutches his dad's hand. " Good luck and take care. Get these people to safety. I'll be back as soon as I can."

Riley grabs my hand and shoves a piece of jagged metal in it. "Remember the four leaf clover I made from a bullet. Keep it. I wanted something good to come from something bad."

I open my palm and see banged metal fashioned into four petals. "Thanks, but I shouldn't accept. It's your lucky piece."

"I want you to have it. It's been lucky for me. You might need more luck now than me." He closes my hand around it and turns his attention to Colt. "Take care of her." Riley shakes Colt's hand. "I promise I'll make sure this group gets to safety. You and Paisley changed my life. Better than that, you gave me a life worth living again. Thanks."

I take off running. Colt races, catching up with me at the train station boarding area. Fortunately, it loads from the other side of the holding area. No movement or conversation signals that not only has everyone boarded, but also the escape of the prisoners has not been discovered. Maybe there is something to the luck of the clover. As the first drop of sun pours on the countryside threatening to expose us, I worry that our good fortune may be short-lived.

We creep around to the other side of the train. No lingering passengers. Good so far.

"Wait a minute." Colt stops me to look around. It is quiet, the only person on the platform is a guard, and he is fast asleep.

I draw Colt's attention to the guard. "Shh! Don't wake him up. Everyone must have already boarded the train."

Hurry!" I grab Colt's arm and look back over my shoulder as the guard rolls from one side to the other, but never opens his eyes. We have to get on the train without anyone seeing us. It's imperative, not only for our safety, but for the others we are trying to save. I pray quietly for those thirty or so we left behind. I hope they find safety, but their future is out of my hands now.

Colt sprints, forcing the door open on the train of the last car. A beeping sound goes off, and the guard once again shifts, but does not wake up. Fortunate for us, he is a deep sleeper. We land in a deserted part of the train. It's obvious we won't be able to stay here for the duration, but we are safe for a few minutes.

A couple of seconds later, the doors close for the last time and lock, signaling no more entries as the train slowly begins to move down the track rocking back and forth.

"Familiar." I whisper under my breath as I realize that at some time in the past I must have ridden on a train, but those memories are just flashes now. How many memories will stir during this rescue trip? It's been so long since I've seen anything but the farm. I close my eyes for a moment memorizing a picture of home and the Ferris wheel. I want to make sure I don't forget.

Alone, at the back of the train, I take a minute to look out the window. The terrain of hills blurs as our transport picks up speed. Buildings of all shapes and sizes come in and out of view. The glorious rising sun mesmerizes me and commands my undivided attention. That moment is interrupted as an announcement blares, "Port of Hamburg, next stop."

Colt winks at me and smiles. "At least we got on the right train."

Chapter 8

Colt's right. We made it on the train. Now what? "Where are we going to hide?" I feel the blood drain out of my face as I lean up against the wall listening to the musical hum of the train. Too bad we can't stay here the whole time.

Colt scrunches in beside me. "Let's sneak in, hopefully unnoticed. Look for any place that looks inconspicuous."

I do my best, hang my head and walk slowly through the sliding door into the back of the compartment occupied by a few sleeping inhabitants. Wonder where they're from and where they're going.

Fliers sit in a rack hinged on the side of the train car so I grab a few and nonchalantly hold one in front of my face trying my best to be unobserved. I hand a newspaper to Colt indicating that he do the same as we enter the corridor of the compartment. Colt motions toward a couple of empty seats facing the back and scoots quickly toward them. I pull him back after I notice a sign on the door in front of us that reads "out of order." We both smile.

Sliding the door quietly and peering in, I whisper, "It's perfect. A large water closet."

I chuckle thinking that it seems fitting we end up in a toilet after the poop we've gone through to get here. Hope the others make it to the caves to hide. Now it's all up to them. I hope we can pull this off. Unfortunately, there is no plan now. Just making it up as we go.

We slip in unnoticed. I talk with a low voice, "We can hide here. We can't have anyone ask to see our marks."

"Or our papers." Colt smiles. "I haven't been on a train in a long time, but from what I remember you have to have tickets, also." He pulls his pockets inside out. "And us, no tickets."

I look around. "Seems familiar, like I've been on a train. But I can't recall—just flashes of memory. It's been such a long time. My whole world as long as I can remember has been the farm."

Colt surveys the room. "I know what you mean."

The bathroom is large, possibly set up for families. On one side sits a sink with a faucet to fill the basin and a foot pedal to drain the water. Housed against the center wall is a stainless steel toilet—full size—although once again to 'flush' a foot pedal has to be depressed. On the other side is a bar attached to the wall. Some graffiti marks up the walls.

One is a picture of a broken egg and underneath is scrawled one word: *Freedom*.

"What does freedom have to do with this picture?" I run my hand over the scrawled egg pictures and survey the rest of the room. Lots to learn about the outside world.

"I don't know." Colt motions to the bar on the wall and points to the blue picture of the circle with a stick figure sitting in it. "You know who this bathroom is for? It's for people in wheelchairs." He puts his chin in his hand. "I haven't seen a wheelchair since before the v—" He pauses. "It's been about twelve years. Do you think people still use wheelchairs?"

"I have no idea. I'm trying to remember a wheelchair." I lean up against the wall of the bathroom. "Right now I just want to be home with my family." I sigh. "All I seemed to ever do was wish I could get out of there and now look, all I want is to go back."

"Don't worry. We should be fine here." Colt spreads some paper towels on the floor area and sits down. "Does your flier say how long till we get to Hamburg?"

I gaze at the crumpled paper. "0600." I look at him. "That's a long time, we might as well get comfortable."

Colt looks over my shoulder at the paper. "The last train got in two hours ago. We have to hope that the ship doesn't sail before we get there."

I don't even want to think that way. I know we will make it, find my family, and be back before anyone realizes we are gone. Gretel and Mom will be so proud. We'll hide in the caves until things go back to normal or, I shiver with excitement, maybe when things get better. Maybe in the future, we will be able to travel. What a nice thought.

Colt points to my pack. "Get the watch out. We'll need it."

I unzip my pack and pull out the watch, but freeze as we hear footsteps outside the door that suddenly stop. Not now, we can't be caught now. We have so much more to do. We sit motionless, tightly clenching each other's hands.

I shut my eyes tight and mouth, "Read the sign. Read the sign." Finally, the steps recede.

Commenting, "Just to be safe." Colt goes to the door and pulls off a shoelace. "I'd better tie this door shut, in case someone else tries to use the broken toilet."

Colt spreads more paper towels out. "I say we get some sleep." He takes the watch from my hand. "This old watch has a vibrator alarm that will wake us."

I distribute more towels around the floor and curl up. "How long

46

should we sleep?"

Colt fiddles with the watch. "I'll set it for five and a half hours from now. That will give us enough time to gather our senses before we stop. We need the sleep if we expect to keep going."

"I know this will work, Colt. It has to." I lie back on the floor and shut my eyes. "Tomorrow, we'll have Gretel and Mom and be heading back. Tomorrow, we'll all be together."

"Nice thoughts. I'll lean on the door so I'll hear if someone comes." Colt leans back against the bathroom door and closes his eyes. "Sweet dreams. Paisley."

I hope that my dreams are sweet. The rhythmic rocking of the train like the singing of a baby's lullaby lulls me to sleep.

"Tickets! Tickets!" The man bellows so loud he can be heard through the door. I awake panicked for a moment, but my fear subsides as the man's voice fades then all is quiet once again allowing me to return to the much-needed sleep.

I feel the vibration of the watch alarm and stretch. We made it unnoticed so far. The door is still tied. We've hurdled one obstacle, but I'm assuming it will be the first of many.

Colt sits on the floor reading the pamphlets from the train that I had gathered earlier. "I feel better, I sure needed that sleep."

"Me, too," I say, stretching my arms above my head. "How long until we get there?"

Colt looks at the watch. "About an hour. We should eat. I looked at your train schedule and this train stops for a good half hour before leaving again. We should stay on the train until everyone gets off, and then we'll sneak off. Don't want to get caught now."

"I'm famished." I pull a jar out of my knapsack and study it. "Pears." I also notice the box and ribbon from my house. Should I look? I can do whatever I want. No one is telling me what to do. I put a hand on the box in my pack.

Footsteps!

I let go of the box and don't move as the doorknob jiggles. Staring wide-eyed at each other, we finally let out a relieved sigh as the movement of the doorknob stops and we hear a woman's voice. "This one doesn't work either."

Colt ears the door for a moment. "She's gone." He shuffles through the fliers. "I'm not sure if you know what you picked up, but these papers tell a lot of what's going on." Colt holds out a paper with a smiling man's face on the front.

I crowd close to him to look as I stuff another pear in my mouth and mumble, "What does it say?" News from the outside world, this ought to be interesting.

He flips the paper over. "This one is kind of like a newspaper. It tells what is going on right now. There is a story of the farm takeover." He hits his leg hard, and then stops to listen to see if the noise was heard by anyone on the train. "Sorry, hope nobody heard that. It just makes me so mad. We don't have anything like this. If we had this newspaper story then we would have known what was coming. Not fair." He bites his lower lip. "Not fair at all."

I wolf down another piece of fruit. "Think about it. If we had newspaper that came around our farms then that would mean that the Mercs were there more often and the Uncounteds would be caught. The Uncounteds like me."

"Still not fair."

"Maybe not, but I'm going to get our farm back from the Mercs. That's my plan to go back to my farm and my life." I pick up another pamphlet with pictures of smiling faces on the front. "Look at this one. Maybe things aren't all that bad, these people seem happy."

He ignores me and keeps talking. "Of course the story says that the farmers weren't owners, but hired ten years ago to run the farms and now the 'Consortium of the World' is going to take it over." He stops talking and slaps the paper on his lap. "What is the 'Consortium of the World'? How are we supposed to know what's going on?" He jerks up the paper again and flips it open making a loud cracking sound.

"Shh! You're going to make somebody come in here." I pick up one of the paper towels from the floor and wipe my hands. "We can't do anything about any of that."

He shakes his head. "Don't you care? It says that all of the owners died from the virus." He flips the page. "All lies. Listen to this; they use our harvest to buy things. We do all the work then they take our harvest and use it to barter. They're stealing from us and we have been letting them do it because we didn't know any better. Lies! All lies!"

He needs to calm down and focus. Besides, those are big world problems. We can't do anything about those issues. We need to concentrate on getting our families back. I take the paper out of his hand using it to wipe the pear drippings from my mouth. "Enough of that paper." I take another pear out of the jar and hand it to him. "Any of these tell about America?"

"Yes, here." He throws a pamphlet at me and I duck, causing it to knock into the wall.

I hear movement outside the door and freeze until all is quiet. "Shush!" I pick up the pamphlet he'd just thrown. "Calm down and be quiet."

"Why?" He asks.

I shake my head. "Oh I don't know maybe somebody might come in here with you being so quiet and all." I smile and he laughs a little.

Seems strange that Colt would worry about such global problems. It's too big to think about. It makes my head hurt. He's just a farm boy and I'm just a farm girl. No reason to fret about such things when there is obviously nothing we can do about it. We need to concentrate on freeing my family.

I study the flier he threw at me. "This one has the map of Europe and America. I didn't know America was so far away. The world is big. If they send them to America, we might not be able to find them."

"You're right. We need to concentrate. One step at a time." He picks up another paper. "This one tells about the virus itself."

"Does it say the virus outbreak is over?"

Colt reads silently for a few moments, and then says, "It's been twelve years, but they don't know much more than they knew before. No deaths reported in the last two years so that's good."

"I guess so. I don't want to get sick or anything." I swallow a pear. "How did they get control of our farms and our people? Does it say anything about that?"

Colt flips through a few of the fliers. "The Mercs, or mercenaries as they were first called, are an army of local militia started when the military evacuated after the outbreak."

I interrupt. "And don't forget that they steal people. They stole Riley and made him a Merc."

A pang of sadness shoots through me. I miss Riley. Strange.

"Very true." He stops for a minute and gazes upward. "I remember playing soccer at that army base. Gosh, I haven't thought about soccer in a while." He looks back down at the pamphlet. "At first, the army's job was to control looting and restore order, but since the outbreak actually began in this region, the quarantine law originated here."

That's something I didn't know. "The virus started here?" I close my jar and pick up my canteen. "Do they know how?"

"No, but I can tell you that there is nothing written about taking farms from people. It reads like they own the farms." He rips the paper in half. "That just makes me so angry that people don't really know what's going on." He pushes the ripped paper back together to finish reading it.

49

"There's something in here about the harvest share, but the way it's written it seems like Mercs are good because they supply food for this region through THEIR farms." He rips the paper into pieces. "It's a bunch of lies." He jerks up to a standing position, sighs for a moment holding the ripped papers over the trashcan, and then stuffs them back in his pocket.

"Calm down Colt." I take a swig of water, stand beside him, and hand him the canteen. "Drink some water. No one knows what's really going on. Maybe after we get Mom and Gretel we might have a chance to tell someone in control what's really going on here. But we can't do that if we're caught." I lift the bottom of the canteen, forcing him to take a swallow.

When did I become the voice of reason? When did I become the grown-up? Guess when doesn't matter.

Colt pulls away from the canteen and gestures expansively around with his arms. "Paisley this is big, really big. People—" He points to the bathroom door. "—people like all of the people riding on this train; they don't know what's really going on. They think all of these things written are the truth. They believe these lies. This is big—world big. They *need* to know what's really happening."

"I agree and maybe we can tell them." I sit, cross my legs meditation-style, and take in a deep breath. "But not right now—after we get my mom and Gretel."

"Gretel, yes we need to save Gretel." He pauses and then sighs.

If it wasn't for Gretel, Colt wouldn't have come and I would probably be stuck or caught or something much worse. Sometimes, it's a good thing to have a flawless sibling.

He's absorbed with his reading so I run my finger over the box from my house. It wouldn't hurt to look for a minute. I carefully open it. It is full of folded papers and a couple of trinkets.

"What's this?" I mutter to myself as I retrieve a lighter with a picture of a winged creature with the words Fairy Princess scrolled along the bottom of it. I light it and place it back in the box. Mother wouldn't mind, would she? I wanted to see the tokens in the treasure chest that my mother had guarded for so many years. One of the cards catches my eye. I have seen it before— the postcard about Orlando. I smile and run my fingers over the picture.

"What's that?" Colt tries to snatch the postcard, but I pull it away, stuff it safely back in the container, and clamp it shut.

"It's the box from my mother's house. It's private. I shouldn't even look at it." I push it back in the book bag.

Colt shrugs. "Your mom's not here. Look if you want."

Chapter 9

Not his business. I quickly shove the box in my pack and grab a paper off the floor. "Look at this flier." I pick the one with the smiling faces. "This one is trying to get rich people to buy people with no families. Look what it says. Help the orphans, give them food and shelter."

Colt sits up straight. "Buying people?"

I hand him the flier. "It says that these people don't have anyone to feed or clothe them. They will most likely die without help. It encourages people to buy these wretched souls to help with cooking or clean floors or help with harvest—look there's a list on the second page."

Descriptors of people complete with ages and health, some listing status of teeth and medical operations, experiences, and languages spoken and understood. Contact information and a haggle free barter price are also listed. It reminds me of the old catalogues around our house for cattle auctions and harvest buys. Sadly, they are not selling cattle, but people. How horrible!

Colt's eyes glare and his face scrunches as if he has just taken a large gulp of year old milk. "You're telling me our world now uses ill-gotten harvest and stolen people to barter. What kind of place is this now?" He shakes his head. "We need to get your family as quickly as possible and go hide with the others before we get sold like slaves. The outside world is seriously messed up."

He's right. Everything we have found out about the world now makes me realize how good I had it. Why couldn't I have just been happy? I am feeling less free with every passing minute.

"What's scarier is that they write this like buying these unfortunate people is helping them. It doesn't make sense. Do people really believe that?" I flip the page for him. "But the most ridiculous thing is that you can buy young people to be used for—" I pause and flip the page over. "Look at that picture of those two. "

I point to the picture. "Don't they look like us or about our age? The rich people buy—"

He interrupts. "They are rich because they sell our stolen harvest and barter using people like money."

I hold up my hand. "No, listen. They buy people our age to entertain their children." I stand for a moment, putting my hands on my hips. "We could be bought or rented." I stamp my foot. "Ridiculous!" I walk stiff-legged. "Look at me, I'm not a person. I'm a doll and you can own me for the low price of—" I stop. "It's really not funny," I say, but can't contain my laughter and fall to the floor, rolling over the paper, clutching my stomach. "I don't know why I'm laughing."

"It really isn't." Colt laughs a little with me. "Maybe we're laughing because we're scared. We may get caught and sold."

The door handle jiggles again causing us to stiffen once again; we silently listen for a few moments until it quiets. I let out a relieved sigh and gather my emotions. "You're right. We had better be careful or we won't be able to do anything for ourselves or for anyone else."

"We need to save Gretel—and your mom, of course." Colt studies the pamphlet. "I think this might be one thing they are doing with the farm people. They might be selling them."

Realizing what this could mean for my family, I shake my head. "We *have* to get Mom and Gretel back."

Colt nods. "We will. But this is the whole world we're talking about. Something needs to be done about it." He looks at me and adds, "But right now, we'll just concentrate on getting Gretel, well, your family back safe and sound."

I smile, and look out the small window at the passing countryside. At first, the scenery is calming, since the hills, meadows, and sprinkling of houses remind me of home, but now there are more buildings and structures, huge, unfamiliar, and threatening. I thought the Ferris wheel large, but most of these structures rival that.

I point out the window and ask Colt. "Who lives in all of those buildings? Do you think it's the people on this train?"

Colt tears off a piece of the stale bread he had brought with him. "Maybe port workers. I don't know. This train only goes back and forth to the port. We really won't get to see what the city of Hamburg is like, but hopefully with so many workers, we won't stand out." He flips another page. "There are some people that work for the 'Consortium of the World,' whatever that is."

"Does it say anything about the ships leaving from Hamburg?"

"This may be a schedule." He picks up another pamphlet. "There's only one ship sailing from Hamburg today, and it leaves at 1800 hours. It's carrying the royals around to different ports telling people about the newly formed 'Consortium of the World.' If your sister and Mom are on a ship, it's that ship. When we get off the train, we'll have about six hours before the ship leaves."

Six hours. A lot can happen in six hours. I chatter without taking a breath. "So we can walk around and see what the outside world really is like? Maybe while we're out, we'll find Mom and Gretel just out on the street." I put my hands on my face and excitedly breathe in. "Maybe before they get on the ship."

"I don't think we'll be able to walk around freely. You're not marked, and I'm marked only for the farming region." He lifts his shirtsleeve exposing the back of his arm. "Plus, it's in the wrong place. We can't chance being caught. Honestly, I don't know how we are going to get around in Hamburg or how we are going to get on that ship."

I touch his shoulder. "Don't worry, we'll figure it out. We can't get this close and not save them. I know it will all work out."

"I hope so. We have no choice now."

Wish he could be a little more positive. Tomorrow we'll all be heading back to the farm and laughing about today. I just know it!

An announcement blares, "Hamburg, next stop."

Colt looks at his watch. "We should be there in about fifteen minutes. We better be quiet until then."

I nod and we collect our belongings in preparation. We separately and without conversation study two different pieces of the reading material.

The train comes to a halt and shuffling sounds ensue. It's a few minutes before quiet sets in again. After another five minutes, we hear the scratching of a broom, and then quiet again.

I like the safety inside the washroom and want it to last. Anxiety of what the outside world holds creeps in to unsettle me. No time to let the fear take over as Colt makes a move to the door.

He gently removes the shoelace from the latch, and fastens it back on his tattered sneaker. "I think we can leave now. We need some clean clothes. People might take notice of these rags."

I smile. "I can't remember other clothes. I haven't had different clothes in a long time. We ended up just letting things out until we both fit into our mother's size and took those up to fit us. Other clothes. I'd like that." I look down at the ragged muddy sleeve of the garment that I've worn for years. "I guess, we kind of smell too." I tend to talk a lot when I'm nervous and I'm definitely nervous. This is not quite what I had in mind when I thought of freedom.

Colt sniffs my sleeve. "Yeah. I didn't want to say anything, but we both smell a little like vomit."

"I could have lived my whole life without the comment that I smell like puke. Thanks for the image, Colt." I am glad there is levity, somehow it makes me feel less afraid.

Colt laughs, opens the door slightly, and peers out. "All clear. Let's go!"

We exit onto a train platform. On my right, the city skyline of buildings juts up from the hills, the tinted gray glass, devoid of any real color, paints a stark contrast to the view on my left side, which consists of barren hills, peppered with a few barns, reminiscent of the farm. The sea is near, evidenced by the smells of salt, organic fragrant mixes of various fish, and seaweed that heavily weigh in the air. Sea gulls fly above, sounding their call.

My eyes grow wide. "I've never heard or seen or smelled so many different things all at one time. It's delightful. It makes me dizzy."

Colt jerks my arm. "Pay attention. We're in danger of being caught. Neither of us can let that happen. Remember that."

I point to a sign that reads: *Port of Hamburg terminal this way.* We follow the arrow off the deserted platform, and onto a sidewalk around a large, blue-gray stucco building that leads to a narrow street.

Stepping onto the street, I whisper. "Listen." Colt and I stop for a moment. "Have you ever heard so many voices in all your life?"

Our farm had an old phonograph, one that had to be constantly hand-turned to play. An antique my mother saved. I remember listening to the albums and the scratchy sounds of the voices. The music helped me pretend to have friends. Friends, that were not there, but friends that I could hear. I didn't feel as lonely when I listened to the songs. They weren't in the room with me, but I felt their presence.

Now here I am and it isn't an inanimate object that I'm playing. This is real. Music, their voices sound like music. Voicing a tune, letting me know I am not alone. The mesh of all those voices opens my mind so I can start to realize how big the world really is.

Colt shakes his head. "Must be a hundred people."

I gasp. "I didn't know there were that many people in the world. Look, there's the ship." I spy the top of a ship's stack on the horizon. It casts an enormous shadow, sitting ominously on the sea about five kilometers in front of us.

Can we make it in time? How will we get on? So many questions and not one answer pops into my head.

Colt grabs my hand to lead me. "We're going to have to get through all of these people, unnoticed, if we plan to make it to that ship."

I allow myself to be pulled. "You think we should cross an open street? We smell bad."

Colt pulls up the corner of his shirt, takes a whiff, and grimaces. "We do stink. Keep moving, maybe they won't figure out who it is until we have passed. Unless you have a better plan, we have to try."

It is a long walk through the open street, to the lengthy, floating pontoon platform, floating in front of the ship. Seems unfair that I can see the end goal, but it seems so out of reach.

The street is filled with people selling all sorts of things. "Fresh bread!" A man yells, holding out a loaf to anyone walking by. The aroma of the fresh baked bread is overwhelming. Another voice competes. "Get your new coats here! New coats here!" A new coat sounds tempting; mine is about ten years old—no, it's my mother's coat—that memory brings me back to the moment. My family, that's why we are here.

We walk a few paces before Colt leans up against a building, pulling me beside him. "I don't know how we are going to get to that ship. Any ideas?"

I peer out and look around for a couple of seconds before plastering myself back on the building. "It's hard to think clearly. It smells so good here. I don't know. Maybe if we sneak from one building to the next. If we go one building at a time slowly, getting closer, a better idea will come to us. It's possible they haven't put Mom and Gretel on yet. We need to keep a lookout for them. We might just fall into an idea."

Colt cocks his head. "That's your idea— to just fall into an idea?"

"I've never seen this many people in one place. I love it and am scared at the same time. Who knows? They might not pay attention to you and me. Using the crowd as cover, we can try to blend in."

"I, honestly, don't know what else to do." Colt nods. "Let's try it."

Coming out from behind the building, we are thrust into a bustling street with many patrons, sauntering in no particular order, with a few venturing in and out of stores. We attempt to blend in with the other walkers, doing our best to imitate, and act as if we belong. Attempts to draw no attention to ourselves prove impossible, as we soon realize, because our scent is so rank. It proves challenging to maneuver through the street vendors that line the walkways, while also intermingling in a nondescript way. We make it a couple of blocks, but it is a crawl like waiting for the sun to set on tally day after hiding all day long. Not enough progress to reach the ship before dark. And what happens when we reach the ship? How will we get on?

My eyes draw to a rack that holds many different kinds of pictures. I yank Colt's sleeve to make him stop, and pick up a card with a picture of a magnificent castle that reads Neuschwanstein Castle, Germany. I show it to him. "Beautiful, isn't it?" I run my fingers over the card. "It looks just like Mom's picture from Orlando."

He pulls the picture from my hand and turns it over. "This is in Germany, not Orlando." He puts it back in the rack, and drags me away.

"No time for this."

No time for anything? Since when is Colt the boss of me?

A young male, on the smallish side, wearing large horn-rimmed glasses and a beige overcoat follows us. "You two need to get off the street."

Colt asks, "Who are you?"

The man lets out an exasperated sigh. "I'm here to help." He pulls up his coat sleeve exposing his forearm and points to the tattoo of a broken egg. "You're on the run, right? Our mark. If you need a place to hide, we can take you in, we can use more recruits."

Pulling my sleeve lower to hide the fact that I have no mark, I reply, "It's okay. We're meeting with some people. My brother and I need to go." I turn back to Colt. "Right?"

A large man dressed in a suit walks toward the three of us.

The shadow person turns his back. "I'll draw him away from you. Get off the street and stay hidden. You're being noticed."

Peeking out from behind him, I spy the man approaching and I nod. "Thanks. I'm Paisley and this is Colt. What's your name?"

"Drake. Lieutenant Drake. No time to talk. Be safe." Lieutenant Drake bolts out from the store area and the suited man trails him, leaving us standing behind a kiosk in the middle of the street.

We duck behind the next building, ending up in an alley. An unusual contraption comes our way. It looks to be a stroller for a baby, but it's a lot larger. Ornate and burgundy in color, it has a curtain draped all of the way around it, except for the front which is covered with a thick, clear plastic. There is a silver button device implanted in the middle of the plastic. A little part of a hose hangs down below the curtain in the back, and is fastened into some sort of apparatus hooked on the buggy. Breathing and whooshing sounds emit from the hose possibly supplying oxygen to its occupant.

The bubbled, decorated carriage is laboriously pushed by a middle-aged woman who appears strong in structure, but is having a difficult time. Out of breath, the driver stops in between the buildings and the occupant, a dark-haired young girl about four or five, leans up. "I want something to eat. I'm hungry!" Her voice is amplified down the alleyway.

"The outside world is certainly strange." I whisper, "Her voice is so loud."

Colt whispers back, "Yes, I remember long ago we had things that could make our voice loud. I think it was called a microphone or megaphone or something like that."

The girl in the buggy and the person carry on a conversation

56

allowing us to remain unnoticed.

Colt crouches down and pulls me beside him. "We'll wait on them to leave, and then we'll go back out into the street and work our way to the ship."

We have to find a way to get to the ship. I have to know if Gretel and Mom are on there. Waiting is unbearable. These people need to move.

The girl beats on the bubbled cover. "Let me out!" Her voice booms again.

The carriage-pushing woman is not bothered by the screaming. She has perfectly coiffed graying hair and is dressed in a light blue suit with a white blouse buttoned all the way to her chin that reminds me of a turtle in defense mode peeking out to survey its surroundings. The woman rolls the carriage with the girl inside until it faces our direction.

The driver pushes the buggy a meter farther into the alley, closer to us, and speaks to the back of the buggy. "Princess Kamea, please be quiet. You will get food when we get back to the ship. How about a doll? I'll find out where we can get you a new doll. I'll be back in just a minute." The woman, who had been pushing the enclosed buggy takes a few steps away from the girl, and walks a little ways down the street. She stops a walking patron and converses with her out of our ear-reach.

The girl locks eyes with us. Colt puts his finger up to his lips.

Princess Kamea leans up. "Miss Brita—" Princess Kamea beats on the plastic cover. "Miss Brita!"

Miss Brita returns, peers in the buggy, and quickly assesses the girl. "You'll be fine here for just a few seconds. I have to let him know where we'll be. I'll be just another minute." Again, she walks away from the carriage, looking up and down the street. She motions to a suited large man. He comes over to her, and the two talk in hushed tones for a few minutes. She points to a store across the street.

"Dirty people!" Princess Kamea beats harder on the plastic cover. "Miss Brita! Dirty people!"

Chapter 10

Desperately attempting to quiet the shrieking girl, Colt puts his finger up to his lips for a second time. At least he's trying, I probably would have run away, and we would have been caught by now.

The girl begins to rock and screech. We approach the buggy and crouch down. I grab the carriage holding my hands on either side and shake it. "Shush!"

The girl rears up as if she is trying to fold herself in half backwards and screams. "I'm hungry!" It's not a pretty sight.

I squeeze the plastic. "Do something, Colt!"

Colt pulls out a jar from his pack and removes an apple. I shift away as he hovers the fruit inches over Princess Kamea, and whispers. "Do you want an apple?" The apple dangles over the top of the buggy and the girl greedily grabs at it, beating on the plastic cover.

Unable to retrieve the fruit, Princess Kamea turns red and beats louder. "Give me! Give me!"

"Hurry!" I whisper to Colt. "The lady is still not paying attention to us, but I don't know for how long." I glance back at the Colt and the little girl for a moment. "Try to quiet her down." I turn my eyes back to the princess's companion still in the street.

Colt presses his hand against the plastic, looking for an opening. This quiets the girl, and she points to a flap, which he locates, breaks the suctioned seal causing the plastic to deflate, and hands the apple to her. She gobbles the piece of fruit, and he gives her another, which she promptly wolfs down too.

I whisper, "Wow, you were hungry." I notice her companion returning. "She's coming back." I reach in and stroke the little girl's hair. "Sweet, girl. Be quiet, little girl." I sing quietly, "Circle up, circle down, the world goes round and round and round—"

The lady walks back down the street, leaving Colt just enough time to close the flap causing it to re-inflate, before the buggy holding Princess Kamea backs out. She is happily humming the circle song.

We peer out into the street. Another child, also walking down the sidewalk with his caretaker, points at us.

"We need to move." Colt grabs my hand.

"This isn't going to work." My eyes widen. I don't see any way out of this. I see no possible scenario in which we end up on the ship and save my family. I'm dejected. "Even if they don't see us, they are going to smell us. We need to get cleaned up. There are no people out here as dirty as us."

"Use the stroller." Colt points to the buggy. "It's big enough to cloak us."

We scrunch down and squat walk beside the carriage. He's right, this is working. The people on the street search around for the source of the stench, but they can't see us. We might get a little farther, but we need a bigger plan. And we need to quit walking like frogs. Thinking about how we must look makes me giggle.

Colt whispers, "I don't understand how you can laugh now. This is not funny. We're probably going to get caught."

"It's kind of funny." I muffle another giggle. "But funnier still is that we're going in a doll store."

Colt shrugs. "I don't care where we go, as long as we get off the street." He rolls his eyes when he spies the doll store sign.

We hide behind Princess Kamea and her massive bubbled carriage, before ducking into the doll store that the princess and her companion enter. Once inside, we sneak toward the back corridor area, as others are distracted by a loud commotion at the front of the store.

We creep down the back wall, discover an unlocked door, and enter it to find ourselves in a large storeroom, divided by beams and an archway. The far side of the room is full of hanging clothes, men's and women's all shapes and sizes, but all basically the same design. A life-size poster, similar to the one in the flier that we saw on the train, stands on the far side of the room, and reads "Coming Soon, Sponsored Companions." The rest of the room is populated with dolls and doll clothes.

"You remember the pamphlet from the train, the one where rich people buy people to play with their rich kids. I think that program was called, "Sponsored Companions."" I flip through the hanging clothes.

Colt shakes his head. "The world has gone crazy. We're in a store where they sell real people for dolls. Unbelievable. We need to get out of here."

I pull out an aproned dress to size it up. "You're right, but I think some of these clothes will fit. We need clean clothes and we need to bathe. We reek." I remove a couple of hang up dresses. "The clothes are all the same, just different colors."

"Okay, but just a few minutes, long enough to get cleaned up." Colt opens another door, along the back wall. "Here's a bathroom. It has soap. Use the sink, get as clean as you can, and put some of these clothes on.

Then I'll do the same. Don't take too long."

A bath, a sink bath, but still a bath. I can do a lot with a bar of soap and running water. Wash my hair and body. The floor will be soaked, but what do I care? I carefully take the four-leaf clover made out of a bullet out of my pocket. We've been lucky so far. Maybe Riley is on to something. I'm not going to take the chance.

"You don't have to ask me twice." I grab a set of clothes, place the clover in the new dress's pocket, and disappear in the bathroom. It takes me about fifteen minutes to wash and clean up. I emerge, wet headed, clean, and dressed in a white ruffled blouse and red satin dress, adorned with a white and red apron. "I put you an outfit in the bathroom. Do you see socks or shoes anywhere?"

"Took long enough, but you do look better and you smell a lot better. As a matter of fact, you look nice." Colt points to boxes. "I think the shoes and socks are in there." He ducks in the bathroom, and when he reemerges, he is clean and clad in beige leather pants, adorned with green suspenders, and a green and white checked shirt. I throw him a pair of shoes, socks, and a felt hat.

He shoves on the hat and makes a face, his tongue sticking out and his head comically cocked. "I can't go out looking like this."

"You *do* look weird." I lean on a box, clasp my stomach, and laugh quietly, but hysterically. "You look so funny."

I'm not sure I've ever seen anyone look so silly. I wish I could enjoy this and laugh loudly. I'm clean and I feel great. These clothes are the newest clothes I can ever remember wearing. I feel better than I've felt in two days. The two days since my world flipped upside down.

"Is this what people are wearing? This is ridiculous." He frowns as he looks in the mirror and readjusts the hat. "I look stupid." He stands by the poster. "I look like a doll, one of these dolls."

I smile, gathering myself and calming a bit. "You're not a doll, you're a person." I can't help it, I start laughing again. "I'm sorry, but—"

He abruptly yanks up the socks. "Shut up!" After pulling on the shoes, he stands, rolling his feet back and forth on the floor. "I have to admit these feel great. They are so comfortable. I'm never taking these shoes off." His smile widens as he walks around.

"You need to wear it all, if we are going to blend in. Look around the room." Dolls dressed in the same type outfits are scattered about, some in boxes with legs sticking out, others neatly packaged and then stacked on the shelves that occupy the front of the room.

"What? We are supposed to look like the dolls?" He holds up a boy doll beside him. "Is this something else this store sells? Doll clothes for

60

people? Yuck!"

"I think they dress the dolls in what people wear. But, maybe I am wrong." How would I know? I haven't been off the farm. I did not see any particular dress on the people on the street. It is true that no one was as grubby as we were, but no one looked as dressed up as we are now. What if we'd gone too far? No way to know that sitting in this storeroom, just have to take a chance. Time is running out.

Colt nods. "Let's find a way out of here and get to the ship. I don't want to wear this any longer than I have to."

Moving towards the exit, we see a few dolls with gouges, or missing legs or arms, which are thrown haphazardly in boxes. I pick up one of the smaller, torn-up dolls. "This must be the garbage." I toss the clothes that we had changed out of into the carton.

Colt places dolls over it to hide the worn, dirty clothes. "What did you do to your hair?"

I admire my reflection in the mirror, pulling at the tips of my newly formed pigtails. "My hair was wet because I washed it, so I braided it. Do you like it?" I toss a magazine over to him. "See, now we look just like the picture."

He glances at the page with a male and female dressed in the exact same outfits. "Aren't these dolls?"

"I don't know. Maybe this is what people wear in the city, or when they go on a ship." I smooth down my apron. "I know these clothes wouldn't work for the farm. Can you imagine trying to get the harvest in this get up?" I laugh and twirl around holding the bottom of my skirt. "All I know is I feel clean and I haven't felt clean in a while."

He goes to the back door, and opens it a crack. "We've been in here about thirty minutes. Guess we better try to sneak out and try to find a way to the ship." He gathers his knapsack, tosses mine to me, and we venture out in the storeroom.

Crouching and tiptoeing through the store aisles of hundreds of neatly stacked dolls, doing our best to hide our getaway, we round the last area and see a clear path to the door. Freedom, or at least escape from this store, is a few steps away.

We are set to run out the entrance, when Princess Kamea yells from her enclosed sanctuary. "Miss Brita. Miss Brita. Those are the dolls I want." She points right at us.

We freeze in our steps. The store worker walks back to us. "These aren't dolls, sweetie. They're people."

Miss Brita crouches down to Princess Kamea's level. "I don't think the "Sponsored Companions" program is in Germany yet, Princess

61

Kamea."

The store worker asks, "Sponsored Companions?"

Miss Brita explains, "It is a program for disadvantaged individuals, where people of means, like my employers, agree to house and feed these pitiful souls, who have no home, and the sponsored young person provides companionship for the child. These abandoned are not supported by anyone. They'll starve, if the people of means don't step in and help. So sad. Queen Nalani and King Ahomana are such kind people; they have just procured six Sponsored Companions or SCs for the princess on this trip. They have two from Egypt, two from China, and two from Africa. You haven't heard of that program?"

The store worker nods her head. "Yes, but I haven't heard the particulars. I can assure you that this store is always current. No one outsells us. I guess it's possible that these are the first of our Sponsored Companions dolls. I assume they transport themselves. Did you come on your own?" She looks at us and I remain quiet.

I think it's best to stay quiet. My only hope is that we can escape soon. The more we talk the more chance we have to make a mistake that will get us caught. Colt is stoic, must be thinking the exact same thing.

The worker turns her attention to Miss Brita. "I would have no idea how to sell them to you. You would have to wait for our manager to come back from lunch."

"We have no time to wait. We are on a ship that sails today and cannot dawdle long." Miss Brita stiffens her stance, fiddles with her collar, and nods toward us. "I have been instructed to purchase the SCs here. That's what I am supposed to buy. Too bad we had to waste so much time waiting for the unpleasant lady to finish spewing that you had sold her a defective doll."

The worker nods. "She actually was in trouble with her employer about bringing home the wrong doll."

"You were good to make it right for her. I'm sure she and her employer will appreciate it."

"That's how we get repeat business."

Miss Brita tugs on my braids. "These two sure look the part, dressed in the native garb of Germany—the dirndl and the lederhosen. For future reference, SCs have no families and are thus unmarked."

The store worker puts her finger on her chin. "We did get a poster. Seems strange that these two showed up, without any word. Trina left for lunch, maybe she left some information. I'll check. By the way my name is Ms. DeVane."

Ms. DeVane asks, "You have purchased other SCs?"

"Yes, I told you my employer purchased SCs from the countries of Egypt, China, and Africa." Miss Brita leans over, and whispers loud enough for us to hear. "It's rumored that some countries are trying to sell people who did not want to be in service or people who have families. Terrible stories of countries stealing children."

"How horrible!" Ms. DeVane gasps.

It's a way to get on the ship. How can I pass it up? I must try. Colt would have to understand. It is time that I become the master of my own destiny. After all, I am fifteen. Rite of passage and all.

I step up and curtsy, as Colt helplessly watches. "Hello. We are poor, wretched souls who need someone to take care of us. Ms. DeVane, you are right. Trina talked to us while you were gone and we are Sponsored Companions. I would—" I stop and point at Colt. "We would love to be companions for your adorable daughter."

Miss Brita says, "She's not my child. She's the princess."

Colt opens his mouth to speak, but before he can, Ms. DeVane reaches for my arm and flips it over. "I guess they came on their own. You were right, she's not marked." She grabs Colt's arm and flips to his forearm—bare. "Neither is he."

Princess Kamea bangs on the plastic cover. "I want them. They're my friends, my dirty friends. He gave me an app—"

Chapter 11

My eyes grow wide, as Miss Brita leans down purring to Princess Kamea. "You can't know them, Princess Kamea. Let me ask the nice lady about them. You don't want to get me in trouble, do you?"

Princess Kamea shakes her head and rocks in the buggy, hitting the sides of plastic. "I want them! I want them!"

Ms. DeVane ignores the temper tantrum unfolding before her. "All people of Germany are marked, it's the law." She pulls up her sleeve exposing her forearm tattooed with a castle with three towers jutting from its top with a number 8. "See. I am marked for Hamburg, 8th district." She exposes my forearm. "They're not marked. Everyone is counted and marked. The only explanation is that they must be the Sponsored Companions." Ms. DeVane looks at me. "You talked to Trina, right?"

It's just a little white lie. It can't possibly hurt anyone, except the little girl who will be disappointed when she realizes she doesn't have us to play with. But she'll get over it. Colt has to back me up; it's a way to the ship. The only way with the small amount of time left.

I nod and Ms. DeVane looks over at Colt, who stands there, silently offering nothing. At least he's not contradicting me.

I slide over to him. "These nice people want to take us on the ship with them."

Colt whispers out of the side of his mouth. "They want to *own* us."

"I don't mean to be questioning you, but you do realize that this is Princess Kamea, daughter of Queen Nalani and the Science Ambassador and granddaughter of the high king don't you? I can't take an illegal on the ship. It would be a nightmare since the ambassador is in the middle of a political race for High Chancellor of 'The Consortium of the World.'" Miss Brita looks us up and down. "Do you have papers declaring their authenticity and your right to sell them?"

This is it. We're going to be caught. All of this for nothing. I hold my breath for a moment.

Ms. DeVane shuffles some papers on her desk. "If they talked to Trina, then the papers must be here. Like I told you, my manager is at lunch." She looks for a few more minutes. "I can make you temporary papers. I could send them on the next ship. I don't even know how much they cost."

Miss Brita shakes her head. "Assets are not the problem. Unfortunately, we can't wait. I need to get her back to the ship. We're scheduled for departure in a couple of hours, but they want all passengers boarded before 1500. They have many indentured servants to clear." She pushes the carriage toward the front entrance. "Princess Kamea, I'm sorry. We can't get these dolls."

My hopes of getting on the ship are riding away in the buggy with a little girl. It's possible we might not be caught, but when the princess leaves and the manager gets back, the truth will most likely come out. I guess we'll have to make a break for it. It'll be a mess. I am dejected. Why couldn't they just take us?

Colt's glares at me and mouths, "Trouble."

Understatement of the year.

"I've stayed here too long." Miss Brita looks quickly at her watch. "We really need to get back. It's time for lunch." She flips the bubbled carriage up to get over a rise at the entrance.

Ms. DeVane makes a funny, squished up face, to peer at Kamea through the plastic at the doorway. "How old is she?"

"I want the dolls!" Princess Kamea shrieks.

"She's four, but sometimes she acts younger, like now." Miss Brita leans around to talk to Princess Kamea. "You can't have them." Miss Brita rocks the buggy, trying her best to console its occupant.

"I want the dolls!" Princess Kamea screams at the top of her lungs, bringing a few patrons from the sidewalk into the store to investigate the commotion, including the suited man from before, a regally dressed woman, and a large burly man.

"Kamea?" The woman of obvious Asian descent, dripping in long flowing robes of chiffon and satin, and perfuming the surroundings with her aura of entitlement, sashays into the store. "Why is my daughter screaming?"

Queen Nalani presses her hand to the plastic covering, and her child mimics her movement, touching through the plastic. Queen Nalani's face softens, as she rubs her daughter's plastic-covered hand. "What does my sweet baby want?"

Ms. DeVane curtsies. "It is such an honor to have you in our store—"

Queen Nalani brushes her hand in Ms. DeVane's direction, hardens her face, and turns to the nanny. "What does she want, Miss Brita?"

Miss Brita points toward us. "She wants the Sponsored Companions from Germany, but they have no papers. I explained we could not take them without authentication."

Queen Nalani runs her hand over my braids, touches my apron, and tugs at the suspenders on Colt's outfit. "They are a good looking pair, aren't they?" She checks our arms for marks. "What are their names?"

Ms. DeVane shuffles papers helplessly. "Not sure."

I feel sorry for the store clerk searching so diligently for papers that don't exist. Everyone's demeanor changes around the queen. They obviously worship her or fear her, I'm not sure which.

Miss Brita looks over Ms. DeVane's shoulder. "We still do not know if they're legal."

"We can find out." Queen Nalani looks at me. "What's your name?"

I had spent many years, mostly listening from a distance at how my Mother handled the Collectors, so I only hesitate for a second before answering. "My name is Paisley, Queen Nalani. I'm very pleased to meet you. It would be lovely to come and live with you and your daughter."

Queen Nalani's grin widens. "Are you in need of sponsorship or do you have a family to care for you? Are you stolen?"

I answer, realizing what I'm about to say is not a total lie. "I need sponsorship, my queen." Partly the truth. I really needed to get on that ship.

Queen Nalani turns to Colt. "And you my dear, what is your name and do you need sponsorship?"

Colt hesitates for a moment, but follows my lead. "My name is Colt. I think your daughter, Princess Kamea, is a forceful child who knows what she wants, but should be respected as a daughter of such a great and powerful Queen. It would be my honor to be sponsored by you."

That was downright eloquent. Who knew Colt had it in him?

"Miss Brita, have her draw up the papers and sponsor these two." She waves her hand at Miss Brita and Ms. DeVane. "First of all, I like the way these two look and conduct themselves. We asked if they needed a sponsor, they said yes, and my daughter wants them. Don't make things so hard, Miss Brita. No one would dare to cross the royal family."

Miss Brita bows. "Of course, my queen."

"How do you want them branded, Queen Nalani?" Ms. DeVane asks.

Branded? As in hot metal iron. Oh no, what have I gotten us into?

"Trivial, I don't take care of trivial." Queen Nalani is miffed at the question. "Take care of this, Miss Brita." Queen Nalani leaves the store and a huge man walks behind her.

Miss Brita looks at Ms. DeVane. "Bodyguard." She looks at us. "We have to mark them with the royal mark, but of course you don't have the branding iron here, do you?"

Miss DeVane answers, "No, of course not."

"Just put a temporary tattoo on them for now. What do you have in

66

terms of temporaries?"

Temporary. I can live with temporary. Colt can too though he won't admit it.

Ms. DeVane pulls out a book and confers with Miss Brita over possible choices, their backs toward us.

Colt grabs our things and whispers to me. "You seem to have a charmed luck thing going for you. Of course we're not on the ship yet." He secretly stores our knapsacks underneath some blankets in the back of Princess Kamea's carriage. "Not completely lucky though, somebody practically owns us."

I whisper back. "We'll be careful. We just need to find my mom and Gretel before the ship leaves."

"Don't forget we also need to get off that same ship too and all within a few hours. We are definitely cutting it close. But I'm not complaining, Paisley. I'm actually impressed."

I smile. "For now, we are sponsored by the royals. Honestly don't worry, the plan is that we'll be off before it sails and no one will have time to own us. I really don't know how else we could have gotten on that ship."

We smile at each other. It could work out. It has so far.

Miss Brita points out an outline of a ship to Ms. DeVane. "I didn't see any crowns, but this will work since we are going on the Queen Nalani. Make sure you write Royal SCs."

Ms. DeVane nods. "I'll get right on that. The Queen Nalani is the biggest ship that has ever come to these ports. Is this your first trip?"

Miss Brita, distracted by the princess, doesn't answer.

Ms. DeVane reaches in her drawer, retrieves two guides for the tattoos of a ship's outline, and motions for us to join her.

Miss Brita rocks the princess back and forth in her carriage. "As quickly as possible. I don't know how much longer I can keep her quiet."

The princess hasn't been too quiet up to now, so what could possibly change? It seems that the only one tiring out on this expedition is Miss Brita. She looks like she could sleep for days. Wonder if we'll get our own bed on the ship. No reason to fret about that, we'll be off before we see our quarters. Silly thinking.

I sit down first, and Ms. DeVane proceeds to draw the tattoo on me, tediously paying attention to detail. "Before the doll store, this is what I did for a living. This paste is made from the Henna plant. I will make yours red and his brown. It will wear off after thirty days. You might want to wait to put the permanent tattoo on until this one wears off." Ms. DeVane ceases talking after noticing that Miss Brita is engrossed in dawdling with the princess. She finishes, calls Colt over, and repeats the procedure in total silence.

The total process takes about fifteen minutes. Colt and I each take a turn entertaining, as much as we are able, Princess Kamea through the plastic bubble. It's the least we can do since we are gaining passage on the ship and plan to abandon it soon after.

As she finishes, Miss Brita inspects each tattoo. "Great job. You are quite good at this. We'll be traveling on the ship for around a month, so the time schedule will work." She fills out and signs the document. "I know you don't know what to charge, but because we're in a hurry, I've taken the liberty of filling in the trade. I put the amount we bartered for two companions in Egypt. It's a fair price. We have deposits of food, and a big selection of non-flawed young girls and boys that you can use as your next SCs to replace these. It's a lucrative trade. An appointed executor at the Trading Bank of Germany administers the royal family's economics. This paper will allow you to withdraw the appropriate amount. I have taken the liberty of adding twenty percent to your rate for handling and the tattoos for you personally. Is that acceptable?"

Flawless people to trade for us? What does that mean? My heart sinks.

"Thanks...thank you so much." Ms. DeVane takes the paper and laughs nervously. "More than acceptable." She walks Miss Brita out of the store. "If you will please let Queen Nalani know that our store is always open to her."

"This is on you." Colt leans over to me. "They bought us with other people. This is *so* sick. Let's find your mom and sister and get out of this freak show."

The pit of my stomach churns. I didn't feel so smart or clever at the thought of others suffering in my place. What can I do now? My bad feeling transfers to my churning stomach.

Ms. DeVane shouts, "Miss Brita, when will you be returning?"

Miss Brita motions for Colt and me to follow her. "I'm not sure. The royals are on a political cruise to garner support and to strengthen their assets by collecting more non-flawed people and labor workers. We will be selling their service, dropping them off at various ports, or taking them with us. I don't make those choices. All I know is we set sail soon."

"Mom and Gretel!" I manage a muffled whisper. What have I gotten us into? What kind of people are they? Buying and selling people like slaves. It's barbaric and wrong. Colt is right, when we get to safety we will find someone with power who can do something about all these wrongs. Unfortunately, it won't be today.

Colt holds up his hands to hush me. "Quiet, we have to make it to the ship first. Do your part. I hope that we can get on and off quickly. I don't like the idea of being of being an *owned* even if it's only for a short time."

I whisper back to him. "What do you suppose Sponsored Companions are supposed to do exactly and where do they stay?"

Maybe he senses my distress because he playfully knocks into me on the way out. "Probably nothing good. Who knows? I'm not planning on sticking around to find out." He smiles at me. "I got to hand it to you though; you did get us onto the ship, legally, and with time to spare."

Colt walks next to me. "Maybe bringing you along was the right choice after all."

I giggle and Colt asks, "What's so funny?"

I giggle some more. "That you thought you actually had a choice."

Chapter 12

Finally, we make it. We're on the way to the ship. I have to admit, I'm proud of myself. It'll be more fun to walk through the streets legally without having to look over my shoulder. Now all that's left to do is to board the ship, find Gretel and Mom, locate a secure way off the ship, make it safely back to Bavaria, and hide while others change the world to a more civilized place. Whew! Thinking about it all at one time gives me a headache. One step at a time. Make it to the ship without incident.

Miss Brita checks her watch. "We have a few minutes before we need to get to the ship." She peers down at Princess Kamea. "But we'd better rush, since Princess Kamea is hungry."

Princess Kamea yells, her voice magnified by the microphone in the plastic. "I'm not hungry. I'm full."

Startled, passers-by stop and look for a moment. One woman points to the royal insignia on the buggy and whispers, "Royals." The rest go back to their routine.

Miss Brita shakes her head. "Fine, dear." She looks over at Colt and me. "She's a handful. Hope you're up for it."

We're not planning to actually do this job, but no reason to hint at that. I tap the top of the buggy. "I'm sure we'll all get along famously."

Miss Brita pushes the buggy. "Let's hope that's true. Since she's not hungry, we can walk a little slower and check out some of the vendors along the way, if—" She points to the carriage. "—if she doesn't get too fussy." Colt takes over pushing the buggy, which brings a smile to Miss Brita's face.

Walking through the streets as a *legal* is a new experience. I'm able to plunder through the wares and offerings of the vendors.

I whisper where only Colt can hear. "Colt, this is the first time in days that I don't feel I have to hide. It's hard hiding all of the time. I feel like I've hidden all of my life."

Dad died a long time ago. Hiding became a big part of my life. I will happily take a break from it, even if it's only for an hour or two. I pick up the paper with the picture of the castle that I located before. I whisper, "Where dreams come true."

Miss Brita pulls the exact same card out for Princess Kamea. "See this picture of the castle in Germany? It looks just like your Cinderella castle back home."

Back home. Where is the princess's home? A castle? It's only fitting that a princess live in a castle. Why is there such a difference in how people live? It doesn't seem fair. Not fair at all.

Princess Kamea snatches at the card through the plastic. "I want it!"

Miss Brita signs a piece of paper for the storeowner and hands me the card. "For the princess."

Clearly, the princess gets what she wants. To get what you want all the time, what a novelty that would be.

I slip the recently purchased picture into the back pocket of Princess Kamea's buggy and ask Miss Brita, "Where do you and the princess live?"

Miss Brita answers, "We're from a place in America called Orlando. The castle there is built to look like this castle in Germany. Have you ever been?" Looking horrified, she quickly puts her hands to her mouth. "I'm sorry. I'm being insensitive. Of course, you haven't been there. You wouldn't have means for that. Sorry." She pats my arm with a "poor pitiful you" look on her face. "But now you can travel with the princess. How fortunate for you to have been chosen."

Chosen? Not really. Owned, bought, purchased—those are better words to describe recent events. But I can't gripe too much, I'm on my way to the ship to retrieve my family.

"No, I've never been." I rub my fingers around the picture of the castle I'd pulled out and smile at Colt. "The place where dreams come true." He nods. I know he remembers.

I place the picture carefully back in the carousel, and continue down the cobbled street with our newly formed entourage.

Princess Kamea starts to fuss and whine, so we speed up. Miss Brita constantly tends to the princess trying to soothe her by rocking her buggy as we walk and stopping occasionally to stroke the plastic. Not sure if the princess can be consoled, but Miss Brita gives it her best try.

Miss Brita finally throws up her hands towards the end of the walk. "Princess, we're almost back at the ship." Miss Brita looks over at Colt and me. "We need to board as soon as possible. You two walk in with me. We will get you registered, and then I'll show you where to go."

"Look." I nod my head toward the massive ship. The original name, "Queen Mary IV," that had been written with raised letters that could not be completely erased has been consigned to rest as a shadow beneath a new moniker in bolder brighter lettering. It is a name that both Colt and I recognize, "Queen Nalani."

Colt raises his eyebrows. "This ship is named for the princess's mother?"

"The queen is the only daughter of King Ahomana. The royal family owns a great many things, as you will soon find out. They are the wealthiest people in the world and the most powerful. See, you are very lucky." Miss Brita guides us around a line of people waiting to board. The great ship is massive in size and dauntingly crowded by people scurrying about helping with luggage, pulling ropes, polishing anything tied or not tied down, and checking lines.

It's a madhouse of individuals, all trying to either talk their way into the front of the line or people trying to reason with those in line as to why they have to wait. I'm confused, intimidated, and long for the simple life of the farm and the serenity of its few occupants.

Colt is stopped, which causes the buggy carrying the princess to halt too. A man's voice booms as the line of people stare at Colt and me with looks of disgust. A woman shouts, "Stop them. They're cutting."

The man yells at Colt. "Back of the line, son."

Another woman in line, with red lips and holding a yapping small dog, steps in front of Miss Brita. This action causes the suited man following closely behind our group to quickly swoop in and push the woman aside. He says, "Stand back. Royal family."

The red-lipped woman, annoyed, announces to no one in particular, "Are you sure? I don't recognize any of them."

The man yanks her out of the line, shoving her face in the direction of the carriage that Colt is pushing. "Princess Kamea."

"Sorry," the embarrassed woman mumbles and retreats into anonymity with her yapping dog.

After this incident, it only takes a couple of minutes for the line to peel back, making way for our group to go to the front, where a uniformed man and lady are checking papers and marks. To the side of this gangway are two more entrances. One of the entrances seems to be filled with poorer people, possibly the Uncounted or farm workers. The other looks to be an opening for loading supplies.

Colt and I walk slowly toward the uniformed man. Off the side of the port, corralled children, being separated from the adults, are hoisted into a truck. They are young. The oldest appears to be no more than ten years old. An adult tries to pull one of the children yelling, "She's my daughter." The man is hauled off by Mercs. A shot is fired and the man slumps. The children and adults scream.

Colt and I gasp. Mercs quickly dispose of him by throwing his dead body into the sea. We hear some surrounding comments.

"All this screaming is upsetting my dog. Undesirables do not know their place."

"Of course that was not that man's daughter. Children are only taken

72

if they are orphans."

"He was probably crazy. Poor soul out of his mind and shot. He'll be better off."

It's hard not to react, but I know we have to get on the ship. It makes me realize how imperative it is that I get to my family and we escape off this ship away from the murderous Mercs.

I whisper to Colt, "Do you think those are the children that are used like money to barter for purchases like us, or maybe their lives pay for the supplies being loaded right now? Killed for trying to reclaim your own child. That is wrong."

"It's horrible, but there is nothing we can do about it right now. Keep to the plan. When we're free, maybe we can figure out a way to help."

I speak low to Colt. "I didn't know there were this many people in the world. It scares me to think how many of them can be evil. What kind of people kill with no remorse? What kind of monsters could possibly think selling and enslaving people is right?" My eyes flip from side to side, taking it all in, paying particular attention to the line of chained people to my right. "That's probably where we need to start looking for Mom and Gretel."

Colt asks, "Do you see them? When we get on, we're going to have to locate them quickly because this ship sails soon."

Stressed by the amount of security stops, I struggle to catch my breath and start to hyperventilate. "This is much more controlled that I had imagined. It's going to be hard to get off."

Colt signals for me to calm down. "No choice. We'll figure it out later. Right now we need to get on the ship." He motions ahead.

He's right. No use worrying about getting off before we make it on. There is no guarantee that my family is here, but we have to look to make sure. If they aren't on here, then we can begin to comb the city for them. The ship has to be ruled out before it sails. We cannot leave them in the hands of the Mercs; they are cold-blooded killers. I know that for a fact, except Riley. I know he's different.

Miss Brita catches up to us and takes over pushing the princess's buggy. "You're wasting time sightseeing. Besides, what is there to see? You two need to stop chattering and move." She steps quickly ahead of us.

Colt and I are stopped again, and a large line forms in front of us. We try to move forward, but are pushed back. Yelling and loud voices ensue. The people in the lines speak freely.

"We need to get on; they are only taking people on for another half-hour. Quit pushing."

"The way we're being treated, you would think we were poor. Don't

73

they realize how important we are?"

"I am a personal friend to the royals. I should be treated with respect."

"We have first class tickets, for goodness sakes. The minute I get on the ship, I'm going to complain."

Unable to make much progress, Colt and I move out to the side, and are soon spotted by the suited man. He grabs both our wrists, searching for the ship's tattoo. "Colt and Paisley, right?" We nod and he continues, "Come with me." He leads us to the front.

At the front of the line, Miss Brita impatiently taps her toe and flails her arms, trying to quiet the princess, when she spies the suited man with us in tow. "Thanks so much for your help. I thought they were lost. It's so crowded here."

As we approach, our forearms are examined and the new Henna tattoos are compared to the papers. Miss Brita asks the uniformed man in charge, "Can we speed this up? I need to get the princess on board?"

The uniformed man nods. "These two, with the princess and Miss Brita, are cleared." He shouts to a woman staffing the next station.

We continue to another desk and Miss Brita steps into a chamber. In a few seconds, a light emits from the chamber, and a beeping sound is heard. The man announces, "Brita Kass, nanny to the royals."

Miss Brita nods, and then pulls the buggy with Princess Kamea into the chamber and again the light glows. A beautiful bugle melody signals the end of the inspection. The crowd quiets and every head lowers. The uniformed people stand at attention, and then each person bows from their waist.

The uniformed woman in charge says softly, "Identified—Her Royal Highness, The Royal Princess, Princess Kamea."

Dead silence followed by hushed whispers of comments such as, "It's the princess. I heard the royal family was going to be on this ship. How wonderful," engulf the room spreading throughout and into the gangway below.

Colt and I wait for instructions. It doesn't take long.

Miss Brita waves towards us. "They need to be initially scanned. They are the princess's new "Sponsored Companions.""

The uniformed woman, in charge, leans down to the enclosed princess. "Princess, you are getting quite a collection of these living dolls. How many does that make now?"

Princess Kamea starts to answer, "I don't—"

Miss Brita answers for her, "She has eight, with these new additions."

74

The woman smiles at Princess Kamea. "We'll take care of entering the specifics on the papers." She motions for me to step in the chamber. "Scanning. Paisley Germany, Royal Sponsored Companion."

After exiting I'm told to sit at a table; another scanner draws on the back of my hand with a light. "This is your code. You can't see it because it is ultraviolet, but when you are scanned from now on, this will come up, letting everyone know that you are owned by the royals."

I seem to be getting preferential treatment. Guess there is something special to be owned by the richest people in the world. Too bad, we live in the world that kills and enslaves people.

The scanner finishes. I stretch out my arm. "It kind of tickles." I smile at the guard. "So do you know how long are we sponsored or have to serve the royals? How long are we owned?"

The guard cocks his head and furrows his eyebrow. "You are always owned by the royals, of course." Then he smiles. "Or until the princess throws you out."

My life is now controlled by the whim of a four-year-old. That's a scary thought.

Chapter 13

The princess might throw us out? Out to where? To the horse corrals, to be sold or to be bartered for? Glad I'm getting out of here.

I take a deep breath. "Of course," I repeat, shaking. Maybe I'm not that smart after all. Looking around, I'm glad that Colt is out of earshot. No need for him to worry. Besides, we'll be off the ship before it sails and long before any of that matters.

I'm relieved to see Colt after his identity announcement.

"Brother and sister." Miss Brita points back and forth to Colt and me.

Colt answers. "Yes." He winks at me and I scrunch my face.

Needing to find my sister, not inherit a brother. I have a family, thank you very much. But it won't hurt for us to go along with it.

We walk a few more steps, and he whispers. "We're off as soon as we find Gretel."

And Mom. He always forgets Mom. I don't like the way his voice drops and sounds dreamy when he talks of Gretel. It's weird. But at least we are both concentrating on getting off as soon as possible.

The ship's common area is elaborately decorated. The main lobby boasts a magnificent crystal chandelier that sparkles with dewdrop shaped crystals, draping like icicles hanging off a cave's edge. Large paintings of Queen Nalani and the princess adorn the walls. I surmise that the massive painting of the large man adorned in flowing robes and wearing a jeweled crown must be the king. Candelabras sit on ornate hall tables and gold encrusted mirrors are prominently displayed. Men and women, dressed with aprons and black and white suits, scurry about picking up cups and glasses that have been discarded.

Miss Brita motions for a bearded man to join us. "Please take this brother and sister to the Sponsored Companion floor (SC)—room 1026. I have to take the Princess for something to eat. We will see you tomorrow." She motions to us. "Take today to get acclimated. Fredrick will show you."

The nanny removes Princess Kamea's bubble and it's the first time we get a clear, unencumbered look at her face. She resembles her mother, with the smooth black hair and almond shaped eyes. "Tell them goodbye Princess. You'll see them tomorrow."

Looking at her this way, it's hard to remember the little spoiled brat throwing tantrums just an hour ago. She looks so sweet, almost angelic. I almost wish we could take her with us. Almost. I stifle a giggle thinking about what a nightmare that would be. Half the kingdom would be looking for us. Still, I should be nice to the sweet girl. After all, the problems in the world are not this little girl's fault.

I lean down. "Goodbye sweet girl, we'll play tomorrow. You be good." The little girl giggles and smiles.

Colt grabs her hand. "See you tomorrow." He cautiously removes our belongings from the bottom of the empty carriage before it is rolled off.

The princess toddles alongside her nanny as they disappear down the long corridor.

"I hate lying to her," Colt whispers to me as we follow Fredrick.

"Me, too." It really does make me feel sad. Unfortunately, the way this world is right now, it won't be the last lie I have to tell before I return. Lies are all that are keeping Colt and me alive. I need to focus on that undisputable truth. I have to lie to survive.

Fredrick leads us down so many flights of stairs it's hard to keep count. "This far down, you'd think you'd be at the bottom of the ocean by now." Fredrick laughs nervously.

"Since we are almost at the bottom, I hope this ship doesn't sink," Colt whispers to me as we walk down another flight of stairs.

With that, I giggle. "We would never survive. I guess we could cut an opening out the side of the ship."

He pulls at his clothes. "Lots of tools to choose from. What are we supposed to cut with, my hat or suspenders, or maybe your apron?" We share a laugh.

The stairs that start out so elegantly carpeted, wear as the flights descend. Each flight down, the level of care declines. The paintings that decorate the landings of the stairs also deteriorate in level of worth. The first flights, so embellished and rich-looking with gold fluted frames surrounding portraits of women and men of days gone by, are replaced with decorations of a smaller, less ornate nature, until finally the paintings disappear completely. As the altitude drops, so does the quality. Toward the end, peeling wallpaper and stained carpet seem the norm.

We aren't at the very bottom, but close to it, when Fredrick finally stops, and guides us down a long corridor with no wallpaper and threadbare carpet. "This is your room."

He takes Colt's arm, runs the back of his hand in front of the door latch, and the door pops open. "Either of your hands will open your door. No one else should be able to open it." Frederick runs his hand under his chin. "Of course, the Mercs and people associated with security could get in, if they wanted." He shakes his head. "They would never come down here to your room. It's beneath them." He smiles. "That is, unless you plan on causing trouble."

"Why would we cause trouble?" I push the door back shut. "I want to try." I wave my hand under the latch and it opens. "I love this."

Frederick bows. "I take my leave now. Stay in your room." He turns and disappears down the corridor.

Inside our assigned undersized stateroom, bunk beds sit to the left, and a sliding door opens to reveal a tiny bathroom, just large enough for one person to stand in, complete with a tiny shower, petite basin and miniature toilet, workable, but very small. A couple of drawers are housed under the beds. Very utilitarian, absent of decoration.

I sit on the bottom bunk. "I like this room."

Colt promptly pulls me off the bed. "No time to get comfortable. We're going to find your mom and Gretel and get off this ship."

I stand up abruptly. "Mom and Gretel. Of course. It's going to take forever just to get back up top."

He looks at his watch. "We have less than three hours before this ship sails and we are stuck. They'll probably pull the boarding plank long before then. We most likely are going to have to swim for it. Whatever we do, we have to hurry."

"I heard Miss Brita tell the store owner that we were going to be out to sea for a month." I enter the bathroom area. "I'm going to the bathroom, before we go. I at least want to use this room once." I slide the door shut.

"Good idea." He yells through the door. "I'll go next, and then we'll find out where they are holding the farm people. Hopefully, it's close to this level."

In a few minutes, we gather our belongings, and exit the door to our room. At the end of the sparsely decorated hallway, a group of three men huddle, speaking in soft tones.

Colt approaches the group. "Hi, I'm Colt and this is Paisley." He waves his hand toward me. "We are looking for some of our friends who came in on the train earlier. Do you know where that group is?"

One of the men, who appears to be about thirty, dressed in clean jeans and a starched buttoned down shirt answers, "I'm Joshua Clarke. You're the new SCs right?" Colt nods and Joshua continues. "There's only been one group today. Actually, we helped unload them when they came in. They're three floors below."

I move closer to the group. "There are more floors farther down? How big is this ship?"

Another one of the group, who looks more the age of a teenager, dressed the same with close-cropped dark hair, laughs. "Yes. My Dad is the overseer of the 13th level. I'm Matthew." He moves closer to me. "I can show you."

I back away.

"You can't look for your friends today." Joshua shakes his head. "You can look another day. You're not supposed to leave your assigned floor."

That won't work. We need to be able to search. We have to talk them into letting us look. I move closer to Matthew and smile at him, cocking my head. He wants to help us. I can tell. He just needs a little persuading.

"Sorry we just wanted to say hi to our friends." Colt crosses his arms. "I know we're going to be here a long time. It's just that we were separated in the transfer and we wanted them to know we made it on the ship. Didn't want them to worry needlessly."

Matthew moves closer to me. "Your brother is just being a good friend. I understand." Matthew hooks his arm around mine. "Dad won't care." He looks at Joshua. "Really, Dad won't care as long as I'm with them. Besides, we're not really following that rule; we're not on our right floor either."

The third man lifts his arm in a halt position. "Matt, I don't know about this. We need to go back where we belong."

"Uncle Leo, I'll be fine." Matt leads me, motioning for Colt to follow, and we proceed down the stairs.

The other two men trot around us, shake their heads with obvious disapproval, and mumble. "You're on your own."

Matt ignores them.

Noticing the similarities of all of the decks, I ask, "Do you ever get mixed up on what floor you're on?"

Matt laughs. "All the time. It's funny the ship's floors are supposed to go backwards all the way down to 1, but someone told us when the royals came aboard they wouldn't be housed on anything that wasn't labeled the first floor. First class all the way so they reversed the order." He points to a small easily missed sign, tacked on the wall at the start of each corridor. "See this tells you the number of the floor you're on. All you need to know is which floor you're going to."

Good to know. "How many more?" I ask, quickening my pace. We have limited time. Can't dawdle.

"Two." Matt emulates my faster movements. "You're in a hurry."

"I want to see my friend." I hop two steps at a time almost falling.

Matt catches up and runs beside me. "Is it a boyfriend?"

I stop for a moment and laugh. "No silly, it's my—"

Colt catches up to us both, runs two steps in front of us, and finishes my sentence. "It's her friend, Gretel."

I nod and roll my eyes toward Colt. "My friend, Gretel.

"Number 13." Matt points to the sign. "We're here."

He leads us in. "This is the common area. This is where she should be."

Double doors open into a large room, crammed with people of all ages and descriptions. Long lines, one for food, and one for the bathroom, take up the east and west of the room. At the front area, men sit around a table and busily write on a piece of paper as questions are answered. The stench of body odor is powerful. The line of people moves first to the information table, then to an area where they go behind a curtain that has showerheads in view that turn on and off every few minutes, the toweled person emerges and is given a set of clothes. Next, they go behind another drape and change into the garments, and then they pick up blankets, and get a lanyard with a number on it.

Tears fill my eyes as I realize this is what my mother and sister had to endure. I need to find them, and we need to escape all of this madness. I swallow my tears. "Will the people at the table be able to tell me Gretel's whereabouts?"

Matt laughs. "Let's hope so, that's what they are here for. Since she's a friend of yours, I'll try to get her an easy assignment."

Colt moves closer to us. "They assign work here?"

Matt nods and the three of them go back behind the table of organizers. Matt picks up a clipboard. "This might be harder than I thought. There are many people on this list. I don't see a Gretel."

I grab at the list. "I don't mind looking."

A man hurriedly rushes up and snatches the list out of my hand. "Matt, they aren't supposed to be down here." He pulls my hand and runs it under a machine. "They belong to the royals." He slaps Matt hard in the face. "You can't take the royals' property."

Matt stands stoic. "Dad, they're just looking for a friend."

Matt's Dad shakes his head. "I don't care what they're doing. I have my orders. You can't have them down here. You'll get us killed. We sail in a little over two hours. Take them back where they belong."

Matt doesn't move.

"Now!"

Matt grabs Colt and me by the arms, and hurriedly leads us out of the double doors. "I'm sorry. My Dad is a rule follower. We'll look for your friend later after we sail when things have calmed down."

"We don't have time." I turn to go back in. "No, we have to find—"

Colt grabs me, pulling me to the stairs. "That's fine Matt. I

80

understand. We don't want to get you in trouble." He pushes me toward the first step. "We'll find our way back."

Matt hangs his head, taking a few steps toward me. "Okay. I should go talk to my Dad anyway." He rubs my arm. "Sorry, I really want to help you. I'll find you later, okay?"

He didn't help at all. I grit my teeth. "Okay."

Colt and I walk up a flight of stairs.

"Colt, what was that all about? Why did you give up so easily?"

Colt stops at the top of the first flight of stairs. "I've got a plan."

Chapter 14

"**A** plan?" I refuse to move any farther. "What kind of plan? You think you can just throw out a comment like 'I've got a plan,' with no explanation, and I'm just going to blindly follow you? You have some—"

A man dressed in black pants and a necktie, and carrying a clipboard, scurries by us. We stop talking for a moment. The suited man stops and turns around. "How much farther to the wine cellar?"

Colt shrugs his shoulders. "I didn't even know there was a wine cellar."

"Careful. Behind you." The man whispers to Colt and me. Turning around, we come face to face with two large square-jawed men.

One the men grabs Colt by the shoulder. "Back to your room." He takes Colt's forearm, waves it under a small metal object, and then looks at the apparatus. He motions to the man who is with him. "He belongs on Level 10, 'Sponsored Companions' Suite." Then, he repeats the action with me. "Her, too." He motions to the other square-faced man. "Take them back." The first man looks at Colt. "You need to stay where you belong. We have to check everyone before we sail. He'll take you and when you get there, stay in your room."

I mouth at Colt. "What now?" I can only hope that his plan will still work.

Colt shrugs his shoulders and points to his watch. "We'll come back— we have time."

The walk up the stairs to level 10 is long and silent. As we reach our designated level, the square-jawed man reminds us to stay on our floor and leaves. We peer down the corridor and see that another man is waiting outside of our room.

Colt reaches the door. "Who are you?"

"I am Jacque. I have been sent to wardrobe you."

Colt shakes his head. "We don't have time to be wardrobed."

Jacque turns abruptly around. "I'm not sure you understand how it works around here. You're new. You follow orders, you don't give them. I don't have time for you either, but I've been given orders to wardrobe the two new SCs so let's go." Colt and I don't move.

"Now!" Jacque shouts. We still don't move. Jacque walks a little ways, then turns back around and shouts. "Unless you want to be locked in your rooms. You will get these wardrobes."

No choice now. "Colt, we better go with him. We can't be locked in our room. We have to find Gretel and Mom."

We follow Jacque to the wardrobe area; fortunately, it is only one floor down. The room holds racks of different kinds of clothes. Jacque measures Colt first. I sit at the end of the corridor, and watch.

Jacque grabs some slacks and throws them to Colt, obviously in some sort of changing area, on the other side of the room. "Here, try these on." Colt grunts, "okay," and then Jacque throws him six more pair. "Seven pair ought to be enough. You put the dirty laundry out daily, and the girl comes by and picks it up." Jacque grabs shirts, shoes, socks, and puts them all in a laundry bag. "Hang these up in your room, and put the other stuff in the drawers. Your room will be cleaned daily. Fresh linens and toiletries will be provided, as needed. Okay, my boy, you're all set. See that wasn't too hard."

Not too hard and thankfully didn't take too long.

Colt is clad in brown slacks and a white buttoned shirt, brown leather loafers and socks, more conservative garb than the lederhosen he had been wearing all day. He says, "I do like these clothes."

I look him up and down. "Thought you were going to wear those other shoes forever?" I laugh.

He smiles, rolling up the toe part of his new shoes. "These are pretty comfortable too."

Jacque motions to me. Jacque pulls out slacks, shoes, dresses of varying lengths, blouses, and socks. "Try a couple on, and then, like I told your brother, as you wear the items put them in the dirty laundry outside your door, the clothes will be returned when they are clean."

I am dressed in a pair of slacks, printed shirt, and slip on shoes. I make sure to move the four-leaf clover from my dress pocket to my slacks. Smiling, I remark, "A little more practical."

Jacque takes us to the outside doors. "I have to go and wardrobe more people on another floor. You're all set." He looks at Colt. "Can you find your way back?"

We both nod, trying not to look too pleased, and rush back to our room to drop the clothes off.

Free of our baggage and standing outside our room, I ask, "What's your plan? We're running out of time!"

Colt pulls the door shut. "I know. I saw a boy that I knew earlier, down in the bottom area. He'll know where they sent your mom and Gretel. We just need to get back down there before anyone else comes by to feed us or pinch us or whatever else these crazy ship people are going to try to do to us. Let's go!"

83

That's his plan. Not much of one. Doesn't he realize that I'm perfectly capable of coming up with a plan? For goodness sakes, who got us on the ship in the first place? Me. He needs to figure out that I am a contributing partner to this—whatever it is. For now, we'll try his plan since we have to find Gretel and Mom and in a hurry. At least we are free of people forcing us to stay in our room. It could be worse. How? I guess it could be worse if we were in jail. That's a sobering thought. I better put that kind of thinking out of my mind.

Sprinting down the stairs, we make our way, passing only a handful of people along the trek, who are scurrying about making last minute preparations for the ship's departure. Conversations run the gambit of benign to ridiculous.

"Room 206 wants their covers turned down."

"They can't turn down their own covers?"

"Room 315 thinks the wallpaper in their room is too bright, they want it changed."

"Room 388 ordered cranberries, not blueberries."

"Where are Room 445's white roses? They were supposed to have white roses."

"Room 178 says that the ocean is on the wrong side."

I comment as we run. "Are you hearing this? Is this how rich people live? The farm was so much simpler. When you're hungry, you eat. When you're sleepy, you go to bed. When you wake up, you work. How I wish I was there now."

"Let's get back there." Reaching level 13, Colt slams up against the corridor, pulling me against the wall also. "Stay here, I'm going to go find out what I can."

Colt disappears.

Leaning up against the wall, I hear a conversation in the hallway. I decide to retreat farther down the hall, out of sight.

One man says, "You need to try to work through the pain."

Another voice says, "I don't know if I can."

The first says back, "You have to. If you don't, you're going to find yourself on the 15th level."

"What's that?"

"That is the throw away floor. The place where they take people who are hurt, like you. They call them the Undesirables."

"I'll work through it, it'll heal. I don't want to be an Undesirable. I hear they leave those people for dead."

"I've heard they do worse. Stay strong, brother."

The voices disappear.

84

How different this world is. I'm still hidden when I hear Colt come out of the door and catch a glimpse of his face as he darts up the stairs.

Is he leaving me? What the heck? I run after him. "Where are you going?"

Colt stops and hugs me. "Sorry, I thought maybe you had to leave, I didn't see you."

We don't have time for these emotions. I pull away. "What did you find out?"

"I know where your mom is."

Mom. My face glows and I lose my breath.

He starts up the stairs. "Follow me."

I run the flights, sprinting after him like a lion running after a gazelle's scent. I don't even care that he didn't tell me the specifics. I don't care that he is running as if he's the king of the world. All I care about at this moment is that I'm going to see my mother.

He finally stops to catch his breath. "She's working in the kitchen. We really are running out of time. Let's hurry."

My stomach flips. "This is it." I rub the dirt off the sign, uncovering the writing and it reads "Kitchen." "How are we going to get in?"

"Watch." Colt bursts into the kitchen, spouting as he enters. "Excuse me. Room 116 wants some pears right away." He grabs a serving tray sitting on a table near the door. "Who has pears?" The kitchen staff rushes around. Pears fly through the air and a white uniformed net-haired woman catches two of the pears and proceeds to cut them up. He turns back, motioning at me and whispers, "Look for your mother."

I scrunch in behind him, surveying up and down and around all of the kitchen equipment. I finally recognize the curve of my mother's derriere, bending over in front of the stove. "Mom!" I say aloud, at first garnering the attention of a few of the surrounding workers who look up momentarily, and then go back to the busy kitchen work they were doing.

Success! We found Mom! I run over to her. "Mom, are you okay? Where's Gretel?"

My mother drops the cake that she was in the middle of pulling out of the oven. "Oh my goodness, I was so afraid for you." Mom hugs me, and points to the cake on the floor. "I think it survived. Can you help me?"

My mother and I manage to scoop up the dropped cake pan, with its sugary contents still intact before we turn and hug each other again tightly.

"Mom, I didn't know what to think when I got back and you were gone."

I'm definitely not going to tell my mother how afraid I had been for

85

myself and for them. I won't share the fact that I had all but given up hope of seeing her again. I will wait until we are all home on the farm and I will show my mother everyday how much she means to me. How wonderful she is and how happy I am to have her as a mother. Later, that will be for later. But for right now, we just need to get off the ship.

Mother looks confused. "How did you—?"

Colt walks up. "Hello, Mrs. Mueller. Remember me? It's Colt, you used to teach me English."

She hugs Colt quickly and we move toward the door. "Sure. Actually, Gretel told me you were watching our girl. Have you found Gretel?"

Colt guides us through the kitchen. "No, but we need to get out of this kitchen."

At the door, my mother stops. "I can't go."

I drop my arms. "Why can't you go, Mom?"

My mother holds both sides of my arms. "Sweet girl, this is the real world. We can't just get up and go back to the farm. Things are different. They have taken over the farm. We have no home to go back to."

"I know that. But we can get it back." Tears well up in my eyes. "Mom, I want to go back to my Ferris wheel."

Mom strokes my hair. "I know you do, my sweet girl. But we are all together on this ship. We can figure out a way to stay together, but not if we get up and walk out on the jobs that have been assigned to us."

Has my mother been brainwashed? Since when did Mom obey and give up so easily? There is something more going on.

She holds my face in her hands. "Do you understand?"

"Not at all. You're not making any sense." I shake my head. "We came all this way to save you."

Colt opens the outside door. "Sit here. Talk and figure this out." We sit on the bench outside the kitchen, while Colt stands as look out.

Mother strokes my braids. "How did you get here? How did you get on the ship without marks?"

What is Mother talking about? Why is she so set on staying? Doesn't she realize it's better for us back on the farm? I hang my head. "What does that matter?"

"It doesn't matter. I just want to make sure that you can legally stay on the ship with me and Gretel."

My mother has lost her mind. Why is she saying all of this? It makes no sense. I don't believe this.

I shake her. "What are you saying? Staying on the ship? We're not staying!"

"Calm down. I'm glad you're here." My mother lifts my head up by my chin. "You did save me. You're here with me, Gretel is here with me, and that is how you saved me. We're all saving each other."

Maybe it's something with Gretel. "Where's Gretel, Mom?"

Colt is interested now. Any mention of Gretel just perks him up. Here he comes over nosing around wanting to know about Gretel.

Mother smiles. "Gretel is working with Ambassador Grayson, Queen Nalani's husband, on some science lab experiments he is conducting. He was so impressed with her medical knowledge. I don't think she told him she taught herself. He's helping to organize the new world. He's going to save us. He's going to change the world."

Queen Nalani the person who buys people as slaves, her husband is going to save the world. Right? My mother *has* been brainwashed. Maybe Colt and I can force Mother to leave for her own good since she is not thinking straight. Colt will help me. We need an idea to get Mom to go with us, and then we'll go after Gretel.

Colt asks, "Who is Gretel with?" Then adds sarcastically, "What a bunch of baloney. Really, save the world?" He angrily mutters, "All lies."

"We don't have a choice. They are *our* truths now and we have to believe in something." My mother glares at Colt.

Colt demands, "Where *exactly* is Gretel on the ship?"

Mother cocks her head. "She's with the ambassador. She said they are locked in the lab until the ship sails. It's on far side of the ship. It's impossible to get to without an escort. I'll try to get you a visit in a few days."

Colt whispers to me, "We'll never get to Gretel in time. I'm staying. I'm not leaving Gretel."

The decision is made. No long thinking associated with it, just logistics. My mother won't come with us; I can't get her off without Colt's help. Gretel is under lock and key. We can't get to her in time and besides Colt won't leave without her. Looks like we are sailing on the ship *owned* by the royals. Not exactly, a great plan. My mother did make a point though, we are all together.

"We are safe for the time being." I hug my mother. "Maybe you're right."

Mother asks again, "How did you get on the ship?"

I hold up my wrist. "We talked ourselves on as Sponsored Companions."

Mother furrows her brow. "What's a Sponsored Companion?"

Colt shakes his head. "Living toys for the princess. We're owned by the royal family." He drops his head. "We thought it wouldn't matter. We thought we'd be off before the ship sailed."

87

Reality sets in. Now we *are* owned, slaves to the royals.

Mother playfully pulls at my braid. "It's okay. I was worried you were stowaways, but you're legal and that's all that matters. You have always been able to talk yourself in or out of any situation. You've always been *my* doll." She smiles at me and looks over at Colt. "You can go back home if you want, Colt. You've done what you were supposed to do. Maybe you should go home. If Colt has a place for you to be safe, Paisley, maybe you *should* go with him. I can't watch out for you here. You'll be on your own."

All that I've been through to find her and now my mother wants to send me away. That's not going to happen.

Colt sits down on the bench outside of the kitchen beside my mom. "I really should go back and help with the revolution. I know my dad and Riley could use the help, but—"

"—but what?" I cock my head, and look at him.

"Gretel, I'm going to stay for Gretel."

Two guards come rushing down the hall. One of the voices is familiar. "I understand there's a problem in the kitchen."

My heart sinks, but then I calm down. I recognize the voice and it send shivers up my spine. Good shivers. Riley.

Chapter 15

It can't be. "Riley?" I mutter under my breath.

"I know them." Riley waves the other guard away. "I'll take care of it."

"You sure?" The other Merc moves back a couple of steps and says, "You got it then. I have another crisis. Someone's dog is running around on level 6."

"No problem," Riley nods, as the other Merc turns around, and takes off down the stairs.

An awkward male hug between Colt and Riley follows a quick hesitant hug between Riley and me. Giggling uncomfortably, I pull Riley in front of Mom. "Mom, do you remember Riley? He used to live on one of the farms near us."

Mom hugs him. "I sure do. Didn't you get caught in one of the Uncounted raids some years back?"

Riley straightens his jacket, which has "Merc Patrol" emblazoned on the lapel. "Yeah, I'm a Merc now." Then he stops. "Actually, I used to be a Merc. Now I'm just pretending to be a Merc." Mom smiles and pats his shoulder.

Riley glances back at Colt. "Once your Dad took over the group at Passau, they didn't really need me, so I sought out the Mercs and volunteered to do security on the ship." He bumps into Colt. "Thought you might could use some help breaking Paisley's mom and sis out."

"Glad to have you." Colt shakes his hand. "How'd you get here so quickly?"

He brushed his hand across his Merc insignia. "I'm a Merc. We can go anywhere."

"Good to know. That might come in handy sometime." Colt nods, and then turns to my mother and me. "Change in plans. We can't get to Paisley's sister in time, so I think I'm going to stay to find her. I don't know if we can find each other again, if we get off this ship. Plus, I want to do some recon for my dad and find out what's going on with the new regime. We'll never have another chance to have this much access again." He takes a breath. "Really, glad you're here. We need to stop getting separated." He bumps into Riley's shoulder. "At least you're in charge. I'm an owned doll."

"Hey, I'm a doll toy too." I pull out the metal clover from my pocket.

"Do you want your lucky clover back, Riley?"

"No, it's yours now."

I blush and shove the clover back in my pocket. "Thanks." I turn my attention to Colt. "I'm so glad you're staying with me especially since you're my brother."

My mom's face whitens. "Brother?"

"Inside joke, Mom." I giggle.

Riley touches both our arms. "I guess since we're all staying we better get back to what we're supposed to be doing." He walks with us down the corridor. "You can't be running around. You need to go back to your room. We'll find each other later." He moves down the hall. "I've got to go. Go back to your room. I *mean* it."

Colt mock salutes Riley. "Promise, we'll go straight there." He hugs my mom. "He's right. We need to go back to our level, but Mrs. Mueller we know where you are so we'll make a new plan. We'll all get out of here together."

I clutch my mom. "I love you, Mom. See you soon. We're on the tenth level, room 1026."

Mother pushes back from me. "In the same room?"

"We're brother and sister." I walk down the hall.

My mother shakes her finger at Colt. "Brother and sister, you remember that."

"Oh, I almost forgot. I brought your special treasure box from the house to you." I turn back around, and pull the box out of my backpack.

Mother gently coddles the container. "Did you look in it?"

"Honestly, just a couple of things." I drop my head. "Didn't have time to go through everything." I look at Mom, consumed with guilt. "Wasn't sure if I should."

"It's yours now." Mother hands the box back to me. "When you have some time to yourself, look through it."

I take the case back. "You sure?"

Mother nods. "Once you look through everything." She gazes down the hall and sighs. "If you have any questions—" She sighs again. "You know where to find me. Now you had better go, before we are caught. The next guard may not be as friendly."

Chapter 16

Colt and I return to our room silently. I sit on my bed. "It's going to be forever before I see the Ferris wheel again, maybe never, but—" I exhale. "At least my family is here with me."

"Home is where your family is, and right now your home is on this ship." Colt's head sags.

"Sorry, Colt. I'm being so selfish. I forgot that you had to leave your family behind." I cup his chin in my hands. "Don't worry. We'll be your family." Yes, we would be a new family, his temporary family. I would be his sister. Gretel and my mom and Riley, yes—Riley, we would become a new family.

Colt says, "I'm not sure if that will work. It's not the same."

"It's better. My family, three in number for so long, just grew by two in a couple of days. You know that's better."

Maybe all of this is a good thing. I won't think of the bad. I know I'm just trying to convince myself. But that's okay. It makes me feel better. It's the best I've felt in a while. Last time I felt good— wind on my face during the Ferris wheel ride. What should I do now? Is there enough free time to go through Mother's treasure box?

An announcement comes over the speakers. "We're setting sail in thirty minutes. Security is cleared. Levels 1 through 10 are invited on deck. Come to the deck and wave goodbye to Hamburg."

Footsteps sound outside the door through the hall and then it falls silent again. "They must be going to the top deck. We're on floor 10! Let's go!" Colt hops down off the top bunk with a thump.

Once again, not enough time for the treasure. I run out after him, and we shut the door, galloping two steps at a time running up the stairs. "Maybe Mom or Gretel will be there."

Arriving at the top floor, we follow the horde of people and claim a spot on the white rail. Worming my way forward, I snag a front perch with Colt standing behind me. I spend a few minutes standing tiptoed on the deck, combing the crowds on the ship looking for Gretel and Mother. "I don't see them, they must not be here."

"Your mother's on level 13," Colt says matter-of-factly. "They only called for 1 through 10."

Most of the people on the sundeck are of the first class nature; clothing varies from evening attire to customary garbs of various countries. I have never seen such exquisite clothing. I am mesmerized by the lack of empathy of the passengers on the deck, for the waiters and waitresses who run around trying to satisfy their every whim. Exhausting work and seemingly unappreciated. I guess they are owned people too. So sad!

Colt panoramically circles the deck. "I don't see anyone familiar. We might as well wave goodbye."

"To who?" I drop my hand off the rail. "We don't know any of these people."

"True." Colt nods. "On the other hand, I don't know about you, but I've never been on a ship. So I say let's enjoy it all. What do you think?"

I turn my attention to the port area. There are masses of people waving, crying, yelling, and jumping up and down. We join in waving and yelling, "Goodbye! Goodbye! I'll miss you! So long! Farewell!"

Thirty minutes later at exactly 1800 hours, the horn sounds, and the ship begins to move. The crowds dwindle to nothing after thirty minutes more. I stand at the rail, wind blowing through my braids. I take my hair down. Closing my eyes, I imagine myself on the ride on the Ferris wheel and I feel free for just a moment.

We linger, long after others go. Colt leans on the rail on his elbows and looks out to the sea. A server comes by, "Do you need anything?"

Colt shakes his head. "We're not anybody."

The waiter waggles his finger. "No, monsieur, you have been called to the top."

Colt furrows his brow. "What do you mean?"

The waiter explains, "Only the level ten and above are called to the top. We wait on you."

I shake my head. "Colt, I guess the toys of the royals are worth more than the people who cook for them."

Colt stands up straight from leaning on the rail. "A lot of things to get use to—to fit into this world."

I nod. The deck is smooth and shiny. Deck chairs line up along the railed area, inviting patrons to sit and linger. I see movement inside the cabins. People watching—a new past time. I never had anyone to watch before, only animals and they were sparse. I notice how different the people are, some walk with their noses in the air, some walk with small dogs yapping in their arms. The one thing they all have in common is walking with an entourage—no one goes anywhere alone.

The top deck houses a restaurant and elegantly dressed men and women descend a staircase to a deck below. I go over to the window to get a better view. These people have all of the money, support, and power in the world, but know nothing of struggle or do they? Now they dress in their finest garb and parade down a staircase. It seems strange to me that people here don't worry about hiding, and people here don't worry about where their next meal will come from. People here don't seem real, but they are.

"If there is nothing else, then—" The waiter turns to walk away.

Colt calls to the waiter. "Wait, do you know where this ship ports?"

The waiter stops, pulls a map out of his pocket, and hands it to Colt. "For you, monsieur." He walks off.

We spread the map out. It shows the ship doing a circle all around Europe stopping at a few European ports along the way, followed by a couple of ports in Africa, and then returning to Germany.

Colt laughs and remarks, "I suppose the princess will get dolls from all over. I won't be able to remember where all of them are from. Hopefully, we can get off the ship before then."

I clap my hands together. "Yes, home. Knowing the princess even the little bit I know her, I think you may be right." I point to a port of call. "Edinburgh. I guess that will be the Scottish dolls. Then Iceland and I don't know what kind of stuff we will do there." I stop for a minute. "Colt, what kinds of things do you think we are going to have to do?"

"I have no idea." He shakes his head.

Gold, orange, and pink lights dance off the water, signaling the setting sun as it shrinks into the ocean.

"It's the first sunset I've ever seen over water." I lean on my elbows on the rail. "It's beautiful. It's like the water is swallowing the day."

Colt laughs. "So what does it do tomorrow? Spit out the sun."

"I guess it kind of does, but yuck, spitting." I shake my head and giggle.

I look at the map some more. "This ship is just going to ports around here, no mention of going to America or to Orlando."

"Your dream place." He smiles.

I hug my arms to my chest. "Colt, I don't even know what to dream anymore."

"Me neither. Maybe we'll start new dreams." Colt leans farther back, lifts his head, and gazes at the stars beginning to peek out on the clear night.

I smile at him. "Maybe so."

After the last drop of light is gulped in by the never-ending ocean, we find deck chairs and slip into them. We sit there until late into the night, looking at the stars in the sky. I remember they are the same stars from home that I've been looking at all of these years. Home — such a distant memory.

Here we are, a family birthed a couple of days ago, venturing out into the abyss of the unknown, *owned* by royals, hiding our family connections, and longing for home. What a pair we make!

Food is waiting in our room when we return. I'm hungry. I swallow my sandwich. "Meat!" I mumble with my mouth full. "I always wondered what it would be like to have all the food I wanted." A bottle of water and a cookie complete the meal. "Chocolate, I've only heard about chocolate." I smack my lips. "I'm going to let it melt in my mouth. This is the best thing I've ever tasted."

Colt nods, unable to talk with his mouth stuffed with libations and eats.

The dirndl and lederhosen are cleaned and hanging on the back of our door with a note. *Princess Kamea would like you to wear your German clothes tomorrow when you come to play with her. Miss Brita*

I run my hand over the dress smoothing it out. "So much for freedom. A little girl is telling us what to wear." I laugh.

"The food was great though." Colt puts on the green felt hat. "The hat too, no freedom in that. At least, no free will to choose." He opens the bathroom door. "I guess Riley doesn't have to wear ridiculous outfits."

"I'm so glad Riley is here. The more people we have—the bigger our family, the stronger we are."

"Me, too. Nice of him to come. We might need the strength of those numbers later. Who knows what else is going to happen?" Colt points to the bathroom. "I'm going first."

I throw him a pair of flannel pajamas, decorated with pictures of dolphins.

He frowns. "Where did these come from?"

"For you, to wear to bed." I point to his bunk bed. "They were right on top of your bed. At least they are warm and clean."

He grabs the clothes and disappears into the bathroom, mumbling. "Dolphin pajamas? No, no freedom here."

Chapter 17

The next morning, a gentle rap at the door signals it is time to rise. The delicious aroma of food permeates the room as Colt opens our door.

An unfamiliar person dressed in red pants, white shirt, and a red bow tie hands two breakfast plates of scrambled eggs, sausage, potatoes and croissants to Colt. "If there is nothing else, then I'll be on my way." He points to the hall area. "You need to be ready and standing at the foot of the stairs at 0800."

We scarf down the food. Food like this every day? I'll be in heaven if I can make it through the gates after the weight I'll gain. I giggle to myself.

We stand at the landing of the stairs at exactly 0800 and a woman dressed in a black dress and white apron motions for us to follow her.

"I feel like an idiot in this outfit." Colt, dressed in the lederhosen, pulls the hat off. "I'm not wearing the stupid hat."

I tug at my apron. "I'm dressed up too." I glare back at him. "Quit whining. We have a good situation here. Better than my mom. We get great food, a nice room, and all we have to do is play with a little girl."

We walk up the stairs, flight after flight. Colt pulls at my apron strings, untying them, and I slap his hand. He says, "You're right, but I hope that's all we have to do is play with a little girl. Besides you look pretty good in your outfit."

I smile at him as I re-tie my strings. "Thanks."

Up on the top level, we are led down the deck toward an ornate and massive gold-plated entranceway. Opening the huge door proves an impossible task for the slight woman leading us, and she grunts trying.

"I'll help you." Cavalier Colt steps in and pulls the door open.

The woman smiles and invites us to enter. Inside, Princess Kamea, who is dressed in a frilly pink dress, walks around freely. Six more people, dressed in what could only be described as their own particular native garb, similar to Colt and my attire, stand behind her. "My new dollies."

Kamea walks over to an elaborate table and climbs on top of four pillows to sit in the chair at the head of the table. Fourteen chairs surround the table and a large stuffed bunny inhabits one chair. A huge Raggedy Ann and Andy sit in two others. "I want my Germany dolls to sit by me today." She points to the chairs on either side of her and Colt and I sit. "Dolly Germany, my daddy loved the song."

"What song?" I inquire.

The rest of the living dolls take their seats around the table.

"The circle song." The princess smiles. "We're going to have our tea now, Miss Brita."

Tea with a four-year-old while the world fights with enslaving its people and injustice. How strange and confusing.

Miss Brita calls for a waiter to roll an awaiting tray, which contains an elaborate silver tea service complete with gold-leafed saucers and cups decorated with pink flowers, to the table. The waiter pours hot tea in each of the cups.

Princess Kamea picks up the silver prongs, grasping a sugar cube. "Do you want one lump or two?"

I lift my cup and saucer to the sugar bowl. "I'll have two, Princess Kamea."

Princess Kamea drops two lumps in my tea, and holds one over Colt's cup. "Well?"

"Two, I guess." He laughs a little.

Six other living dolls sit around the table.

The attractive coffee colored couple dressed in African garb of bright material rise for a moment, and the female, who wears a purple colored kanga, extends a hand to me. "My name is Adanna and this is Baako."

The dark-haired Asian dolls wearing teal colored silk robes with a gold embossed, fire-breathing Chinese dragon, rise next and bow. The male introduces himself and his partner. "We are Pandi and Wei. We are from Taiwan."

The other two dressed in white linen tunics and wrapped pantaloons, accessorized with snake arm bracelets, and massive headdresses stand for a moment. "Suma and Naeem from Egypt."

Princess Kamea squeals, "I love all my dollies, new and old." She picks up her cup. "Drink your tea."

Uncomfortable glances circle the table. We sip our tea.

Miss Brita stands beside the princess. "Princess Kamea, we need to do your lessons now."

"No!" Princess Kamea jumps out of her chair, falls on the floor, and starts kicking and screaming. "No! No lessons! I want to play!"

Miss Brita quietly repeats the same verse over and over. "If you don't do your lesson, the dolls will be removed." Her voice rises a little in volume each time, continuing until she finally catches the princess's attention.

The princess stops, gets up, sits in her chair with a loud thump, and

96

angrily crosses her arms. "Okay, Miss Brita. Please don't take my dollies away. I'll do the lessons."

Miss Brita motions for another more modestly dressed woman to come over, and for the next four hours, the princess and her charges, which include all of us "living dolls," participate in lessons. We practice speaking and writing the different languages of English and German. Literature, science, and math follow.

Participating in school is a normal kind of thing to do. Of course, I remember on my farm we did "normal" every day, Mother insisted on it.

Colt pushes into me. "I feel like I'm back in your mom's class."

I giggle. "I guess you do. I don't remember those classes with you, but I do remember her giving me and Gretel lots of lessons. I like learning."

Colt nods. "Me too." He looks over at the Princess. "This might not be that bad."

Baako overhears us. "Don't speak too soon. We haven't done the games yet."

"Games?" Colt furrows his brow.

"Time for lunch!" Miss Brita announces and the SCs take their places at the tea table while waiters bring plates of sandwiches, chips, and glasses of lemonade.

"Adanna and Baako, how'd you get to be in the service of Princess Kamea?" Colt asks.

Adanna finishes a bite of the sandwich. "Our parents were killed in the great uprising that happened five years ago. We were living in an orphanage in Africa. We were recruited to be Sponsored Companions and went through six months of training. We are very fortunate that Princess Kamea picked us out of all of the SCs of Africa, and gave us a place to live." She smiles at the princess, who gobbles down her second sandwich.

I ask, "SCs, now is that short for Sponsored Companions?" Adanna nods as I swig a drink of lemonade. "What was the orphanage like?"

Baako pours another drink for himself. "You really don't want to know." He swings his head toward the princess. "The princess does not like to hear about anything that makes her sad and—" He looks at Miss Brita. "No one here likes to talk about how bad it is in our country."

I eat a chip. "I understand." I look over at Pandi and Wei. "What about the rest of you?"

Pandi gathers her plate with the half-eaten sandwich and puts her napkin on top of it, as Naeem answers. "We were not in an orphanage, but from the island of Taiwan. We lived in the mountains, and we were taken from our homes in the middle of the night. We were made to be servants of the people running our country."

"How horrible!" Colt asks, "Who is running your country?"

"Mercenaries." Pandi continues, "I think you call them Mercs here. They run everything."

Miss Brita holds her hand up and the waiter clear the plates. "Enough of that negative talk. You will be happy to know that all of that is about to change. Ambassador Grayson and some of the leaders are meeting to form the Consortium of the World and restore communications and bring order back to the chaos for all of us who survived the virus." She claps her hands together and looks up. "Praise be. It's about time. Consider yourselves lucky to be here. We will be making history or rather the ambassador will be making history."

I help to gather the plates. "What exactly are we doing on this ship, and where are we going?"

Miss Brita stops me. "Put those down. We have people to do that. You must do only what you are supposed to do. It restores order. Everyone knows his or her place and what is expected. You, all of you, are expected to entertain, and make life fun and easy for the princess. That is your *only* job."

"And is it okay for us to know where we are going, and what's this ship's mission?" I repeat.

Miss Brita smiles. "Of course. We are on a mission to gather support for Ambassador Grayson and fact finding so the ambassador can have proof of what is happening in each country. We are also collecting for the princess—living dolls from all over. All of you are very important to all of us. You have first-hand knowledge of your countries. The ambassador thought of everything. Ambassador Grayson is a great man."

I open my mouth to inquire more, but as if on cue, Princess Kamea announces, "Game time!"

Miss Brita rises from her seated position in the corner. "What game do you want to play today, Princess?"

"Dress up!"

Baako leads the rest of the group, sans Colt and me, in a collective groan. It's hard to play knowing the misery all around, but it is a requirement if we ever hope to go back to our real lives.

"What's dress up?" I whisper to the rest.

Adanna sighs. "You don't want to know, but I'm afraid you're going to find out."

Miss Brita claps her hands. "Okay, dolls let's go to our dressing areas, and let the princess pick out your outfits. Remember, you are to dress in the clothes, and then come out, and the princess will let you know what kind of play you are to participate in." She walks over to a closeted area, amply supplied with full clothes racks. "Princess, do you know which outfits you want on which dolls?"

Colt rubs his chin and whispers to me. "You're kidding me—we really are dolls."

Princess Kamea busily picks out clothes for each of us, while we huddle waiting for her choice and our fate.

Colt snaps his fingers. "I say, let's take charge of this."

Baako puts his wrists together, as if jailed by imaginary handcuffs. "We're basically prisoners. How's that going to work?"

"With a little finesse and a lot of manipulation. Watch and learn." Colt sashays over to the princess, and bows very low. "My Queen, my princess, the most beautiful girl in all of the land. Shall we set up an obstacle course for your loyal servants?"

Princess Kamea turns. "An obstacle course? What's that?"

"You sit here on your royal chair, and we will show you." Colt walks her back to her chair.

"What are you doing?" I grab him by the arm.

"If we're going to have to be down here every day, let's at least make it fun."

I shake my head. "Do you know what you're doing?"

"Not really. Time to fake it." He winks at me. "Let's all work together and wing it."

"Wing it?" I cock my head and look to the others. "Sounds dangerous."

"I'm willing to give it a go," Baako chimes in, "Anything is better than dress up. You start, we'll follow."

Colt moves four chairs to the four corners. "This will be our course." He grabs a set of clothes, drapes it over two more chairs, and climbs under the tablecloth coming out on the other side. "The first obstacle is to climb into the caves of—"

"The caves where the evil dragon lurks under the seas of —" Pandi pipes up.

Suma dances around the draped chairs. "The seas of Egypt."

Princess Kamea squeals, and claps her hands. "I love this story. We'll try to hide from a dragon in the Egyptian Sea. What's next?"

I pick up the teacups and saucers and sit them on the floor very close together. "Next, you need to avoid the backward icicles of the Bavarian Forest." I tiptoe in and out of the cups. "Make sure you don't break them otherwise—"

Wei runs at her with fingers held to his head like horns. "The dragon

99

will capture you and bring you to his lair that is—" He looks around, picks up a table and turns it upside down. "—in the Pyramid of the Forevers."

"You must compete, also." I pick up a bouncing ball from a toy chest. "You must land a ball in the bucket." I drop a ball easily in the bucket so I back up. "No, you have to stand here and bounce the ball in the bucket." I land the ball in the bucket once again, and then I shake my head once more. "No, you have to land the ball five times in the bucket before you can move on. It's a work in progress." I smile.

By the time we finish, we have an obstacle course that takes up the entire area. It consists of ball throwing, ball bouncing, tiptoeing over the cups, crawling under the table cloth, putting on an outfit over clothes running around the outside of the area three times then taking the outer clothes off, balancing a ball on a plate, spinning a ball on a finger, and hopping around a course drawn on the floor with chalk. Maneuvering through the course three times leaves all of us competitors including the princess breathless and tired.

Miss Brita takes the princess by the hand. "That's enough for today. Say good night to your new little friends."

The princess giggles and hugs each living doll. "Fun! I can't wait until tomorrow. Goodnight, my sweet dollies."

After she leaves, we are led back to our rooms that are all located on the same floor, adjacent to each other.

Colt opens the door with his wrist ID. "We should get together."

"I agree, but not today. I'm tired." Naeem opens his door.

I stand at our door. "Is everybody brother and sister?"

Adanna nods. "Of course, you have to be to be on the living doll registry. You knew that right?"

"Of course, I don't know why I asked." I rush through our door mumbling.

Colt shuts the door behind us. "Be more careful, Sis."

I sit on my bed and lean back. "Can we trust them?"

Colt opens the door to the bathroom. "We have to. We have no other choice."

Chapter 18

That next morning, after four hours of lessons, Princess Kamea claps her hands. "Miss Brita, I want my surprise now!"

"Yes, I think it's time. Everyone, follow me." Miss Brita leads our troop on a trek, down the stairs with Princess Kamea in tow in her carriage with the four male living dolls carrying it.

"This is an ancient Chinese marriage carriage. It's what the Chinese bride is carried in. See the markings," Pandi tells me as we walk along side of the carriage.

Miss Brita turns around. "Yes, we acquired it when we were in China. The princess loves it."

Colt smiles. "I can see why. She just sits, while we do all of the work." He asks Miss Brita, as we are descending. "How many levels are on this ship?"

Miss Brita looks and counts on her fingers. "I'm not sure, we're going to fifteen. That may be the last level. I've never been down this far."

Colt takes a deep breath. "And what level are we on now?"

Miss Brita looks at the sign as they cross the threshold on the next staircase. "We're on twelve."

Baako exhales. "Whew. We might want to slow the pace."

Princess Kamea opens the sliding door of her carriage, and peeks out. "Are we there yet?"

"It's a surprise. Be patient." Miss Brita slides her door shut.

"Okay," the young voice says through the door.

After the flights down, Miss Brita opens two large factory-like doors revealing a floor with a group of about forty people, corralled in the corner. Debris consisting of leftover parts, broken machinery, ripped clothing, and small kitchen paraphernalia clumped haphazardly litters the large area. The princess escapes her carriage and runs around the open area, squealing and twirling. "I love it! Can I play here? It's so big."

Miss Brita motions to the people in the corner. "Who's in charge?"

A man who appears to be in his thirties, sporting a crew cut, and wearing beige worker's clothes steps out from the group. "I am. My name's Victor." He limps a few steps. One of his arms is burned badly.

"What happened to you?" I ask.

Miss Brita holds her hand to stop me. "You do not speak here. Undesirables are not allowed to speak unless asked a question."

I frown. "I did ask a question."

Miss Brita glares at me. "I allow you some leverage because the little one likes you, but do not get confused. You are owned. You are not allowed to ask questions. You entertain the princess, nothing more."

I shift slightly on my heels.

Colt whispers, "Not now. Stay calm. Remember, this is only temporary."

Miss Brita turns her head towards Victor. "We are taking this level over. You need to move."

Victor looks around at the rest of the group of men, women, boys, and girls with varying types of limps, bandages, and burns. "We don't have a place. I'm not sure what you want me to do."

Riley and two other Mercs come through the door. A shorthaired guard, in a rigidly starched uniform, pulls his holstered gun and points it at Victor. "Halt, don't come any closer to the princess."

Princess Kamea runs around, still squealing, paying no attention to the unfolding scenario.

"I don't want any trouble. I don't know where to send my people." Victor waves his hands, indicating the group of people huddled over in the corner.

The dark-haired Merc waves his pistol at the group. "Not my problem! Move! Now!"

The huddled group slowly moves to the door of the room, whimpering. One of the group, a badly crippled man, falls, and the others attempt to pick him up.

"Leave him!" The dark-haired Merc screams.

Everyone retreats to the door, leaving the crippled man crawling on the floor.

The dark-haired Merc cocks his pistol and points it at the man.

Riley holds his hand up to the Merc. "Lamar, wait a minute."

"You're right. No use wasting a bullet on a nobody like him." He uncocks the gun, walks over to the crouched man, and pistol-whips him on the head. The man starts bleeding profusely.

"Careful, Lamar, you might scare the princess." Riley desperately pulls Lamar off to stop the beating.

Lamar stops and looks for the princess who is still running around the room, oblivious. "See, she doesn't care."

Riley jerks Lamar up. "Think, Lamar. Think. You just lucked out buddy, you don't want her to tell her grandfather, the king, do you?"

"No, no. I don't want that." Lamar backs off and lowers his pistol. The crippled man is left bleeding on the floor. I run over to him, putting a towel over his wounds. I pull his shirtsleeve up, exposing his upper arm. I notice the broken egg tattoo. I whisper, "Shadow? We met Drake." The crippled man manages a weak smile as I pull his sleeve down to cover his secret.

Lamar holsters his pistol, and looks at Miss Brita. "Sorry, I didn't mean to scare anyone. I didn't get the message in time that this room needed to be cleared. I'll get this garbage out of here." He makes a move toward the group. "We can throw everyone overboard."

I open my mouth to speak and Colt bends down to my side, helping to clean the crippled man's wounds. "Not now." Colt leans over and whispers to the man. "What's your name?"

The man grabs Colt by the collar, pulling him close, and whispers. "Morgan."

Turning to Miss Brita, Riley asks, "What's the problem with these people staying in here?"

"It's wrong!" Lamar pipes in. "These people are garbage. They aren't supposed to be here. They should have been dumped at the last port."

Riley looks to Lamar. "I understand that, but they aren't in the way. Can't you wait and put them off at the next port?" He doesn't wait for an answer but turns to Miss Brita. "What is the princess going to use this lower level for?"

Miss Brita answers, "We are going to use this floor to build and to play the new game. It is a surprise for the princess." She looks over at Colt. "She loved the game. Her mother told me to make the game bigger and permanent." She points around the floors. "This is the only free floor."

Colt shakes his head. "Well, it's not exactly free." He points to Victor and his group. "There are people living here."

"Colt, you do not have permission to speak. Why are you questioning me? I am in charge. You are a SC." Miss Brita shakes her head. "And just so you know, these are not people. These are Undesirables."

Lamar turns his gun and points it at Colt, and Riley steps between the gun and Colt, talking to Miss Brita. "I understand what you want, what about these people?"

Miss Brita raises her voice. "I don't care where they go. They just need to go now."

"Tell them that I have an idea." Colt whispers to Riley.

"This SC has an idea, does he have permission to speak?" Riley asks Miss Brita.

Miss Brita nods.

Colt walks around from behind Riley and Lamar lowers his gun.

"The obstacle course will take a lot of work, if we are going to do something that the princess's mother will be happy with. It'll take a lot of people power." He points over to Victor and his group. "Why not use—" He gulps. "—the Undesirables to help us?"

Riley nods and looks at Lamar. "What not, Lamar?"

Lamar says, "I really don't like the idea, but if it'll save us from having to come down here all day and do manual labor then I guess it's worth it. I can just see it now. Lamar, send some people down to help build this. Lamar, send some people down to carry this—to move this— we have better things to do. No offense to the little one." Lamar looks over the princess's way.

Miss Brita nods. "None taken."

"They can work at night," Riley says, "and during the day they will stay in the corner, or help man parts of the obstacle course while the princess is using it."

Lamar points to Morgan. "All except this one. We'll throw him overboard."

Not on my watch. No more killing. I jump up. "Morgan just told me that he is a—" I stammer for a minute. "—a carpenter and we probably need carpenters to build the most fabulous obstacle course in the world."

Lamar points his weapon at me. "SC, I don't think you had permission to speak."

Chapter 19

I freeze, staring down the barrel of the gun. Then I stand up straight. "Are you going to shoot royal property?"

Lamar cocks the gun and cracks an evil grin. "You didn't have permission to speak."

Riley and Colt move toward me, but I put my hand up to stop them. "Why would I speak without permission? I know my place." I turn to Miss Brita. "Didn't you give me permission?"

Everyone looks to Miss Brita.

The room is quiet for about thirty seconds. Finally, Miss Brita breaks the silence. "What I care about is the obstacle course. If this Undesirable can help us, then we'll patch him up and use him, and drop him off at the first port when we are finished with him." She looks over at Victor. "I take it you are in charge of the Undesirables down here." Victor nods, and she continues, "There is no room for mistakes. Can you keep them in line and most importantly out of our way?"

"Of course, it would be an honor." Victor bows his head towards the princess. "We serve at your princess's pleasure. We'll be happy to help make her an obstacle course."

Miss Brita claps her hands. "Problem solved, but this is just a temporary solution. When the obstacle course is finished, we will only need a couple of you."

Lamar raises his pistol and points it at the group of Undesirables, then lowers it. "I can keep anyone in line."

Miss Brita adjusts her tightened collar and speaks to Lamar. "No need for that. We have it worked out, but we should have some security, just in case."

"I'll stay." Riley pipes in.

Lamar nods. "I sure don't want to be around these non-people. So that works for me. Thanks for volunteering. I don't know how you can stand these Undesirables. Just looking at them turns my stomach." With that, Lamar turns and walks out muttering, where Miss Brita and the princess won't hear. "We have better things to do than play nursemaid, royal or not."

"Can't say I'm sorry to see *him* go." I whisper sarcastically to Riley.

Riley sighs. "Probably not the last we'll see of him. Unfortunately, he's a freak. A sadistic control freak!"

"I wanna play! I wanna play!" Princess Kamea is jumping around the room.

"Okay, Mr. Germany." Miss Brita points to Colt. "Make her happy."

Colt claps his hands together. "I'm sure if we put our minds to it, we'll come up with something spectacular that will need lots—" He looks over at Victor. "—lots of people to work on it."

Victor shuffles over. "Yes, what exactly are we making?" He whispers to Colt and Riley. "Thanks for saving us. But sooner or later they're going to find a way to throw us overboard."

Colt brushes Victor aside. "First, let's make sure you survive the night. We have to sell this. We need a good plan. Actually, we need a *great* plan."

We eight SCs spend the next few minutes sharing ideas and describing how we built the makeshift obstacle course the day before with Victor and a few of the Undesirables.

Victor nods. "I get the idea. The first thing we need to do is a temporary obstacle course. We can have some of our little ones play with her." Victor motions towards his group. "Amanda, Thomas, Judi, Mike, and Gregg come here." Five children, previously hidden by the adult women's skirts, emerge from the shadows. "You will stay with this girl." He points at me. "You do what she says. She's the boss." The children nod.

I stand by the children. "Why are they Undesirable?" I look at Victor. "What—?"

Victor interrupts my questions. "Undesirable is a term used for throwaway people. They call us garbage. We are only good for—" He stops when he catches a glimpse of the horror on my face.

"There's nothing wrong with any of you." I softly slap Victor on the back.

Victor moves me to the side, and whispers, "There's a lot physically wrong with me. I used to be a Merc until my accident." He pulls up his sleeve, revealing the rest of his arm. "My arm was burnt, and my leg caught in a machine, leaving me with a limp." He points to the others. "These children are Undesirable, because they are children born of the Undesirables or children with no home. They are not old enough to be SCs like you, but they are too young to be of much service. They have no place in this world."

Colt says, "You all have a place now." He smiles at me.

"We're going to make the best temporary obstacle course ever." I take one of the five by the hand and motion for the princess to join us. "Princess, let's look for things that we can use. Like hide and go seek."

The princess stops running. "What's hide and go seek?"

I smile. "It's where you hide, and others look for you, but today we are going to find things that are hidden to make our obstacle course." I motion around the room. "This room is filled with treasures like this." I pick up a rag off the floor and wrap it around my head. "I am now Duchess Phoebe, a wise woman who can see the future. It's your job to find all the treasures and bring them here. "

The children run from one end of the room to the other, bringing back a variety of loose items including tea saucers, broken and unbroken, clothing, blankets, cups, trash, and anything else that isn't nailed down.

"Can you use this broken saucer?"

"What about this blanket?"

"I found a lot of clothes. I'm going to pile them up."

I unwrap my headdress and direct them to arrange the found treasures on the floor in designated piles. We build an obstacle course, similar to the one from yesterday.

The obstacle course consists of four parts. The first part, the children layer newly found clothes over their clothes. Next, they run down a marked racetrack about one kilometer long, stop, and remove the clothes and race back. The princess proves to be especially coordinated for this competition. Probably because she has experience with changing clothes and the children of the fifteenth floor do not.

The second part, the children have to recreate an intricate pattern of cups and saucers by drawing it. One of the Undesirable children obviously has a lot of natural artistic ability and wins easily while the rest including the princess are left wanting. Thoughts that Kamea will pitch a fit for not winning are quickly squashed as she giggles her way over to the next competition.

The third part, the children have to flip a ball in a bucket. This is a close battle with one of the boys pulling ahead with a last minute ball in the bucket to win. Cheers erupt.

For the last part, the children run around, crawl under, and hop over chairs and tables. The fastest person wins. All six children complete the obstacle course. Kamea is declared the winner as the girl in front of her slows at the last minute. Interesting how children instinctively know what to do even if they are not told.

I stand by Colt, watching the children squeal as they misstep, fall, and succeed. "They seem to be having a good time. How can anyone possibly call these children Undesirable?"

"The farm sheltered us." Colt pulls out a long piece of paper. "We didn't realize how good we had it."

I sigh. "I know. I just want to go back. But, first, we have to help these people."

Riley motions over to Miss Brita. "You also have to do that with her watching you. She reports directly to Queen Nalani. Watch your step. Be invaluable. A good start is to succeed in making a great obstacle course that the princess will love. She likes you though, I can tell."

"I can set up a target practice with poison darts, although I don't know if they have the plants here that I would need to make the poison," Baako nonchalantly states.

I cough. "You do realize that we are setting up a course for a four-year-old. I don't think we need poison darts."

"I suppose not." Baako drops his head.

I skip over to the princess and give her a drink.

Kamea hugs one of the Undesirable children. "I want my friends to get drinks too."

"Of course."

I walk over by Riley to retrieve more fruit punch drinks when Lamar storms in the door and stomps towards Riley. Lamar yells in Miss Brita's direction. "I'm just checking in." Then he angrily points over to Morgan, who is quietly sitting by himself with a bandage on his head. "I guess I needed to check in. I thought he was going to help."

Riley nods toward Morgan. "He is. He's an ideas' guy."

Morgan struggles to stand up, and Lamar starts toward him. "Maybe I should just take him and throw him overboard." He reaches Morgan and grabs his arm. "He's too much trouble."

I start toward the fracas and Colt holds my arm. "Let Riley handle it."

Riley locks arms with Lamar. "Honestly, he had the best ideas for this obstacle course they are planning." Lamar tries to pull away, but Riley holds tight. "Lamar, think of what King Ahomana will think when the little princess brings her grandfather down here and she tells him how much of a help you were to her." Riley points to Morgan. "If you throw him overboard, it might be impossible to get the others to work. Is that what you want the little princess to tell the king?"

Lamar stops moving for a minute and then pulls viciously away. "Okay, but keep them in line Riley. I'm counting on you."

Lamar stops for a moment to tip his head to the princess and Miss Brita, then storms out of the room.

Riley whispers to us. "He doesn't want to be down here, but he loves being in charge."

"Maybe it wouldn't hurt to train a little for defense." Colt whispers over to me, "Some of these Mercs are crazy." He glances over at Riley. "No offense, Riley, but we never know when we might need some defensive moves. Is anyone planning on staying here forever?"

"No." I say and the others shake their heads. Our group sits together discussing the specifics of the course.

"Wait a minute. What if you make the obstacle course adaptable and use it to train?" Riley slaps him on the shoulder. "How about if you use the blow pipe and put colored flour in it, like a paintball?"

"I remember. We use to play paintball on the base with the military. Good thinking, Riley." Colt writes on a piece of paper. "Paintball, target practice. Now we're getting somewhere."

Riley cuts his eyes to Colt. "Plus, you can practice how to blow the darts should you ever need to defend yourselves. I mean, besides me, who knows how to protect themselves?"

"I know how to use a machete," I blurt out. Mouths drop open, and then I add, "I learned during harvest. We could train after the princess goes to bed."

"It's settled. We'll train using this obstacle course." Colt smiles.

I say, "It's worth a try."

Riley touches my hand. "It'll work. I'll be security." Riley is a good person to have on our side.

Colt sketches. "It only works if we make a great obstacle course that the princess loves. We'd better get started."

With newfound direction, everyone works on specific tasks.

At the end of the school day, Riley asks Miss Brita, "We're in the middle of something. What if I stay, and escort them back up later?"

Miss Brita hardly acknowledges the question, but gives the okay sign.

"Four are needed to carry the princess back, and then they can return."

The four SCs each take an edge of the carriage. "We'll be glad to escort our sweet princess," Naeem says to a smiling princess. "Did you have a good time today?"

The princess nods. "I love my dollies."

In half an hour, they return. That night, we spend time planning the obstacle course, and also discussing strengths each of us can offer in terms of defensive maneuvers. Riley is an expert in hand-to-hand combat since he was trained in the Merc training camps; I am a machete master, learned from many years of harvesting; Adanna and Baako, are proficient in the art of the poison blow dart; Suma and Naeem excel in spear throwing; Pandi and Wei can wield the Chinese gun, a simple bamboo staff. Victor shares that he used to make bombs as a former military soldier.

Colt spreads paper out on the floor. "What we need to do is incorporate each of these ideas into the course so we can practice technique."

With input from all, we devise an obstacle course that will take weeks to build, thus insuring the survival of the Undesirables at least for that time.

I comment, "We must give everyone a job, so if Lamar comes down here, he'll have no choice but to keep everybody until we can make a plan to get everyone off the ship. We could set up locations to paint targets, mix flour, water, and dye for the paint blow-dart part, make dummies to practice moves with the bamboo stick, put plastic suction cups for the end of a dart to practice machetes and spear throwing." I stop and look over at Victor. "Of course, we can't teach them to make bombs." We share a laugh.

Victor sighs. "You're probably right about that."

In a couple of hours, we complete a workable plan consisting of six stations: blow paint darts, plastic headed spear throwing, dummies and bamboo sticks, short plastic suction tipped machetes for throwing target practice, and wrestling. Every one of the safe games can be converted to lethal for training purposes and all under the guise of entertaining the princess. It's a magnificent plan if we can just pull it off before anyone finds out.

"Not a word to anyone." Colt rolls up the plans.

Riley nods. "This is treason. Any word of this and it's certain death."

I shudder, "Why are they are so mean? Why do they kill people?"

Victor grabs both my arms. "You really don't know, do you?"

I shake my head. Victor lets go of me. "It's better that way. You're too young to remember the horror. Maybe most young people won't remember what happened right after the virus outbreak."

"You keep this down here." Colt hands the drawing to Victor. "We've been on the farms since the outbreak. We've been sheltered. Why is all of this happening now?"

Victor secures the rolled up drawing under his arm. "It's about power. It always is. See you tomorrow."

Chapter 20

The next morning, the four males report to the first level to carry the princess while the rest of us go to the course on the fifteenth floor.

As I enter the fifteenth floor, I immediately notice a familiar face. "Gretel!" I smile at my sister. Maybe this would be the start of a plan to get off this ship and go back home. Mother told me that Gretel was fine, but somehow hearing it and seeing it are two entirely different things.

My sister swings me around. "I missed you. I'm glad you're okay. Mom told me where you were. I only have a few minutes before I need to be back. I sneaked out." She looks around. "What exactly are you doing here?"

"What I'm good at." I kiss my sister's temple. "— playing." I love being able to talk to my sister. Now I wish more than anything that I could see all the shoes lined up just perfect. I bet it wouldn't bother me at all.

Gretel swings me again. "You *are* good at playing." She puts me down. "Mom told me that you were a Sponsored Companion." She playfully tugs at my hair. "That's a good job. You don't have to do much."

"I'm still not helpless." I slap her hand away. "I'm going to get us home. You'll see. I'm going to figure out a way. I'm going to come up with a plan."

Gretel pushes her hair back around her ear. "Yeah, I heard Colt was here. He kept his promise to take care of you. I want to thank him." She smoothes the front of her dress. "Where is he?"

"He had to get the princess. When he comes back, she'll be with him. He won't be able to talk."

Gretel kisses me on the cheek. "That's my cue to go. Don't take any chances. I'll try to get down here to see you again." She turns to go. "Tell Colt I'll be back."

Colt? Is that all she can think about? Colt? I grab her. "Wait, what do you do in the science lab? You work with Princess Kamea's dad?"

"Yes, that's right."

Gretel is in the perfect spot to help our cause. We must find out as much as we can if we hope to escape. Gretel must want to go home as badly as I do. Or does she? No time for *that* conversation now, but I want my sister to stay a little longer. "Wait, what kind of experiments do they run? What do you have to do?"

Gretel holds my face in her hands, as people staff their posts in the makeshift construction site. "Everybody's coming back. I will tell you everything, I promise. But what I have to do now is go. Greverstand." She hugs me again and whispers, "Mom wanted to know if you've gone through the box yet?"

The box. I had forgotten about that box—odd because I had daydreamed about its contents ever since I had discovered it so many years ago. "No, not yet. Tell Mom I'll go through it soon."

"I will. See you soon, Sis." Gretel slips out the door.

Too quickly, the visit is over and I forget to tell her about the ribbon I brought her from home. Nothing is decided. Will this nightmare ever end? In a few moments, the boys carry the princess in.

Miss Brita busily lines books up on a table.

I ask, "Are we going to have classes down here too?"

Miss Brita sits in a folded chair behind the table. "Yes, it'll be easier."

"You seem different, Miss Brita. More relaxed. Did something happen?"

"I had the best talk with the queen this morning. It's the most pleased she has been with me." Miss Brita opens a book. "The princess is totally engaged. She is doing better in her classes. I think it's because of the obstacle course."

It's more than that. I can feel it. Her mindset has changed. I sit on the floor crossed-legged beside Miss Brita. "You're owned too, aren't you?"

Miss Brita closes her book. "I don't like to call it owned. I have been in the service of Queen Nalani for many years, before the queen married Ambassador Grayson and the princess was born."

"How long have they been married?" I need to find out whatever I can. I like Miss Brita, but it's obvious her allegiance is with the royals, not the servants. Wonder if she could be turned to our side? How can she watch the killing and not want to change things?

Miss Brita motions for the princess to go with the tutor. "First, lessons."

"After I take her, can we talk?"

"I was hoping to get some reading in, but I suppose when you return we could talk some." Miss Brita reopens her book.

I walk the princess to the table with the tutor and the princess settles into her language arts class. I return and sit on the floor by Miss Brita. "Well?"

She quickly closes her book. "Queen Nalani and Ambassador Grayson married almost five years ago. The princess was born that first year." She opens the book again.

"What's the ambassador like?"

"I might as well put this down." She closes the book again. "I guess I'm not going to get to relax."

Don't want to make her angry. "I'm sorry." I place a foot to the floor, to get up.

"I haven't had anyone to talk to in so long, it feels strange. Something about you Paisley just makes me open up." Miss Brita puts the closed book on her lap. "Actually, I like it down here. We're in charge down here."

I sit back down. "You're always in control, Miss Brita. "

"I wish." She leans back in her chair, looking up at the ceiling. "There was a time when I was in charge, but not now."

Stay on topic, stay on topic. "What is the ambassador like?"

Miss Brita sighs and smiles. "He is a kind and good man. A brilliant scientist. I think his brilliance is what made the king work so hard to marry him off to his daughter. Everyone knows the ambassador found the immunization for the virus. Who wouldn't want to control that mind? There is sadness to him, though. I know he misses his son. The princess has a half-brother, who lives in America. I know that seeing his son again will make him happy."

I flip my leg back under me, and sit cross-legged again. "The ambassador was married before?"

"He said he lost his wife to the virus." Miss Brita shakes her finger at the princess, warning her to get back on task. "He doesn't talk much about it. After the mission, we will be going back to America. "

The mission, that's the first time I've heard it called a mission. Must be important. "So, what's the mission all about?"

Miss Brita stiffens and picks her book back up. "You need to get back to work."

Why did she cut me off? Confused, I turn around to face a battalion of six Mercs.

Lamar questions, "What's going on, Miss Brita? Queen Nalani asked me to check on the princess."

"I've got it under control." Riley trots over. "She has security."

"There are a lot of Undesirables." Lamar surveys the room. "I think we might need some more men down here."

Riley taps his holstered gun. "I can handle anything."

Wonder if they know Riley keeps the gun and bullets in two separate places? He can handle anything, what a joke! I had him pinned at Colt's farm. Still, we don't want extra security.

Miss Brita stands up, and motions to me to stand too. "This

Sponsored Companion was telling me about the princess's success with her English paper today. SC Germany, go back to your post. I appreciate you coming to report to me." Miss Brita nods her head toward Lamar. "I thank you for being so diligent, but I hate to take a detail away from where they are truly needed. We have our security guard, and he has a communicator. We also have the emergency speaker communicator on this level. I think we'll be fine."

"Miss Brita, you overstep." Lamar holds up his hand. "It's really not up to you."

Miss Brita grabs his shoulder. "Of course, it's not, but I think the princess will start getting upset if too many security people are walking down here disrupting her lessons and her fun. I would hate to tell Queen Nalani—"

Just when I think Miss Brita is totally for the royals and against the servants, she surprises me. Of course, without the security Miss Brita is in total control. No idea where her allegiances lie; maybe she doesn't know either.

Lamar bows and backs away. "Of course, let us know if we can help you or the princess."

Miss Brita clutches her book in hand and extends the other. "Thank you. I appreciate what a great job you are doing. I will apprise Queen Nalani about how wonderful you've been."

"That would be nice." Lamar shakes her hand and turns to Riley. "Keep up the good work and let us know if you have any problems or need any help."

Riley nods. "Will do."

As they exit, I glance over to Miss Brita. "You handled that very well."

Miss Brita sits back down in her chair and opens her book. "Lots of practice, dear."

Chapter 21

The next few days are hectic. The ports of call are suspended at the last minute because the meeting places are still being decided concerning the organization of the Consortium of the World. No schedule of stops. An unfortunate turn of events as we attempt to plan our escape.

Staying on the ship with no excursions is boring. We are glad for the distraction of constructing the princess's new game. Making the obstacle course fun as well as useful for our defensive practice demonstrates to be a difficult task. With creative juices flowing, we work together and at the end of the week, the obstacle course is usable. Colt and Victor are pragmatic in making sure that every one of the Undesirables has a job. A much-needed advantage as we don't want to worry about anyone being thrown overboard. The princess enjoys the people bustling around and is happy and productive with her schoolwork. Miss Brita's mood is lighter since she has some free time; something that I surmise is not always true.

I operate the target practice with three of the Undesirables. Victor joins us so I ask, "I don't understand why some people are classified as Undesirables?"

Victor answers, "You really don't see it, do you?"

"I really don't." I shake my head.

Victor surreptitiously motions to specific children. "Sasha is deemed overweight, Troy stutters, Lizzy is blind in one eye, Mary hurt her arm, John is clumsy, the list goes on."

That's crazy. I furrow my brow. "If they have one thing wrong with them, they are Undesirable."

"I didn't say it was right. I just said how it works." Victor shrugs.

"What kind of world do we live in?" I let out a large huff. "We need to change it."

Victor nods. "Us and what army?"

I spread my arms out indicating the whole group. "This army."

Victor smiles. "I like your thinking, but you're getting a little ahead of yourself. This is just another way of staying here longer. Besides, don't you have a goal?"

He's right and I say, "To get home."

"And that goal does not address our problems. Just concentrate on that and staying out of trouble."

Princess Kamea yells for me. "I guess you're right, besides I have a job." I turn back around as I head off to play paintball with the princess. "Things could be worse."

Victor puts his head in his hand and mutters, "You have no idea."

Sadly, I have seen some of what he means. The useless murders, the thievery. But my guess is that he has seen lots worse. I shudder to think.

The next two weeks, we perfect the obstacle course and stay late to practice shooting blow darts, using bamboo sticks, throwing spears and machetes, the real ones. I see Gretel and Mother in passing, but even the limited contact is the jolt that keeps me on track. Colt lights up when Gretel comes in a room and those visits motivate his creativity. Happy people are productive people.

"We're docking in Britain tomorrow," Princess Kamea announces as she is carried to the fifteenth level. "I'm getting some new dollies."

I look over at Colt. "Do you think she means Sponsored Companions?"

"Yes that's exactly what I think."

New people. New ears. Constant change just when I'm getting used to everyone. I lean over to him. "It's going to be harder to keep the Undesirables useful if she keeps adding to our numbers."

"I know, but we just need to go with it. We don't have a choice."

Not right. I sigh. "We should always have a choice."

Colt nods. "Wouldn't that be nice?"

"Princess Kamea has chosen you two to come with her to London," Miss Brita announces, "We will be going by Stonehenge first. Ambassador Grayson is meeting with a delegation to discuss some terms of the agreement of The Consortium of the World."

A road trip to London. I should be concentrating about how I can get my family off the ship, but right in this moment my stomach is flipping, I'm exuberant, more excited than I've been in a very long time. London! Wow!

Riley adds, "I'll make plans to accompany you as your security."

"Sorry, but Lamar has assigned one of the other guards." Miss Brita shakes her head.

"That's fine." Riley turns to Colt. "Besides, you have Colt."

Miss Brita furrows her brow. "He is a Sponsored Companion and not a security detail."

"I know, but he'll protect you."

Miss Brita asks, "Without a gun?"

Riley laughs a little. "I think you're better off with him without a gun."

116

They think they are so great. I interrupt. "I'm sure there will be no problems tomorrow. I'm glad you're here to protect the people on the fifteenth floor, Riley."

Riley cocks his head. "I won't be down here. I'll be on patrol."

"Don't worry, I'll hold down the fort." Victor slaps Riley on the back.

With the way the world is, I shouldn't be so happy about this trip, but I am. What does that say about me? Have I grown up at all? I'm not going to worry about it. I am going to London tomorrow. And I'm going to try to have fun!

Chapter 22

Before disembarking the next morning, Colt shakes his head as he admires himself in the mirror. "Don't get me wrong, I'm glad we are getting off the ship for a while and I am excited about going to London." He swipes his hand in front of his clothes. "But do we have to wear this get up?"

I laugh. "I like the lederhosen and dirndl." I shove him over and admire myself.

He opens the door. "Because you look great in your outfit. I look like an idiot."

"Quit whining." I follow him to the stairs. Reaching the first level, I am awestruck by the cliffs. Glimmering and vast, the large head of chalk rock bows to the tranquil sea and welcomes travelers.

"The White Cliffs of Dover are unbelievable!" Colt gasps and holds a deep breath for a moment before releasing it. "So much more fantastic than what I thought when I read about them. I think I might have travelled here when I was younger, but those memories are so jumbled now. How could you ever forget these?"

I am mesmerized. "I feel like I remember these cliffs too. Mom and Gretel say we've never been out of Germany. It couldn't be a memory, could it? Do you think I saw a picture in a book or something?"

"Probably so. I see Miss Brita. Oh goodness, does the princess have to be in that big carriage? She hates it, plus she is so loud in it."

The troupe of six consisting of Princess Kamea in her bubbled carriage, Miss Brita, Colt, Trevor, me, and a Merc assigned as our security detail, gather at the end of the gangplank.

A rotund man dressed in flowing gold silk robes and surrounded by an entourage of Mercs walks by the group.

"Tutu Kane!" Princess Kamea shouts, and then the large man bends to see her.

"Why is my granddaughter in this hideous contraption?" He shouts as Miss Brita cowers and bows.

With head still bent Miss Brita speaks, "I'm sorry King Ahomana." She lifts her head slightly. "Ambassador Grayson asked me to keep her safe from the virus."

This is the king. I thought he would be more regal. He has a savage quality to him much like the wild animals that inhabit our farm. "King" is a good title, he carries himself like the king of the jungle; he rules with a roar and intimidation.

"Where is my son-in-law?" King Ahomana asks.

Queen Nalani joins the king. "Papa, he is coming up from the lab." The queen waves to Miss Brita to pick up the child. "Princess Kamea does not need the bubble carriage today. I'm sorry; I think Miss Brita is thinking of Germany." She announces, "Ross is coming."

Ambassador Ross Grayson hikes up. He is a lanky graying man with a kind aura. He is out of breath from slogging the stairs. "What's that about Germany?"

Queen Nalani hooks her arm in her husband's arm. "I was just telling Papa that Kamea does not need the bubble carriage unless we are in Germany."

Ambassador Grayson glares at his wife. "Our daughter was not to go out in Germany—bubbled carriage or not. I told you it's not safe." He leans over to his wife. "The virus."

Queen Nalani jerks her arm out of his. "The virus is gone. We are negotiating a peace and new world order. Quit scaring everyone!"

King Ahomana holds up his hand and bellows. "Quiet!" The stillness in the room is instantaneous and complete. King Ahomana turns his head and stares at his son-in-law. "Does the princess need that monstrosity in London?"

Ambassador Grayson bows his head. "No, not in London."

King Ahomana puts his hand on Ambassador Grayson's shoulder. "Then it is settled. The princess will be taken out of the carriage." He squeezes his son-in-law's shoulder. "I trust that you will bring better negotiating skills to the table in London than you have practiced here today with your wife. I am putting a lot of trust in you. I don't want war."

"I agree. War will cause more death than the virus. We both know that is not the answer." Ambassador Grayson straightens his tie and buttons up his blue blazer. "But, you know how your daughter can be."

King Ahomana nods and smiles. "Yes. She can be a handful. I raised her to be strong willed. Good practice for you to make the peace we all need." He motions for us to follow him down the gangplank. "Let's go!"

Colt and I help Miss Brita free the princess from the carriage.

Miss Brita sends the contraption back into the ship with a servant. "Bring the fold-up stroller."

The princess toddles ahead. "I don't need a stroller. I'm not a baby."

Miss Brita pats her head. "I know you're not, but you might get tired of walking. We'll take it just in case."

A flank of long limousines waits at the harbor's edge. A security detail gets into the first vehicle. King Ahomana climbs into the second one along with Ambassador Grayson and his wife with four security men stationed alongside standing on an attached foot plank. The next limousine is inhabited with security and other diplomats.

Trevor opens the door to the fourth car. "This is ours." Our group gets into our assigned sedan and a ship's steward brings the stroller and puts it in the trunk.

Miss Brita closes the door. "We're all set."

"Where we going?" asks Princess Kamea. "I want new dollies."

Miss Brita hands her a piece of a banana. "Our first stop is Stonehenge. Your father and grandfather have to meet some people there. We will have lunch and then we will go into London and look for new dollies. Okay?"

Princess Kamea takes the banana and settles back in her car seat.

Miss Brita retrieves a piece of paper from her pocket and opens it. "Here's our itinerary. It's an all day trip in the car. It takes around an hour to get to Stonehenge. We will be staying there for two hours and eat brunch."

Brunch? What is brunch? No memories of brunch. But Stonehenge— rocks in the middle of nowhere, *how could I know that?*

I whisper. "I remember something about Stonehenge."

Colt shushes me. "You must have read about it in a book."

He always has an answer for everything, but I really need to know what we are doing. I shake my head. "Sorry Miss Brita, please continue I really want to know where we are going."

Miss Brita holds the paper out to us pointing to the list. "After Stonehenge, we will be going to London— that takes about two more hours. From what I understand there are a couple of shops that sell dolls."

I cross my arms. "You mean Sponsored Companions?'

Miss Brita flutters her eyes. "Yes, SCs. But it really is a good program, don't you think?" She thumps me on the arm. "You and your brother would probably have starved if we hadn't bought your service." She puts her hand to her chin and shakes her head. "Just think of all of the poor hungry people."

"Not all starving people are saved." I jerk my arm out of the way. "What about the Undesirables? They are people too."

Miss Brita's mood is sullen as she sits back hard in her seat. "We can't save them all."

"What about our reason for this trip?" Colt waves his hand to the front of the car. "Up in front of us are people who can change how it is.

120

Maybe they will be smart, make good decisions, and stop some of this craziness."

"I hope that same thing." Miss Brita squeezes his shoulder. "But for today let's just concentrate on what we are doing, shall we?"

Colt and I both nod, as Princess Kamea is enthralled with drawing and playing with a magnetized picture made by her father.

Colt points over to her. "At least she's busy or it'd be a long ride."

I smile. "True. I'm sorry, Miss Brita. Please continue and tell us more. It does sound exciting."

Miss Brita unfolds the paper again. "We stay in London for about three to four hours. We can eat a late lunch there. They are just rebuilding from what I understand. We can see what monuments still stand." She folds the paper and puts it back in her pocket. "We have to hope that our world will be better and trust that the right people are making the big decisions."

"Of course." I slide over by Princess Kamea. "It's not for us to say."

During the hour ride through the townships of the countryside of Great Britain, it is evident that the last twelve years have taken their toll. There are few signs of civilization. The people roaming the streets are like paupers, wearing ragged clothes. There are no signs of cars or farm equipment. Mass graves, marked only with the amount of dead and the date they were buried, are prevalent on both sides of the poorly maintained roads. What starts as a fun day quickly changes into a gruesome and depressing one.

A tear runs down my cheek. "I'd heard about how bad the virus was, but I never saw proof. I hadn't realized how many died." I point to a burial site. "It seems that this whole town died."

Miss Brita shakes her head. "Yes, I remember the panic. No one could go to work so communications stopped. You don't realize that people actually are needed to work at television stations and at towers to keep computers and the worldwide web running."

She purses her lips. "I bet you don't even remember television or computers."

Colt looks up at the ceiling. "I remember a little square box that had words and pictures on it. I don't know if that was television or computer."

"It could have been either." Miss Brita remarks, "When the virus came everyone was quarantined. We lost many people. We knew about those close to us, but we don't know how many people were lost all over. The virus spread and kept killing for many years."

"How many years has the virus been eliminated?" Colt asks.

Miss Brita shakes her head. "It's not eliminated, only dormant. Ambassador Grayson is working on a cure. He's given an immunization to a lot people. A child can't take it until he or she is five. That's the reason he is so careful with the princess. She does not have the immunization yet."

I look over at Miss Brita. "I don't think we have the immunization."

"Of course you have. All SCs are immunized." Miss Brita taps my shoulder. "But that doesn't matter, since you were from Bavaria. You *were* from Bavaria, right?"

I nod.

"Bavaria is where the virus started." Miss Brita continues, "It should have wiped you all out. If you survived, then you probably have a natural immunity."

Colt smiles. "That's a good thing."

Miss Brita shakes her head. "It is according to how you look at it. If you survived, people might want to study you. Ambassador Grayson is a scientist trying to stop people from doing that."

I hug the princess. "Is that why you think he's a good man?"

Miss Brita nods. "He *is* a good man, but he *is* only one man. King Ahomana does not necessarily agree with him about everything and the king has the real power. Why do you suppose there were so many people gathered from Bavaria and Germany on this trip?"

"Why?" Colt asks.

"King Ahomana wants Ambassador Grayson to conduct experiments on them. The only thing that is stopping the Undesirables from being experimented on is the ambassador."

I shake my head. "The world is a sad place. I wish I could go home. Life was simple there."

Princess Kamea stops her game and looks up at me. "I don't want you to go home. I want you to stay with me forever, I love you, dolly."

I smile. "I love you too, Princes Kamea, but why don't you call me Paisley instead of dolly?"

"Okay, Paisley." The princess goes back to playing with her magnetized drawing game.

I stare out the window. As we get closer to our destination, the burial sites grow.

The desolate farmland countryside is so barren it makes me sorrowful. Then out of nowhere in the middle of all of this nothingness, huge stones protrude like royal pillars from a faraway time, so out of place that it astounds me. "Stonehenge," I mutter. "I've been here before. I couldn't have dreamed this. I *know* I've been here."

122

Chapter 23

The huge stones, jutting up like fingers pointing to the sky, sit in a pasture in the middle of nowhere. The color of the stones is not exceptionally noteworthy; it's the surprise of these natural structures existing in this barren field. A mysterious, overwhelming, mesmerizing, and utterly beautiful site.

Colt sits up straight. "Unbelievable."

I sigh. "One you would remember, no matter how young you were." I wipe the window with my sleeve to get a clearer view. "I've been here. I just don't understand why Mom would not tell me the truth about it. I'm going to ask her next chance I get."

Colt looks out the opposite window. "Probably had a good reason not to tell you." He snaps his finger. "I bet they didn't want you to try to leave the farm. They knew you were quarantined and you had to stay."

"Possible." I nod. "I was a headstrong girl."

Colt leans back from the window. "*Was?*"

"Okay, I *am* a strong willed girl."

"We're almost there." Miss Brita unhooks the princess's seat belt and pulls her arm through a jacket sleeve.

Princess Kamea helps pull her other arm through. "I want some new dollies."

"First, we tour this historic place and eat. I think you will like it, Princess Kamea." Miss Brita opens the door.

Miss Brita gets out of the car and motions for us to follow. "We'll walk around first and then we'll sit and eat brunch later. "

Walking around the stones seems surreal. I touch them. "I remember we couldn't get close to them. It seems that we had to stand back from them. There was a roped off area and sidewalks, but I recall pictures."

How could I remember them so vividly? Why aren't Gretel and my parents in any of my memories? Did I mix up a picture with the real thing? How could that be? This is a site that once you saw it you would never forget it. This is one of those places that pictures don't do justice.

Miss Brita takes Princess Kamea by the hand. "You can sit for a minute, Princess." The princess takes a seat on a bench that is located away from the stones. Miss Brita says, "Stay here. Trevor will keep his eye on you. I'm going to walk around with Colt and Paisley." Miss Brita waves to Trevor. "She can run around a bit, but just in this area."

Trevor nods his understanding.

Miss Brita joins Colt and me on a path to the stones. "You must have been here Paisley because many years ago the stones were being mutilated by the public so it was decided that there would be a roped fence around the stones. You could take pictures, but not touch them. I guess during the quarantines, someone removed the barriers or maybe they rusted away."

Colt caresses the stones. "After the quarantine, rules went out the window."

Miss Brita places the side of her face on the stones. "Some think these stones are magic. I bet a lot of people came out here looking for answers or at least trying to get some of the healing powers during the outbreak."

I touch the stones. "I've heard the stories. Maybe from something talking in my ears. Does that sound crazy?"

"Not really." Miss Brita calls up to Trevor. "Watch her a few more minutes. I'm going down below to see if the shop is still here."

Trevor acknowledges with a head nod.

Miss Brita, Colt, and I find our way under the mound to a boarded-up shop.

Miss Brita pulls off one of the boards. "There was a listening device that told the story of Stonehenge."

Colt crawls in and returns holding three headsets. "Is this what you are looking for?"

Miss Brita and I say together. "Yes."

"I remember these." I put my earplugs in my ears. "They don't work."

Miss Brita opens hers. "The batteries are dead. Colt, see if you can find any packaged batteries. They might still be good."

Colt disappears and returns out of breath with new packages of batteries. "These were in the area of the recorders. See if these work?'

"Yes." Miss Brita removes the corroded batteries, takes a stick from the ground to scrape out the rust, and then puts the batteries in the player. She puts the ear buds in her ears and turns the recorder on. "It works. You two put batteries in yours and I'll go get Princess Kamea's stroller." She hurries off for a moment before stopping and calling back. "Colt, get a player for the princess and Trevor. This will be great!"

Miss Brita pushes the princess as we walk around, touching the stones while listening to the history, myths, and legends that surround Stonehenge. One of the security details interrupts the history lesson to tell us that it is time for brunch.

"Can we come back out and finish up after we eat?" I ask Miss Brita.

"Not sure." Miss Brita asks, "Are we eating here? I hope so, this is great."

Trevor guides our group back to the limousine. "No, ma'am. We are eating at another location. We won't be coming back here. Sorry."

I groan.

Miss Brita puts the listening devices in the vehicle's console. "I didn't realize we were going to eat elsewhere. That's okay. We'll take the headphones and listen to the rest of the story about Stonehenge on our way to London."

"Yea!" Both Colt and I cheer.

After a few minutes' ride, we pull up to an old farmhouse that looks as if it has been recently been renovated. Servants line the steps of the porch. We are welcomed into the house and shown a table in which to sit. A head table is set up with places on one side for King Ahomana, Ambassador Grayson, and Queen Nalani; and on the other side sit four well-dressed men.

For the next hour, servings of poached eggs, grilled bacon, potato cakes, bread, baked beans, and grilled tomatoes fill our plates. Beverages of orange juice, grapefruit juice, and espresso flow freely.

Colt picks up his third helping of the potato cake. "I haven't had this much food since—forever."

I drink the entire glass of orange juice in one gulp. "This orange juice is great." A waiter comes around and refills my glass. "Thanks." I empty it again. I consume five more glasses before I finally say, "I better stop, or I'll have to go to the bathroom too much."

Colt leans over to me. "I don't know what's being discussed at the head table, but Ambassador Grayson is not happy."

I stuff another potato cake in my mouth. "I agree." I pick up another piece of bacon. "This is so good." I look over at Miss Brita. "I would love to take some of this back to the people on the fifteenth floor."

Miss Brita shakes her head. "I don't know how we could make that happen."

I sit quietly for a moment then say, "I know." I lean over to the princess and whisper to her.

The princess walks over to her mother, Queen Nalani, speaks to her, and returns to the table.

One of Queen Nalani's security detail comes over in a few minutes. "The princess has asked that all of the left overs be packed up and given to her people building her toys on level fifteen and King Ahomana and the queen say that will be fine." The security man looks over at me. "Can you show me which limo you want it in? I would really appreciate it."

I nod and he leaves.

"You're learning quickly, my dear." Miss Brita shakes her head. "But you need to be careful using the princess like that. You might get in trouble. King Ahomana and his daughter Queen Nalani can be quite vicious." Fear glints in her eyes. "But you never heard that from me." She looks up toward the head table. "The only person at that table with any kind of heart and not out for themselves is Ambassador Grayson. Please watch yourself."

I nod. "I will."

The king motions to one of the security force who taps a glass to get everyone's attention and announces. "Time to go. Everyone back to the limos."

Walking by King Ahomana, the queen and the ambassador, I overhear their heated conversation. King Ahomana says, "Ross, You need to watch yourself with the European delegation. Not everyone shares your ideas about democracy. The dictatorship suggestion is a viable one. The world does not know what is best for them now and we need to make good choices for them. We know what's best for them. We must tell them what to do."

Tell people what to do. Does the king think everyone in the world is in need of someone to tell them what to do? His way hasn't worked so great. There are slaves, starving people, and Undesirables. Things need to change.

"I'm not sure that we know what's best for the people. They need to decide that for themselves." Ambassador Grayson bows. "Respectfully, the United States of America put me in charge of this delegation. The USA believes in democracy. What you suggest could be a great abuse of power."

King Ahomana motions to his daughter. "Go ahead, dear. We will catch up with you in a moment."

Colt and I are caught behind King Ahomana and Ambassador Grayson.

King Ahomana holds his hand up stopping the ambassador. His face is angered and red. "I only put up with you because you are married to my daughter."

Ambassador Grayson stands hands on hips. "I love your daughter, but you and I know for a fact that this was a political move on your part. Our arranged marriage was to cement your foot in the Consortium of the World."

King Ahomana grabs the ambassador's arm and jerks him. "I am in charge. You are just my mouthpiece. You will vote the way I want or you will suffer the consequences. Do I make myself clear?"

The ambassador stands tall to the king, raises his voice, and spews his words. "I will support the laws that are best for all people. You will not dictate how I vote or what I say."

Maybe Miss Brita is right and the ambassador is a good man. Only time will tell. But he will have to survive the election.

Two of the security detail nervously stand behind the men. One of the security men asks, "Problem?"

The king holds onto the ambassador's arm. "Of course not. Just a family disagreement."

The ambassador jerks his arm away. "No problems here."

The king orders the security detail. "Please put the ambassador in the third limo. I only want to ride with my daughter."

Chapter 24

The king talks with some of the security people as Colt and I make our way around the fray. Ambassador Grayson huffs off and changes limousines.

Security men follow with the boxes of leftovers. I point to our car and they fill the trunk. We file into the back seats of the stretch limo, heavy now with boxes and ice chests full of leftovers. I buckle my seat belt. "Where to next?" I know the king and ambassador are upset, but I'm not because I am still going on a trip to somewhere I've never been. Or at least I don't think I've ever been there.

Miss Brita gets out the tape players from Stonehenge and passes them around. "London. It will take two hours driving through the countryside. We might as well listen to the Stonehenge story. Enjoy!"

Something to distract and pass the time makes me smile and I put in my ear buds. "London here we come!"

On the road, I notice the highways. How could I remember these? I *must* have travelled off the farm. "What are the roads called?" I pull out my ear buds. "I remember something about a blue sign with three white marks that look like roads."

Miss Brita turns off her player and puts it on the console. "That's the mark of the autobahn. I haven't traveled on the autobahn since the virus scare. The roads in England are called motorways, but in Germany they were called the autobahn." She puts her finger to her chin and sighs. "It's been twelve years."

"Not much wear and tear on this road. It's in great shape." Colt follows suit and puts his player up too.

"I guess that is because it hasn't been used very much." Miss Brita points over to a "WC" sign. "You know in America they call water closets bathrooms. It's funny how different parts of the world name things. It would be interesting to see what kind of shape the water closets are in. But it could be really nasty since they possibly haven't been cleaned out in twelve years."

I laugh. "I'll pass." I sniff. No discernible smell, but then the car windows are rolled up.

There are only a handful of cars on the road. The countryside seems untouched by the virus crisis. No burial sites and the houses peppered on the side of the roadway appear to be in good shape albeit overgrown in terms of lawn care. Skeletal remains of what appear to be cattle or other farm animals are scattered about the large pastures. Grape vines are dense. There is a light on in a deserted gas station and the limos pull in.

I watch as the security detail scrambles to fill up the tanks. "Who is running these gas stations?"

Miss Brita opens the door, stands beside the car with her hands on her hips and twists her waist, and then waves her arms back and forth across her body to stretch. "They are run by the consortium. It's been a long time since there was a need for gas. What we are using was stored before the virus. It's very limited and we have to have special permission to get it. It costs a lot. Do the rest of you want to stretch a little bit?"

We all unbuckle, jump out, and begin exercising outside the car. Colt raises his arms above his head and then bends over, grunting as he moves. "I've been meaning to ask. How do people buy things nowadays?"

Miss Brita bends from her waist. "Mostly bartering. That's how the king got so powerful. People from his island had an antibody in their blood that gave them a natural immunity to the virus. That's how he met the ambassador. He sold the right for the ambassador to use the antibody to work on the vaccine."

Colt lifts the princess out, twirls her, and then puts her down so she can run around for a couple of minutes. "Let me get this straight. The king traded blood antibodies that could have saved people from dying to make himself rich. He could have just given the immunity away and saved so many more people. Kind of barbaric."

Miss Brita chases the princess and catches her before answering. "I guess you could think that way. The king had a valuable commodity and he chose to use it for wealth instead of giving it away. It was his right. The root saved a great many people. Life, it doesn't get more valuable than that."

One more reason not to like the king. He's selfish. It's funny how nature works, even though this area hasn't been used for years and death has been the norm since the outbreak, new grass sprouts out and nourishes the area. As I take a deep breath in, everything smells fresh and new. I run after the princess. "So why are they worried about Princess Kamea? Doesn't her blood give her a natural immunity?"

Miss Brita slides back into the limo. "Unfortunately, she has gotten some antibodies, but because she did not spend her early years eating a root that grows only on the king's island she is susceptible to the virus. The ambassador has found a way to make a vaccine from the root. But it's very strong so the princess has to be older. He's working on a cure so this virus even if it is contracted cannot kill anymore. He has a greater purpose in this world, that's for sure." Miss Brita calls to Kamea. "Time to get back in the car." We all load into our vehicles.

"The limo with the ambassador hasn't pulled out yet." The driver says, "Do you think it's okay if we go in front of them since they're still waiting to be filled up?"

Miss Brita buckles the princess in her seat belt. "I'm sure it's okay. I don't think there's any specific order."

"Never mind." The driver motions behind them. "He's pulling out behind us now. Now we're out of order."

Miss Brita smiles. "Not many cars out here. I don't think it matters what order we're in."

Interesting about the virus. If you were lucky and lived on the island that had the root, you survived. How is that fair? Why should the king's people all live while the rest of the world suffers? How is it fair he became rich and powerful because of a root and on the back of all of that suffering? The world is a baffling place.

Out the window, brick pieces of structures choked into submission by the thick vegetation protrude every so often as a testament that this area once housed a viable community. Road signs in varying levels of decay remain on the side of the road. One raggedy sign advertises the "Eye of London" with a picture half torn down of a giant wheel-looking contraption.

I light up. "Is that a Ferris wheel?"

Miss Brita nods. "I doubt that is still standing, and if it is I'm sure it doesn't work. It was a giant Ferris wheel. The glass-covered pods filled with tourists boasted a birds' eye view of London from every angle. A popular attraction."

Colt hits my knee with his knee. "She has a thing about Ferris wheels."

I nod. "I really do. I love Ferris wheels. If that thing still works, I sure want to go on it."

A loud noise rings through our car which swerves, slides sideways down the road, and then veers off the roadway slamming through the pasture. The driver slumps over the steering wheel and Trevor screams, "Gunshots! He's hit!" We bop up and down in our seats secured only by our seatbelts as the car rides over the uneven field. The steering wheel whips out of control slamming into the dead driver each time it turns. Trevor unbuckles and struggles from his back seat post to maneuver the lifeless driver out of the way before he finally forcefully throws his own body in the front seat between the front door and the driver. He yanks the deceased driver's head back and blood spurts into the back seat. My face warms as I am hit with the wet red blood; I gag for a minute, but quickly recover as I see the rest of the back seat passengers being showered by blood too.

"The driver's been shot!" Trevor quickly unhooks the driver from his seat belt. He shoves the limp dead body over with his shoulder and grabs the wheel yelling to us, "Get down! I'll try to drive us out of here!"

I freeze for a moment holding my blood soaked hands in front of me. I hear screams, but I don't know if they are coming from me. I scan the area out the window and see the rest of the limos are still on the roadway, but stopped. Security people have left their limos and are running towards us.

Trevor turns and squeezes Colt's collar with one of his bloodied hands. "I have to stop the car." He yells, "Protect the princess!" He jerks his head side to side trying to get a view out of the windshield splattered with blood.

Colt unbuckles his seat belt and throws himself over the princess, shoving me onto the floorboard of the car in the process. "Get down and stay down. Don't move!"

The princess screams. The smell of the blood trickling down from his shirt gags me and I cower. The princess, burrowed in between both of our bodies, clutches my shoulders, and cries softly.

Trevor shouts that he has control of the car. As I lay vulnerable, it gives me solace as I hear Trevor yell each of his successes letting us know that he has finally gained control of the vehicle, is pushing hard on the brakes, and is steadying the steering wheel. The car comes to stop. I breathe a sigh of relief and Colt lets us up. I hold the princess's head in my lap as she sniffles quietly. Two strangers run towards us after getting out of a mysterious car that suddenly materializes from behind a barn in the field. A man, brandishing a gun runs to our limo, shoots the door handle off, and wrenches the driver's door open. Trevor struggles to gain access to his weapon, but he's too late. The stranger shoots Trevor in the head. I scream. Blood gushes out as he slumps over into the front seat.

The unknown assailant points the pistol at us and cocks it. "Where's the ambassador?" The menacing voice of the stranger booms through the car.

"Help! Help!" Miss Brita screams trying to roll her window down.

"Shut up!" The man pistol-whips her in the head with the butt of his gun and she collapses over, bleeding profusely, still buckled in her seat belt.

The man points the gun at Colt as the princess screams. The man furrows his brow. "Who is this child? What is this child doing in this car?"

His question allows Colt a few seconds to grab his gun. Colt holds the gun barrel toward him and slugs the man hard in the jaw with the butt end of the gun, he sways but does not fall. The stunned man backs away from our car and is plummeted with shots by the security detail that have now made it to our limo. His dead body jerks with each shot and the sound is deafening until he finally drops with a loud thump. The mysterious car accelerates towards us avoiding the barrage of gunshots and the other unknown man is able to dive into the car as one of the two occupants of the car opens the passenger door as it races by. The security detail chases the racing car by foot, but are soon unable to keep up and the unknown assailants escape.

"What happened?" I yell. "Was anyone hit?" I realize how ridiculous that sounds since obviously the driver and Trevor were not only hit, but also killed. Tears well in my eyes as I loosen my grip on the princess and rub her looking for wounds. "Are you okay, Princess Kamea?"

Princess Kamea screams and death-grips my arm, refusing to let go.

Finding no apparent injuries, I cradle her head. "It's okay. You're okay. It's over." I get out of the car carrying the princess with Colt following closely behind. The security men shadow us forming a protective circle around the princess and me. Lots of shouting and orders are yelled, but I am in a fog and cannot make out what is being said. We run towards the other cars and meet Queen Nalani.

Queen Nalani shrieks. "My baby! My baby! Are you okay?" She snatches the princess from my arms.

Ambassador Grayson's limo dashes to the fray and he jumps out of the door before it stops, tripping, and falling first before picking himself up and running toward his family. "What happened?" He envelopes his wife and hugs his daughter. Colt informs him about the gunshots and about the shooter. "He was looking for you."

The ambassador asks, "Were you hurt? You both are covered with blood."

I look at my blood-splattered clothing. "No, it's blood from—" I choke up unable to finish the sentence.

King Ahomana trots toward the group on the side of the road. "Is my granddaughter hurt?"

"She's fine." The ambassador cradles the princess and then takes her to his car as the king follows. "From what I understand, they were after me. During the gas stop, we inadvertently switched our lineup. I was supposed to be in that car."

How did the gunman know where the ambassador would be? Were

they getting inside information? Why do they want to kill the ambassador? I have to hold it together for the princess's sake. I can't fall apart. I keep repeating in my head: "Be strong. Be strong."

One of the security men says, "We can load the bodies in the trunk and transport them back to the ship. We might be able to identify them and I don't want to leave any bodies behind. We shouldn't stay here too long. We don't know who they are or if they'll come back."

"Yes, we should get out of here. We are too exposed." The king points to the ambassador. "Take the princess to my car. She will ride with me where she will be safe."

The ambassador reaches in his car, gathers the princess, and nods. "That's a good idea."

Another security man trots beside us out of breath. "The driver and Trevor are dead. We can take their bodies back with us, but the nanny is alive just hurt. She said that the two SCs saved the princess."

The queen passes by us stroking our arms. She cries softly. "Thank you for saving my baby. We are in your debt."

What does that mean? That they will let us go? Probably not.

Colt shakes his head. "No need for debt."

"We love the princess." I curtsy. Seems like a lame thing to do, but I can't think of anything appropriate. What is the protocol during something like this? I'm too stunned to process.

"The SCs did their job. They are right, no need for debt." The king lets out an exasperated sigh. "I can't believe they almost hurt our precious princess. They better be glad they didn't make that mistake."

The ambassador hugs his daughter and hands her to his wife. "Take the princess to King Ahomana's car. I will go to London by myself. I cannot put any of you in danger. This has to be because of my stance on democracy."

The king lovingly gazes at his granddaughter. "That's probably best."

We separate. Ambassador Grayson and a security detail go to London in one limo while Colt, an injured Miss Brita, and I go in another, with security following the rest of the royal family back to South Hampton.

After about a half an hour on the road, we stop as the security men discuss altering the route back for safety reasons. Colt and I get out of the car for a minute to breathe the outside air, stretch and wait on the conversation to end. We walk silently out of earshot. The severity of the situation hits me, and I cry on Colt's shoulder. I whisper, "I was so scared."

Colt runs his hand through my hair. "Me too. I thought being with the royal family would protect us, but now I'm not so sure."

Where can we be safe? The world is in turmoil. My bottom lip trembles. "I'm glad the royal family is okay, but I've seen too much death. Trevor and the driver—"

Colt sighs. "I know. We need to step up the training. We need to find a way out of here."

"I agree." I sit up straight. "We need to get home and out of this madness. We were safe there." I look over to Colt. "We need a plan. A concrete plan." I lean on his shoulder. "To survive."

Chapter 25

The ride back is distressing. In pain, Miss Brita cries most of the time. I try to make her comfortable. How did this happen? I am now in the middle of a war.

Miss Brita grits her teeth. "You'll need to take over being the nanny, Paisley, until I can return. I will try to get back as soon as I can." She grabs my collar. "Can you do that?"

What choice do I have? "Of course, if the queen will let me."

Miss Brita moans in pain, and then breathes shallowly. "She will. I'll talk to her."

I wipe Miss Brita's brow with a moistened cloth. "Don't worry. Colt and I will take care of everything."

Miss Brita sighs. "I am so glad you two are here."

Back at the ship, things are less controlled. The limousine ahead of us containing the queen, her father, and the princess is driven to the ship's gangplank and the three royals get out of the car with security personnel flanking them on every side. Colt and I are directed to go immediately to our room and await instructions. Medical personnel rush out to take Miss Brita on a stretcher.

I spy my sister dressed in pink nurse scrubs tending to Miss Brita. "Gretel? What are you doing here?"

"Oh, no! Paisley, you're covered in blood." She pulls at my sleeve. "Are you okay?"

I stare down at my blouse, red and stained. "It's not my blood." I peer down at the nanny. "What about Miss Brita?"

"Glad you're okay? Don't worry. We'll take care of Miss Brita." Gretel gives Miss Brita a shot. "The ambassador signaled the ship from the car and asked us to take Miss Brita to the medical lab. It's been a long wait for all you to arrive." She strokes my cheek. "When we heard— I was afraid that you—are you okay?"

I nod and point at the syringe in Gretel's hand. "You're getting good at that?"

Gretel puts the spent syringe in a red waste bag. "I have all of the right equipment here. The ambassador has taught me a great many things." She lifts up the stethoscope around her neck. "I really love helping people, I always have."

Gretel has a purpose now, how wonderful for her. I'm so happy for her that I almost forget about the horrific incident. I furrow my brow. "They tried to kill the ambassador today."

Gretel motions for the others to take the stretcher. "I know. I'm thankful he is not hurt. I have to go. We'll talk. I'll try to find you later." She gives me a quick hug, and then she disappears.

The leftover food in the trunk shoots through my mind for a second. Too much anguish to try to get that to the 15th floor. Too much security. Sad. They would have loved that treat.

Colt and I make our way onto the boat through the added security on the first level. We are guided around others who are milling about, showing credentials and having their wrists scanned to gain entry. I hope the scrutiny on this ship is tight. With someone out to kill the ambassador, I wouldn't want any of us to be an innocent bystander casualty.

Colt and I arrive at our cabin and he unlocks the door. He pauses and says, "Before we go in, let's check on the others, and see what happened here today."

"Good idea."

We lock our door back and walk down the hall to Adanna and Baako's cabin. Colt raps quietly. Baako opens the door slightly and peers out. When he sees us, he opens it wider and grabs us in a hug. "Oh my goodness, you two. I thought you might have gotten killed today."

Hearing the commotion, Suma, Naeem, Pandi and Wei come into Baako's room. It is crowded, but we make do sitting six across one of the twin beds.

Suma rubs her hands together. "It was crazy today. When word got back about what had happened, they shut down the fifteenth floor and sent us all back to our rooms. We've been sitting here ever since."

"What did they tell you?" Colt asks.

Naeem jumps to his feet. "They said that there had been shots fired at the royal limousines, that no one knew who was hurt or wounded, but there were at least a couple of people killed."

Pandi whimpers. "That's why I've been crying all afternoon waiting for you to come back. Is the princess okay?"

"She wasn't hurt, but Miss Brita was." I cradle my chin in my hands. "It really was scary. The driver and our security man, Trevor, were killed."

A knock at the door startles us. Baako shushes the group, and calls out, "Who is it?"

"Me." Riley answers.

136

Baako opens the door and lets him into the crowded room. Riley elbows his way inside and hugs me first. "I was so worried. Glad you are okay." He releases me after a long embrace and turns to Colt. "Do you know what it was all about?"

Colt shakes his head. "There was some kind of altercation at Stonehenge with the other two men who were there. It seemed to me that they didn't agree on politics."

I embrace Riley again. "Politics? I don't want to be involved in politics. I want to go home." I can't help crying, but I try to hide it by sinking my head into Riley's chest.

Colt inches his way over to me. "Don't worry." He grabs both of my arms and looks me right in the face. "We'll get there and all in one piece."

Sweet of Colt to try to comfort me, like a brother. I sniffle a little. "You really believe that?"

Colt looks over at Riley. "I'm curious. How do they get messages here from the limousines? I mean how did you know what happened?"

Riley pulls a square box out of his pocket. "One of the Undesirables rigged up some sort of a radio gadget. They use old communications towers." He flips the gadget around. "Somehow this sends signals to other boxes like these and we can communicate with each other."

"Signals?" Colt takes the device and studies it.

"It can only beep. I had to learn this thing called Morse code." Riley shifts his weight from one foot to the other. "It's so crowded in here. You probably should get back to your room. They're not sure what they are going to do about anything, but we're shipping out tonight. At least we'll be safe on the open seas for a while."

I hope he's right about being safe. I haven't felt secure since I left the farm. Wonder if that is what freedom really feels like? Always afraid.

"You're probably right." Baako stands up. "Everyone go back to your cabins and get some rest, it's been a stressful day for all of us." He opens the door for everyone to exit. "We'll see each other tomorrow."

Outside the cabin sits a tray, which Adanna picks up. "It looks like we all have dinner trays. The help doesn't miss a beat."

Of course they don't. The help is worried about being thrown overboard or being sold at the next town. The help does what they are told. *I am now the help too.*

Colt and I make our way back to the cabin and take our meals inside when I pick up my meal, a piece of paper falls out, and I open it. "Colt, Mom sent me a letter with my food."

Colt pulls the cover off his tray. "What does it say?"

"It says that she's glad we're okay. She was worried. Says that she'll

137

try to send more messages. That's the first good news I've heard all day."

Colt and I eat in silence. I can't believe we wolf our food down as if it's just any other day. What's wrong with us? I would have thought we would have been too upset to eat, but I'm famished. It's strange how a person reacts to stress.

Colt finishes his food and puts his plate outside the door. "I'm going to take my shower first if that's okay."

Sitting on my bed and savoring the last bite of the meal, I pick up the treasure box from home. What could possibly be in here that Mom thought should be guarded all of these years? I open the box and the first thing I pull out is the postcard from Orlando. I smile, study it for a while, and put it to the side. Something about that card calms me down.

Colt comes out from the bathroom. "Your turn."

I place the opened box over to the side and grab my bedclothes to take a shower. I remove my blood soaked clothes and carefully take out the four-leaf clover. I decide to put my and Colt's clothes in the bag to be put outside for laundry. Can't imagine they can be cleaned, but really don't want the reminder in here with us.

As the water runs over me, my mind wanders to the postcard. "Where dreams come true" How are my dreams coming true? For the longest time all I wanted was to get off the farm and venture out in the world. That wish had come true, but at what cost?

The farm was home. I could sneak out and ride Hershey when I wanted or I could run through our land as long as I was careful. We had to study every day and I griped about that. I wouldn't complain now.

Exiting the bathroom, I hear Colt's rhythmic breathing, signaling that he is fast asleep. I quietly crawl back up to my top bunk and flip on the light overhead. I pull the chest close.

There is a long piece of cord. It would be perfect to tie around the four-leaf clover bullet. I pull the bullet out and loop it a couple of times then tie the cord around my neck so it hangs low on my chest. All of my new clothes will cover it. I am afraid I'll forget to switch it from one set of clothes to the next. This will make sure I always have it. That makes me smile. The next item I uncover is a scarf with an unusual design, with swirly colorful abstract figures. Pretty. The tag reads: *Made in America, Paisley Design Scarves, INC., New York, New York.* I mumble, "This scarf's design is the same as my name. Wonder why Mom kept this?" I tie the scarf around my neck and reach back into the box. I retrieve a delicate yellowed piece of paper and unfold it carefully. Scrawled on the paper in cursive writing: *If I don't make it, take care of her. JG.*

What could that mean? Who is JG? Who is *her*? Maybe there are other clues I continue searching. Next, I pick up a handkerchief and unfold it once. An initial embroidered on the handkerchief is a "G." Must be Gretel's, I smile thinking of my sister. I unfold the rest of the initialed handkerchief and out fall two pieces of jewelry. One is a ring with a large diamond in the middle surrounded by three smaller diamonds on each side. I slide the ring on my finger. It fits perfectly. I hold my hand up to admire the way the light hits the stones. Why would Mom keep something this valuable when she could have traded it for food when we really needed it? I admire the other piece of jewelry, a necklace with a diamond encrusted initial 'J'. Who is J? I clasp it around my neck, but am unable to see my reflection in the mirror from the top bunk. Why did Mom hide these? It makes no sense.

I toss and turn that night unable to fall asleep, still wearing the ring and the necklace. I am in the delirium between awareness and sleep when an image flashes through my mind. It is a woman. I can't see her features, but I recall her sweet smell. It feels like—home and makes me feel safe. A flash pops into my mind just as sleep sets in. It's an image of the woman and around her neck is the "J" necklace. Is this some memory of Mother at a younger age?

The next morning I replace the treasures back in the box and lower myself from the top bunk.

"Tried to wake you." Colt yells from the bathroom. "You were sleeping so I thought I would brush my teeth first." The water quits running and then Colt emerges dressed, a few moments later. "No word yet on what we do today."

The morning drags. After eating breakfast, we sit with nothing to keep us occupied. I fiddle with my sock. "At least we didn't have to put on the Germany outfit today. Ought to make you happy."

"It does. I doubt they'll ever get those clothes clean." Colt nods. "Do you want to play a game?"

Nothing better to do. "Sure, what do you have in mind?" I sit beside him on his bunk.

Colt surveys our space. "We don't have a lot of room here. But what if we play a game that's fun and will help train us?"

"I can't imagine what that would be."

Colt grips my hand. "Put your other hand behind your back."

Colt unclasps my hand. "Now we are going to try to counter our own moves." He moves his hand in slow motion to my head. "See, if I was to try to hit you on the head you need to try to block that move."

"Interesting." I move my arm up to block. "But not much fun."

Colt smiles. "No, I guess not, but we need to practice how to fight."

What in the world, is he talking about? I frown. "Fight?"

"You never know, Paisley. We might need to fight one day."

"I guess." I block his next move.

The better we get at it, the more intense and involved the game becomes, until we are doing nothing but defensive moves. For the next hour, we practice until there is a knock at the door.

Colt opens it and Riley stands there. "They sent me to tell you the princess is not up to lessons today."

I scoot in beside Colt. "Is she okay?"

Riley nods. "She's shook up a bit. They thought it best she sit out of school for the rest of the week."

Colt makes a loud sighing sound. "What are we supposed to do until then?"

Riley walks into the entranceway. "That's the best part. They want you to work on the fifteenth floor. They think the obstacle course will help her feel better. They want you to complete it as quickly as possible."

Colt claps his hands together. "That *is* great news."

Riley points to me. "You better put on some pants. You want to make sure that you don't get your cute little dress dirty."

I see that my choice of wear is not suitable for the job. I just didn't think Riley would notice or why I like that he did. "The princess likes this dress and I was trying to please her. Give me a minute and I'll change."

"Sure we'll wait out here." Colt walks to the entry with Riley.

Before they close the door, Riley says, "Colt and Paisley you need to both hear this. You can order anything you want or have anyone down there you need to help with the obstacle course."

This is my chance. I turn quickly. "Like someone from the kitchen or the lab?"

Riley nods. "The kitchen for sure. Don't know about the lab. The ambassador is always excited about whatever it is that he does there. Not sure if he will let anyone go."

I'll take whatever family time I can get. "The kitchen it is. I'll get to spend the whole day with my mom." I smile as I slip into the bathroom.

In the next few minutes, we proceed to the 15th floor.

Victor is waiting on us. "Ever since I left the city, I've been saving these." He drops open his backpack and out falls a bunch of lighters. He picks one up, flicks it up, and watches as the flame burns. "I thought we might find a use for these."

It seems weird to hoard lighters, but even stranger that he would save them for all of these years. They must hold some sentimental value. I pick up one with a picture of a beer and the word *Munich* written below it. "Why did you collect these?"

Victor shakes his head. "I'm really not sure. I think it's because it is something that could help me remember." He flicks one on and off and lays it down. He pulls out another with a church outline and *Nuremburg* scrawled across the bottom. "I used to live in Nuremburg or close to it when I was younger. When life was good. Before the virus hit. Every one of these is from a place I've visited. I guess you could say this bag of lighters represents my history. The history of Victor."

Victor, an Undesirable, has a "history bag." No matter what label you put on people, their spirit will shine through. I hope that's the way it is with the rest of the world. I pick up another; this one has a picture of a cup and reads Poland. "What's this one's story?"

"Boleslawiec, Poland." Victor rubs his fingers around the lighter, which is white with blue embellishments on it. "That's where they used to make pottery. Polish pottery was famous. People from all over the world would order the pottery and have it shipped to their houses."

I flick it on. "It is very pretty." The flame goes out. "Tell us about before."

Victor gathers his lighters and puts them back in his backpack. "That is too long of a story; it would take all night or more. I'll tell you one story and then we will work some on the obstacle course."

How wonderful to know stories from before. "Then later you'll tell us another story?"

Victor chuckles. "Then I'll tell another story and then we will—"

"We'll practice some of our moves." Colt adds, "We need to train."

Victor flings the backpack over to the side. "Sounds like a plan to me. Story then work, another story and more work."

Victor motions for everyone to come and sit around him. All of the Undesirables with the children in the front sit to listen. Victor pulls up a chair and starts, "I used to work for the government communications company of Germany."

I sit cross-legged on the floor. "The government?"

Victor nods. "Before the virus, you could call anyone anywhere, and when you talked to them you could see them on a screen just like you were there. So like you, Paisley, if your mother was not here, you could call her and the two of you could make a cake with each other over the computer screen. It was actually pretty cool."

The younger children giggle and look wide-eyed at each other.

Victor points to them. "Some of you are too young to remember it." He surveys the room. "Most of you are too young."

I ask, "Do you think we'll ever be able to communicate like that again?"

"I really don't know. It didn't help us much. When the virus hit, we had all of the communication in the world, but all that did was spread the word faster. The message was dire. There was nothing to be done about the virus then. No cure."

Colt leans back on the wall with his arms crossed in front of him. "I heard the people of Germany had a natural immunity."

Victor nods. "I've heard that too. If we did, I didn't see it. Many died." He stops for a moment. "So my first story is telling you about these wondrous machines that made the world small because we could communicate no matter how far away we were." He stands up. "Unfortunately, communications was one of the first things we lost."

One of the children, Amanda, raises her hand. "Why did it go away?"

Victor picks up a rolled-up paper plan. "Everyone had to stay home so the virus wouldn't spread and people wouldn't get sick."

"Are we going to get sick?" Amanda asks.

Groans sound from the young ones. I guess we should have told him upfront, we only wanted pleasant stories. No one wants to hear these sad stories.

"Of course not." Victor smiles. "We are going to make the world a better place."

Amanda raises her hand again. "And no one will be an Undesirable."

This is too much. I pipe in. "You are not an Undesirable. You and I and the rest of us are all just regular people and don't you forget it." I walk over and hug Amanda. "That's enough for right now."

Victor claps his hands. "She's right, time to get to work." Victor hands the plans to Colt. "Let's divide up into teams and each one work on part of the obstacle course. We'll train with the time we have left."

Colt motions to the people sitting on the floor. "Come with me and we will complete the paint gun field."

I gather another faction. "We're going to practice throwing the suction cups darts, and after that we will practice with real machetes." I look over at Riley. "We have two actual machetes. I said we needed them to cut the background parts."

Riley slaps me on the back. "Good thinking."

Victor takes a group to practice moving undetected. This is the part where you move and touch people without them realizing it.

Riley has a unit training for hand-to-hand combat while the others are training in spear throwing and poison dart throwing. All under the guise of building an obstacle course as a play area for a four-year-old. The progress of completing the course is phenomenal and the practices are even more impressive. Too bad that the princess is so upset, but it is a wonderful opportunity to rehearse defensive tactics and fight strategy.

We've been at it for about an hour when I feel a tap on my shoulder, I turn. "Mom!"

Mom hugs me. "I brought you some lunch. They said I could visit for a little while."

I yell. "Lunchtime!" A long line forms and the group takes turns getting their bag lunches.

Colt announces. "We'll take about half an hour. Eat your lunch wherever you want."

Mom and I find a place over in the corner and sit on the floor. I pull out a peanut butter and jelly sandwich. "My favorite."

"I remember." Mom smiles, taking a bite out of her sandwich.

I take a swig of juice. "I looked through the box last night."

Mom stops midair with her sandwich. "And?"

I retrieve an apple. "I found a scarf that has a design with my name on it, an old note, a ring and necklace and old postcards. What does all of that mean?"

"There is something that I've been meaning to tell you. Do you remember any of your younger days?" Mom pats my knee.

I shake my head and bite into the apple. "How young?"

"From before the virus?" Mom puts her sandwich down.

"Not much. Some flashes here and there."

Mom scoots close. "What kind of flashes?"

I stare at the ceiling. "When I saw the necklace and ring I thought I remembered a woman who wore them and I don't think it was you." Just a dream, it had to be just a dream.

Mom sits up straight. "What exactly do you remember about the woman?"

"It's strange the only thing I can remember about her is her smell. It was sweet. Who was she?" I shake my head and take another bite of the apple. I chew trying to make sense of it all.

Mom has a weird look in her eyes. I've never seen that look. It scares me. She leans over and whispers, "She was—"

Just then, Lamar busts through the doors yelling, "What's going on here?"

143

Chapter 26

Riley rushes to confront Lamar. "What do you think is going on here? They're working on the obstacle course. It's what the queen wanted."

On cue, Lamar points over to my mother. "We have to beef up security. What's a person from the kitchen doing here? She's not working on the obstacle course, is she?" He cuts his eyes at Mom and then back at Riley. "It looks like she is sitting here gabbing." He motions to Mother to get up, which she obeys. "Get up and get back to the kitchen. No playing around. You need to keep everyone in check down here, Riley."

Riley stands tall to Lamar. "She brought lunch. Just saying hello. What's the harm in that? I'm sure she was planning to leave soon."

Lamar bumps into Riley. "Maybe you are *too soft* to watch this group."

Riley bumps back into Lamar. "I'm just as tough as you are."

Their respective guns are pulled simultaneously and they point them at each other. The room gets quiet.

"What are we Mercs shooting each other now?" Riley laughs, nervously, training his gun on Lamar.

Lamar cocks his gun. "Scared?"

Colt walks quickly toward them, but Victor pushes Colt out of the way and dives in between Riley and Lamar. The movement and fray cause Lamar's gun to discharge hitting Victor in chest and he falls backward.

Screams and gasps fill the room.

Lamar growls at Riley. "I wasn't going to shoot. Why did he come at me? Thank goodness, he's a nobody. If he dies, it doesn't matter. You make me crazy, Riley. Quit disrespecting me. You're one of us. I'd never shoot you!"

Riley is stunned for a moment, but then drops his gun. "Get a towel!" He rushes over to Victor.

One of the Undesirables hands Riley a towel and he covers the gunshot wound to stop the spurting blood. "Why would you wave your gun around?"

"Why not?" Lamar waves his gun. "I'm a Merc. I can do whatever I want."

The Undesirable who brought the towel takes over applying

144

pressure to Victor's wound. Riley stands up. "I'm a Merc too, but I don't go around shooting people."

Lamar waves his gun at Riley. "You seem to like these Undesirables a little too much." He walks over to me. I'm standing horrified at what just transpired, as is everyone else in the room. It's as if we're frozen in place except the woman helping to douse Victor's wounds. The rest of the Mercs cock their guns and aim them at various people in the room. Lamar grabs my hair. "I've heard you've spent a lot of time with this Undesirable. Is she your favorite?" He jerks my hair again. "Maybe I'll throw her overboard. Then you can concentrate."

I'm disgusted, but I squirm and break free as Colt steps in front of me to square up against Lamar and his gun. "She is my sister and not an Undesirable, she is a favorite of the princess. We are SCs and from what I understand, protected. Which means you can't mess with us. Besides, I'm not sure what the princess would say if you hurt any of us who are building her play area." Colt pulls me in closer behind him.

Lamar backs away. "I don't know if any of that is true, but believe me, I'll find out." He lets out an exasperated sigh. "I'll go for now, but I'll be back. You can count on that." He looks over at Victor. "If he does not recover, he is to be thrown overboard before we dock, or he will be put off at the next port."

Lamar glares at Riley. "Your choice, Riley. Prove you are indeed a Merc. You are in charge for now, but I'm watching you." He waves his gun to the crowd and they cower as the gun barrel points their way. "I'm watching all of you. If it were up to me, I'd throw you all overboard, every last one of you." He storms out of the room.

Victor moans as the door slams shut.

I rush over to Victor. "Victor, are you okay?"

Victor manages a small smile. "I won't be running any races, but I think I'll survive."

This is all getting way too real. We have to help him, but how? I huddle with Colt and Riley. "We have to get him some medicine and get that bullet out and stop the bleeding, or he's not going to make it."

Riley shakes his head. "What do you suggest?"

Colt grabs both of our arms. "You two go to the lab and get medicine from Gretel. I'll get the bullet out and do what I can to mend the wound and stop the bleeding. We have needle and thread here. It's not great, but it will do." He looks at me. "Tell Gretel he needs some pain medication."

Riley looks around. "While I'm gone, you're in charge Colt. Keep everyone else out until I get back. We have to hope Lamar doesn't come back while I'm gone. He's is looking for a reason to use that gun."

Colt nods. "I see that and—" He grasps Riley's arm. "Thanks for being on our side." Colt holds Riley's arm by the wrist and elbow. "Brothers forever."

Riley nods and squeezes back. "Forever."

Colt gets another cloth and puts it in Victor's mouth. "I've done this before. We've had some gunshot wounds with some of the Uncounted that tried to escape the Mercs. This is going to hurt." He grips Victor's hand. "Hurt a lot."

Victor nods. How can he be so brave? I just want to crawl into a closet or under a table and hide. But I can't. We're in too deep. It's not just our own families we have to save. We have the rest of these people, the Undesirables, to think about now. I feel a lot older than my fifteen years.

Colt takes one of Victor's lighters from his backpack and motions toward the machete. "Bring me the knife. It's crude, but it will have to do." He runs the flame over the blade and begins his cut. He stops and looks at Riley and me. "You two need to hurry and get back with that medicine if he is going to have any chance to survive. It's the infection that will kill him."

Riley and I walk out of the room together.

I'm shaking. "It all seems so real now."

"Let's just concentrate on this. Okay?" Riley points to the stairs. "We have to go up ten flights. That's where the lab is."

I take a deep breath. "Gretel will find what we need and Victor will be fine. I just know it."

We run silently until we reach the 5th floor. Riley leads me to the massive double doors labeled "LAB" and big sign that reads, "Do Not Enter."

I point to the sign. "This says not to enter."

"When did that ever stop you? Leave it to me." Riley opens the door and walks in.

Gretel is standing in a white coat dropping some sort of substance into a test tube. She sets the test tube back in its holder when she spies me. "You're not supposed to be here."

I hug her quickly. "I know. We had a—" Probably shouldn't burden her with the gory details. I stop for a minute and gulp. "—an accident on the fifteenth floor and we need some medicine."

Gretel pulls me over to the side and Riley follows us around the corner. "What kind of accident?'

"It wasn't an accident." Riley says, "A Merc shot one of the Undesirables and Colt is trying to save him, but we need some medicine to make sure that the wound doesn't get infected."

146

"We have some antibiotics over here." Gretel nervously looks around, walks over to a cabinet, and pulls out a couple of containers. "I usually can't walk around this lab so free, but the ambassador has other things on his mind."

I take a bottle that Gretel hands me and whisper, "Because of the assassination attempt?"

"Keep an eye out, Riley." Gretel finds a bag on the counter and drops some medicine bottles, gauze, and tape into it. "No, you haven't heard? It's his daughter, she's sick."

"The princess is sick?" I squeeze Gretel's hand.

Gretel nods.

"What's wrong with her?"

Gretel opens the bag again and puts another package of gauze and packing in it. "I don't know. The ambassador thinks it may be the virus."

Riley turns his gaze to Gretel and stops her from what she is doing. "The virus? The *real* virus? I thought that had been eradicated a long time ago."

Gretel hands the filled bag to me. "Yeah, he did too."

Riley's mouth drops open as the ambassador comes around the corner and spies us. "What's going on here? Why are you visiting instead of working?"

Gretel switches the bag from me to Riley who hides it discreetly in his jacket. "Oh, I'm not visiting. These two heard about the princess and want to help. They have asked if they can donate blood to be tested to see if it can be used for the antidote."

The ambassador sighs. "Of course they can. I'm sorry." He looks over at me. "You have the same eyes as—" He drifts for a moment, and then continues, "You're one of my daughter's SCs right?"

I nod and he smiles. "She talks about you all of the time. She really likes you and your brother." He stops. "I can't remember his name."

"Colt?"

Ambassador Grayson nods. "Yes, Colt. You two are her favorites. And you're Paisley, right?"

"Yes."

He looks over at Riley. "And you're a Merc?"

"Yes, sir." Riley answers, "My name's Riley."

"Paisley and Riley." Ambassador Grayson brushes Gretel's arm, absentmindedly. "Of course they can give blood. Thank you, Gretel." He walks off mumbling.

Gretel cocks her head and points to a chair. "Sorry about blindsiding you about giving blood. It won't take but a few minutes. You will be back in no time. Sit here."

I watch Ambassador Grayson walk off. "He really is worried."

Gretel ties a rubber hose around my arm. "Make a fist. Yes, he's worried. You might want to look away." She inserts a needle and draws the blood. "I just need a vial to test. Who knows you might have the magic blood." She points to the other vials of blood. "Heaven knows, we're testing everyone." She finishes up.

Afterwards, she hands me some orange juice. "Sit here for a minute." She points to Riley. "Take a seat here." Riley sits in the chair beside me. "We need to do the same thing to you."

She hands Riley his juice a few minutes later. "I have to go, but sit here for a couple of minutes and take the bag to your friend. I hope he's okay."

My sister really does seem to have found her niche. She is so comfortable in the lab. A place where her perfectionist ways can be used, not to drive me crazy, but to help others.

I hug her. "Keep us updated about the princess. I hope she recovers soon."

Riley shakes his head. "The princess is the least of our problems. If that virus is back, and we are stuck on this ship, we're all in danger. It could be an epidemic like it was before."

"Let's hope it doesn't come to that." Gretel sighs heavily.

I get out of the chair and Riley and I head for the door. We make our way back to the fifteenth floor. Upon entering, we see Colt covered in blood, sewing up a wound on Victor. Riley drops the bag.

"Any pain killers in there?" Colt bites the last pieces of thread with his teeth.

How could we have been so stupid and got so sidetracked? I tear up. "We didn't even think to ask."

Colt holds up the bottles. "Don't worry. You got some here. This is a local anesthesia rub." He looks at Victor. "It won't help much, but it's something." Victor nods and Colt rubs the salve on his wound. He looks over at the women standing around. "Get some water and clean him up as much as you can." He pulls out the gauze and tape. "Then put this on top of it. We have to give him these antibiotics every four hours and hope for the best."

Victor grabs Colt's hand. "Thanks." He mumbles through the fabric still clenched in his teeth.

"Rest, my friend." Colt walks over to the sink. "I think I might have ruined these clothes."

How could he be worried about clothes at a time like this? I stand by him. "You have others," I whisper to him, "I need to tell you something."

Colt scrubs his hands and arms, pulls off his soiled shirt, exposing his bloodied undershirt, and throws it in the trash. "I don't have another shirt. I'll have to wear this back."

One of the Undesirables pulls off his raggedy shirt. "You can have mine. I have two."

Colt shakes his head. "I don't want to take your shirt, but I'll wear it back and return you one of mine tomorrow. Thanks, Buddy."

Colt pulls off the undershirt and puts on the Undesirable's shirt. "What did you need to tell me?"

I take in a deep breath. "It's about the princess."

"What she wants us to play a game with her?" Colt furrows his eyebrow.

I shake my head solemnly. "She's sick. They think she might have the virus."

Colt draws up a breath and holds it for a moment before letting it out. "*The virus?*"

I shudder and nod. "If the virus rears its ugly head then none of this really matters, especially on this ship. In these close quarters, everyone who isn't vaccinated or doesn't have the immunity will die. We will no longer be a traveling peace mission ship. We'll be a ship of death."

Chapter 27

The next two days I try to push worry about the virus from my mind while we work on the obstacle course and train. Victor is on the mend and thankfully, Lamar has not been back.

On the third day, our group practices poison dart throwing, machete handling, hand-to-hand combat, and spear throwing. I am tutoring the young Undesirables. Since being assigned to build the obstacle course, food has been plentiful. Even though Mom has not been able to deliver the food since the Merc encounter, she passes me notes of encouragement on the trays.

Some of the messages contain niceties such as "I saw you today walking back to your room"; "Hope everything is okay"; "Thinking about you"; "I am having a good day"; "Thinking of the Ferris wheel farm"; "You have a good day." These little notes put me in a good mood despite the oppression of the situation.

Halfway through the third day, Lamar bursts into the room, bellowing through a megaphone, loud and unruly, interrupting our practice. "Everyone report to the upper deck. There is an important announcement."

"Everyone, even the Undesirables?" Riley asks.

"Don't question me." Lamar shakes his fist in the air. "Everyone."

Riley links hands with Victor and pulls him to his feet while Colt and I take each of his arms to guide him up the stairs. Others pull up Morgan in a cradle carry to take him up the stairs.

Victor hobbles and almost falls. I warn them, "Some are not in any shape to be moved."

"I agree, but no choice." Colt half-bobs towards Lamar who glares at us.

"I can drag them if you want." Lamar hisses.

"No need, we can do it." Victor hugs our shoulders. "Don't worry about me. Let's get up there and see what's going on."

The entire group travels up the stairs in single file.

"I've never been to the top level." Amanda clutches tightly to a red-aproned woman's hand. "I wonder what's up there."

"Do you think they'll throw us overboard?" An Undesirable man whispers to his group.

Another answers, "They're not going to pin a medal on us. Watch yourselves and stick together."

One of the Undesirable women excitedly exclaims, "Maybe they've decided to let us go."

Another woman walking beside the other whispers, "Maybe there's another outbreak. I'm scared."

"Stick with me." A muscular Undesirable male with missing fingers cups the two women's shoulders. "Don't get separated. Whatever happens, don't get separated. Hang onto each other's hand and keep the children safe."

On the top, I look out onto the ocean, half-expecting land to be in sight. Only clear blue water as far as the eye can see. "What do you think this is all about?"

Colt shrugs.

King Ahomana stands on a pedestal before the crowd. "As some of you know, my granddaughter has been gravely ill for many days now. Her father thinks she has the virus. I demand to know who infected her. Who is sick?"

Everyone cowers and inches away from the side railings.

"I am going to have you thrown off the ship until someone tells me something."

The Mercs flank the king. He growls, "Tell me! I demand it!" The king's face turns red and he spits his words out, "Now, or the first of you dies!"

The king spies crumpled up Morgan. "He's looks sick, throw him overboard." Mercs toss Morgan's frail body over the side. He is lost forever.

The group freezes is disbelief.

As Colt and I prop up Victor, Colt speaks, "Why do...?"

The king whips around and glares at Colt. Colt stops speaking mid-sentence. Victor's eyes grow wide and he flings his body in front of Colt. He totters in between the king and Colt steadying himself with a hand on a railing and says, "Please your majesty, calm down. I don't think you're thinking straight because of your granddaughter's sickness. If any on board were carriers of the disease, the whole vessel would be sick. I know this virus—I lived through the outbreak. Our group may not be the source. Could it have been contracted from one of the ports we visited?"

King Ahomana jerks his head to face with Victor. "Why is this man questioning your king?" The king spits in Victor's face. "Dirty Undesirable." The king yells at the Undesirable group huddled together. "He will be the first, you cowards!" The king raises his hands up above his head and yells to the Mercs standing guard, "Throw him overboard!"

151

The Mercs rip Victor from Colt and me. I yell, "No!"

Victor is no match for the three men who lift him up and cast him over the rail. Gasps and screams fill the silence. Two Undesirables lunge forward to try to get a hand on him before he goes air-born, but are unsuccessful. The side of the railing fills with onlookers weeping and wailing, staring into the abyss. Victor disappears into the blackness of the sea.

The king orders with a booming voice, "Quiet and back away or you will be next! Tell me what I want to know! Tell me now! I order it!"

Colt grabs at me and catches my arm as I charge the king. Colt locks me in place, but I scream through my tears, "He knew nothing! You didn't have to kill him!"

The king waves his hand, dismissively and shouts, "No one questions me, throw her off the ship too."

Three Mercs attempt to pick me up, but Colt keeps a tight hold. I struggle, the Mercs finally wrench me out from Colt's grip, and I fly through the air. I shut my eyes waiting on the inevitable. Crazy thoughts about the possibility of me treading in the icy water until a friendly fisherman saves me from the watery grave shoot uncontrollably through my mind. In a few moments, those flashes are replaced by visions of the Ferris wheel and my farm. I'm doomed and I know it. What was all this for?

Sailing through the air, I feel a tug and realize my ankle has been snatched by someone. I recognize Colt's touch. My body jerks as my momentum is suddenly halted and I slam into the side of the railing, dangling upside down like a rag doll. My mind fogs for a second then I hear Colt's voice, "I got her."

I hear a loud voice I recognize as an Undesirable. "Don't let her go, she'll fall."

Riley shouts, "I'll brace you. Don't let her go." I am flopping over the side eyeballing the ominous water below.

"Treason. You dare to disobey me." King Ahomana barks, "Throw all three of them over the rails." His eyes bulging, he shouts, "Drown the traitors!"

Screams and sobs engulf the area. The king yells, "Everyone quiet!" Voices are suddenly silence as if they have all been shoved underwater. Gasps are cut short like a recording that had abruptly been turned off with no warning. Fear spreads and the only sounds left are the heavy broken breathing of the Undesirables standing unmoving.

Mercs surround us as Colt jerks me back on board. I stand face to face with Lamar who pulls his pistol. "It'd be easier to shoot them."

A child moves and an adult quickly picks him up cupping her hand over the young one's mouth.

King Ahomana yells, "Shoot them then. Shoot them all."

Heads shake, cries are contained as terror sweeps the top level.

The lone gun points at me, I scream and wave my arms. Colt shoves Lamar's arm as the gun discharges. Lamar and Colt struggle to gain control of the weapon and Lamar pulls the trigger again. Bullets lodge in the planks from one side to another as Lamar discharges his pistol again and again attempting to hit his target, one of us. Fear takes over the Undesirables and they creep backwards huddling together. The other Mercs don't try to intervene, but rather jump around dodging the wayward bullets. Finally, the gun clicks empty and Colt releases Lamar's arm.

"Stop! Stop!" Gretel breaks through the crowd, shoves into Lamar's weapon dislodging it from his hand. It tumbles over the side of the vessel plopping safely into the sea. "The princess is cured!"

The Mercs and Lamar snatch Colt, Riley, my sister, and my arms behind our backs rendering us defenseless. We all struggle, but are unable to break free.

King Ahomana points to Gretel. "Let her go!" The Merc releases Gretel, she falls to the deck, and the king snaps, "What did you say about my granddaughter?"

Gretel stands up and takes a big breath. "The ambassador is on his way up. He'll tell you. Please wait."

Colt, Riley, and I are yanked to our feet by our arms and held. The other Mercs swing their guns back and forth pointing at the Undesirables. The groups clutch each other and remain silent. The next few moments pour slowly like honey through a sieve.

I whisper to Colt. "Do you think Gretel was just trying to save us or do you think the princess is cured?"

Colt whispers back. "I hope she's cured. Then there would be no reason to hurt anyone else."

Lamar marches to the gun wielding Merc pointing at Riley and shoves the gun down. "Not him. He's one of us." He glares at Riley. "You *are* one of us. Right?"

Riley agrees with a small movement of his head as if he is contemplating what to say and finally mumbles out, "Of course." The Merc motions for Riley to join the rest of the Mercs who are imprisoning us.

"Let the ambassador through." Someone yells.

Ambassador Grayson breathlessly runs up to the king. "I found the antidote. I found the cure. After all of these years, I found a cure. Not just the immunization, but a real cure. Do you know what this means?"

"My granddaughter?" King Ahomana holds up his hand. "Is she well?"

Ambassador Grayson smiles. "She is cured. The blood that I created an antidote from was given by one of your Undesirables. It was the one we needed."

"Great then drain that person's blood and make antidote. We will sell the serum to the highest bidder." King Ahomana matter-of-factly says.

The ambassador gasps, "I don't need to do that, sir. Now that I have a sampling of the blood, I can synthesize the cure. No one needs to die."

King Ahomana puts his hand to his chin. "Let it be written that King Ahomana in his great wisdom decided to let even the meek live because he is such a good king."

The ambassador bows to the king and everyone else does too. The king sashays through the crowd. "I will see my granddaughter now."

Gretel grabs me. "I was so scared. I am so glad you're all right."

My voices catches, "We lost Victor, though." I hug her back.

"I'm sorry, I tried to hurry." She squeezes my shoulder. "I wish I could have gotten here sooner, maybe the information would have saved him."

I shake my head. "It's not your fault. I don't know what the children will do without him and what the group will do without their leader. He was their force, the glue that made them strong."

I look over at the women hugging and crying as they shield the two children, Thomas and Amanda, in the folds of their dresses building a protective cocoon around them. The Undesirables will have to lean on others to lead them now. It's so sad and his death made no sense. Such a wasteful and inhumane act. I shudder as I think about the bigness of it all.

She hugs me again. "I'm so sorry."

I take a big breath and turn away from the Undesirables for a moment trying to distance myself from my inner thoughts. "The ambassador really found a cure?"

"Yes and you won't believe whose blood it was."

Lamar menacingly marches up to Colt and handcuffs his arms behind him. "You are under arrest."

"What's going on—?" I scoot in close to Colt.

"What's the charge?" Riley asks Lamar.

Lamar yells at Riley, "What's it with these two and you? Why do you care?"

Riley stutters, "The princess loves them both."

"That's true and anyway—" I chime in. "He's my brother."

Lamar jerks Colt around. "Yeah, right." He snaps handcuffs on him. "He may be your brother, but he's my prisoner now. If you have any questions, take it up with King Ahomana. This was a direct order from him."

"I know *why* they are taking him." Gretel shakes her head. "I don't understand why they are arresting him."

"What do you know about this?" I twirl around to face my sister.

"It's the blood. When you and Riley came to donate blood, I told the ambassador that one of yours had the right antibodies."

I ask, "Which one?"

"Yours." Gretel points to me.

"So why is Colt being arrested?" I shake my head.

Gretel lifts her hands palms up. "Because you said he was your brother. They think his blood may contain the antibodies too."

"They're going to find out that we're not related." I drop my head in my hands.

"Yeah, they're going to find that out and they'll know you lied." Gretel puts her hand under my chin trying to pull my head up.

"We need to get out of here." I grab my sister's hand.

Gretel squeezes my hand. "You're right. It's too dangerous for you." Gretel swallows a tear. "You and Colt need to get out of here and off this ship as soon as possible."

I sniffle for a moment, before a thought crosses my mind. "Wait a minute. Did your blood work?"

Gretel trembles and stifles a sob fest. "What do you mean?"

I look up at Gretel through teary eyes. "Aren't you in danger too? You checked your blood too, right? You're my sister, shouldn't your blood contain the antibodies?"

Gretel's face drops. "It should, but it doesn't." She turns and walks a few steps.

"Why not?" She walks farther. Why is she leaving? There's trouble here. I ask, "What about Colt?"

"I can't answer your questions now." Gretel says, "I need to go, they're taking him to the lab. Don't worry, his blood won't match so he should be back soon."

"Will they arrest me?" I tremble at the thought.

"Hope not." Gretel stops. "We all need to get off this boat." She twirls back around. "Let me check into something. I'll get back to you. Be careful, Sis."

155

Chapter 28

"Riley, can we free Colt?" I ask as Colt is led away down the stairs in handcuffs.

After Riley whispers to one of the other Mercs, he says to me, "He said that they are taking him to a lock down area in the lab."

I glance over at Riley. "It should be me."

"What are you talking about?" Riley cocks his head.

I sit down with Riley on a bench. "Remember when they checked our blood? It was my blood that they found had the right antibodies."

Riley peers over at me. "So you think they're not after you because of the princess?"

I shake my head. "Sounds crazy now that I hear it out loud. I just don't know what to do."

"Why?"

I hit Riley on the knee. "The biggest problem is that Colt is not my brother, and you know and I know they are going to find that out when they compare our blood. And—"

"What else?"

"I'm never going to get back home since my blood is so special. Once they find out that Colt can't give them what they want. They'll come after my sister, my mother, or me. We need to get off this ship. Now."

Riley pulls a paper out of his shirt pocket. "I have the itinerary. I know where we are docking next."

"Where?"

Riley slaps the paper on his hand. "Pisa, Italy. You could maybe find your way back to the farm using the underground if we could manage to smuggle you off."

I smile for a quick moment, but then my grin quickly disappears. "What happens to the rest? What happens to the Undesirables if we leave?"

Riley folds the paper back and puts it in his pocket. "Unfortunately, that is the rub. If you save yourself, the rest will suffer."

"I need to think. I'm not sure I can live with myself if I leave the rest of you." I sigh, "I can wait. Nothing is going to happen tonight."

One of the Mercs announces, "You are all free to go back to the fifteenth floor."

I pick up Victor's backpack of lighters. "What should we do with this?"

Riley points to two of the young children clinging to each other. "Give it to Amanda and Thomas."

"Why?" I ask.

"You didn't know?" Riley takes the backpack. "Their mother died before they got on this vessel and Victor was all they had left. He was their father."

"Victor is a hero. He gave his life for Colt." I tear up again. "What will happen to his children now?"

Riley drops his head in a defeated manner. "What's going to happen to all of us?"

He walks over and hands the backpack to the two children, who hug him. He murmurs, "Be proud, your dad is a hero to all of us."

A couple of the women of the Undesirable group sit with the two children as Thomas unzips the backpack. He hands Amanda an object and she hugs it, then the two of them hug each other as a couple of women stroke their hair whispering to them. "It'll be all right."

"Go back under where you belong." The Mercs order throughout the crowd.

No one moves.

Lamar grabs one of the other Mercs' guns and shoots it in the air. "Move or I swear you will go over the side and into the sea. King or no king. Go now!"

After the shot, everyone scurries. Adults grab children by the hand, lift the youngest up in their arms, and run to the stairs. After a few minutes, the stairwells are full of chatter.

One man whispers as he passes me, "They are going to kill us all. They have us out in the ocean." His grim voice continues, "They can throw us overboard any time they want to."

"What are those children going to do without a mother or father?" One of the women lowers her head and she slumps her feet as she walks in a doomed way as if it's taking every ounce of energy she has. "It's hopeless."

"That Merc wants to kill us."

"Did you see the king order them to kill Victor?"

"The king is wicked."

I make it back to my room and fall into bed, unable to hold back my emotions. I sob uncontrollably until finally falling asleep.

The next morning, I hear a rap, open the door, and am greeted by a waiter. He hands me a note, my breakfast, and a bag of cleaned laundry.

The note reads: *Princess Kamea will be at the fifteenth floor today. You are to wear your dirndl.*

I open the bag and am amazed at finding the dirndl is clean. I'm not hungry and pick at breakfast. I dress unenthusiastically and walk out of my room escorted to the fifteenth floor by a Merc I've never seen before.

"Paisley!" Princess Kamea runs and jumps into my arms.

I'm unable to show much enthusiasm, but I do miss her, worry about her, and am happy that she is going to live. My blood was able to help her. "I'm glad you're feeling better." I manage a weak smile and embrace her very tightly.

"You're squeezing me!" Princess Kamea yelps.

"Sorry." I put the princess down. "I'm just so happy to see you."

The rest of the Undesirables and the other SCs are scattered about. Princess Kamea and I walk over to them.

"Miss Paisley, what shall we do now?" Baako asks.

"I don't know." I rub Princess Kamea's hair. "Why are you asking me?"

Baako continues, "You have to decide. You're in charge now. You're the new nanny."

I fear I know what this means and I tear up. "Is Miss Brita not coming back? Did she die?"

"We don't know, they don't tell us anything. We only know that she is not here right now. They told us you are in charge." Baako sits beside the princess and me.

"Oh," I look around the room. My gaze catches the two children, Thomas and Amanda, their eyes red from crying. I glance toward the princess. "I think the princess should play with the rest of the children today. No school or lessons. Just fun for the next few days."

Princess Kamea's eyes get very big. "Really, no lessons, just fun?"

I stroke her hair again. "I think we've all earned this." I motion to Thomas and Amanda. "Why don't you play a game with these two?"

Princess Kamea smiles. "What should we play?"

"You should play hide and go seek." I explain the rules of hide and go seek. The rest of the children join the group and run around together. Princess Kamea shrieks with delight. Shrills of laughter fill the room. The happiness of children is without a doubt the best medicine of all.

"You made a good choice." An Undesirable helps me corral all of the children. "We all miss Victor, but this is not the time."

I spend the next few minutes regaling the children with the ins and outs of the game, assign the princess the 'it' position, and they begin. I take a deep breath. I feel so alone even in this room full of people. Colt is now a part of me and I miss him. I guess he really is my brother now. Not by blood, but in the way it counts.

"Time to grow up." I mumble to no one in particular. "We need a plan." I survey the room and motion for the other SCs to join me. "We need to do something soon. Today let's train. Riley told me that we are docking in Pisa, Italy. We need to have a concrete strategy that gets us all off at that harbor before the king chooses to throw any more of us overboard."

Baako grabs a bag of flour. "I agree. We need to get out of the way of those vying for control of the new world consortium before we get caught in the crossfire."

I shake my head. "We're in the middle now. If we stay here, we are going to be innocent casualties."

Baako pulls out some flour and blends the paintball mixture. "Who are we going to take with us?"

What did he mean by that? I look around. "Everyone. We leave no one behind."

"You are talking about a lot of people." Baako coughs uncomfortably.

"We can't make that choice. We have to try to take them all."

Pandi fiddles with a dart. "Yes. We must take everyone."

Princess Kamea skips up to me and grabs my hand. "Come and play with us."

I also need to do my job, so I go with the princess and call back, "Everyone needs to be thinking of a way we can pull this off and it has to be soon. We port in Pisa in two days."

That night, the SCs come into my room.

"We need a viable plan to get everyone off." I begin. "It is as simple as that. Once we are free, we simply do not come back on."

Baako suggests a few ideas. "What about if we say we need to gather food and we need lots of Undesirables to bring the buckets and bushels of food on the ship."

I like the simplicity. Simple is always better, especially with this many people, not so many moving parts. "That's not a half bad idea. Plus, I could get my mother in on it and we could pull the others from the kitchen who are willing to go."

Wei chimes in. "No, they already have workers who bring food on. We need to think of something that only we could accomplish."

"Also, I know we want others to come with us, but we need to be careful about who we tell." Pandi warns, "There are a lot who are happy with their situation. They want to stay. They might tell the king or the

Mercs to gain favor."

"Do any of you want to stay?" Everyone shakes his or her heads "no."

Good, that's taken care of. I smile. "Okay. I agree with Pandi. We need to be careful and not get ourselves in trouble by telling those who could turn us in."

Wei clasps his hands in front. "I think we should concentrate on the Undesirables and a few others who we trust." He looks at the group. "It needs to just be family, or friends we consider family. Even if they decide not to leave, they should be loyal and not turn us in. The only way that this works is for us to be smart."

Naeem shakes Wei's hand. "I agree brother. I have three extras in mind. I will tell them where they need to report, and what time."

Adanna uncrosses her arms. "So we're in agreement. We need to make sure that the group thinks we need all of these people to get off to help with whatever we decide."

"What if we tell them we need some goods and supplies to complete the obstacle course? That would make more sense." I tap my chin with my finger.

"She's right." Pandi says, "We control the obstacle course."

"It's settled." I clap my hands together. "I need a list of things we need to purchase from Pisa. Make it a lot and big and bulky so the extra help will seem right. I will put in the order since I'm in charge. "

"What about the extras?" Pandi asks.

"We will set on a place for them to meet us." I say, "We might have to disguise them as Undesirables. As long as it isn't too many, we ought to be okay."

The next day I send a note to my mother to meet me. She finds her way down to my floor under the pretense of bringing the meals. She is disguised with a bright green kerchief tied around her head and a flowery kitchen coat. "I need to be careful, I'm taking a chance."

I talk quickly and quietly. "Meet me when we dock in Pisa on the 15th floor. We have a plan to escape."

She pulls the green scarf farther down on her forehead. "Too dangerous."

"It's too dangerous to stay on the ship. Others are depending on me. I have no choice. Please come with me."

Her eyes dart from side to side. "How many?"

"Everyone. All of the Undesirables." I grasp her arm. "Please. Trust me."

She gazes into my eyes for a moment. "I know you're right. I'm scared, but if my young daughter can be this brave then I can too. I'll join you. Tell me quickly what I need to do."

I briefly explain our idea. On the 15th floor, we will have Undesirable clothes for her to change into, and then she simply walks off with the rest of our group. We hug and she leaves.

For the next step, I ask Riley, "Can you get me to the lab? We have to figure out how to get Gretel and Colt out too."

Riley walks along side of me up the stairs. "I'm going to escape with you and the rest."

"I'm not sure about that Riley." I take his hand. "You might want to stay here where you are safe. You can come back and forth. You are a Merc. You're freer than anyone I've seen, besides the royals."

"I have my reasons. Besides," Riley smiles. "I want to see that Ferris wheel again."

The thought of him coming with us causes butterflies in my stomach. I stroke his face. "Even when we break out of here, we still have to win our farm back. The Mercs are in charge of it."

Riley places his hand on my back guiding me down the stairs. "And that is where I can help."

I reach around and hug his arm. "Okay, if you really want to come. Don't get me wrong, we would love to have you. You are a great asset, but you don't have to come."

Riley crooks his arm and his hand envelopes mine. "I know. But I feel I owe it to the Undesirables. I owe it to you and Colt too, but mostly to Victor to make sure his two children get off safely. I have to make sure they survive. The only way that I can know for sure is to go myself. Plus, I would kind of miss you." Riley turns red for a minute, then points at the double doors with the sign "Lab" on it. "Here we are."

I enter and spy Gretel right away. "Where is Colt and what did you find out about the blood?"

Gretel points to a cage in the corner and there sits Colt. He jumps to his feet when he sees me. "Paisley!"

I rush over and hug him through the bars. "We have a plan. We're going to get all of the Undesirables and you and mom and Gretel out."

"Me?" Gretel drops her head. "I can't go with you. I need to stay here and help the ambassador with the cure. It's really important."

I hug her. "We are important too. You have to come with us."

Gretel shakes her head. "I can't, I have to stay and see this through. But I can help Colt get out."

Colt holds Gretel's hand. "I will try until the last minute to get you to come. I can be quite persuasive."

Gretel smiles. "I *know* you can."

Riley and I share the plan with Colt and Gretel.

I need to know about the blood and how much trouble we are in. I pull Gretel to the side. "What did you find out about the blood?"

Gretel scrunches up her face. "Nothing. The ambassador wanted me to find out if Colt was really your brother. I did the test and he found out he wasn't, which we already knew. Then he asked me a lot of questions about you."

Why does the ambassador care about me? Is he going to try to drain me of all of my blood? Scary thought. "About me?" I ask, "What kind of questions?"

"A lot about exactly where we lived?" Gretel purses her lips. "What did I remember about life before the quarantine? A lot of questions about you before your third birthday."

I furrow my brow. "Seems strange. What did you tell him?"

Gretel pushes her chin with her fingers and then takes a deep breath. "You were supposed to ask Mom, but you are not my blood sister."

Not her blood sister. What is she talking about? My eyes get big. "Not blood sisters." I wring my hands. "Was I adopted or something?"

"Mom really should be telling you." She lets out a heavy sigh and pauses for a moment before continuing. "But right after the virus outbreak, you came to live with us. Mom said you were abandoned from one of the farms and no one knew who you were but —"

How could they have kept such a secret? Didn't I have the right to know? I sniffle. "Is that where the stuff in the treasure box came from?"

A single tear runs down Gretel's cheek. "I'm sorry, Paisley. But I feel like we are real sisters in every sense." She hugs me. "You got your name from that scarf you had with you. It had the word Paisley. Mom thought that was such a nice name."

This is unbelievable! "My whole life has been a lie?"

Gretel hugs me tighter. "No, your life has been as my sister." She looks at me. "You are and you will always be my sister. Greverstand?"

It's too much. I will have to think about it later. I swallow a whimper. "Greverstand. Where did I come from?"

Gretel takes a deep breath. "I really don't know. When I told the ambassador this story, he got quiet and I haven't seen him since. I honestly am not sure what it's all about."

Riley clears his throat and gets our attention. "Talk later. Quit worrying about anything else, but getting out of here. We need to figure out a way to get Colt out. Okay?"

We need to go soon or risk being caught. "He's right. We have a plan."

We sit at a table and outline everything. Gretel agrees to think about escaping with us and says she will make sure that Colt makes it to the fifteenth floor.

Later that night, we port in Livorno, Italy, the harbor city for Pisa. The lighthouse stands regal and invitingly welcomes us. I'm glad to see the old structures seem untouched by the horrific disease that ravaged the land. Were their dead buried beneath the sea? An unnerving thought. I decide to push that kind of thinking to the back. I try to enjoy the beauty of the city that surrounds me, majestic and timeless. Will our world ever recover? Will we survive? I hope so. Everyone is to disembark the next day at 0800 in the morning.

I fitfully sleep trying to absorb all Gretel said. What did it all mean? What happened to my real family? Did they die from the virus? Why did I survive? Would I ever find out the truth?

The SCs meet at the door the next morning. The plan is that the rest of the group planning to escape is to gather on the 15th floor and make their way to the top deck. We will all congregate and go out together.

Baako sits on the bed. "Are we ready? Is the plan a go?"

My truths have to take a back seat to our escape; too many lives depend on me. "Yes, we're all meeting on the first level. We have to go out with the princess. I will need time to hand her over to her mother or to security before we disappear."

We arrive on the first level and the smiling princess is there with her mother and father, the ambassador and the queen. I am overcome with emotions. I really do love that little girl. I hug her. "I missed you last night. I am so happy to see you."

The princess giggles. "I love you, Miss Paisley. I love you more than anyone. You are my favorite dolly."

I catch a glimpse of Colt, Gretel and my mom dressed in the dirty clothes of the Undesirables. The group is all together, even Gretel who I guess reconsidered after talking to Colt. Riley is here too. It is all going exactly to plan. We walk down the gangplank. I will not be coming back to this ship, but I smile because I know that I'm going to find my freedom and freedom for the Undesirables whose future is certain death.

I lean down to the princess and whisper, "No matter what happens I will always love you. You do know that, don't you?"

The princess smiles and hugs me again. I reach the end of the gangplank and turn to the ambassador standing beside the queen. "I am going to go with my group and get some supplies. I'll be back later. Will it be okay to leave you with the princess for a little while?"

The ambassador furrows his eyebrows and his face expresses a hint of a smile. "Of course it will, my dear. It will be completely okay. I look forward to seeing you this evening. I actually have something I need to talk to you about."

That's not going to happen. I cock my head. "Okay." What could he possibly want to talk to me about? I will never know. We reach the street. It is littered with individuals crowded to the point that it is hard to maneuver. I spy Colt two steps behind me. This is going to work. I lean down one last time to hug the princess. The ambassador leans over to pick up his daughter.

"No!" Colt jumps in front of me and shoves me to the ground as I lean up to stand. A loud noise deafens me for a moment. Colt jerks backward falling down and holding his shoulder, shrieking in pain. The security unit bolts away with the princess, her mother, and the ambassador.

Blood splatters all over me. I scream. "Colt!" I cradle Colt's head in my hands. Blood covers him.

Riley appears. "What happened?"

I wail hysterically. "I don't know?"

Pandemonium ensues. Everyone is screaming and people are tumbling over each other. Fallen children scream in pain as adults try to upright them. The Mercs take over and everyone is shuttled back onto the ship including our group. I trot alongside Colt with Riley and Gretel in tow. Our trek down the stairs ends in the ambassador's lab.

The ambassador washes his hands, pulls on gloves, and motions for the group carrying Colt to place him on a table. "I can save him."

"I'll need your help Gretel. Wash up!"

"Colt?" Gretel sucks in tears.

"Now! Gretel now! Colt needs your help." The ambassador elbows her dirty clothing. "Change quickly! Clean clothes, now!" Gretel hastily complies stripping her dirty Undesirable's clothes and replacing them with pink scrubs and a clean white coat.

As Gretel changes, the ambassador gives Colt a shot which puts him to sleep.

I hold Colt's hand and chant. "You can save him, I know it. I know you can. It's not his time to die."

The operation is bloody and messy. I never knew the human body

164

held so much blood. Colt is so still that I think at one point he must be dead. I am calmed as I feel his pulse beating slowly in his wrist as I hold his hand. I see Riley crouching in the corner, bowing his head, and whispering. I think he is praying. A good idea at a time like this. The surgery takes about half an hour. A long half hour. Gretel silently dispenses medical instruments to the ambassador while he operates, removing the bullet, and stitching him up.

"Will he be okay?" Gretel pleads with her eyes to the ambassador who nods that he will survive.

Afterwards, Gretel sobs hysterically in my arms. I wrap my arms around her. "Your ambassador saved him."

The ambassador motions for us to follow him. "Gretel, I'm not going to ask you why you were dressed that way. I don't think I want to know. But your friend needs morphine. Why don't you go and get it? We need to keep him asleep as long as we can."

Gretel leaves to retrieve the painkiller and I ask, "Why did someone shoot him?"

Ambassador Grayson shakes his head. "They weren't shooting at him. They were aiming for me. It's this whole World Consortium. Everyone is taking pot shots at me."

"Why?"

The ambassador face turns ashen and his cheeks sink in his face. "That's a good question. It seems that even though everyone has been wishing for the world to get back together and have rules. They have been living without regulations so long and there are those who like it that way. They don't want to have laws now or at least they don't want someone from America, an ex-military soldier to be making those rules."

I stare at him, "*You're ex-military?*"

"I like the song 'Circle up, Circle down' that you taught Kamea." He stares at me and it makes the hairs on the back of my neck stand up.

"Thank you. That's a song my mother taught me when I was a baby."

He smiles and his eyes fill. It's weird, but I repeat. "You're ex-military?"

"Your mother taught you. That makes sense. Yes, I'm ex-military. I was stationed in Germany. I'm from Orlando."

"Orlando." I smile. "I saw a postcard from Orlando that mother kept. It says that Orlando is the place where dreams come true."

He removes his gloves and washes the blood off his arms and hands in the sink. "That used to be the case before the quarantine."

I am so happy that the ambassador saved Colt. Even though the ambassador is acting strangely, I want to let him know how impressed I

165

am. "But you cured the disease."

"I did with your blood. Want to know why your blood worked?"

"I assume it's because there are those with immunity in Bavaria." What if the only reason he saved Colt was to get my blood? All of these crazy thoughts dance through my head so I ask, "Why *did* my blood work?"

He pats my hand. "You were given a prototype as an infant of an immunization that was developed by the military when the virus was discovered about thirteen years ago."

The ambassador has lost his mind. I frown. "How is that possible?"

The ambassador takes a deep breath. "Because I gave the immunization to my family first. To my wife who was pregnant with our son. She was lost during the outbreak, but my son survived and is immune. He is thirteen and lives in Orlando. I also gave it to my daughter, as a baby. She was three-years-old when she went missing."

I shudder and look wide-eyed at the ambassador. "What are you saying?'

He stands. "The mother who taught you that song was my wife. I think you know what I am saying. You are my daughter."

"That's impossible."

He holds my hand for a second, but I quickly pull away.

"It is not only possible, but it is true. I ran the blood tests many times. I tested Gretel and even had your so-called brother brought down here when someone told me about him."

I sit unmoving. It is a lot to digest.

He talks fast now. "I know you have a lot of questions, but I don't have time to answer them all. I will do whatever it takes to insure your survival, but you must not tell anyone who you are. The only reason that your brother is still alive is that I have him at boarding school and he was able to appease the royals about their succession. After my wife, the queen, next in line for the throne is Princess Kamea unless there is an older child who can claim the throne. My son had to relinquish any claim on the royal title to save his life before we were married. The king wanted him dead, but I told him I would not marry his daughter if my son were executed. I don't have that threat to hold over him anymore. He has Kamea, he has his heir. You won't be able to do relinquish the throne because I am considered a royal now. It could possibly cause a war. If anyone finds out, you will be in grave danger."

Now I have a king trying to kill me. Great. "But I'm not their blood." I look at him.

"It doesn't matter." He shakes his head. "I'm royalty. You are my daughter and my oldest child. I'm not sure I can protect you if this comes out. I always worry that I'm not going to be able to protect your brother in Orlando, but I will do my best to protect you both. You are all I have left of your mother."

A warm tingling sensation travels through me and I smile. "A brother. I have so many questions. My real name. What's my mother like? What's my brother like? I have so much family now, blood and otherwise."

My father's face lights up. "I'll try to answer all of your questions. Take a pause and digest everything you've been told. I don't want to overload you with information. We have time."

Do we have time? I am processing through what I've just been told as my smile disappears and I have to ask, "You think it's the king who is trying to kill you, right?"

The ambassador affirms with a head bow and a faraway look in his eyes.

"Why don't we all escape?" I ask, "We can go back to our Ferris wheel farm."

He smiles. "I remember that farm, it was close to our base."

I grab his head in my hands. "Come with us and we'll all live on that farm."

He shakes his head. "I can't."

"Why?"

"I can't leave Princess Kamea and my wife. She's pregnant again." He drops his head.

"You're my father too." I jump up. "And the king is trying to kill you."

"You don't understand responsibility and commitment. I have to stay, but as your father, I know the only way for you to survive is to escape. I can't think of any other way. The longer you stay, the more in danger you are in."

I don't know why, but I trust him. "We had a plan—until your attempted assassination thwarted that plot. Now we'll have to wait until the next port."

"I love you, daughter. I always have and I always will."

Those words cause my heart to race and butterflies once again invade my stomach. A father. Another question creeps into my mind, am I an American?

My thoughts are interrupted by his words. He says, "Let me know and I'll help you. I promise. When you escape, make it back to the farm, and I'll find you. I really have to try to organize a democratic world consortium. If I don't the Mercs or, even worse the king will be in charge.

167

It is more important than you and me. It could save our world. Do you understand?"

"Yes." I weep in his arms. "I am more like you than I thought."

Just then, Lamar breaks into the lab. "We have orders to take the prisoners. It was discovered that there was a planned escape from the ship at this dock. We will be executing all of the involved parties."

The ambassador stands up. "Who are the accused?"

Lamar reads from a list. All of the "Sponsored Companions," your lab assistant, Gretel, a Mrs. Mueller from the kitchen, and all of the Undesirables."

I slump to the floor. Lamar had all of the names of those who were planning to escape except Riley. Who turned us in? Who is the traitor? Was it Riley?

The ambassador holds his hand up. "There must be some kind of mistake."

Lamar wrenches my hand behind my back and I feel the cold metal of the handcuffs locking around my wrists. Gretel and Colt are handcuffed and the three of us are marched from the lab to the ship's deck.

On deck, I huddle in a group with the others who are sentenced to die. I scan the crowd for the turncoat. It's not Riley. I see who it is, it's Baako. The traitor. The betrayer. The main instigator. He has signed all of our death warrants. He has killed us all as if he pulled the trigger. Why did Baako choose to save Riley? It's a code. I think I understand. There Baako sits, smugly talking to the Mercs. He wears the Merc mark. He is a Merc now.

How could he? Fury bubbles inside me. I wish I could spit in his face or worse. Two Mercs grab me and I thrash about trying to break free to no avail. Finally succumbing to their brute strength, I am dragged out while my newfound father looks on horrified.

I am stunned to see my mother who is identified as the woman from the kitchen. I walk by her mouthing, *I'm sorry.* If only I hadn't gotten her involved. My heart hurts.

She whispers to me. "Think of the Ferris wheel farm. We will always be on the Ferris wheel farm. I love you, Paisley and Gretel, my daughters, my loves."

All hope is lost. Everyone I care about is going to be executed and it's my fault. Tears blur my vision as I see Gretel being gagged. One by one, the Mercs rip a dirty sheet in strips and muzzle each of my co-conspirators. With each one, I sob uncontrollably. I see the young ones, Thomas and Amanda, and almost lose it.

Lamar forces me to watch by holding my face up. "You killed them all with your arrogance. Who do you think you are?"

Riley is over to the side. He is not bound or gagged, something for which I am grateful. His look is one of helplessness. At least his cover is not blown. Small concession, since my whole family is going to be wiped out. His lucky charm, the four-leaf clover isn't helping me now. I would try to give it back to him, but he doesn't seem to need it now, he's safe.

I kick and wrench trying to break free without success. I am hauled in forcibly to stand before the king with Colt to one side and the rest of the SCs sans Baako and Adanna, with all of the Undesirables standing behind us.

The king paces back and forth and yells, "You have been charged with treason against the crown of the King Ahomana and are hereby sentenced to death. I do not want to kill you here, as your rotting carcasses will mar our beautiful ship. I want all of Europe to witness my power and what happens if they go against their king. We will travel back to Hamburg and you will be publically executed there." His voice booms to the crowd. "Let this be a lesson! You will not go against your king or you will be put to death!"

Queen Nalani holds her hand up. "Not the SCs. The princess loves them."

The king puts his arm around his daughter. "We will get her more. She will love them too. I have no choice. My granddaughter will have to understand."

Queen Nalani whispers to him. He looks at her and touches her belly. How could the king not realize how Colt helped to save not only the princess, but also the queen and her unborn child? Could the king be so heartless?

I can tell him, I have nothing to lose. I have to try. I'm the reason all of this happened. I mumble through my gag. The king looks at me. "Remove her gag. I will hear what she has to say."

My head is jerked viciously as a Merc rips my gag off. I face the king as I speak. "I want you to know that if it was not for Colt you would not have your granddaughter or daughter. His heroic act saved their lives. He deserves to live. As for the rest of this, I take full responsibility for the treason and the conspiracy. I was in charge, you can ask anyone. Please let the others live. You don't have to keep them on the ship, but let them go at Hamburg. Let them make their own way. I beg of you, merciful king." I bow my head. "Please, just execute me. Let the others go."

The rest of the group tries to speak. Since they are gagged, they are not heard.

The king looks at his daughter. His face softens. "I will take all of this

169

into consideration. You are very brave. You are right. The boy saved their lives. He took the bullet." He points to a Merc. "Take the boy's gag off and let him speak."

A Merc yanks Colt's dirty muzzle from his mouth and it drops around his neck allowing Colt to talk. He looks over at me. "Let her live too. The rest did not have anything to do with any of it. I take full responsibly for all of it."

The king waves his hands to the rest of the group. "We have two people who promise to take responsibility for all of the wrong doing and have pledged their lives to save yours. I am the king. I only need to make an example of my power. I do not need you all for that. I will take these two lives to pay for all wrongdoings. The rest of the dolls will stay for my granddaughter and the Undesirables will be put out at Hamburg to spread the word about what happens when people dare to cross the king. You will make your own way. No deaths of any of the Undesirables."

Cheers erupt among the Undesirable group.

Colt and I smile at each other. Amanda, Thomas, and the Undesirables are freed from their gags. Tears well up in my eyes. I'm afraid, but it'll be worth it.

King Ahomana nods. "As you travel off this ship, let others know how powerful I am. I will execute only these two." He waves his scepter in our direction.

Groans follow his announcement. A couple of the male Undesirables lunge forward and grab the arms of one of the Mercs yelling, "Let everyone go. No deaths." Mercs trounce on the two Undesirables and free their comrade.

The king motions to the Mercs to hold the others back. "If anyone comes forth to try to save them, then I will have no choice but to execute all of you." He grabs Thomas and Amanda. "Even the children. Do you want that?"

Quiet overtakes the group. They step back cowering. Women hold on to their children. The king lets go of the two children who are quickly hidden behind the skirts of the women. The king is truly evil.

"This is just." King Ahomana continues, "I am a just king. These two will pay with their lives. These two will be carried off when we dock at Hamburg and they will be publically executed per my orders. The rest of you will be pardoned. You will be thrown off the ship at our next port and will get no more support from the royal family or any crew member of this ship." He looks to the group. "Do you understand?"

Heads nod.

The king motions to the Mercs. "Take the prisoners away."

"I was planning on saving everyone." I look over at Colt. I hate that he is here, but happy in a selfish way that I don't have to do this on my own. What kind of a monster does that make me?

Colt smiles weakly. "You thought you could get rid of me that easily." He would make a joke at a time like this. That is so Colt.

Why did he do it? He really wanted to be the hero, I guess. Maybe he did it for me. Maybe for Gretel? I don't know and I would probably never know.

"You realize that we are going to die." I half-heartedly smile back.

Colt nods. "Yeah, but we are dying for a good reason." He is a hero. I always knew he had that in him.

"The best reason of all." A warm feeling glows within me.

Our bindings are removed and we are put into the same cell to sit, waiting on the inevitable. A quiet calm encompasses me. Not sure why.

After two hours, our cell door opens and Gretel enters. "Paisley I don't know what to say. I don't want you to die."

I grab my sister's hand. "This is just payback for all of those times that you saved me. I owe you. I need you to take care of Mom. Get off this ship as soon as you can and find the underground. Tell them everything. They should let you in, and then you can survive until someone figures all this out. Greverstand?"

Gretel nods and tumbles to her knees crying. "I can't believe you're still worried about me, I'm supposed to be the big sister and look out for you."

I smile at her. "If I didn't worry about you, then what was all of this for? I did it for you, for Mom, for Thomas, and for Amanda. For all for you. There was no reason for all for us to die."

Colt hugs Gretel. "I still remember your mom's classes. Tell her to make sure she teaches the new kids English. Make sure she does that."

My mom enters the cell and says, "Tell me yourself."

I cry and hug Mom. "Mom, the treasure box is in my room. Will you please make sure to get it? I brought a scarf for Gretel from home, makes sure she gets that too." I whisper, "I know you took me in after the virus. Thank you. I am sure that it would have been easier not to hide me all of those years when I wasn't even yours. I love you Mom. You will always be my mom; it doesn't matter if you didn't birth me."

"How did you figure that out?" My mother starts crying hysterically. "Paisley, I wanted to tell you. I had always planned to. I was waiting until you were older."

"You got my name from the scarf didn't you? What about the

jewelry? Where did that come from?"

My mother clasps my hands in hers. "The scarf and jewelry were in your pocket along with the note. Maybe whoever left you hoped that someone would find you and accept it as payment for your care."

"But you didn't cash it in?"

"No," my mother says, "I didn't need payment to take care of such a beautiful child. You have made my life complete. I tried to take your place, but they wouldn't let me. I have to report to the kitchen. The ambassador made sure of that and that Gretel would stay with him. I have lived most of my life, but you my daughter had your whole life in front of you. I wish I could take your place."

"I know you want to, but you can't. You would risk all of those lives." My eyes brim with tears.

My mother's voice cracks as she speaks, "I know. I am so proud that you are my daughter. You are truly a treasure."

"You raised me right. I love you, Mom."

"I love you too, Paisley."

I turn to Gretel. "I love you too, sister."

We three hug each other and sob for another few minutes, before the Mercs come and separate us.

Colt pulls Gretel to the side. "Before I die, can I ask you for a favor?"

Gretel wipes her eyes. "Anything."

"A kiss."

Gretel kisses Colt, holding him tight.

As their lips part, he says, "I've loved you since we were kids." Colt pulls her back one more time to kiss her lips and then her forehead. "Have a good long life. Don't forget me. You're the real reason I came."

"I know." Gretel buries her face in his chest. "I love you, too."

It is the most romantic thing I have ever witnessed. I wish that Colt could survive. I am not sure that Gretel will ever find anyone who will love her that much. It makes me sad to think of that. But the two of us, Colt and I, are giving up our lives for those we love. What more noble cause can there be?

Finally, the Mercs pull Gretel away from Colt and Mom walks out with her.

"See you on the other side." I shout to them as they leave. "I love you both." I cry and Colt holds me as tears roll down his cheeks.

Colt says, "It was the right thing to do."

He's right, but it still is hard to do. "You scared?"

"Yes." Colt nods. "You?"

"Of course." I hug him hard. "It'll be over soon."

172

Chapter 29

Things move quickly the next day. We are once again gagged with filthy strips of sheets that taste like grease and sweat. Our hands are cuffed behind our backs. I lose sight of Colt after the Mercs blindfold me and drag me up the stairs. I'm on the deck, I smell the ocean and hear the waves break against the ship. Blindfolded, I am unaware of exactly where I am. I strain to hear sounds that will clue me in, but it is eerily quiet. No crowds gathered? Strange. I assume I'll be hanged or shot. Possibly the king has changed his mind about throwing me overboard. Maybe I will drown quickly before the sharks have a chance to rip me apart. What a morbid thought, but morbid thoughts are all I have left.

I'm lifted off the ground and shoved onto a wood surface. A splinter lodges in my elbow. Someone jerks me up into a seated position, unlocks my handcuffs, and then locks them back in front of me. I would try to make a break for it, but what would that accomplish? Being in this situation is the only thing keeping many others alive. I sigh and sink into acceptance of my future. Where are the Mercs taking us? Is Colt with me? I wish I could see him. I am angry they are taking such a long time to murder me. It must be part of the torture.

My fury transforms into curiosity. My initial fear morphs into intrigue as time passes. I'm shuffled, pulled, pushed, and thrown down for so many hours now that I can't keep up with the amount of time that has elapsed. I didn't get a chance to see the Undesirables released. That would have been a nice vision to hold in my mind as I die. I try to conjure up the image of the Undesirables, and Thomas and Amanda smiling and waving, as they are finally set free. I try to imagine the future. My mind wanders, dreaming that my mother and Gretel escape too. Maybe they will erect a statue in my memory. I smile. How can I think such silly thoughts now? Will Riley miss me? I feel the corded four-leaf clover bullet close to my heart. I wish I had given it back to him. He needs the luck now. What does a dead person need with luck?

I feel an arm brush mine. "Colt?" I whisper with no idea of who is listening.

He rubs my arm. The clanging of cuffed wrists lets me know he is a prisoner too. "I'm here. I hear horses."

"I hear them too. Kind of soothing." I turn my head toward his voice. "Are we going to die soon?"

"Who knows? We're traveling by a horse drawn cart now going somewhere." He runs his hand down my arm searching for my hands clamped in front of me and takes one in his. "Are you blindfolded?"

"Yes," I reply. "Why are they taking us so far if they just want to kill us?"

He sighs uncomfortably. "Probably taking us to the biggest crowd to make their case. You know how they lie about everything. We know better, don't we?"

My voice catches. "Be careful. We don't know who is listening."

"I don't think it matters much now." He squeezes my hand. "You afraid?"

"Surprisingly, not." I sigh. "I know I should be, but it's been a long journey. I guess in some ways it'll be a relief for it to be over." I laugh nervously. "We did have a good run though didn't we?"

He clasps both hands around mine. "We did at that. Hope it's not too painful."

"That would be nice—a quick death." I move as close as I can to him and rest my head on his shoulder. Instantly, I feel better. "I'm sorry you have to die too, but I'm glad you're here."

He squeezes my hand. "Me too."

We whisper, reliving our escapades and talk about the others imagining their future. Colt is apprehensive and cheerless when he talks of Gretel. It makes me sad to hear him, but he tells me he is ultimately happy that he is one of the reasons why she will live. I know my end is near as some of the vegetation I smell reminds me of home. The sounds through the branches are reminiscent of home too. I guess when death is near your senses take you to a place that makes you happy. A half a day of bumping up and down on rocky and uneven terrain is followed by a rest. As we travel farther, the smells and sounds become so much more familiar. Strange, how my mind is playing tricks on me. It's hard to tell the difference between night and day, but we travel a long way. Finally, we come to a complete halt.

Pulled apart, I am thrown off the wagon onto the ground. I await my end.

Someone jerks me to my feet and removes my blindfold. I squint as the brightness blinds me for a moment. As my eyes adjust, I see we are knee deep in a meadow with vegetation growing all around us. I recognize this meadow. But how could I? No crowds, just Colt and me and two Mercs. One stands in front of us holding a paper. The other Merc unlocks our restraints and stands behind us. We hug each other.

"See you on the other side." I fight back tears.

174

Colt nods and lifts his face, jutting out his chin.

The uniformed man in front of us, unrolls a paper, and reads from it. "Colt and Paisley Germany."

We look at each other for a minute. Our homeland still follows us as our last name. Even though, certain death is ahead that makes me smile.

The reader continues, "For acts of treason upon The Consortium of the World you are hereby sentenced to death by a firing squad."

My flesh gooses and my stomach churns. This is it. I suck in a big breath, waiting for the inevitable. I know the end is near, the air smells like home. Leaves rustling soothe my ears with familiarity. Panic and calm battle inside of me.

Where are the shots? They are drawing this execution out. Why?

The man keeps reading, "Because of service to Ambassador Grayson and his family in protecting their safety, your sentence is commuted to life imprisonment. You are hereby ordered to stay on this land. Guards will check periodically, and you are to stay here and never leave."

My mouth drops open.

The Merc rolls up the paper. "We will be going now." He joins the other Merc and they quickly load in their buggy and ride off leaving us standing there.

Colt grabs me and hugs me tight twirling me around. He lets go without warning sending me flying through the air where I land hard on the ground.

I stand and rub my derriere. "Why'd you do that?"

Colt throws his arms around me. "Don't you realize where we are?"

I shake my head.

He takes off running. "Follow me!"

I trot after him. Hoof steps sound behind me and I turn to see a horse. It's a familiar and welcomed sight. "Hershey, where have you been?" I nuzzle the horse and then look beyond the beast to a magnificent metal giant. "We're home, Colt."

In front of me are my farm and the Ferris wheel, a little weathered, but for the most part just as I left them. I fall down and kiss the ground. "We're home, I'm so glad we're home."

Colt nods. "It's over Paisley. We can relax now."

Right at that moment, I can't help myself. I sob uncontrollably. We're alive!

That night, I sleep in my own bed with Colt on the blanketed floor beside me. I know we need to figure a way to get Gretel and Mom off the ship, but tonight, I enjoy my restful slumber.

The next day, we take stock of our supplies, raiding our farm's underground stash. We wearily walk the grounds making it back to the concrete slab that holds the Ferris wheel as dusk sets in.

"We should go inside before it gets too dark. We have enough reserve food to live quite comfortably here for months." Colt matter-of-factly states as he pulls the Ferris wheel lever back to the "on" position.

The Ferris wheel groans and turns slowly. "It works!" I shout, "How is that possible?"

"The solar panel must be hooked up to it." Colt flips the lever on and off. The metal giant creakily starts and stops. "I'm not sure for how long."

"I'm taking a ride." I jump into the chair and Colt follows, clanging the door shut. We are on our third revolution when I notice movement in the woods. "Do you think the Mercs are checking on us this soon?"

"Shouldn't take the chance." Colt grips the chair. "I'll unlock and we'll jump out when it rounds the bottom. I'll turn it off. No use letting them know it works." We slide out of the carrier. Colt pushes the lever and the metal giant screeches to a halt.

"Is that—?" I can't believe my eyes. How could this be? Colt and I grab each other in tears. We watch as the Undesirables from the ship walk, limp, and run out of the woods. Each greets us with a handshake, hug, or a smile. I am overcome with emotion especially when I recognize two familiar faces—Victor's children, Thomas and Amanda.

Amanda walks over and lays a book bag gently at my feet, almost as if it was an offering. "It was Dad's."

I pick it up and open the bag to discover the butane lighters—all shapes and sizes with the different pictures and logos. "Your Father's history."

Amanda tears up. "He shouldn't have been killed."

"You're right." I lean down and hug her. "Leave the bag here for right now. It'll be safe. We'll find a special place for it later." I look up at one of the men in the group. "How did you find us?"

"We tracked your buggy." He answers, "Took us a while since we were on foot. We had no place else to go." He drops his head. "We have no papers. I was afraid we would be caught, so I led our group here. Remember, we are Undesirables."

"Not anymore." I interject, "You—all of you—are very desirable now."

Colt grabs the man's elbow and shakes his arm. "You made the right choice."

It takes a while for us to sort out all of the Desirables and decide where they will bunk. Eventually, we use the barn, the house, and blankets draped as tents set up under the stars.

That night as I lay in my own bed, I toss and turn. Everything worked out, but somehow it's not enough.

I get out of bed and walk outside. Colt is standing by the Ferris wheel. When he sees me, he says, "Do you want to ride again?"

"We have to save the rest of them. We've seen too much." I take a deep breath. "I really want to be free, Colt. I want us *all* to be free *all* the time."

Colt smiles. "I can see a plan forming in that brain of yours. What do you have in mind?"

"We said we needed to change things. We can't stay here on this farm knowing what we know. We have to make a stand. We need to do something. Something grand." I spy Victor's bag on the ground, dump it out, and the lighters scatter. I pick one of them up. "Start the Ferris wheel."

Colt obeys. The Ferris wheel creaks at first and then groans to a start. It's a beautiful sight, the magnificent metal beast coming to life.

I take the lighter and sit on the bottom chair as it passes. The Ferris wheel turns slowly. I ignite the lighter and the flame goes around with me. "We need to light the way." I yell to him as I circle. "Circle up, circle down," I sing, quietly at first and then louder.

Colt puts the Ferris wheel on automatic at its slowest pace, grabs another lighter, and joins me in my chair. We are loud and others notice and come out. At first, they watch without joining.

Eventually, one of the Desirables picks up a lighter and slides into the next car with the flamed lighter singing. In a few minutes, another joins.

One by one the chairs fill up until the entire Ferris wheel is lit up like a Christmas tree.

I quit singing and start to chant. "Freedom for all." I pull the cord holding the bullet four-leaf clover and twirl it in my other hand. This lucky charm has to keep working.

The others join in. As we get louder, my eyes glisten, and I choke up.

"The fight to change the world has just begun," Colt says, looking over at me. "This is the beginning of our army."

Our orders to stay or be killed shoot through my mind, but I smile. "We need to take back our world. We can't let it stay the way it is."

"Agreed." Colt motions to the field. "We have right on our side."

I was willing to die before and I am willing to die now. As I round the top, Ferris wheel ablaze, I know.

Sometimes it's just the right thing to do.

Book 2
Take the Helm
Chapter 1

Slavery. Human trafficking. It's strong and alive here in my world. A world controlled by royals who only care about power and who think it's acceptable to own and to buy and sell other human beings. If those were the only things wrong with this world, we might stand a chance, but there is so much more.

Perched at the top of the abandoned Ferris wheel, I conduct my daily exercise. Twelve children ranging in age from six to thirteen scale the monster, swinging from one end to the other. Each child brandishes a stick, our substitute for weapons. I count off the steps, one two, three...Only a few missed beats, no hesitation. We're improving. An army of children. How sad!

We've practiced this next drill a zillion times, but this time Mike, the oldest, slips and bullets from the high rusty beam of the Ferris wheel. A throaty scream slashes through the air. I'm not sure who owns the piercing shriek, but a thud ends it.

A pang of responsibility shoots through my heart, as I fight my urge to go to Mike. I have to follow the contingency plan, which means waiting for Colt. Today, it's Colt's job to be the medic. I can't help Mike. I have to make sure the other eleven on the metal giant get down safely. Been lucky about injuries, a miracle since we live on an isolated farm with twenty or so people who are training for a war that may or may not happen.

Out of the corner of my eye, I see Colt bolt to the crumpled boy. "Paisley, I got him," Colt yells. "Bring the rest down."

Scaling the prongs of the Ferris wheel is like walking for me now. I've done it so many times. I bark orders to my subordinates and they plunge downward in a manner that replicates a fly lighting for a second then fluttering to the next point. A slip of a hand and a few narrow escapes make the descent anything but ordinary. They are improving, but not perfect yet. After all, they're only children.

They complete their task with no mishaps. As the last trainee safely hits the ground, the edges of my mouth curve and an unintentional proud smile grazes my face before I force its disappearance. I stiffen and say,

"That will be all for today. Go get some food and I'll see you in the morning."

My orders are not immediately followed. They mill around and a couple march over towards Colt.

"What about Mike?" Amanda brushes past me to the crumpled boy in front of her. She reaches for his hand. "Are you okay?" She drops to her knees. "Is it your leg?"

Colt presses on parts of Mike's leg. When he reaches the calf area, Mike grimaces in pain. "Ouch! Might be broken," Mike groans out an answer to Amanda, "but don't worry I'll be fine." He turns his head toward the others. "Go ahead with them. They'll patch me up and I'll be back at the camp in a few minutes."

Amanda reluctantly joins the others. Colt retrieves a piece of wood and splints Mike's leg. Colt and I have to be the soldier, medic, parent, teacher, trainer, or whatever the situation calls for. We know we have to start teaching the recruits to fend for themselves. Colt and I won't be around forever.

Our small group cares about one another too much. That will probably be our downfall. We can't stay in our protected corner of the world forever. We have to join the fight. It's our mission. What a joke! Don't even know exactly what that is. Our world? An epic mess up. Colt and I are actually under house arrest, or I guess farm arrest. We're not supposed to leave for any reason.

"Don't worry." Colt wraps his arm around my shoulder. "I patched him up. He'll be ready in a week to continue training. At least it wasn't broken."

A pang shoots through me. I slap his arm away. "How do you know that? You're not a doctor." It's not like me to be so curt. I know I'm missing Gretel, my sister. She was the doctor or as close to being a doctor as she could be with no formal schooling. She would know exactly what to do. One of the big reasons I must escape this farm is to find her.

When we arrived a month ago, we were a group of thirty-one. Sixteen of us range in age from eight to seventeen. The rest are older and frail, encumbered by disabilities and injuries. We've lost nine of our oldsters since then, and are in danger of losing two more. Now our group numbers only twenty-two. The losses have been disheartening. At first, Colt and I only trained with the older children. Now, no choice. We must prepare those of us who are healthy and strong even if they are only eight years old.

"We can't fight or teach them to fight if we don't show a united front." Colt plants his feet directly in my path and forces me to stop. "If we expect to win this war and change the world then you and I need to work together. Stop whining."

I shove him. "What are you talking about? How can we leave the children alone? We can't win. They can't even scale a Ferris wheel that's not moving without misses. It's hopeless."

"They're not alone." He motions toward the barn.

I nod. "I know the adults are there, but they need more help than the children. Our plan seemed so solid before, but now I'm not so sure."

"Paisley, it's not hopeless. Something is going to happen, and when it does you'll see why all this training was the right thing."

Does he really believe what he is saying? Maybe he'll understand sarcasm. I keep walking. "Sure, it's the right thing. We'll leave the children. They'll get stronger when we go." I wave my hands around, "Who knows? Maybe Mom and Gretel will escape. The Consortium of the World will decide democracy is the best path and put the ambassador in charge." I step in front of him and stop. "Who is dreaming now? It sure isn't me, Colt. Wake up!" I turn around and face him with my hands thrust firmly upon my hips. "I know we planned to leave soon, but how can we?"

I turn on my heel and Colt follows behind mumbling, "It'll work out, have faith."

I struggle to hold back the tears as I throw open the front door of the two-room shack that I have called home for as long as I can remember. Home? Home is where your family lives. This is not home now. This empty shell houses Colt, twenty misfits, and me. People who were once deemed unfit to live to the point that they were labeled Undesirables because of their disabilities, flaws, or lack of loved ones with the means to take care of them. This world—messed up.

"We should have information from the outside soon." Colt follows me and stands in the doorway. "I sent Thomas on a mission to locate a newspaper so we can find out what's been going on, and maybe the location of the ship your family is on. I hope he makes it back soon." He sighs and looks up at the ceiling. "Wouldn't it be great if he brought us good news?"

"The eternal optimist." I couldn't help but love Colt. He had been like a brother to me during one of the worst times of my life. We almost died together and now we work together in charge of our misfit army.

He smiles. "Always." He squints. "Someone's coming from the woods."

"He's back. Thomas is back!" Mike yells from the yard.

Colt and I rush through the door and see Thomas falling to his knees. His clothes are ripped and he is covered in mud. He shakes as he pulls out

180

a wadded-up paper from his pocket.

Colt lifts the papers carefully from Thomas' clutched hand. I grab a jug of water. Thomas jerks it from my hand and greedily chugs it. The commotion brings the rest of our drill group in and they crowd around us.

Colt and I sit on the ground beside Thomas. News from the outside world. But is it news that we want?

Colt asks, "Is it good news or bad news?"

Thomas jerks the jug down, water dripping from his chin. "Not good, not good at all."

Chapter 2

"What kind of bad news?" I ask as Thomas drinks again. My mind wanders to every kind of horrible news I can imagine. What if the ship sank and my family drowned? What if the ambassador was killed? Goose bumps arise as I think of the worst of all, what if the virus that wiped out millions and forced a twelve-year quarantine has returned?

Thomas releases the jug. "He's losing. The ambassador is losing." He pokes at the print that Colt is holding.

"Let me see." I pull part of an article from Colt's hand. The two of us silently read for the next few minutes as the rest of the group welcomes Thomas back.

Thomas is right. It's not good news, but do we really need to tell everyone? We've had so many setbacks and deaths, I worry that this might deflate our group. It's sad to me that Thomas is only nine and is already privy to the unfairness of this world. That I can't change. But we can control this bad news. I lean over to share my thoughts and hesitations with Colt.

Amanda, not one to stay in the background long, scoots in beside me. "What's it say?"

"Nothing interesting." I shuffle the article to the side. "It's time for you to rest now. We have an early practice tomorrow. You need your sleep."

Amanda stands up and stomps her foot, knocking dirt all over me. "You're not telling us! You're keeping it from us. We demand to know!"

I stand up and hug her. "Of course, you should all know. Colt and I haven't had a chance to read everything. We might tell you something that's not true. Please, give us time to look through everything. We won't keep anything from you." I hold Amanda's chin in my hand and gaze into her eyes. "I promise." I have become such a good liar that I scare myself sometimes. But, it works.

The children reluctantly make their way to their assigned sleeping quarters, makeshift tents of sheets. In a few more minutes, it's quiet once again.

"Mike needs to stay in the house until his leg heals, and—" Colt shoots a knowing glance my way and then back to Thomas before continuing. "Thomas, move to the house until you gain your strength back. Can you both make it on your own?"

Mike hops on one leg toward the door and stops to study Thomas's face. He then looks at Colt and me. "You can fool them, but I know there's something in that paper that you don't want the rest to know. Tell me. I'm almost grown. I'm thirteen." Mike stands, jutting his chin out defiantly and crossing his arms.

Thomas nods. "He's right. He's old enough."

This secret, we can't keep. At least not from these two. Thomas knows, and he will tell Mike. I walk toward the Ferris wheel. I dread this conversation. I know that it's time for Colt and me to go. We should tell them. We should tell every one of them tonight, the oldsters too. My shoulders droop as I announce, "I'll gather the rest."

Hiking through my farm to the barn housing the oldsters is surreal. No more harvesting our farm for the Mercs, hiding from them, or worrying about being an Uncounted. My worries now are of the global kind. The battle for control is immense and in my mind unwinnable. Why are we trying? Simple, we must.

"Heather?" I spy one of the women fretting about outside the barn, portioning our dinner for the night. "Help me gather the rest. We need to talk." I help her divvy up stalks of corn. "Are Joe and Arlas doing any better?"

Heather shakes her head. Entering the barn is like visiting a hospital. Beds contain what's left of the former Undesirables. Bandages cover most of their limbs and the stench of disinfectant and sickness permeates the hay that surrounds them. It would be easier to have the meeting here, but Colt and I had decided long ago to keep the children out of the barn. Too much sadness, too much sickness. It just didn't feel right.

I move a blanket to cover the oldest man, Joe. "We need to have a meeting in the house. We have news that we want to share."

Only four decide to attempt the trek across from the barn to the house. Three women and one man. How can we possibly make a difference with so few? I push the negative thought from my mind. We move at a turtle's pace from the dilapidated barn, dodging the rusted turbines and cars. All reminders of the decades before the virus, before the royals, before the Consortium of the World, before the struggle for democracy, before human trafficking was the norm.

Inside the house, we take our places around the room on the threadbare sofa, the rundown chairs, and decaying stools.

"What's the news?" The man, Jack, asks.

I feel my shoulders drop.

Jack takes in a deep breath. "That bad, huh?"

I don't answer, but spread the articles on the chipped coffee table

183

that sits on blocks. Its legs rotted off long ago. "There is some good news; others are attempting to do what we are doing so we're not alone."

Jack asks, "How would we know that? I thought the media was controlled by the royals."

I nod. "Unfortunately you are right, it still is. But newspapers report problems. We think this is the handwork of the resistance. There are articles about them throughout the newspaper. They destroy meeting places."

"How do they destroy them?" asks Gina, a pretty older woman with a mangled arm.

"Some use explosives," Colt answers, "but mostly by axing out support beams and causing the structures to collapse. It's easy to do with most buildings being in such disrepair."

Gina breathes out. "Good, I didn't want our children to go into places where bombs were set. I know it's dangerous work, but –" She stops for a moment. "I'm just glad we're not planning on going into bomb-riddled places."

I add, "The children aren't going at all." I stop for a minute. I might have said too much. I explain, "I mean they still have to train."

Jack lets out another exasperated sigh. "Let them finish. I want to hear the news."

I report. "There are many factions of unrest, but we are all spread out. This article is about the ambassador's trip. He has completed his voyage around Europe on the "Queen Nalani" ship and—" My voice cracks, "—is planning on traveling on the same ship to America in two weeks."

Jane, a rotund woman, scoots over to me and slips her arm around my shoulder. "Aren't your mom and sister on that ship?"

"Yes."

"That's why we called you together," Colt interrupts. "We need to figure out what to do next."

"We need to join with the other groups." Mike sits up, rubbing his splinted leg. "The only way that we defeat them is to have a bigger army, one that can make a difference."

A nine-year-old boy, Beau, slips out from his hiding place in a closet. "I agree with Mike. We're too few, like fleas on a lion. We need to join the others."

Mike smiles. "And be like a club knocking that lion's head off."

Beau laughs and shoves his fist in the air. "Yes!"

How can these children speak with such maturity? They have grown up too fast. Here is a nine-year old talking with wisdom far beyond his years. Children. Children must be included in any plan. Why? Because they have to soldier the army. We have to be realistic. We can't leave them out.

I'm not sure how long the others, the old ones, will survive. Deemed as Undesirable because of their flaws, their years have been cut short because we have no usable medicines to make them better or any real food to make them stronger. They brought the children here to give them a fighting chance at survival, but in doing so, they signed their own death warrants. It's part of what makes the Uncounteds and Undesirables so strong, their sense of duty and sacrifice. Traits that have eluded most of the Mercs and royals. So unfair!

"We need a plan of action," I say. "Mike's right. We need to search others out." I nod quickly at Colt and scan the rest of the room. "Gina and Heather and the rest of you need to stay here on the farm. You are too weak to leave." They open their mouths in what I can only surmise will be a protest so I cut them off, "The children need you. You need to take care of Joe and Arlas. It's the only way."

Gina drops her head. "I guess we really are still Undesirable."

My face burns with anger at the mention of that word. "You are not Undesirables! None of you ever were!" I stop and catch my breath.

Colt finishes my thought, something we do now. "It's important that we know those left behind on the farm have the best care. We have to take into account physical limitations."

"Plus we plan on kicking butt and coming back with news of a better world. A world of freedom. Everyone free, not just the rich." I gain calmness as I speak.

"Everyone needs to be in on this decision," announces Thomas as he heads for the door. "I'm going to get the others from the barn." He disappears into the night.

"We have to get on that ship," I whisper to Colt. "Mom and Gretel are on that ship."

Colt's eyes go dreamy for a moment. I'm sure it's at the thought of seeing Gretel. Colt's in love with my sister. I guess if I really thought about it, Colt will probably be my brother one day. Only problem, my sister and my mom think we're dead. My mind conjures up Riley. Guess he thinks I'm dead. It makes me happy to think about him being on that ship too.

"We need a plan." Colt hides his mouth as he talks. "We can't leave those young ones here without us unless we know they'll be safe. I don't know how long the adults can hang on."

He's right. I guess if we're honest about it, we're part of the young ones. Colt's turning eighteen soon and I'm only fifteen. I feel grown-up.

185

Maybe we skipped our childhoods. I turn my back to the group and speak softly to Colt. "What do you take me for? I'm not heartless. I know we have to make sure they're all right. I don't plan to leave anyone in harm's way. Don't worry. We'll figure it out."

"With a real plan?" He smiles, still voicing low, "Or letting it happen? You're better when you just luck into things."

I laugh. Laughter is so scarce here. I like it when something is funny even if it's only for a fleeting moment. It's hard not to melt into it, but right now, we need to be serious. The adults need both my and Colt's care. We know we are the caretakers. Some of the children even call me *Mom*. I'm fifteen, but I still feel like a mother hen, a responsible mother hen.

Half an hour later, our entire group crowds into my house. We occupy every free space in the room.

Colt clears his throat. "I think we should let Thomas speak about what is going on outside this farm. After all, he did make it there and back."

Thomas stands and thrusts his hands in his pockets. One hand pushes through the fabric lining. Thomas's eyes widen and he shifts uncomfortably before he attempts to use his other hand to free the stuck hand to no avail. The more he jerks, the more the hand disappears into the lining leaving him standing crooked and totally flustered. The more he moves, the more ridiculous he looks. Beau laughs. Thomas turns red and Mike tries so hard to hold a laugh that he moves his leg, hurting it until he yelps in pain. A couple of the women rush to help Thomas right his jacket.

If I don't do something, no one is going to take him seriously. I decide to rescue him, something I do a lot of nowadays.

"Thomas, we'll hear from you in a moment." I fold my hands together in front of my chest, like I saw a speaker do once in a picture. That gesture made me want to hear what she was going to say. I hope it has the same effect here.

The room quiets down. So far, so good. I talk in a low, whispery voice. "We have a couple of problems. One, we need to work with a bigger group and unless there are some people hidden in the forest that we don't know about then this—" I wave my hands around. "—is all we got."

"What about the families that you and Colt saved from the other farms?" Thomas pipes in. "We've heard those stories over and over. Where are they?"

He has a point. We liberated a large group of farm families after the

Mercs took over their farms. Saved them from human trafficking. Colt's family was among them, but unfortunately, we've lost touch with them.

They were not where they were supposed to be and we have no way of tracking them. Maybe we shouldn't have left it that way, but we wanted them to be safe. We can only hope that we will run into them or that democracy will win then everyone will come out of hiding.

On a positive note, the fact that we couldn't find them means the Mercs won't be able to either. Patience. It's easier to talk about than actually do.

"Good point, Thomas." Colt scoots closer to me. "We don't know where they ended up. They might be right around the corner. They might have been caught or they may have relocated elsewhere. We can't wait on them. We've been here a month and—"

"I want to wait!" Gina yells out. "We need them and—what did you say? There might be as many as fifty?"

Joe struggles to hold his hand up. "Me and Arlas ain't gonna be no help. I say we wait on the others."

Thomas jumps up and down. "I didn't say *to wait*. I just wondered where they are." He sits back down with a thump. "Sorry I brought it up." He looks at Colt. "Colt, what's your plan?"

Colt doesn't move or comment.

Can't wait any longer. I shout, hands on my hips, "Listen, we have three major problems. One, we have too small of a group. Two, the only healthy people are children." I stop for a minute and wave my hand toward Joe and Arlas. "No offense, but we've got to do something."

"Why?" Amanda rubs her eyes.

I must have asked that question a thousand times when my mother homeschooled us. Now it just irks me. How can I answer why about a question or plan of action that I'm not sure about myself? I lie, that's what I do and hope for the best.

I answer like my mom always did. "Just because." Amanda doesn't ask another question so I continue, "Number three is that my mom and Gretel are on that ship and that ship is going to America in a couple of weeks."

Thomas asks, "Why does that matter?"

"Because I'm leaving to find some groups for us to join. While I'm gone, *you* still need to train. You need to take charge of yourselves. You need to have a concrete daily plan for survival and you need to stick to it. You need to do all of that because *I'm* going to search for that ship and try to free Mom and Gretel.

And if I don't succeed," I pause and take a deep breath, "I'm going to

187

America and I won't be back for a very long time."

Chapter 3

The reaction and noise accompanying it is deafening. Our entire group sits on the floor and in various chairs facing each other. There is not much space in between, but everyone still seems to feel the need to speak loudly. Maybe it's because they think no one will listen. It's understandable. They have been ignored for most of their lives, labeled and cast aside as Uncounteds or Undesirables. Sadly now with so many voices speaking all at once, *no one* is being understood.

Finally, Colt stands up and holds his hands up demanding to be heard. He shouts, "Paisley will have company!" The room quiets. Colt shoves his shoulder into mine. "I'm going with her."

"Have you both lost your mind?" Gina stands and wags her finger as she speaks. "You can't leave. You're under house arrest. If they catch you, they'll execute you."

"For Mom and Gretel, I'm willing to take the chance." I grab Gina's wiggling finger. "I know you mean well, but to be honest I don't want to live this way. Not being able to go anywhere. The first part of my life I was imprisoned by the quarantine because of the virus. The next part of my life I'm going to be free or die trying to be free."

Arlas is unable to stand so he shifts on the couch, and puts his thoughts in the conversation. "We were *all* quarantined."

"That's true and now we're searching for a way to be free." I nod at him as I speak. "I don't want anyone to think I don't realize what you've been through, but you've got to understand it's my family. My plan is to not only save them, I want to save everyone." I point to the children. "That's what all of this has been about. All this training, every day we've been working toward our freedom."

Mike jumps up from his spot on the rug, hops on his good leg, and shouts, "If you leave, who's in charge?"

"I'm looking at the new army leader." Colt throws an arm around Mike. "You're ready. With you training the younger ones and Thomas running reconnaissance, your group will be strong. Heck, with your fire and determination, you might just be unstoppable."

Mike smiles, pulls Thomas to his feet, and the two stand shoulder to chest since Mike is taller. "We *are* a pretty good team."

"You're a *great* team." I smile at them. "You don't really need us anymore." I say it, but I'm not sure if it's true. I hope it's true, but they must believe that they can make it on their own. If they believe it, then maybe they can do it without us. I'm not sure if I'm making this argument because I believe it or because I don't want to feel the guilt that I feel now. Either way, we have to leave them in charge of themselves. It's the only choice.

Jane sits quietly on the tattered couch and shakes her head. "But we do need you. I am fearful about what will happen when you go."

I plop down beside by Jane. "You don't really need us to run the farm. You, Gina, and the others know how to do that. You know how to get the harvest. With fewer of us here, it'll be easier. Less mouths to feed."

"But what happens if the Mercs come back?" Jane chokes out.

I put my arm around her shoulder. "If the Mercs come back, you'll deal with it. Hide. None of you is supposed to be here anyway. The only difference if we were here is that the Mercs could take us to prison. Then none of us would have this chance. We have to seize this opportunity before the Consortium of the World is decided. If democracy doesn't win out, then none of us will be able to do anything about it. It has to happen now."

A tear runs down Jane's face.

I choke. "If you cry, I'll cry." I swallow a sob. "It's time. I have to try to save Mom and Gretel." I grab her hands and squeeze. "I probably won't get another chance. You understand. It's family."

Jane wipes her eyes and nods too. "We're your family too."

I sigh. "Don't you think I realize that? I have to do this. It's what's best for everyone."

Nods around the room signify that all agree.

Colt shakes Mike's hand. "Then it's decided. I never doubted that Paisley would convince you. She can be quite persuasive when she wants to be."

"And I want to be." My smile is shaky. "I *have* to be."

Gina hugs me. "Let's get Joe and Arlas back to their beds."

I shove my shoulder under Joe's arm. He lets out a groan of pain, but quiets after that. Colt and I will discuss when to make our move. But it has to be in the next couple of days or the ship will be gone and then it will be too late.

The next two days are full of last-minute instructions, strenuous drills, and sad good-byes. Unable to sleep the night before we plan to go, I tiptoe out to my Ferris wheel, throw the switch to the lowest speed, and sit in the bottom chair. I want that ride one last time just in case I don't make it back. Moving this slowly, the wheel lulls me to a half-sleep. I don't know why I want to sleep on the Ferris wheel, but I do. I pull out my four-leaf clover bullet that was owned by Riley and roll it in my hand. He fashioned it as a good luck piece. It's brought me luck so far, I hope it can continue. It's easier to keep up with since I put it on a necklace. Riley is on the ship too and the thought of seeing him again excites me. My mind fills with of all the things that can go wrong. It's a struggle to fall asleep.

"Wake up sleepy-head." Colt's voice. He opens the door to the Ferris wheel carriage with a creak. "I've been looking for you in the house. Should have known this is where you'd be. It's time to go. Are you packed?"

I see the sun peeking above the horizon.

"I packed last night." I rub the sleep out of my eyes. "What time is it? Is it morning? I thought I'd never fall asleep last night." I step out of the carriage and look toward the house. "Is anyone awake yet? Should we say a last good-bye?" I stretch my arms over my head. "Did you stop the wheel?"

"Yes. You're full of questions." He pulls at my sleeve. "Did you sleep in your clothes?"

I slap at him and throw on my backpack. "Of course, so I'd be ready just in case you left me. I planned on running after you."

He chuckles a little. "I hate good-byes." He sighs. "It'll be sad. Let's go. No use making a big scene."

I take a longing look at the Ferris wheel. I love that old metal rusty giant. It represents home. But home is people, not an object, home is Gretel and Mom. I turn my back on the wheel and cut my eyes over at Colt. "I don't know about you, but I plan on trying my hardest to make it back to this farm. With Mom and…"

"Gretel." He smiles. I'm positive I know what he's thinking and it makes me blush. We have definitely been together too long.

It's been a while since I've travelled this far off my farm. The snow hasn't fallen yet so the ground is still green. Bavaria is so beautiful this time of year. When my family was together, we were too focused on getting the harvest to enjoy our scenery.

Being locked on the ship for so long made me appreciate nature and our forest. The open sea is nice but it sure doesn't compare to the Bavarian green hills. A few deer gracefully hop in our path giving us a scare. We fear running into the Mercs, the ones who imprisoned us in the first place. Mercs are just in it for the wealth and power. That's something that the royals and Mercs have in common. While the quarantine was in force, no one challenged their authority, but now that the world is slowly waking up, everyone is jockeying for a position of power. The Mercs still murder first and ask questions later. We don't want to be on the receiving end of one of their killing sprees.

The red and yellow foliage paints a spectacular canvas, as if nature is communicating that there is still good in the world. The beauty surrounding me makes me forget everything else for the moment. As breathtaking as this path is, it is a reminder that things and people who are pleasing to the eye get the most attention. I realize that as we pull the wine berries off the most unattractive vines. The beautiful meadows are wonderful to look at it, but they don't feed you. In contrast, the vines in the vineyards are not only unpleasing they also are scratchy and downright ugly, but what do they do? Their berries feed you when you're hungry.

Makes me think of the rich people on the ship who got all of the attention. Everyone caters to them, but do they do anything for anyone else? Do they make a difference in the world? Most of the time, no.

But the less fortunate, the Undesirables and the Uncounteds, they do all of the work. They bring in the harvest that feeds the world. I could drive myself crazy thinking about how the world is not fair, but today Colt and I just need to keep moving.

Getting out of our forest without discovery proves to be a formidable task. We finally decide to go down Dead Man's Row. It's the most disturbing route, but also the less travelled. It's where the Mercs bring their murdered and throw them into a deep ravine. Savages!

"I hear someone. Quick!" I dive into the bushes, yanking Colt beside me.

It's a Merc riding alone dragging a lifeless body behind his horse. His horse grazes our bush and we have an unencumbered view of the corpse. It's a boy. He couldn't be any older than twelve. A tear escapes my eye and I swallow a gasp.

I want so badly to run over and knock that Merc off his horse. I want to pound him into the ground. The dead body of the child proves this Merc is dangerous. But I can't chance discovery. What could that boy have possibly done that would have warranted death?

The Merc crawls off his horse and ambles slowly back to the lad, like a wolf circling his prey. Prey? His prey is dead. Is he taking pleasure in admiring his work? How sick! He heaves a large knife high over his head. I can't watch.

I hide my eyes for a second before the gore of it draws me back. I let my breath go as I see him whack the rope a few times near the boy's feet. At least he's not mutilating the body. Not yet. I shudder. He pulls the free rope away and walks toward his horse, leaving the youngster in a heap in the middle of the dirt. Like trash.

Colt and I haven't spoken since we hid in the bushes. I glance at him. His horrified expression matches exactly how I feel. There is nothing to be done for the poor dead lad, but still my heart aches.

The Merc takes his time to roll up the rope. My only thought is that he wants to make sure he has it for the next time he plans to murder someone. If we kill this Merc, then he won't be around to slaughter any more innocent boys. I make a slight movement, but Colt's hand pressures my arm. I move again, and he squeezes harder. The more I move the more he presses until my arm goes numb. I look up at him. He shakes his head with a slight move. I know he's right, but it's just so hard not to do anything.

The Merc takes his time collecting the corpse and heaving it over his shoulder. Some blood drops on his boot. He shakes his fists, curses, and slams the boy's dead body down. He stomps the corpse a few times, swearing about how the lad has messed up a perfectly good pair of boots. This boy's life is worth less than a pair of boots. What kind of a person is this?

He lifts the youth up one last time, yanking him over his shoulder and walking to the edge of the ravine. Instead of throwing the body over, he slams it on the edge and kicks the corpse over the side, leaning over to watch the body fall. One thing for sure, the boy's soul is now free. Another thing I know for certain is that this Merc doesn't have a soul.

I'm so horrified that I shift my position. The bush moves. The Merc is on us quickly, slapping me hard in the face. My face stings and I fall backward toward on the ground, struggling to keep my footing. He snatches Colt by the collar. Colt squirms to break free. I grasp at the Merc and scream. He shoves me harder and I slam against a tree. Pain shoots through me, but I go after him again slapping at his arm. He yanks a hunk of my hair with his free hand. I yelp in pain as he jerks me away from Colt. Even with both of us struggling against him, he holds fast. He has a death grip on me and Colt is in a clutch wedged firmly to the Merc's side by the Merc's massive arm. I see Colt struggling, but his arms are locked. Colt's kicking him though. Good for him. Murderers are strong, or at least this murderer is.

"Let us go!" I shriek.

The Merc laughs. "I plan to in just a minute, but you better watch it girlie, that first step is a long one." He laughs again. "Let's get rid of your friend. We don't need him. Plus, he's a little hard to hold onto. Heck, I might keep you around for a bit after he's gone."

The Merc shoves me once more away from him and I crash against a tree, hitting my head. I'm dazed for a moment. He then concentrates his full strength on Colt. He dangles Colt, hanging onto his collar almost choking him over the deep crevasse. "It'll be over quick. Thank you for giving me the girlie. You're just in the wrong place at the wrong time, boy."

I grab up the closest branch. It's not much, but it's the easiest thing I can snatch. I slam him in the back of his head as hard as I can. He swings around to face me. When he does, he loses his grip of Colt. I yelp as I see Colt fall feet first into the ravine.

Colt's gone. He's dead. I didn't help anything. Colt might have overtaken him. I lost Colt. It's all my fault.

I'm so enraged, I can't see straight. This Merc will die even if I have to go with him. I sprint full throttle toward him. "I'm ready to die, you coward!" I squeal, and charge as fast as I can. I reach out to grab him, but he steps out of the way at the last minute and I stumble. I try to catch myself. I tumble headfirst. Not a good death is my last thought as I swan dive to a certain fatal end.

A jerking motion halts my forward thrust. I feel a death grip on my ankle. I smile as I see Colt hanging onto a vine with one hand and my ankle with another. He didn't go over. There's still a chance, but the vine won't hold us both for long. He's just extended the inevitable, but in a way that makes me happy. At least we'll go together and on our own terms.

A horrible scream pierces the silence. The Merc's flailing body sails over us and hits the bottom with a thud. How is that possible? Maybe we have a guardian angel looking out for us.

"Swing her up to me!" A voice yells out. "I'll get her. I'll pull you up after."

I dangle for a minute before I'm yanked up. I glimpse the arm of the uniform of the person who drags me to the dirt. It's a Merc! Are we going to be prisoners now? Worse, he'll turn us in for the bounty in trade for power or rewards. Either way our quest is over. Colt follows quickly using the vine to walk his way up the side, easy for him now without my added weight.

I turn to face the Merc—ready to pounce.

My heart leaps. I recognize him.

Chapter 4

I can't believe it. I swallow my breath. "Riley? How?"

Riley clutches me under my arms, drags me to my feet, and squeezes me in a long hug. "Is there ever a time when you aren't in trouble?"

Colt slaps him on the back. "Glad you happened by when you did or we wouldn't be here." He wallops him again so hard that Riley lunges forward and loses his grip on me.

I fight tears. "He's right. I'm so glad to see you. Once again you saved my life." I hug him again quick and let go. "What's going on with Mom and Gretel? Are they okay? But how..."

"Too many questions. In a minute." Riley slips his arms around both of our waists. "We need to get out of here right now."

"I'm not moving until I know that Mom and Gretel are okay."

"They are." He glances around with a suspicious look. "I'll tell you everything. I won't leave anything out. But it won't matter if we don't move because we won't be alive. Let's go, now!"

He's right. The sun threatens to give away our location. The forest is eerily silent, except for the painfully obvious exception of our gasping breaths and the snapping sounds of leaves as they are crushed under every step. Periodically, we stop and listen for enemy movement. Hearing none, we venture a little farther.

After winding our way down the path for a few minutes, Riley points to brush. "We need to get off the trail. I have no way of knowing if someone will be here, but I can tell you it will be a Merc one hundred percent of the time. Wish we had a good hiding place."

Colt's face lights up. "I know a place!" He glances at me. "Remember?"

We clomp through the underbrush. "The cave." I inhale in an excited breath. "We're going to our cave!"

Colt leads and I am relieved that he remembers where it is hidden. He signals our arrival to our secret place by motioning toward some bushes. He directs us to pull the overgrown greenery aside, revealing the shrub-covered door. We quickly enter.

"I've sneaked up here a few times hoping to find my Dad and the survivors from our rescue, but they didn't make it." He drops his shoulders. "This was the rendezvous point. I thought he would have at least left me a note to tell me where they ended up."

I knew Colt sneaked off the farm some, but I had not thought he was looking for his family. I am so focused on saving my own family that I forget others have family too.

He shoves the brush around. "No one else has been here. See? No sign anyone ever came to this cave."

A dejected look erases my grin. I pat his back and I follow him through the door.

Colt picks up matches conveniently propped up by the door, easily lights a kerosene lantern, and illuminates the contents of the haven. Boxes of jarred and canned foods, some half-opened, are scattered about. I see the discarded jars of fruits we consumed last time we were here. Colt's right, no one has visited since we left. Huge water jugs rest on the dirt floor. It still smells musty like the barn back on the farm after it's been closed up for the winter.

I pick up a jar and open it. I take in a big whiff savoring the sweet aroma. "Peaches, my favorite. Let's eat!""

We plop down in the middle of the cave surrounded by the food and the water jugs. The other two open jars too and for the next few moments, slurping sounds fill the air.

Colt swallows a piece of fruit whole. "Riley, about time you tell us what's going on."

"Let me start by saying that I'm glad you are both alive. For the longest time, I thought you had been carried off and executed. Wasn't that what was supposed to happen?" Riley tosses another piece of fruit in his mouth.

Colt picks up the jug of water. "Yeah. Our sentence was commuted to life imprisonment on the farm. That's where we've been since then. The guards actually took us there." He turns up the jug and starts gulping water.

"Save some for me." I try to pull the jug down. "Yeah, we weren't supposed to leave. We were on farm arrest. We were supposed to stay there forever."

Riley chuckles. "And of course you decided not to follow orders. Why does that not surprise me?"

I giggle. A little water dribbles on my shirt. "Riley, did you know that the Undesirables or Desirables as we now call them made it to the farm? They followed our buggy when we left."

"I heard that." Riley dabs my chin with his finger. "Missed a spot."

I push his hand away and wipe my mouth with the sleeve of my jacket. "What I want to know is why you're off the ship, and what happened to Mom and Gretel?"

Colt nods. "Yeah, what's going on with Gretel? Is she *really* okay?"

Riley slaps his stomach. "That's enough for me right now." He scoots to the side of the cave and leans back. "They're both fine. The ship is here for two weeks, and then it leaves for America. One of the guards let it slip last week that you two had been taken to the farm and let go."

I put the lid back on my jar of peaches. "It was a secret. Do Mom and Gretel know?"

Riley shakes his head. "I thought it best not to tell them since I wasn't sure you were still alive. Sometimes the Mercs say something but in the end, it might not be true. I've seen them go back and kill the person." He drops his head. "The boy you just saw. Like him, he was supposed to be taken back to his parents."

I lean up. "Why didn't the Merc take him back to his parents? That was a child."

"Lazy." Riley shrugs and sighs.

"I don't understand." And I don't. What does being lazy have to do with being a cold-blooded killer? Riley is not making any sense.

"I was with the boy and the Merc." Riley shakes his head. "The Merc decided he didn't want to waste his time and energy taking the boy back to his parents. He thought it was easier to kill him. So he knocked the boy in the head at night and he was dead in the morning."

Colt jerks up from his leaning position. "Why couldn't you do anything? Couldn't you at least attempt to save the child?"

"I was sleeping when it happened." Riley slams back against the cave side. "What could I do?" Riley asks. "In the morning, the boy was dead. The Merc already had him tied to his horse to take to the ravine. He tried to tell me it was the right thing to do. It was easier to kill him and then report back we had taken the boy to his parents. He also said that we could say that the boy had an accident and died on the trail."

"That doesn't make sense. Why would someone do that?" I ask and look over at Colt. "Does that make sense to *you*?" Colt shakes his head

"Not at all. Of course, it doesn't make sense to good people." Riley twirls the half-empty jar of fruit on the dirt floor. "Unfortunately, we don't have many good people in the Mercs. Some are bloodthirsty criminals. The Merc organization gives them a legal outlet to murder."

"So sad." A tear runs down my face. "That child was supposed to be back with his parents and now he's dead and his parents will never know what happened to him."

Colt slides up against the cave wall and crosses his arms. "Why are you here, Riley? How did you find us?"

"I volunteered to go with the Merc to take the boy back. I was hoping to slip away and go by the farm and see if you two were still alive." Riley sighs. "When he killed that boy, I told him I was going to go back and report him, but he pulled a gun on me."

I shift on the floor. "He shot you?"

Riley taps the jar on the ground. "No, he shot *at* me. He didn't hit me, but he didn't know that. When the gun went off, it startled me so much that I lost my footing and fell down a hill. Fortunately, it was a short drop and just stunned me. Guess I was *still* long enough to convince him I was dead. I followed him when he left and..." He stops for a minute and shrugs. "You know the rest."

"We're glad you're here." Colt slaps Riley's leg. "Really glad or we'd be dead."

"We need to get Mom and Gretel off that ship." I rest my hands on my knees. "Will you help us?"

Riley stops moving. "Wait a minute." He furrows his brow. "I came here to find you and help you train for the resistance. I just escaped the ship. I don't want to go back." His shoulders droop. "I can't go back. They'll wonder what happened to the other Merc." He glares at me. "What about the people living on your farm? Are you just going to leave them?"

"Of course I'm going to find help for the people back at the farm. Colt and I are planning to search out other resistance groups. We heard they were all over. And then after that...I mean we have two weeks..." I let out an exasperated groan. "Don't you understand? If Mom and Gretel leave for America, I might not ever see them again. I *have* to get back on that ship."

"How?" Riley taps my forehead. "Everyone thinks you're dead."

I sit up against the cave wall and let out a deep breath. "That *is* a problem, but I'll figure out a way around it. I always do."

Colt nods. "That's true. What if we just concentrate on trying to get Gretel and your mom *off* instead of us *on*?"

"That'll work." I cross my arms. "Now all we have to do is leave here." I hold my hand up, pointing one finger up, and count the rest as I list our tasks off. "Make sure we don't get caught by the Mercs, find other resistance groups, give them information about our farm, make sure that is working..." Running out of fingers on one hand, I start counting on the other. "Find our way to the ship, figure out a way to get Mom and Gretel off, make our way back to the farm with them, end human trafficking, defeat the royals and those not wanting democracy, and do all of that in..."

Colt laughs. " ... the next two weeks." He pauses. "We do have a bit more time for that end stuff."

"Exactly." Riley says, "No problem. Let's do all of that."

198

Riley catches my eye and starts laughing. I laugh too.

I know it's probably not appropriate, but I'm stressed. It's hard to live in fear for your life constantly. That laughing, that down to your toes, bottom of your stomach, fall on the floor laughing with my two best friends makes me feel better than I have felt in a long time. I need this and I'm sure that Colt and Riley do too.

It's been a hard few months. My world, and the entire world, has been turned upside down. The virus that kept us all separated is eradicated. Now it's all a battle for control, with the different sides lying, stealing, and manipulating—whatever it takes to make sure their side wins. It's a battle to choose the color of our future. I'm determined that in this new world, everyone will be free, democracy will win, and the royals will be nothing but figureheads with no real power.

Is that too much to ask?

Chapter 5

Our sense of urgency returns the next day. We refresh supplies and venture out with a new plan. First order of business, to find at least one of the small bands of resistance. Our farm children need some support. I wouldn't feel good about it, if we don't at least try to send them some help. If we get enough small groups together, we might become a force to be reckoned with. We might actually make a difference. What a nice positive thought! I try to hold onto that positivity all day long.

I refuse to think about Mom and Gretel too much. If I do, I'll run full force to Hamburg. That wouldn't be wise. I need to be smart so I am not caught. Only problem is that finding people who are trying very hard not to be found proves a difficult task.

We come across no one for two days, as we travel towards the ship. Occasionally, I notice the gorgeous countryside. I feel guilty enjoying its beauty. We need to complete our mission. The longer we go without seeing anyone, the more discouraged I become.

On the third day, we close in on Hamburg, the town where the ship is docked. I hear a rustling in the forest. I crouch into the brush alongside the trail. "Colt!" I whisper, but he doesn't hear me.

A young girl about seven years old sprints down the trail and runs full throttle into Colt. She crashes into him and he grabs her arm.

She yells, "You can't take me. I won't tell you anything!" She kicks him hard, but he holds fast.

"I didn't ask you anything." Colt clutches the squirming girl. "Quit kicking!"

The girl freezes for a moment and shouts, "Are you a Merc?"

Colt shakes his head. "No." He rubs his chin. "Are you?"

"No! Girls can't be Mercs, everyone knows that!" The girl spies Riley. "Even if you're not, he is." She twists out of Colt's arms, lands hard on the ground, and falls backward into a prickly bush. "Ouch!"

I squat beside the girl. "Are you okay?" I grab her hand and pull her out of the bush. "Sit here on the trail for a minute."

She cuddles up to me and I pull the thorns out of her arm. "I know *you're* not a Merc." She says, "You're a girl. Did they catch you?"

"No. I'm Paisley." I nod toward the others. "These are my friends, Colt and Riley. Who are you, and why are you running?"

"Kelley, my name is Kelley." She wipes the dirt off her pants. "I'm running from Mercs. They're trying to capture me and make me work for them. Like a slave."

I sit beside her, pick up her foot, and retie her shoelaces. "Where are you supposed to be?"

"Not supposed to say."

"There." I pat her neatly tied shoe. "Why can't you say?"

"It's a secret. We cause problems. I find out where the Mercs are and I go back and report. But they saw me and started chasing me." She flexes her feet in front of her, admiring her laces. "I can't tie them that good. They always come untied." She smiles at me.

Riley says, "She could be part of a resistance group. That's the people we've been looking for." Riley sits down beside Kelley. "Tell us where they're located."

"I'm not telling you anything, Merc," responds Kelley, jutting out her chin.

I rub her hair. "First, we all need to hide so the Mercs don't find us. Then we'll tell you who we are and what we're about. Okay? Will you come with us?"

She studies me for a few minutes. She frowns at Riley, and then looks at Colt. She half-smiles before refocusing on me. Her face breaks into a full grin. "I know a place where no one will find us. Come on."

"Lead the way." I stand up and pull her to her feet.

Colt squints his eyes. "Are you sure about this? It could be a trap!"

"Even if it is, do we really have a choice?" I whisper to him. "I hope she's taking us to the rest of her clan. Maybe we can convince the others in her group."

Colt smiles. "You're always thinking."

I feel the edges of my mouth curl. "I'm always doing that, but sometimes I *think* us right into trouble. Like right now, we really don't have time for this. We need to get to Hamburg and onto that ship."

"You're right. We *also* need to find some help for our people. Let's hope we can do both." Colt hugs me. "Remember, I want to get to that ship as bad as, or worse, than you do."

I sigh and nod. "I know. Gretel."

Colt waves his hand at the trail. "Lead on, Kelley."

For the next half-hour, we wander the German forest in a serpentine pattern, circling around and back more times than I can count. I'm not sure if she's doing it on purpose, but if someone put me at the starting point and asked me to retrace our steps, it would be impossible. A great tactic, one I had hoped to teach the charges back at our farm. Unfortunately, time ran out and plans sometimes have to be broken.

Flexibility must be the rule if we plan to make any headway in the war. Hard to do when your family is so close yet so far and you ache to see them.

The green countryside is alive making it a little easier to maneuver. In a few weeks, winter will set in. Snow-covered trails make it harder to hide footprints unless the snow falls constantly.

Kelley runs ahead. I turn to Colt. "I have a bad feeling about this." We are standing in the middle of a clearing. Kelley is nowhere in sight.

"Don't move!" A loud voice bellows from the woods. In a few moments, five large boys surround us. "Identify yourself and give us the word." They hold huge sticks.

"We don't know the word." I say without thinking. Not a great idea since we might be clubbed to death any minute now.

"Stop, these are my friends." Kelley emerges from out of the forest leading a horse-pulled carriage. Its only inhabitant is an age-weathered woman with a shawl draped around her shoulders. "Make them stop, Aunt Sandra!"

Aunt Sandra is helped out of the carriage by a couple of the boys. She doesn't say anything. The boys still have their makeshift weapons held above their heads, but they stand still while the woman hobbles around, studying each of us. She stops at me. "You saved my niece?"

"Yes." I nod. "We all did." I motion to Riley and Colt.

One of the boys pipes in. "This one's a Merc, Auntie." He grabs Riley's bare arm, revealing his Merc tattoo. Riley jerks his arm away.

"Quiet, boy!" Aunt Sandra looks at me. Her eyes squint almost closed. "Do you want to tell me what's going on?"

Colt opens his mouth to speak and Auntie holds up a gnarled hand. "Not you, *her*." She points at me.

"It'll take a few minutes." I manage.

She shuffles into the forest a ways and pulls back the brush to reveal a circle of rocks. "We better have a seat then."

All five boys take seats on the single rocks. Auntie, Kelley, and I huddle together on the same long rock, leaving Colt and Riley to sit on the dirt. I tell them of our troubles. I'm not quite sure if I should reveal everything, but I do. I know I'm taking a chance, but our time to get to the ship is growing short. If we have any hope to reach Mom and Gretel in time, we have to trust someone. They listen intently, not interrupting, even when I explain how Riley became a part of us because he was an Uncounted who had been recruited by the Mercs. I tell them that he was born on a farm in the Bavarian forest not too far from where I live. So in reality, he wasn't really a Merc, but a farm person like me.

I stop when I finish my story. Aunt Sandra rubs her chin. "I think that joining the resistance groups together is a great idea. Since you plan to go to the ship, you'll have to trust my boys to go to your farm and help your little ones. Do you trust me?"

"Is this your family?" I ask.

"Yes." She looks at the boys with fondness and love.

I stare at her. "These children that I told you about may not be my blood, but they are my family. I need to know you are telling me the truth before I give you information about where to find them."

One of the boys asks, "Even if we threaten to kill you."

I nod. "I'd die before I put them in harm's way."

Aunt Sandra studies me for a moment then says, "I believe you just might do that." A boy helps Aunt Sandra limp to her feet. "We'll show you so you'll know you can trust us."

The same boy cocks his head. "You sure? They may be lying. This may be a trick to find our hiding place."

"I'm not lying. I promise." I bow slightly in her direction. A sign of respect.

"They aren't." Aunt Sandra hobbles to the carriage and gets back in. She pulls Kelley in beside her and says, "Follow us."

"I'm grateful to you," I say.

Aunt Sandra motions to the other boys to get Riley and Colt to their feet. "I've lived a long time. I've seen a lot. I know when I'm being fed a story. In a few minutes, you'll see we aren't lying to you either."

Our group tramps deep into the forest until we come upon a vineyard with vines so thick they are almost impassable. We make slow progress until we come to a clearing. In front of us stands a large concrete barrier fence covered with greenery. Until you are standing right in front of it, it is completely hidden.

"Does this wall go all the way around?" I ask.

"Yeah," A boy who hasn't talked before answers.

One of the boys finds a tree and starts counting a path around the wall. He counts his steps to one hundred and thirty four before he stops. He reaches into the mass of vines and locates a gate. It takes him a few minutes to unlock the latches. Aunt Sandra gets out of the carriage and the boys hide the coach in a hollow area in the bushes and cover it with brush.

I'm surprised when we walk into darkness instead of light. "Is this a cave?"

"Yes." The same boy answers. "Duck or you'll bump your head." When we all clear the gate and crouch in the cave, he turns the handle on the latch. "It's a secret, how you open it from the inside. Just in case someone breaks in, we can trap him or her here. My brothers and I built this cave. You like it?"

I nod. He doesn't respond. It's dark so I guess he can't see my gestures. I mumble, "Yeah." In a few feet, we are able to stand without crouching.

One of the other boys retrieves a lamp and lights it. We walk a good distance before we come upon two sentries guarding a threshold. They bow when they spy Aunt Sandra. We are allowed to pass. A few more steps lead to another door that opens into an unbelievable sight.

A high hedge blocks our passage. About a kilometer ahead beyond the maze sits a sprawling tall structure, its pinnacle castle-like in its appearance. From this vantage point, we can see it is crowned by several tower spikes.

The boys take a piece of cloth and blindfold the three of us.

Riley holds the cloth over his eyes while someone ties it behind his head. "You *are* serious about no one finding you."

I cringe a little as they tie the cloth over my eyes. "I'm not a fan of blindfolds." I flash back to being blindfolded and supposedly being led to my death that turned out to be house arrest, but just the same, it isn't a happy thought.

Colt quietly lets them blindfold him. He whispers to the group. "Anything that will get me a step closer to saving Gretel, I'm okay with."

Aunt Sandra says, "The boys will take each of you by the arm and lead you through the maze." It takes a little while and we bump into the sides and stumble on the uneven terrain. A couple of turns we go forward then backwards, one time we have to jump over what sounds like a stream. We have to climb a ladder to move ahead at one point. Blindfolded or not, if you didn't know how to get through this maze or have a map, I don't think you'd make it. It must be quite a puzzle, and huge as it takes a while.

Finally, our blindfolds are removed. In front of us stands the most magnificent castle I've ever seen. The structure sits in a valley like a crown cushioned on a pillow. Its regal splendor begs for a royal bow of respect. It's surrounded by forested hills on all sides and is hidden mostly by the natural terrain. Spires of stone with triangular spiked crests and a gazillion gated walls mesh together in an intricate pattern that rivals what I read about Versailles. I don't know how they ever kept this a secret.

A deep valley devoid of water surrounds the structure. We follow Aunt Sandra across an open drawbridge. The inside structure houses a mammoth courtyard where giggly children run, holding waving flags. Kelley says a quick good-bye as she joins the fun with the rest of the children. A metalwork shop and stables for horses are located near the entrance.

What kind of place is this? I squint and make out a structure even farther up the mountainous hill. It looks like the pictures of ruins where wealthy landowners would build gigantic castles at the highest point of their land to not only watch and rule over their kingdom, but as a vantage point to ward off enemy attacks. Men roam the ruins and I wonder if they are operating the same type outlook post now.

Colt, Riley, and I shoot glances at each other as we make our way to the main structure. The two men guarding the gate bow slightly to Aunt Sandra and open the massive outside doors that allow us to pass into the main house. Colorful rugs of all shapes and sizes lay on the floor. People sit around on the rugs. Some are sewing. Some read aloud or to themselves. Some are talking.

When Aunt Sandra enters, the room immediately falls silent. They all stand and bow. She makes her way to the center and sits on a simple chair of wood and iron, devoid of any decoration. The chair is surrounded by more rugs. She indicates that we all sit.

"This is my house," Aunt Sandra says. "My family owns these lands, and I have been sheltered by this house my whole life."

I shift my legs out in front of me. "Even during the virus outbreak and quarantine?"

"Especially then. One of my son's friends worked on the military base and we got word immediately what was happening. Some of his friends were mistakenly left during the evacuation. My son brought his friends and some of the villagers here. From time to time, we have brought others into our hidden sanctuary. We are self-sufficient. We grow our own food. We have been undetected for all these years."

"You're showing me this so I'll trust you, right?" I ask.

She smiles. "Of course, dear. I want to help your... what did you call them...Undesirables."

"They're Desirables now."

"Of course they are, my dear. Everyone here is desirable too. Please let me help you."

I look over at Riley and Colt. "What do you think?" They both nod. Why would she show us this if she wasn't planning to help us?

I tell her about the farm and its location. I explain who is there and what shape they are in physically, being specific about their disabilities, injuries, and limitations. She shares some information she has garnered

205

from the outside. It's dire. The king is gaining support for a dictatorship of the world with him as its master and chief.

"That can't happen," I tell her. "He is a bad king!"

She nods. "I know." She sighs. "The information my couriers have brought back paint a picture of children being kidnapped to be used to serve the rich. Horrible stories of mistreatment. It must be stopped."

I glance at some flyers on her table. An advertisement for the Sponsored Companion Doll Program catches my eye, and I point to it. "We were Sponsored Companions, living dolls for the princess." I stop for a moment, frowning at the glossy advertisement. "Anyone who they don't deem as in perfect health, they label as undesirable. Anyone without a family, they label as Uncounted. I was an Uncounted."

"Then you have firsthand knowledge of how it is. I have one more thing to show you." She hobbles toward one side of the room. We follow her through the doors. Inside are beds filled with people with varying degrees of injuries.

"What's this?" I point to a bottle hanging upside down.

"This is our hospital." She hugs a woman carrying a clipboard. "We conduct raids on the Mercs. We confiscate medical supplies, radios, weapons, food, all sorts of things. We smuggle them back here to supply our army. We plan to take back Europe. At first, we had to wait to make sure that the virus was truly eradicated. We've just been waiting for the right time."

Colt picks up a pill bottle. "Some of ours could use some medical care." He picks up a yellowed newspaper. "Do you get news from the outside?"

Aunt Sandra smiles at a patient sleeping in a bed. "Some. We have actually used their news sources to find out where and when shipments are coming. You wouldn't believe the medicines we found."

Riley, silent for a while, pipes up. "Some people are trying to organize the Consortium of the World."

Aunt Sandra fluffs a patient's pillow as she talks to us. "I've heard that. What are your thoughts on that matter?"

I offer, "We used to work for the ambassador. I think he's trying to bring democracy back."

"I've heard he was a good man, but the king..." She shakes her head.

Colt huffs. "Don't get us started. The king is not one of our favorite people. It might have to do with the fact that he sentenced me and Paisley to death."

"You're not dead." Aunt Sandra pinched her lips together. "Why is that?"

"Too long of a story. But he's right, the king did try to have us killed. But the ambassador is really nice, an honest man. He would be good to lead our world into a democratic rule."

"Come, come." She walks towards the door. "We must let these nurses and doctors get back to work." As she reaches the door, she turns. "What are your plans now?"

"If you promise to take care of the people at my farm, we'll continue from here to try to rescue my family."

"I give you my word. I ask only that if you come across any others in trouble or on the same quest as us that you send them our way. If you're not sure if they're telling you the truth, don't worry about it. It'll be fine. My boys and I will figure out if they're truthful or not." She bows slightly. "You are welcome back here when you find your family."

"Are you joking?" Riley laughs. "We would never be able to find this place again."

"You don't have to. My boys will find you. They always do." She motions to a huge table heaped with fresh fruits and other foods. "But first, eat. Stay the night and start fresh in the morning."

"Sounds like a plan." I take a seat and chomp into the best-looking pear I've seen in a long time.

I feel safe. Even if it's only for a night.

Chapter 6

We venture out on our new mission after being awakened. Better than an alarm clock, children run around the compound signaling the start of the day. "Time to wake up! Time to wake up!" they yell until everyone is awake. Makes me wonder who wakes *them* up.

Fortunately, Aunt Sandra sends a guide to help us off their land and point us in the direction of Hamburg. It takes a while to get back through the maze, through the entrance cave, and out of the surrounding woods. We would have never found it.

We estimate it will take us three full days to reach the port town. With our food rationed and our path clear, the only obstacle standing in our way is the ever-present danger of being discovered. Mercs roam the countryside with no formation or clear plan, making them impossible to guard against.

Two and a half days in, while searching for a place to rest, we find a group of children huddled in a cave. After sharing the few morsels of food we have, we tell them about Aunt Sandra. We give them specific directions to find the area close to the sanctuary.

I say, "Don't worry. When you get close, they'll find you. Take care." We send them on their way with a message to Aunt Sandra, that we have almost made it to Hamburg.

A large hill stands in front of us.

"We're almost there." I breathe. "I can smell the ocean."

Riley points to a seagull circling in the sky. "You're right."

We scale the hill and crawl on our bellies to peer over the side. The color of the terrain has changed somewhat from the lush green to bald bushes, announcing the change of season. Fall has always been my favorite time of year. I loved the weather and the anticipation of snow. Always loved the winter too. It meant no chance of Mercs. Now winter means it's too hard to travel. Strange how situations change your outlook.

"There it is." Riley points out the obvious. The stack protrudes from above the deck of the great ship. "I don't know how we're going to get on it."

I flip from my belly to my back. "We'll figure out a way."

"You always do." Colt stands and pulls me up. "No one down there to see us. If we're going to get Gretel, we have to stand tall and make it happen."

Riley flips over to his back and grabs at my leg. "We're taking a chance. You are both on house arrest. If I'm caught, I'll be thrown in the brig for abandoning my post."

"Take a chance, Riley. Stand up. They probably think you're dead anyway." I pull at him.

Riley stands up beside us. "We need to be careful, whatever we do."

"I've got a crazy idea." I hoist on my backpack.

"Why does that not surprise me?" Colt chuckles. "Give it to us."

"Let's go back to the doll store and try to get sold to the royals as Sponsored Companions again." I take off running down the hill.

Riley yells after me. "That *is* a crazy idea." He pauses for a minute. "Or stupid."

Colt catches up to me. "I agree with Riley. Stupid. You *want* us to be owned as dolls to play with the children of the rich again. That doesn't make sense." Riley runs alongside and Colt continues, "They would recognize us. Plus didn't we get tattoos?"

I shout to him as I run. "Tattoos! That's right! My temporary is worn off." We all stop to catch our breath halfway down. "Let's at least go by the store," I plead. "To see if it's a possibility. There are more rich people on that ship, besides the royals. We could be owned by someone else and probably stay out of their way."

Colt nods. "It's such a crazy idea that it just might work. To the doll store." He takes off after me as I run again.

Riley follows us and says, "Only if *I* get to play with the princess this time."

Entering the town of Hamburg is easier this time around. We don't smell as bad as we did the first time. We don't draw much attention as we navigate the streets looking for the doll store. The alley is easily recognizable because of its proximity to the ship and the shouts of the street vendors. Locating the alley gives us a starting point, which makes it easier to find the doll store. Peering in the window, we see Ms. DeVane sitting, prim and proper, while tending to a patron. It's been a while. Will she recognize us?

"Let's sneak in the back like before and see if they have any new costumes. We might be able to pull it off if we just put on a new outfit." Colt flattens against the alley wall adjacent to the store.

"I'm with you." Riley settles in beside Colt. "Remember, I haven't been here before."

"We look like we're criminals with you two pressed against the alley wall like we're under arrest or hiding or something. C'mon you two." I walk nonchalantly toward the store picking up brochures from the kiosks that sit in front of its door. "Wait until she isn't looking," I whisper to Colt.

It doesn't take long. Ms. DeVane turns her back to show a customer a doll.

Colt leads the way, crouching along the back aisle, through the doors, and into the back storeroom. "Here we are once again. In the doll birthing room."

Riley scrunches his face. "Birthing room?"

I pick up a doll from the trash bin. "He's just joking. Don't listen to him. It looks just the same as it did before."

Riley thumbs through a pamphlet. "More propaganda for the king. Rubbish!"

Colt proudly displays a poster. "New Dutch Dolls," he reads off. The poster displays a picture of two people dressed in the traditional dress of Holland. The female wears a white triangular hat crossway on her head, a blue-checkered dress, with a white apron and wooden shoes. The boy is dressed in navy knee-length pants, a navy blazer, a white shirt, a blue cap, and wooden shoes.

I look around and spy a box labeled: *New/Just In*. I open it. Wrapped inside the box is a pair of complete costumes, one for a boy and one for a girl, representing Holland. "These are brand new. The people from the boat can't possibly have them yet. This just might work."

Riley sighs and picks up the outfit. "It will for you two, but not for me. What are we going to do with two boys, one girl, and only one of each outfit?" He sits on the floor, head in hands. "I really want to help, but I can't chance getting caught. I wouldn't even be able to lie my way out of this. I've been gone way too long. Lamar will know, if he's still there."

"Lamar? I hope he's not still there. I can't stand that guy." I slump down beside Riley. "If he is, we'll figure out something." That Merc, Lamar, is one of the most bloodthirsty Mercs I've come across. He wants to kill all the time. Most of the time his conquests are the Undesirables, people with disabilities, or those weaker than him. He probably preys on them because they will be less likely to be missed. It's so sad! I had a dream once that Lamar got his due. His arm was burned badly and he became an Undesirable. That would make him think twice about wanting to kill people who aren't perfect physically.

Colt hasn't moved. He stands by the boxes looking at the outfits and studying the wooden shoes. "I have a much better idea." He brings the shoes over and sits down beside us. "What if you and Riley went as the dolls?" He points to the shoes. "Believe me, I don't want to wear this get up, especially not these."

I frown. "Are you going to just stay here on shore?" I slap Colt hard on the arm. "That's not very nice. What about Gretel? I thought you couldn't live without her. That's all you've been moaning about since we got to the farm."

Colt grabs my hands and holds them down. "Hear me out. What if you two went as the dolls and I take Riley's clothes and go in as a Merc?"

I jump up, hands on my hips. "A Merc? Are you out of your mind? What do you know about being a Merc?" I look over at Riley. "Tell him, Riley, tell him why that won't work. Tell him why that's the craziest idea you've ever heard. Tell him, Riley."

Riley sits, silent.

I flop back down. "You're not thinking this is a *good* idea are you? How can he pass?"

"The only real thing he needs that he doesn't have is a Merc tattoo. The only thing I would need to do would be to hide my Merc tattoo and get a Holland doll tattoo." Riley pulls up his sleeve.

"It can't be done then." I shake my finger at Riley. "Do you know how to hide a tattoo, or make one?" I wag my finger at Colt. "Do you?"

Colt and Riley both lean out and look at each other.

"Any ideas?" Riley asks.

"One." Colt gets up and walks toward the door to the store. "But it's a gamble."

The two of us follow Colt into the store. Ms. DeVane sits quietly focused on a piece of paper. There are no customers.

Colt approaches the counter and gently rubs his fingers on the wood to get her attention, and he meekly talks. "Ms. DeVane I don't know if you remember us but I'm about to bet my life that you are not going to turn us in, and that you will, in fact, help us."

Riley and I freeze, fearful of the answer we are about to get. What if Ms. DeVane turns us in? Then all of this has been for nothing. We travelled for nothing. We might even be tortured into giving up the location of our farm or Aunt Sandra's compound. How long would I be able to hold out? I don't know. Torture, I don't know how much I could take without folding. I don't want to find out. All of these horrible thoughts run through my head for what seems like forever.

Ms. DeVane sits and quietly studies us. She reaches under her desk. She's probably going to bring out a gun to shoot us dead or take off into the street to announce our presence. What kind of trouble has Colt gotten us into?

211

Chapter 7

Ms. DeVane moves in slow motion. I hold my breath wondering what will come out from under that desk. She pulls out a piece of paper and slaps it on the table. I gasp!

"Are you okay?" Ms. DeVane peers out at me from under her starkly cut bangs.

"Uh-huh?" I manage to answer weakly before my body relaxes.

Colt fingers the end of the paper, trying to pull it across the desk to him. "What's this?"

Snatching it back, Ms. DeVane lifts her sleeve exposing the back of her upper arm and reveals an etched tattoo of a broken egg. "I'm with the resistance. Thought you might need some assurances." She quickly rolls the sleeve back down. "Of course that part of me must stay hidden. You understand, don't you?"

I nod in disbelief.

Colt's mouth drops open and he asks, "How long?"

The corners of her mouth turn into a shy smile. "Like I thought you were *really* Sponsored Companions." She shrugs. "I figured if the royals didn't know any better… and if you two had enough of a reason to get on the ship that you were willing to lie to get on illegally." She chuckles. "Let's just say, I thought it was my duty to help you." She shuffles the paper. "This is just for show in case someone comes in. You are asking me about buying a doll." She peers over at me. "And by you, I mean *you*, not the boys." She picks up a pen. "Now what can I help you with?"

I sit in the chair in front of the desk. "It's complicated."

She taps the desk with her pen. "I'm okay with that."

Riley pulls up his military jacket sleeve to reveal *his* Merc "M." "It's a little more complicated than you might have thought."

Ms. DeVane motions to the empty seats in front of her desk. "You two have a seat."

Colt and Riley flop into the chairs. A patron, sporting an elaborate hat full of pink feathers surrounding a white glittered bird, saunters in, carrying a blonde dog with a pink ribbon tying up a tuft of hair.

"Be with you in just a minute." Ms. DeVane pushes a page over in front of us. "If you'll look over this contract while I help this customer. I'll be back with you in a minute." She fires us a quick look and disappears down one of the aisles.

Riley shifts around to look for others. Seeing none, he turns back to us and whispers, "I say we just lay the plan out. Tell her exactly what we need and see what she can do."

I nod. He's right. No use trying to candy coat it or manipulate her. If we hope to get on that ship, we need Ms. DeVane's help.

The bell sounds at the front of the store indicating an arrival or departure of a customer. We are hoping for the latter. Our wish is granted. Ms. DeVane takes her seat behind the desk in a couple of seconds. "What do you need?"

The three of us explain our plan. We tell her of my family on the ship and a little of our journey since we last saw her, omitting the gorier events like the killing of the boy and the biggest secret, the existence of Aunt Sandra's sanctuary. Ms. DeVane listens intently, writing notes on her paper as we talk.

"The Holland dolls, I can do." She opens her file and pulls out a folder. "In fact, there is a couple on the ship who have an order in for the Holland Living Dolls for their seven year old. I can easily fake the papers and the tattoos." She reaches for Riley. "Let me see your Merc tattoo." She pulls his arm over and studies it for a moment. "Yes, it can be done. Plus with this as a guide I can put a temporary on for Colt." She leans back in her chair. "I can do all of this for you, but I want something in return."

I slump back in my chair and sigh.

Ut-oh here it comes.

Chapter 8

What can Ms. DeVane possibly want in exchange? She is going to fake papers and copy tattoos. That's worth a lot. What if the favor is too big? We all scoot closer to her desk waiting for our hopes to be squashed.

"I have a son. He was taken as an Uncounted three years ago. I want you to see if you can find out where he is. Come back here and tell me after you get your family off the ship." She lifts her eyeglasses to wipe a stray tear.

I squeeze her hand. "What's his name?"

"William," she whispers meekly. "He has blonde hair and the cutest smile." She stops and sighs. "He used to have the cutest smile. He also has a scar above his eye from when he fell off his bike. And a birthmark on his leg. It's in the shape of..." She buries her head in her hands.

I stand up, walk around her desk, and hug her. "How old is William?"

"Eight." She glances up to the ceiling for a minute. "He was five when they took him."

Colt says, "Do you know who took him or where?"

"The Mercs, of course. But where?" She shakes her head. "Not sure. I heard rumor to America, but I don't know for sure."

I look at the others and walk back around the desk to face her. "I'm going to be honest with you. We can promise to do everything we can to find information about your William, but in the end we might not be able to tell you anything." I clasped her hands in both of mine. "I don't want to promise you something that I'm not sure we can deliver."

Riley leans in. "It's hard to find the missing. They send them as far away from home as they can to keep them from escaping. Look what happened with me."

"If you want to back out on our agreement, since we can't promise you results, we totally understand," Colt says. "It wouldn't be right for you to take all of these risks."

Ms. DeVane scribbles on the paper. "Of course I'm going to help you. If it's possible, I want you to look for him or information. I might not ever know where my sweet William ended up, but I have to try to find out." She stares at us with a tear-streaked face. "You understand, don't you?"

I sit and clutch her hand. "Of course, we will do what we can."

Riley pokes at the paper. "Give us his full name. Date of birth. Any other identifiers like that birthmark or something unusual about him. We will see what we can do. Absolutely! Who knows? We might just get lucky and bring him back."

She smiles. "Wouldn't that be wonderful?" She motions to the back of the store. "You two…" She points at Riley and me. "Go get dressed in the traditional Holland outfit. It's in the back in a…"

Riley finishes her sentence. "A box. Yeah we already opened it. Sorry."

Riley and I go to change into our new garb. When we return, Colt's arm is elevated, protecting his newly drawn Merc tattoo. "See?"

"Unbelievable! It looks like the real thing!" I smile at Ms. DeVane. "Great job! You *are* an artist!" I pull my white apron out and curtsy. "What do you think of me as a little Dutch girl?" I ask Colt.

"Cute! Cute!" He thumbs-up with his free hand. "Where's Riley?"

Riley sheepishly ambles out of the dressing room. "Now I see what you mean, Colt. I feel like an idiot in this."

I nod. "But it's for Gretel and Mom."

Riley points to Ms. DeVane. "And William."

Ms. DeVane works quickly drawing the SC tattoos on Riley and me. We leave her store with hugs, information about William, and legal boarding papers.

"Feels like we've done this before." Colt pulls out the postcard from the kiosk as we pass by with the picture of the Neuschwanstein Castle. "Where Dreams Come True," remember?"

It was sweet of Colt to remember the postcard from my mother's treasure box. I tell Riley about a postcard from Orlando with the same picture of a castle from America that had that saying. I smile as I tell the story, but it only makes me more homesick to see my mother. I hate that she thinks I am dead. How horrible for her.

I smile and rub my fingers over the postcard before placing it back in its holder. "Do you think we'll be able to see the princess or the ambassador?" I can't tell either of them that I not only hope to rescue my mother and sister, but I really want to see the ambassador.

Riley crinkles his brow. "What reason would you have for wanting to see any of the royals?"

"The ambassador *did* save us." Colt spouts the truth although he doesn't know the entire story. The ambassador told me before I was forced off the ship that he was my real father. It's tough to get news like that and not be able to talk to him about it. Thankfully, I did get to have a conversation with my mother who confirmed his story. She found me wandering alone after the virus outbreak, took me in, and raised me as

215

her own, a fact that made me love her even more.

"We *really* need to get on that ship." I quicken my walk.

Colt takes one step to my every two. "I agree. I *have* to see Gretel."

As we walk, Riley coaches Colt about how to act like a Merc. We decide that Colt will take us in with our papers. Our hope is that no one will inspect Colt or his tattoo too closely. We label that Plan A, then we discuss Plan B, running. Finally, we discuss Plan C, which is how to escape if we are caught. I shake my head at the boys. "I guess our real plan is that plan A or B better work."

We share an uncomfortable laugh as we spot the gangplank to the ship. The former name— "Queen Mary IV"— rests as a shadow under the new moniker in bolder brighter lettering, "Queen Nalani," the name of the king's daughter, the ambassador's wife, and the princess's mother. The ship is massive with at least fifteen floors. Colt and I spent a month traveling up and down them.

The ship has been docked for a week now, so the hustle and bustle is minimal. I don't know if that is a good or bad thing. We hang back to watch for movement. The timing is critical. One wrong move and it's Plan C whether we like it or not.

A huge group of patrons following a guide cuts in front of us. The tour guide bellows, "Stay with our group. You are very fortunate to have been granted permission to tour this great ship, *The "Queen Nalani."* This ship leaves for America in three days. King Ahomana asks that you consider this a small payment for your support in the upcoming election. Search your hearts! Is it really better for the people to have a democracy? We can have a democracy any time, but King Ahomana should be making those choices for us. He will know the best plan of action. He is a brilliant king."

I shake my head and mouth, "Really" to Riley and Colt. I can't believe my ears. This is the king who wanted Colt and I executed. This is the king trying to kill the ambassador, his own son-in-law. The king and the Mercs want to have complete and total power over the world. Don't they see? Don't they know? How can anybody possibly believe these lies? But here they are seventy or so men and women, listening intently to this speech, savoring every word, as if it was the rarest chocolate they would ever have. No, worse than that, listening to his jargon as if it were completely true.

The man continues talking, "Thank you. The king appreciates your support. After our tour is completed he asks that any or all of you feel free to join him for a king's banquet in the great dining hall." He motions to the group. "Follow me."

"This is our chance." I scrunch behind the large collection of people being funneled to the thin gangplank. Riley and Colt follow suit and we all finagle our way to the middle of the crowd. I tell them we'll worry about security later if we need to.

A redheaded woman dressed in a blue blazer pushes up to me. "I can't believe they are crowding us in like this. Don't they know who we are?"

I nod, not wanting to say anything for fear of giving our deception away. She continues, "I love that Amsterdam sent you in the native dress. What a nice touch! Do you speak the Hollands?"

I don't have to answer, thank goodness, as she is pushed back behind me and I lose sight of her. Although I can speak the Hollands, a Dutch language mix between German and English, my dialect might not be what she is expecting. I move farther up in the front of the mob. No one else attempts a conversation. I glance at Colt and Riley moving on through. They seem to be more interested in getting out of the close quarters than talking.

My instincts are right. It's too large of a crowd. Security is more worried about upsetting the king than they are about making sure that everyone in the group belongs. We walk with the others as they herd us into the first floor. We use them as cover for the three of us to escape down the stairs. We take two stairs at a time until we reach the tenth floor. No time to notice the disrepair this time, or the differences between the upper and lower floors. I remember how the floors are so luxurious on the top and dwindle as we descend to the tenth floor. A floor we know well since it is where all of the Sponsored Companions are housed. It's the floor we spent most of our time on when we were on the ship before.

Colt says, "Let's stop here. We have three days before we sail."

I scrunch my face and look at him. "How do you know that?"

He smiles. "It was the only part of the speech I listened to."

"Let's see if we find any of the SCs." Riley pushes us down the corridor.

We round the corner. I come face to face with Suma, the female Sponsored Companion doll from Egypt. "Suma," I whisper.

Her eyes get wide. She faints.

Colt catches her. "So much for subtle entrances."

Chapter 9

"Good thing I remember how to open the door." Colt carries Suma down the hall. "Which is hers?"

I smile and point. "Good thing I remember which room is hers."

Riley pushes us forward. "Quit patting yourselves on the back. We need to get out of the hallway."

Colt waves Suma's wrist in front of the door lock. It opens. Naeem, her brother, stands as we invade his room. Riley covers his mouth before he has a chance to scream. "Remember Colt and Paisley?" He whispers.

Colt gently pats the back of Suma's hand as he delicately lays her on the bed. "Suma, Suma."

Suma wakes up with fear in her eyes for a quick moment before they fill with tears and she throws her arms around Colt's neck. She then reaches out for her brother and me. It's a few minutes before Suma releases any of us from her hug. I'm crying by this time.

Naeem plops on the edge of his bed and drops his head in his hands. "They told us you were dead. Said they killed you as an example for all of us."

I scoot in beside him. "Do we look dead?"

"No." He shakes his head. "I'm glad you're not, but why would they lie? What happened?"

Colt says, "They took us back to Paisley's farm and said we were to stay there for the rest of our lives, but the Undesirables tracked our horse and buggy. They've been with us ever since."

"We are still training for the war," I add. "We don't have many of the original adults. They're dying because they're sick and we don't have any medicines they need."

Suma sighs, "How sad. Who is taking care of them now that you're here?"

"We found some pockets of people who were with the resistance." Colt sits on the floor. "A couple headed back to the farm to help the children with their training."

Suma nods. "I'm so glad the children are alive. It worried me when they forced them to leave the ship."

"Do you ever see my Mom and Gretel?" I hate to be blunt, but Colt, Riley, and I need to find them and get off. We have three days to find them and plan our escape. Three days should give us time. Should be easy.

"They're still working in the same place. They're fine the times I've seen them. But they seem sad. Probably missing you, Paisley." She claps her hands. "We should go right now and surprise them, let them see you're alive!"

Riley overhears. "Be patient. I know you and Colt are anxious, but we have some time. Night might be a better cover. Let's wait."

Colt's shoulders droop. "Guess a few more hours won't hurt. We don't want to be caught."

I sigh, sharing his disappointment. "I'll try to wait, but it's going to be hard. I miss my family." I ask, "How's the princess?"

"Spoiled as ever." Suma laughs. "Miss Brita is still having a lot of trouble. She comes down in a wheelchair for the princess's lessons."

"Scoot." Riley pushes Colt over. "I want to sit too. What about the obstacle course and Lamar?"

Naeem lets out a long sigh. "The obstacle course was stopped because of Lamar. I heard the other day that he thought two of his Mercs had been killed. I think your name was one on the lists, Riley."

"Yes, that makes sense. I'm sure they thought we were killed on the trail." Riley crosses his arms. "Of course I am sure that Lamar's crying over the loss."

Naeem chuckles. "Not so much."

"The queen is bed-ridden." Suma leans around to talk directly to me. "She's having a difficult time with her pregnancy." She sits back. "The ambassador is worried about her, which is why we are heading back to America. There is supposed to be a doctor there who might be able to help her."

Colt stretches his legs out as much as he can. "A lot has changed."

Riley starts. "Then we found a castle where..."

I interrupt him. "Along the way we saw all kinds of castle ruins."

Riley shoots a confused frown my way. No time to explain to him now. We shouldn't share everything with these two. Some of these secrets could get them killed. I'm not sure if I'm telling myself that because I truly believe it or because the major betrayer last time was one of us SCs.

I have to ask, "How is Baako?"

The room goes silent for a minute. Suma is the first to speak. "He's been on the outside looking in. I think he thought when he turned us all in, he would get special treatment, but he hasn't. Lamar is still in charge and on a major power trip, killing for no reason. Scary times. We wonder if we can actually survive the travel to America." She averts her eyes. "Sometimes we talk among ourselves that you two were the lucky ones.

At least you were out of this."

"But that would mean we were dead, Suma." Colt laughs. "I think it's better that we are alive."

"That's true." Suma continues, "Adanna, Baako's sister, was saved because of him and cries all the time. I feel so sorry for her."

Naeem pulls at my triangular white hat. "Why are you dressed like this?" He waves his hand over at Riley. "Better yet, why is he dressed like a Sponsored Companion doll? Aren't you

a Merc?"

Colt pulls up his sleeve. "I'm the Merc now."

Colt, Riley, and I spend the next few minutes explaining

our plan to rescue my mom and sister, and then go back underground.

"You can't leave us here!" Suma buries her face in the bed cover and starts bawling. "You must stay and help us."

I shake my head. "Help you what?" I rub her hair. "I need to get my family off before they go to America and we can't find them."

Naeem folds his hands in front of his lap. "She wants you to stay to save the ambassador."

"The ambassador is still in danger?" I ask. "I thought he was heading back to America. Isn't he from there?"

"Miss Brita says they are holding his son hostage." Suma speaks through sobs. "They're going to kill his son in America if he doesn't do what the king says. It's so sad."

Naeem comforts his sister. "He has been so sad ever since you two left."

I know that I need to find my Mom and Gretel and save them. But I have to ask myself—can I really leave when my father is in danger if there is something I can do?

"We might be able to stay and help. Could we go to America?" I say before thinking.

Colt and Riley jump up at the same time. Colt towers over me. "What are you talking about?" He looks over to Naeem and Suma. "I mean, we would like to help, but you don't understand. Paisley and I are supposed to be at the farm, and Riley is a wanted Merc. We'll die if we stay. How would that help you?"

I need to be smart about how I phrase this. I can't force Colt or Riley to stay. In fact, if Colt and Riley would take Mom and Gretel back to the farm, then I could just stay and try to help my dad and save my brother. Even saying that inside my mind sounds crazy. What could I accomplish all by myself? Who could I trust to help me? The better question is who could I possibly help? Could I save my brother all by myself? Was it possible? Probably not. I sigh loudly, ready to give up.

"I'll stay with you." Riley hugs me. "I owe you that much."

I look at Riley, such a good person. He doesn't owe me anything, but him saying he'll stay with me makes my stomach flip. I take a deep breath and manage to muster a question. "Where would we stay?"

"With us of course!" Suma stands and hugs me. "You and I can sleep on the bed together, and Naeem can take his bed and Riley can have the floor." She grins. "See, it's settled. We have it all figured out."

Colt pulls my arm. "Except the part where we save Gretel and your mom."

I hug up to him. "I thought we'd help you get them off the ship, and then you could take them back to the farm. When Riley and I get back, we'll find you."

A knock at the door interrupts the conversation. Riley, Colt, and I cram into the small bathroom while Naeem opens the door. A mumbled conversation goes on for a few minutes. Then all is quiet.

Naeem carefully opens the door and the three of us roll out. "That was news from the captain. You need to make your move in the next two hours. That's when we leave for America."

I tap my foot trying to come up with a plan. We all start a plan with "What if..." but we do not complete our thought. I guess we are all having the same trouble. What can you really do with only two hours left?

"We can't possibly get out of here. It would take us that long to find them. We're stuck." Colt decides for us. "It'll be cramped, but I guess I'll sleep in the tub." Colt places his cheek on top of my head. "You get your wish. We're *all* off to America, where all your dreams come true."

Chapter 10

The ship's speaker booms, "Decks one through ten are invited to the top deck to wave your good-byes as we move the ship from the port out into open ocean for our transatlantic cruise."

I squeeze around Riley who is standing in the middle of the floor, or what little there is of it, in the small cabin. "I need you all to get out of the way. I need to go to the bathroom for a minute. It can't wait."

Sitting on the toilet, I hear them discuss how we can't go to the top. "You might be recognized. This is going to be a tricky ride, not much room in here—" Naeem says, "—very close quarters and a long trip."

I remember seeing the map of the world before, the world is big. We're going to be on this ship an uncomfortably long time. I open the door of the water closet and announce, "We need to try to find Mom and Gretel and at least let them know we're alive. I wouldn't want to have either of them bump into us not knowing. How horrible would it be for them? Plus, they would most likely blow our cover with their reaction. They need to know as soon as possible. Could one of you tell them?" I look at Naeem.

Naeem squirms his way to the door and motions for Suma. "We can try. Right now, we will go to the top deck. At least there is more room there."

"I'm not sure this is going to work." Colt pulls up his sleeve and looks at his Merc tattoo. "It has Riley's identifiers and besides it's not real. I guess since I'm already on the ship and as long as I don't get off, there should be no security checks for my tattoo. Or at least, I hope not."

Riley nods. "I've never been checked on the ship so you're probably fine."

Colt bops me on the forehead. "That means that I can walk around and scout out another safe place to stay."

Riley shifts his shoulders before maneuvering his way over to the bed and flopping down on it. "That's probably a good idea. Try the fifteenth floor."

"The old obstacle course floor?" Colt asks.

Riley stretches his legs out. "Yes, they haven't been using it and they rarely send any guards down there because that is where all of the Undesirables took refuge."

I smile, remembering the obstacle course and Mom and Gretel's visits. How we all worked together; the SCs, the Undesirables, the princess and her nanny, Miss Brita. Fun times! The princess was happy down there, we all were. Will we ever be happy again?

"Fifteenth floor, it is!" He stretches his arms over his head and hits the ceiling. "We have to find something or we'll kill each other on this trip."

Suma cracks the door open. "Just thought I'd let you know the ship's not leaving on time. They didn't have time to let everyone know. There is a large group of visitors touring the ship so we have to wait for all of them to disembark." She almost shuts the door before adding. "I'm going back up there, but it's a mess. Lots of people milling about."

"Chaos." Colt stretches his arms in front of his chest and knocks into a shelf protruding from the wall. "Sounds as if a Merc like me needs to do some reconnaissance." He opens the door slightly and peers out, before disappearing down the corridor.

I sit on the bed beside Riley. "Brother, looks like it's just me and you now." I tug at my apron and pull off the wooden shoes. "These are cute, but way too difficult to wear all of the time." I rub my feet. It feels good to stretch out my toes.

Riley scoots back on the bed using it as a chair. "What are we going to do for clothes? We can't keep wearing these."

"Wait a minute." I open the door and peer out into the corridor. "There are always clothes to be cleaned." The laundry cart with bags full of clothes from the SCs stands unguarded in the hall. Since one servant gathers the clothes before the other collects, the cart stands in the hall for a while. I grab a couple of bags and duck back in the room. "These clothes are not clean and the fit might be off. Let's hope not too much, but they will have to do. SCs wear a certain kind of clothes when they are not clothed in their native garb." I unclasp my hat, tossing it on the bed. "Like this." I pull out a shirt and pants for me and one for him.

"Shoes?" He pulls his off and lets them clatter to the floor. "You could use these shoes for weapons."

I laugh. I retreat to the bathroom to change. When I emerge, Riley is dressed in the casual clothes.

For the next few minutes, we wiggle our toes and sit without talking. I have to find Mom and Gretel soon. My mind wanders to the Ferris wheel and all its glory. A tear runs down my cheek as I think of the army of children I left behind. I only hope that Aunt Sandra's boys have found them. Sad to think that most of the adults that were once deemed Undesirables probably won't be there when I return. I'm traveling to the unknown, America, but remain strong in my conviction that I will return.

A knock at the door startles us both. "Paisley? Riley?" It's Colt. We crack the door just enough for Colt to squeeze in. "You were right about the fifteenth floor, Riley. I found us a place to hide."

"With more room, I hope." I say.

Riley pulls his legs up on the bed sitting as crossed-legged as possible. He looks very uncomfortable. "I'll have to fold myself in half to stay in here any longer with this many people. When can we go?" He leans over to retrieve his shoes and tumbles onto the floor. He hits his shoulder and grimaces. "We also need other shoes. Something needs to be done about these."

We change back into the Holland outfits, but we take the other clothes with us. It is a catch-22, if we wear the comfortable clothes with the clunky shoes we will stand out. We decide that it will be better for each of us to wear the whole outfit, wooden shoes and all.

There is actually an art to sneaking out, not looking like you're sneaking. The three of us try our best to master this.

Colt decides to make it a competition by sprinting down the stairs. Although he is out of sight, I hear him stomping. Riley and I keep up as much as we can while wearing wooden shoes.

Riley clotheslines me with his arm. "Wait." I fall with a thump and he sits beside me and holds a finger to his lips.

"Why?" I whisper.

"Listen."

I strain my ears and I hear voices. I recognize one as Colt. Oh no, he's been found. I whisper to Riley, "What do we do now?" Riley shrugs.

We don't have much time to wait. Colt walks slowly back up the stairs.

Riley and I stand. We see who is shoving him from behind. The SC who turned us in. The one who told all of our secrets. The main reason we were sentenced to die.

Baako, the betrayer.

Chapter 11

Riley jumps in front of me and reaches around Colt to slap Baako on the back. "Hi, Baako. So glad you joined us."

"Huh?" A stunned Baako lets go of Colt's collar. "Is that you, Riley?" Baako makes a scrunched-up face. "What kind of outfit are you wearing? You look like a girl." He points to Riley's feet. "Are those wooden?"

"You won't believe why I have to wear this get up!" Riley lifts his feet. "I can't believe I have to wear these awful shoes. Let me tell you..."

Baako interrupts, "What about these two?" He cuts his eyes at me and my stomach churns. I could knock him in the head and sleep fine tonight.

"Let's go where it's quiet." Riley pushes Baako back, gently guiding him down the stairs. "We can talk on floor thirteen."

Baako hesitates, but relents and goes in front. Riley turns to us for a moment and whispers "Follow my lead."

I shrug and Colt and I follow Riley. I have no idea where we are going or what we are doing, but we really don't have a choice. I think Riley may be going to kill Baako and with what Baako did to me, I'm not that unhappy about that prospect. Every time I see his face, it brings me back to that time we were set to free all of the enslaved Undesirables and Uncounteds, but Baako told the king of our plan. I feel my face flush with anger. I try to walk without shooting glances full of hate at Baako, but it is hard.

We finally arrive at Floor thirteen. Riley steps out into the corridor and walks to an open room. My heart races with anticipation and fear. I do hate Baako, but I'm not sure I can be a part of whatever Riley has in mind for him. Not sure at all.

We step into a storage room. Large cans of beans, tomatoes, and corn line the shelves on one side. The other side is stacked with boxes of tissue, paper towels, and toilet paper along with bottles of cleaning products.

Riley flips on the overhead bulb and closes the door behind us. He crosses his arms and stares at Baako. "They told you, didn't they?"

Baako looks at Colt and me. "Told me what?"

"I thought so." Riley places his hand on Baako's' shoulder. "I told them you could handle it."

"Handle what?" Baako shakes his head.

Riley crooks his finger, drawing Baako in closer and says in a low voice, "Colt, Paisley, and I have been on a secret mission since..." Riley stops talking and looks at Colt. "How long it's been Colt?"

Colt hesitates then says, "A long time. I can't remember now."

Riley smiles. "That's right. See how long it's been. Not even Colt can remember when it started. What about you Paisley, do you remember when we were recruited?"

I shake my head. I guess Riley is doing a good con job because Baako is wide-eyed and listening intently following every word. It's sad. He's so gullible. No wonder the king and his goons were able to get Baako to tattle on us. He is so naïve he doesn't know when people are telling him the truth or when they are making up a whopper of a lie. Right now, it's the whopper variety.

"What kind of mission?" Baako breathes in.

Yes, he's hooked. Riley spins an intricate story about how, when he was collecting the harvest at the farms, Colt and I were his secret contacts. We had been placed there as spies to report. For all these years, Riley has always been our contact. When the farms were disbanded, Colt and I were brought back on the ship to infiltrate the Undesirables and the Uncounteds. We had planned to tell the king about the escape plot, but Baako beat us to it.

"Hold it!" Baako stops him and stares at both of us. He crosses his arms defiantly.

For a moment, I think we might have to kill him after all. Then he asks, "Why should I believe you?"

I know the answer to this one—an answer that he'll believe. "Because we're alive. The king made a big thing about killing us. You saw that. Don't you remember the whole *I'm going to execute you two and save the rest?*"

Baako looks up as if he is trying to conjure up that memory. "That's right."

It scares me how good of a liar I am becoming.

Colt joins in. "Why would he leave us alive if we weren't telling the truth?"

I hold my breath. Will Baako believe this whole made up story? It doesn't take long.

He drums his fingers on his lips. "What's your new mission?"

I shouldn't hate Baako, I should feel sorry for him. He thought he was doing what was best for his family. He really doesn't know what's going on. With all the unrest in the world, it behooves people to know whom they can trust and whom they can't, and when someone is lying. Poor Baako's so dumb, he can't tell the difference

Between the three of us we convince him that Riley and I are disguised as living dolls (SCs), representing Holland to spy on the SCs and make sure the princess is protected. How Colt is now pretending to be a Merc so he can protect the two major and very secret, special relatives of the king, who we describe differently, but who are in fact, my mom and Gretel. I threw that part of the story in. It would give Colt a reason to spend time with Gretel; it would give them some protections while we made the transatlantic trip.

"We have to hide while we're here, Baako, so we'll be living on the fifteenth floor." Riley concludes the pack of lies.

Baako shakes Riley's hand and then mine and Colt's. "Is there anything I can do to help you?"

I pipe up. "It would be easier if you could bring our food every day then we wouldn't have to sneak around."

Baako salutes. "Just have to clear it with Lamar."

"No!" Riley shouts. "Lamar can't know! Remember, he was the one who thought you couldn't handle it." Baako nods, then Riley continues, "Besides, just think when we complete our mission and we tell Lamar how much you helped us and..." He salutes Baako in an exaggerated move. "I wouldn't be surprised if you didn't get a promotion out of this."

Baako puffs out his chest. "You really think so?"

We all nod. Baako slaps his knee. "I'll do it. You three just go down to the fifteenth floor and *do not worry* about a thing. I'll make sure you get three squares a day. A promotion?" He grins. "Anything else you need?"

A wry smile crosses Riley's face. "Shoes."

Chapter 12

Baako trots off. I guess to find shoes.

It's funny, seeing him run off so giddy and happy. It's difficult to wait for him to get out of sight before we look at each other and break out in a laugh.

We need to get back on track. Enough of this playing around. "Let's go find Mom and Gretel." I am afraid to wait any longer.

Riley gathers his composure. "With the chaos of everyone trying to get the people on and off the ship, this might be the perfect time to find them." He points to a waiter who rushes by. "Everyone is busy and no one's paying attention.

Colt claps his hands together. "Gretel. You don't have to ask me twice. Let's go, but to the lab first."

I'm okay with seeing Gretel first, if it makes Colt happy. I have to see my family. Now.

The lab is easy to find with Riley's help. We decide to send Colt in first since he is dressed as the Merc.

It's been a half an hour. I'm patiently waiting, but Riley paces back and forth. "What's he doing in there?"

"How would I know?" I crack the door open to peer in.

The door flies open and bonks me in the face. Gretel rushes out, her face lit up like a child seeing her first Christmas tree or the first time I saw the Ferris wheel lit up. She grabs me. "Colt just told me you were out here! He and I've been sitting in there talking—well doing other things too." She flushes. "Never mind. You don't need to know about that." She throws her arms around me. "But I'm sorry I didn't come out right away." She backs off, as Colt comes through the door. She smacks Colt hard in the face. "I can't believe my sister has been out here the whole time and you didn't tell me." She whacks him one more time in the arm before pulling me into a hug again. "Paisley! We thought you were dead!" Tears stream down her face. "Come in, you two." She moves through the open door into the room.

Colt must have had a good visit. He has a grin on his face reminiscent of a cat with a gut filled with an angler's load of trout. "She couldn't wait a minute longer."

Riley, Colt, Gretel, and I enter the lab. We fill Gretel in about what happened after we left.

"The ambassador's perfected the cure." Gretel smiles. "I like the fact

228

that I helped. It was all with your blood, Paisley."

Colt slaps me on the back. "Glad you have that *special* blood."

Riley shoots his eyes toward me and blinks in a strange way. "She is special in every way." After that comment, he blushes.

Him turning red makes me feel funny. My stomach flip-flops. "Special for getting into trouble." I shift uncomfortably.

Gretel hugs me again tightly. "I wouldn't have it any other way. Enough of this talk."

I love my sister. I especially love her when she reads my mood and knows it is time for her to intervene. At times like this, when she covers for me to make me comfortable in an uncomfortable situation, I love her even more.

The ambassador breaks through the door. He spies me and his face turns ashen. "Paisley? What are you doing here? Being on this ship puts you in great danger." He looks over at Colt. "Both of you."

I stand up and fight the urge to hug my *real* father. No one else knows our secret. "We had to come back. We appreciate you saving us, Ambassador Grayson." It sounds formal, but I'm trying not to give the connection away. "I heard that it was my blood that you used for the cure." The ambassador doesn't say anything so I add, "Don't you want to talk to me about my blood?"

He looks confused for a moment, and then plays along. "Yes, if you could come this way." He glances at Gretel and the boys. "I'll bring her back in a minute. I might need another sample of her blood."

Riley hovers protectively. "You're not going to hurt her, are you?"

Gretel slaps at Riley. "Of course he's not." Riley sits down and the ambassador and I move toward the back of the lab.

When we are safely out of their sight, he pulls me into a hug and kisses my cheek. "Why did you leave the farm? You were safe there." He pushes me out and stares at me as he releases the hug. "You have no idea what I went through to assure your safety."

"I understand, but when I found out the ship was going to America..." I stop, hearing other voices.

He puts his fingers to his lips. "This way."

We walk down a corridor and enter a secluded area. It's an indoor office. The back of the area is stacked with books and has a porthole looking out to the ocean; two of the walls are half-full of marked charts with bookshelves full of books lining the bottom half. The inside wall is made up of the entrance, a door on one side and the other half of the wall is part wall and part windows with opened blinds. The office is full of papers strewn about in no logical organizational pattern. Two rolling

229

chairs are stacked high.

This looks just like him. Brilliant, but unorganized. He is an exceptional scientist, but probably the only person in the world who understands how his own mind works. I can see a small part of that in me. It makes me smile that a part of my father has found its way into me though we weren't together during my childhood years. He peers out of the inside windows. He closes the blinds and shuts the door. "We won't be disturbed in here."

"How did you find out about America? Have you been leaving the farm?" He asks. "Sit." He points to a rolling chair. "Might need to move a few things."

I roll the lab chair toward me. "We had people going out to scout the newspapers and media so we could keep up with what was going on."

He picks up the papers off the stool and moves them to yet another pile on the counter. "Who else was with you on the farm?"

"The Undesirables. They followed our horse and buggy." I stop for a moment and sit. "I think their plan was to save us. So sweet." I sigh, thinking about our army of children back on the farm. It makes me both happy and sad at the same time.

"I cannot protect you on this ship." He empties his chair and sits. It is noisy, rolling across the plastic guard on the floor. He moves beside me and grabs my hand.

I jerk my hand out of his. "I'm not asking you to." My face flushes. Why does everyone think I have to have someone to watch over me? Colt, Riley and now my father.

"I didn't mean to make you angry." He leans back. "I'm just worried."

I stand and pick up an empty test tube from the counter and roll it in my hands. "You should be the one worried. I heard rumor that they have my brother, my real brother, your son, held hostage so you will do what the king wants." I stop, watching him to get a glimmer of a reaction so I'll know if it's the truth. The ambassador flinches.

I shout, "So it's true!"

He stands up and takes the test tube out of my hand motioning for me to sit back down, which I do. He takes a deep breath. "Yes."

I jump up again. "We need..."

He pulls me back down into the chair. "No, you don't *need* to do anything. You *need* to keep out of sight until we get to Orlando. I can't help you on the ship, but I can do a lot for you in America. I'll help your brother too. Hide until then. I have a plan."

I start to ask him about this plan, but there will be plenty of time for that. I want to know other things. "You never told me his name."

230

He frowns. "Whose name?"

I let out a frustrated gasp. "My brother."

He smiles. "Your brother's name is Oliver."

"Is my name really Paisley?" I ask.

He takes my hand in his. "It is now, but you were born with the name Penelope. Your mother was a big fan of *The Odyssey*."

I smile and sit back with a big sigh, causing the chair to roll. There is something about knowing my real name, even though I'll never use it.

"What was my mother like?"

"She was one of a kind. You are like her in many ways. She was always the first to fight for what she thought was right." His eyes gleam. "She was a brilliant scientist in her own right."

"She was?"

He pats my hair. "Yes, you probably have inherited her brains. I know your brother has. He is young, but he is a genius with communications. They have him working to restore all of the communications for the world. He is the expert in that field and he's only fourteen." He sighs and taps my head. "Of course, I know that if you'd been given the schooling your brother had been given all throughout your life you would probably have been working right by his side." He smiles. "It makes me smile to think of my children working together on something. Your mother took care of us. She was the heart of our family. I see a lot of her in you, especially your eyes. You have the same eyes."

It's nice to know that about my mother and realize we share the same color eyes, but it also makes me realize that she was just my birth mother. Without her, I wouldn't be here, but my mother and my sister are my real family. I must always remember that.

My father and I talk about what my mother was like and life on the military base and a little about America. It all sounds wonderful, but of course, the stories were all from before the virus. He is so animated, reliving the stories I realize how much life has been sucked out of him by these piranhas he calls family now. His wife, the queen and her father, the king.

"Did you get enough of her blood?" Riley calls out.

"I think you have a bodyguard." My father opens a cabinet and pulls out a sticky bandage and puts it across the inside crook of my elbow. "For show."

I press the edges of the bandage down. "In here."

I hug my father one last time before I depart.

We decide to give Colt a few alone minutes with Gretel to say a proper good-bye. I have to admit I've never seen my sister so happy. Her eyes glisten when she looks at Colt. Love is written all over her. I think it's great that in the midst of all of this turmoil and death the two of them have found each other. It makes me hopeful that one day I will find my own Colt.

As we exit, I look over at Colt. "Now, onto Mom?"

He nods.

Once again, Riley is able to maneuver throughout the passages with ease and finds the short cut to the kitchen. In order to reach the kitchen we have to travel to the top deck. People are scurrying about. The ship hasn't left port yet, but most of the ship's inhabitants seem to be on the top deck. The elite leisurely stroll the deck occasionally barking orders at the servants as they scurry about trying to obey or anticipate the ones in charge's every whim. Not knowing how much time we have before the ship leaves, we try to hurry.

Finally, we walk into the kitchen. It's chaos. Cooks are emptying trays of food and pulling baking sheets out of the oven. We travel through the entire kitchen and at first, no one takes any kind of notice of us.

I spy my mother frosting a cake. "Mom!"

Mom turns and drops the spatula she is holding. It clangs to the floor. People fall silent for a moment before returning to their chores. She bursts into tears and grabs me. "Oh Paisley! I just knew you weren't dead. I could feel it. I would know if you were dead. I'm so glad. Oh, Paisley!"

Our crying and hugging garner the attention of a couple of workers, who are basting a turkey on the counter next to Mom. One of the workers chastises, "You need to be quiet. We have work to do."

Mom pushes us toward the back door and swings it open. "In here. There will be a little more privacy. No one is in here right now. This is clean up."

"I missed you, Mom." We spend the next few minutes telling her about how we planned to get her and Gretel off, but how we didn't have time because the ship is leaving early.

"Now we're stuck going to America with you and Gretel."

She hugs me again. "Together, but you'd better make sure that you don't run into the royals or any of the Mercs that know you two or Riley. Be careful."

"I promise." I hug her again. "We will be on the fifteenth floor."

I don't want to leave her. My heart is filled. I'm home. Home is here.

I memorize my mother's smile as we take off out the doors.

By the time we get back to the fifteenth floor, we can feel the ship's movement and the scurrying is down to a minimum, sure signs that we are on our way across the Atlantic Ocean heading to America. I don't know if that's a good thing or a bad thing.

Riley laughs as we shut the door behind us. Sitting in the middle of the floor are two pairs of camel colored leather everyday shoes, one for me and one for Riley.

Baako came through.

Chapter 13

Ten days is a long time to hide on a ship, but we try to make the best of it. It only takes one day for Riley and me to figure out the schedule. We have six hours in the daytime when most of the SCs are busy with their child owners. It seems that the rich like to laze around in the morning. We have not run across one of the royals or any of the Mercs in the early hours. The Mercs must stay up late keeping order when the wealthy are awake. I love it. Special moments for ourselves. We use this time to gather food, visit Gretel in the lab, and Mom in the kitchen. I even find a few minutes every day to sit and have a coffee with my father.

Riley and I are thrown together daily because of our Dutch SC status. It makes it more believable if we travel as one unit. I haven't been alone with Riley this much and I enjoy it. So much of my life has been bringing in harvest. Now that I've experienced it, playing is an activity that I look forward to.

"How about a game of shuffleboard?" He says one morning. I had never heard of shuffleboard before this trip, but here we are playing it daily and quite competitively too. Riley wins handily at first, but I catch on later, even beating him a few times. We work out in the gym. It seems silly to me since I have always gotten all of my exercise doing chores on the farm, but I go anyway, enjoying the treadmill the most. Laughing at the idea that I need a machine to help me run. We play a few games in the bowling alley and the crazy golf course.

"Stole you something today." Riley holds up a piece of cloth no larger than my arm.

I grab the blue polka-dotted fabric out of his hand. "What is it, a hat?"

He holds up a pair of underwear looking things. "No, it's a bathing suit. I got one too."

I frown. "Why do I need a bathing suit? Are we going to swim to America?"

He points to a closet door labeled "Women." "No silly, we're going to swim in a pool. Go in there and change." He hands over a white piece of meshy fabric. "This is called a cover-up. Put it over your suit. There is a heated pool on the third deck."

I shrug, holding up the suit and cover up. I'm not really sold, but I am willing to try.

I emerge in a few minutes, tugging the meshy white shirt over the bathing suit. I feel naked. Riley stands there in the swim trunks and shirt. I look away. The sight of him tingles something strange inside of me. Maybe it's because we've spent so much time together, but the thought of not seeing Riley every day makes me sad. Not seeing him would be as if a piece of me wasn't here. I try to concentrate on something else. Like his feet. Thanks goodness he's wearing his other shoes. The wooden ones I am wearing look ridiculous with the swimsuit. I smile when he hands me regular ones. He thinks of everything.

We travel to the third floor and I follow as he leads me into a large enclosed room with an inviting pool. The water is the most beautiful turquoise. It is like a large tub and the water is just as warm. The swim is wonderful. There are no other people there.

"Our own private island," he says.

I continue with the fantasy. "We are rich and off for our exotic getaway at the island of..."

"Paisley and Riley," he finishes.

I giggle. "Not very original, but okay—the Island of Paisley and Riley. I like it that you put my name first."

"I always put you first." His eyes gleam.

I jump in the water. What he said makes me happy and uncomfortable all at the same time.

Colt has the run of the ship, as long as he stays out of Lamar's view. It's nice how Baako is helping with this. Baako has completely bought into being one of the king's secret spies. He warns us when Lamar is close, and checks on Mom and Gretel daily since he thinks they are long lost relatives of the king and royalty in their own right. We had to fill Mom and Gretel in on it, since the first time he saw Gretel, he bowed.

"Don't bow," I told him. "You'll get them killed by the royals' enemies." Every day he brings Mom and Gretel extras such as food that he confiscates from the royals.

Between what news Colt gets and Baako slipping us information, we keep apprised of the daily happenings in the outside world. It is that knowledge that is the most disturbing. We read stories of the dissidents and their raids on harvest stockpiles and the growing unpopularity of democracy. There is a strict censorship on the news. A powerful machine spins every story to sway the populace the king's way. The ambassador *may not* be safe on the ship. I don't know why I have such a bad feeling about that, but I fear for my father's life.

Day four, I meet with my father for our daily coffee in his office.

"I think your brother Oliver is being held at what used to be a theme park in Orlando," my father confides. "That is where I will head first when the ship docks. I want you to come with me. I have a group of supporters who will hide both you and him until the election is over."

"What about you?" I take a sip of coffee.

He picks up a square of sugar. "Sugar?"

He knows I cannot resist sugar. I slide my cup over for him to drop in the cube, which begins to dissolve as soon as it hits the coffee. "I can't go and walk out on Colt, Riley, and my family. Not even for my brother." I ask again, "What about you?"

He stirs his coffee and leans back. "I can't abandon the cause especially since my wife is pregnant." He pauses. "I will just be able to work better knowing my children are safe."

"We aren't your only children."

He takes a sip and then sets the coffee cup on the table. "I know, but the princess is being taken care of and the queen is not due for months."

"How is the queen?"

He picks the coffee back up. "She's having a difficult time. I am afraid the virus medication that I gave her early in the pregnancy—the same virus inoculation that I gave you as a child and your mother when she was pregnant with your brother—has had an adverse effect on her." He holds his coffee chin high, not drinking. "I didn't realize that because she already had the immunity, from eating the herbs on her island, that it would make her so sick."

I pat his knee. "You couldn't have known."

"True." He drinks. "Tests show that the baby is fine."

"Do you know what it is—boy or girl?"

"Boy." He smiles. "I will have two of each. You, your brother, now the princess, and this little one. You have a big family, Paisley."

It is a big secret family, one that I cannot reveal for fear of death. I feel sorry for my father, caught in the middle of this war, and in the middle of two families. Of course, I can identify because I have three families now. The one I was born to, my father, my brother, and my half-sister—the one I grew up with, Gretel and my mom—and the family that isn't related but has become my family, Colt, Riley, and the army of children at our Ferris wheel farm. For someone who grew up so alone, the space in my world has suddenly filled up. Not sure if that is a good thing or not.

236

Chapter 14

Days five through nine on the ship are uneventful. Day ten, land is sighted. That morning, we go through the same schedule. Riley and I wait until mid-morning, while Colt goes out early in his Merc outfit to scout the ship.

Riley and I are still in the room when Colt returns. "Something's going on in the lab."

"Gretel?" I ask. "Is anything wrong with Gretel?" I start for the door. "What about the ambassador?"

Colt grabs my arm to stop me from leaving. "It doesn't seem to have anything to do with Gretel. They had a crew in there taking all of the ambassador's stuff."

"What stuff?" I ask.

Colt searches for words. "You know, his papers, files, test tubes."

Riley leans up against the wall with his hand. "Was the ambassador there? The king? Lamar?"

Colt presses his head between his hands. "Wait a minute. Too many questions." He takes a big breath. "Lamar wasn't there. The king wasn't either. There was some talk about the cure and the virus. All I can tell you is that the ambassador was going ape-crazy and yelling that he would never try to hurt his own child or his wife."

I cross my arms. "They think he did something to his pregnant wife?" I look at Riley. "That's crazy!"

Riley nods. "It's possible the king is beginning a case to discredit him before we land in America. It would make sense that they would want an article that paints him in an unfavorable light. They want to hurt his credibility. They want to discredit him. I heard the king is worried. The ambassador is too popular in America and now he's gaining popularity in Europe. That's dangerous for anyone who does not want democracy."

"Stop for a minute and answer my question." I jerk up. "Tell me. Who said he hurt his wife?"

"It doesn't matter." Colt interrupts, "I'm worried about Gretel." He opens the outside door. "I'm going to the lab. You two worry about the politics."

I watch Colt leave and then turn my attention to Riley. "Should we go to the lab?"

Riley says, "No, not with the Mercs there. Colt will make sure they are okay. Let's wait until it's all clear. And I really don't know who said the ambassador hurt his wife."

"Thanks. Promise that we'll check on everyone later."

Riley nods.

I am worried too. Although the one thing I shouldn't worry about is Gretel with Colt checking on her. That's a better job for someone pretending to be a Merc than for me or Riley pretending to be SCs.

"I don't want to stay here." I ask, "Where can we go?"

Riley shrugs. "We're all packed here. I guess we can walk the decks and see if we can figure out exactly when the ship is going to dock. After we know everyone is fine, are we going to try to get off, or lay low while we are at the dock?"

"I'm not sure. I guess we can walk up there and see what's going on. Want to?" I ask.

"Sure, why not?" Riley opens the outside door. "It won't hurt anything. And to make certain, we can dress in these adorable outfits." He pulls out his Holland garb. "I'll even wear the shoes just to make sure we are covered if we get spotted."

He pulls on the wooden shoes.

I smile. "You can always use them as weapons."

After changing, we take our time ascending. The top deck is a bustle of movements. Waiters balance trays full of drinks on their hands, offering beverages to the elegantly clothed patrons, while other waiters fill their trays with empty glasses.

"Over here." Riley pulls a couple of chairs to the side. "I think we can sit here incognito."

I look around. "We might not be able to see anything." I smile, sit, and crouch to peer through the gates. "If I scrunch down, I can see everything that happens."

"You let me know if you see something interesting." Riley sits and stretches his legs in front of him, kicking off the wooden shoes. "I'm going to enjoy the fresh air. Don't you miss the outdoors?" He rubs his feet. "We've been inside the belly of this ship way too long." He takes a deep breath. "Fresh air, I miss fresh air."

"You're right!" I lean back and take in a deep breath. "It's great!"

He grabs my hand. "We can pretend we are a wealthy couple. Here on our…" He winks at me. "Our honeymoon."

I laugh. Normally, I might have knocked him in the arm or said no, but somehow it doesn't bother me that he mentioned honeymoon and me in the same sentence. I remember when I first met him, he seemed so skinny. I don't know if it's because he's grown up a little or…I guess I don't know what it is, but he seems so handsome now.

I hold his hand. We sit there for a while. It's nice.

"I don't understand why I am going to jail. What's going to happen to all of my research?" The ambassador's voice booms from below. "That research is important! Don't you understand?"

I peer over the edge to the scene unfolding below. Four Mercs surround the ambassador. The king stands in front of him and bellows, "My daughter is ill. You have given her medicine that made her sick. I'm not sure you didn't do that on purpose."

"I didn't!" The ambassador pushes his glasses up on his nose. "Why would I hurt my own wife? My unborn baby boy?"

The king waves his scepter in a dismissive way. "I don't care what you say; she is sick and until she is well you will be incarcerated. You'll be transported to jail as soon as we land in America."

The ambassador holds his palms together. "Please let me out. I have to present to the members of the Consortium of the World. I have to argue for democracy. I have to let them know that I have found a cure for the virus and that I plan to give it to every man, woman and child for free." He bows to the king. "These things are important. Our world will be better when I do this. Please my king, I must finish my mission. I've sacrificed so much."

The king jerks his scepter and slams it into the ambassador's chest. "You have sacrificed nothing. You have lived like a wealthy man. I have given you my only daughter as your wife. You have gotten a state-of-the-art lab. I have given you everything you want." He clenches the edges of his robe in his hands. "How do you repay me? You make my daughter ill and you refuse to give me the formula to your new vaccination even though it is my wealth and power that made it possible." The king slams down his scepter. "You want to give everything away. You want my daughter and me and even *your* daughter to live like paupers. I will not allow that to happen." He presses the scepter into the ambassador's chest. "Don't you forget who is king. Ambassador Grayson, you are hereby placed under arrest. You will be transferred to a prison cell when we port. That is all."

I jump up from my hiding place, leaving Riley sitting. "No, you can't!"

Everyone stops and looks at me. I peer up at Riley, who makes a move to follow me. I shake my head slightly, begging him not to move. I realize too late, I have made a bad mistake. My only hope is that Colt and Riley won't be caught so there is someone out there who might be able to rescue me from my own idiot reactions.

"Help," I whisper to myself. I clutch my bullet clover necklace. "Find me a way out of this."

The king's eyes train on me.

Chapter 15

The king walks around me. My father holds his breath. I hold mine. I expect Riley is holding his breath too.

The king stops in front of me. "You look familiar. Do I know you?"

I try to disguise my voice by speaking Dutch while keeping my words to a minimum. "No."

The king's eyes narrow. "I've met you before. Just can't think of where."

It's not a question so I don't answer.

The king shakes his head. No way out of this or at least no scenarios that I play in my head that end with me and my father being released unharmed. I don't think my father has breathed a complete breath since I found my way down here.

King Ahomana says, "Why do you care about what I do with the ambassador?"

I shrug, trying to buy time to come up with a good answer. What would make sense? Absolutely nothing comes in my mind.

I open my mouth to spew some kind of nonsense I hope that the king won't be able to understand when I hear a voice from behind me shout. "*Her*, that girl. She can tell you about me."

I turn. Standing in all of her glory is the woman who talked to me when I sneaked onto the ship with her group. I try to recall what we discussed as we squeezed in during the tour. I can't remember.

"What do you need me to tell them?" I ask her in my best Dutch accent.

She says, "She's the Holland representative. The tour..." She pauses looking to me to fill in the name of the tour.

I don't know the name of the tour so I fake it with nonsense talk. "Yes, we were on our way with our guide and he was telling us about all the wonderful things about the king and..." I run out of things to say. I can only hope that the king's vanity will kick in and he won't look too closely at me.

The navy blue suited woman completes my sentence, "Then the ship started moving and we were caught on it with no security papers or anything. Right, dearie?"

I nod. "Yes that's right and we've been..." I wait again for her to fill it in. Might as well let her. She's doing a great job. If the king buys all this bull.

"Yes, we've been or at least *I* have been, at the mercy of kind servants ever since. What about you, dear? How did you make it for these ten days?" The woman asks.

"Same as you," I lie.

King Ahomana waves his scepter. "Enough of this nonsense. Both of you leave my sight. Your chatter bores me." He glares at me. "You will not interrupt your king again. Do you understand?"

I bow and back away. I finally hear my father let a breath go and begin to breathe regularly. The only thing I accomplished was not being thrown in jail along with my father. But what can I do to help him? I'll ask Riley. Maybe between the two of us we can come up with a plan.

I separate quickly from the suited woman to make sure she doesn't continue our conversation and waste no time making my way back to the deck. Riley jerks me down beside him by one arm in the hiding place and hugs me. "Quit doing stuff like that! You're going to get yourself killed."

Tears flow. Guess I was more scared than I thought. I bury my head in his shoulder. I must look like an idiot, tightly crouched in an almost fetal position bawling my eyes out. "Sorry," I mumble.

He rubs my hair. "Some of us would miss you if you got thrown in jail." He lifts my chin and forces a soft chuckle. "You wouldn't be there long though. You'd talk someone into freeing you."

I dry my tears. "I would, wouldn't I?"

He nods.

I peer over just in time to see the Mercs haul off my father. "What *are* we going to do about the ambassador?"

"Not sure there's much we can do." Riley shrugs. "We could get off the ship and try to find out where they are holding him, but that is a dangerous choice." He stands up. "How would we ever get back on the ship? You *do* want to return to Bavaria, right?"

He pulls me to my feet and I stand beside him. "Of course, it's just…"

Riley knocks into me with his shoulder. "You want to save them all." He reaches his arm around my waist. "It's one of your best traits."

Riley likes some of my traits. I smile. His arm around my waist makes me all tingling inside. Before, I felt the same about Colt and Riley, like they were my brothers. Now it's different; if this were a race, Riley would win.

He moves his arm. "We'd better go below before we *really* do get caught."

I rest my elbows on the railing. "Just a while longer. Look, you can see land. We should dock soon. Can't we stay up here and at least *see* America even if we're not going to be able to touch it?"

He slips his arm back around my waist. "Guess it can't hurt anything."

It takes about an hour to get close enough to make out anything but outlines. I try to imagine what I think this world looked like before the twelve years of deterioration. I cradle my hand over my eyes like a sailor I once saw in a picture. I try to look as far as I can see. No hills, mountains, or rises of any sort. Seems strange that they can actually call this land, since it is so flat. The only protrusions are buildings taking the place of mountains, clumped together densely and standing proudly. I read somewhere that this once was a bustling metropolis of people, art, and business. The skyline is now consigned to serve as a reminder of how desolate, quarantined, and sad our world has become. I think of our army of children waiting patiently back home on the farm. Standing erect and ready to pounce on this new world, fighting, scratching and clawing, whatever it takes to mold the future into something they can be proud of.

It takes about fifteen minutes for the ship to maneuver for docking. The crew shouts orders to each other. I am amazed at how well they work together to bring the magnificent beast to a standstill.

Riley and I are quiet for a while. I enjoy standing with his arm around my waist. Makes me feel normal. Like two friends on a cruise, waiting to disembark. How funny! Nothing farther from the truth.

It's a few more minutes before they lower the gangplank. I'm jealous. I wish I could get off the ship. I want to see America. I long to travel to Orlando, where all your dreams come true. How awful to get this close yet not be able to get off the ship.

I sigh. It hurts to watch. I pull away from Riley's arm. I stand knowing I need to make my way down the stairs, but for some reason I am unable to move.

After a few more moments, my senses return and I ask, "Riley, you ready?"

His eyes are sunken and sad. "I guess we really should go find Colt. He might have been looking for us."

"That's true." I haven't thought of Colt all morning, or Mom, or Gretel, or even Baako. The ambassador's fate has been the only thing on my mind.

A few workers leave the ship first. A couple of minutes later, I see my father being led away by a group of Mercs. I assume he is being taken to jail. Will I ever see him again? That thought blows through my mind and for a moment, the loss makes me sadder than I have ever been in my life. Why do they feel the need to surround him with such burly men? What's he going to do, run away? I watch, unable to move. He is taken to a waiting car, shoved in, and the car disappears from my sight.

It must have been my distress that made me let my guard down and not be aware of my surroundings. After ten days hiding on the ship, I turn and face the one person who could blow my cover to smithereens.

The princess.

Chapter 16

"Miss Paisley! Miss Paisley!" The four-year-old breaks from her companion's grip and dashes toward me. What can I do? Absolutely nothing. If this is my last act, I'll make it a good one. She's my sister, even if she doesn't know it. I reach down and hug her tight. My cover is totally blown now. I let out a long sigh; one of resolution.

I grit my teeth and plant my feet. I know in my heart one thing and that is that I do not give up. Ever!

I shoot Riley a quick look and mouth, "Stay. Don't follow me." I pull off the wooden shoes, hug them to my body, and take off running.

The princess thinks it's a game. She trails behind me. "I run too!" She yells, giggling. "Wait, Miss Paisley! Wait for me!"

In a flash, we are surrounded by Mercs. Fortunately for me, the princess's safety is more important than my escape. While the princess unknowingly runs block for me, I safely sprint across the plank onto the American shore.

What now? I have no idea. I'm completely alone. I dash across the shipyard, dodging the myriad of workers. I use them as cover, occasionally glancing back over my shoulder, half-expecting to see a Merc hot on my trail. None, so far. I sprint, no idea who is chasing me, or what I am running to, gasping for breath.

I heave, fall to my knees, and throw up breakfast. I look for cover. I'm still clinging to the wooden shoes. I might need them later and I don't want to leave any clues behind.

There are many structures. I choose one. There is a large rolling door at the entrance and I push it up just enough for me to roll under before sliding it back closed. I hope this will give me a few minutes to hide. Basically, the building is a huge roof over water. Boats are tied up with wood docks surrounding them. A few large water vessels hang from the rafters tied up and forgotten. It makes me think of a graveyard. A graveyard for boats that were once used for fun and now dust covers their once pristine hulls, who knows maybe their owners didn't survive the outbreak. There is a walkway in the middle of the dock with stairs leading to an office. A boat covered with a shiny yellow tarp catches my eye—it's big like a yacht. It's hoisted and tied up to the top of the roof, impossible to get to on foot. The good thing about it is it seems unreachable. That's the kind of hiding place I need. If I can figure a way on the hoisted yacht and use the tarp as covering, I might have a fighting chance. I know that shouldn't be a good thing, but it is. I will have to be creative in order to heave myself on board. It's so high, maybe no one will think to search there. I look around for other options. None comes to mind.

The first hurdle is to reach it. A rope, all I need is a rope. I search through some boxes on the dock—no luck.

A little higher starting point might give me more of an opportunity to pull myself up to it. I need a rope. I climb the stairs to the office, scanning the large shelter. No sign of a rope. So much for that idea. I wonder if I can jump it. I back up. No. It's impossible. I don't have enough space to get a running start. I run down a couple of stairs and hear shouting. The Mercs are closing in. No way out! I have to hide now!

I turn the knob on the office door. It's unlocked. Finally, a break! I examine my surroundings and quickly locate a box large enough for me to crouch in. They'll most likely search it, but what choice did I have? I open the latched lid and there sits the most beautiful sight I've ever seen. A rope. I sling it over my shoulder and shut the lid. I glance around, making sure I haven't disturbed anything in the room.

I knot the end of the rope and throw it like a lasso around a beam in the ceiling. The shouts get louder. First try, I miss. Oh no! I throw it again. It falls back down to me! I toss it as hard as I can. Almost! I will be able to think of that *almost* while I'm sitting in jail. Desperate, I heave it again. It hangs for a moment, but falls again! I hear the Mercs right outside the door. I'm running out of time. I toss the rope as hard as I can and at last, it catches. I take my time inching the rope up so it will come down the other side. Finally, I get both sides of the rope together. I tie the ends together. I shimmy up the rope. It reminds me of scaling my Ferris wheel's prong. I make my way to the edge of the yacht's cover. I hold onto the edge making sure I have a hold of the boat and not just the yellow covering. I heave myself up. The entry door begins to slide open. I untie the rope quickly and drag it to me. I lift the cover and slide in the rope. I flatten myself inside the boat. I haul the tarp over me. I hear the access door thump signaling that it is fully open.

I hold my breath. Booted footsteps thud.

A voice yells, "Any sign of her? Search the office!"

Another voice asks, "What about the boats?"

The first voice answers, "Search them all!"

My heart sinks. I hear covers being thrown off. Metal clangs. I shut my eyes and try to imagine how strewn the boat shed is now. I clutch my four-leaf clover necklace hoping to compel its luck to me now. I roll my head to the side and force myself to focus on something, anything. I spot a blue stuffed toy. It looks like the whales I've seen pictures of in books.

Maybe this was a child's toy. Might have been left on from before the virus, when everyone took boats out for fun. I blank the noise and slow my breath. All I think about is the toy.

A voice breaks my concentration. "What about this one?" Are they talking about my hiding place? I hold my breath.

"Can't get to it!"

"Are you sure?" The first voice asks.

One of the Mercs yells, "I can try to jump." *Thump!* I could have told him that wouldn't work. The boat shifts a little as two or more of the Mercs bang on the sides of the boats, taunting, "Come out girlie! Come out if you're in there!"

I concentrate once again on the whale.

A voice yells, "Let's move to another building. She's not here!" Booted footsteps sound before I hear the entrance door come down. I wait. The voices disappear.

I wait a little longer before I stir. I decide to search the yacht for items I might need later. I tiptoe gingerly because the boat rocks slightly with my every movement. I enter through the outside door to explore the living quarters. Inside the cabin, I discover an area that looks like it hasn't been touched for years. I could only surmise that this yacht was left when the virus ravaged and the owners either died or were quarantined. The beds are stripped and sheets and blankets stored. I open the cabinets and find them filled with canned goods and various staples. I stumble upon a box of fruit bars. I pull one out and eat it while I go through the rest of the drawers. The fruity smell's overwhelming. Tickling my taste buds, it's delicious. Guess these things last forever. I can't stay here too long. But I need to be smart and wait long enough to use the darkness as cover. I find a wind up clock and set it one hour. I need some sleep so I can think a little straighter before I figure out my next move. I have no idea where I'll go or how I'll get home or what will happen to Riley or Colt.

For the first time on this journey, I'm completely on my own. Scary!

Chapter 17

I nap for an hour. Afterwards my mind is clearer. I'll organize first then try for some more sleep. I find a backpack and load it full of fruit and cereal bars. I gather a clean shirt, a pair of socks, and a large pair of sneakers. I change into these, hoping to blend in more with this culture than I did before with the Holland outfit. I stuff my Holland outfit and shoes in the backpack. I also find soap, deodorant, shampoo, a flashlight, and a pocketknife. I cut off the end of the sneakers with the pocketknife to make them shorter. I don't have a choice; I have to make them fit me somehow. A baseball cap completes my ensemble. I'm able to stuff my hair underneath it. I disguise my appearance as best I can. An advantage that might become useful. I guess at the time and set the alarm for 0200. Everyone should be asleep by then. Should be safe to leave.

When I wake up, I take my time knotting the rope and shimmying down. I carefully untie the rope and sling it over my shoulder.

Sneaking out of the boat shelter is not as difficult as shimmying down the rope. I throw the rope in my pack for later. I find an unlocked door on the side of the shed and walk out. I have no plan except to get as far away from the ship as possible. I make a mental note of how to find my way back should that need arise. It makes me feel better just knowing where the "Queen Nalani" ocean liner is located. Nothing good has happened on board that ocean cruiser, but it's my connection to home. Or maybe it's the fact that Riley, Colt, Mom, and Gretel are on board making that ship my pseudo home for now.

The shipyard is deserted except for an occasional sentry. I see no one searching for me. I take my time, not wanting to draw attention to my movements. A few shards of sunlight illuminate the area with just enough light for me to attempt escape. I scan for sentries as I look for a way out.

The boats hanging from the rafters and floating in the slips provide no accessible place to hide as I travel through. Fortunately, a few rusted cars speckle the area, enough to use as cover. One harbors a nest of birds that scatter when I walk by. I stop for a moment to see if the movement perked the interest of the guards.

Still unnoticed, I sneak toward the place with the biggest cluster of lights. The only road in or out is guarded. A line of delivery trucks awaits their turn to be given the all clear to leave the compound. It's now or never. I creep up beside a truck with lots of crates in the back. It stinks like garbage. A truck full of fish. Not fresh fish; it's the garbage. Heads, guts, and lots of blood. Decaying fish. I shake my head, hold my nose, and shimmy over the side of the truck bed. I hope that it's a smart move, but certainly not a pleasant one. I dig deep in the smelly fish. If this stench doesn't kill me, I should be fine. No way anyone is going to look through here. I have no way of knowing where this truck is going, but I will let myself be taken as far as it drives or until it delivers this garbage of fish and me.

After the truck clears the gate, I try to find a hole for my nose. The fresh air helps a little. I concentrate on my Ferris wheel. No way to make a plan. I am in a foreign country with no help, riding to who knows where. It's probably not the best decision, but jail as an alternative definitely was not a better choice. No way for me to judge time or how fast we are going. I am completely and totally lost.

Sadness takes over and I have a good long cry. It has a releasing effect on me. Afterwards, I decide to trust that the universe will give me an idea of what to do next.

After many hours, the truck stops. I creep down farther into the fish. I listen.

"Garbage pickup." A man's voice says. The truck starts to move again.

Shortly, the truck stops and the driver slams the door. I peek out; he disappears inside a building. I seize my chance, heave myself over the truck bed, and creep into the shadows.

This area looks like a drop off and pick up point. I put on my backpack and slink out, trying not to be noticed. It might work here since my surroundings reek and I stink of fish. Once I get to a less smelly area, my stench will give away my whereabouts.

It doesn't take long before I'm noticed. A couple of men stack boxes in front of me. One of them looks at me. "Hey are you the new loader?"

I must look like a worker. I fit in here. Filthy, with my hair stuffed in my cap and wearing these disheveled jeans and cotton shirt. But the big giveaway is the pair of cut-off sneakers on my feet. How poor does that appear?

I shrug. Another stands with hands on one side of a box. I figure it won't hurt me, so I grab the other end. For the next hour, I haul boxes. Maybe I can keep hiding as a box loader for a while until I figure out what to do next.

"What's your name, boy?" A man with blackened, broken teeth asks.

I look around and spy a box with the name *Sara Lee* on it. In the lowest voice I can muster I say, "Lee."

The man smiles his non-toothy grin. "Lee, you're a good worker.

Were you just purchased?"

Another of the men says, "They like to buy the young strong ones. They last longer."

I nod and grunt out an affirmative answer. We are in America and people are still being bought, still owned. Human trafficking is alive and well in this part of the world too. Unfair and unacceptable! The reality checks as a good reminder about what all of this is about. Bringing about change.

It seems like hours before a man in better clothes stands on the stairs and yells, "Quitting time! Make your way to the grub hall. Eat first, and then get a bath and change of clothes."

The thought of a bath is welcomed since I reek of fish. I follow the bunch into the grub hall. A large pot steams with what smells like fish soup. If I weren't so hungry, I would have passed. I sit at the end of the table with the other three. I wolf down my food. After we toss our used plates on a stainless steel cart, I am led to a table heaped with clothes. The clothes aren't new, but they are clean and smell a lot better than the ones I'm wearing. I gather a pair that appears small hoping they will come close to fitting.

"Lee, get you a better pair of shoes. Those you have are going to make your feet sore." One of my group advises.

I pick out a pair, hold them up to the back of my foot for size, and add them to my pile. Next, I follow them to the showers.

Ut-oh I'm in trouble. They are all showering in the same big stall.

Chapter 18

It's a large shower stall full of men. I avert my eyes. The men are all faced to the middle with their backs to me, and no one is paying attention to anyone except themselves. This is not going to work for me. I'm in trouble.

One of my group members pulls off his shirt. "Here, Lee." He hands me a bar of soap. "Don't be shy. I know, it's strange. It took some getting used to—showering with everyone."

I hold my palms up and he stops undressing. "I can't." My voice is high. I forgot to go low. Fear shoots through my body. I shake.

The three of them surround me outside the showers. Fortunately, they are all still mostly clothed.

"C'mon Lee." One of the men grabs my cap. "It isn't that bad." He smiles, rocking the hat back and forth on my head. "You're one of our crew now. We'll take care of you. Nobody will bother you. Just throw your old clothes in a pile. They'll be thrown away later."

I don't move. "What's your name?" I ask him.

"Sam," he replies.

"Sam, can I trust you?" I say.

Even though Sam is the one I asked, all three nod. I crouch down so as not to let others see. I pull my hat off, letting the hair fall down to my shoulders. "I don't belong here. I'm a girl."

Sam gasps. "Ned, they're buying girls for work now." He looks over at the other two men. He pushes my hat back to my head. "Put that back on while we figure this out."

The three talk in whispers. "She reminds me of my daughter." "We have to protect her." "We can't let them have her." The voices run together. I can't tell who is talking, but they seem to want to help. I hope so. I have to trust them. I have no choice.

Ned holds my shoulders. "We can help you tonight. There's a separate shower on the side. We'll take you there. After that, we can probably only hide you for a couple of days. We need to get you into the underground."

"Underground?"

Ned continues, "We'll explain later." The three men push me into an alcove in the showering area while they finish showering. It's a few more minutes before all is quiet.

Sam says, "You should be able to take a shower undisturbed now. We'll keep watch just in case."

I nod and sneak to the separate stall and shower. Carefully, I make sure that the four-leaf clover necklace stays on my neck. I change into the clean clothes and disguise myself as best as I can. I follow them out to the sleeping quarters. A bunch of men are haphazardly stretched out on the ground on makeshift beds of blankets and rags. The three huddle on both sides of me.

John hands me a blanket. "We hate that they are buying and selling people, but we are not going to let them start sending girls to work down here with a bunch of men. That's crazy."

Ned nods. "They've gone too far. We may have to speed up the take over."

"Take over?" I pull the blanket up to my chin.

"Lee, don't worry about it. We'll make sure that you are taken care of. I hate to think what would have happened..." He stops and drops his head in his hands.

"What?" I am so confused. These men need to fill me in on what they mean.

John shakes his head and leans on his back looking up at the ceiling. He rolls toward me and whispers. "They sent a girl down here before. A Merc got a hold of her. He was a mean one. He was mad that she couldn't keep up with the work and he beat her badly. She died before morning."

Ned nods. "We have to get her out before tomorrow night. Send out the message. We have one for extraction."

Sam, the quiet one, finally speaks, "My daughter was killed by a Merc. I'm not going to let that happen to someone else's daughter. I'll send the message to Lieutenant Thai." Sam pats my head. "I will die before I let anything happen to you."

"I don't want you to die." I had not known these men for long, but I already knew for sure that they were good people. They deserved better than to be owned people. Why is the whole world under the control of the Mercs? That *had* to change. If I escape, I will come back and save them. I have to. To traffic humans is wrong! It's just wrong! "If I make it, I'll come back for all of you."

The men smile at each other. Sam says, "That's sweet, but let's plan on getting you out first."

He's right. I can't save anyone until I'm free. I pull out my bullet four-leaf clover. Riley told me he wanted to make something lucky and good out of an object used for meanness and violence. That's what I like about Riley, always positive. I miss him. I roll the metal clover around in my hand. The thought of him soothes me. Somehow, I don't feel so alone now.

251

The next morning, Ned wakes me. "Time to get up. Be ready to move."

Sam explains, "When we get our breakfast, the three of us will create a diversion. When you see the guards and everyone distracted, run behind the serving table. I will point out the man who will help you as we go through the line." He hugs me. "Good luck, little one."

I nod. As we walk through the breakfast line, Sam points to a boy serving eggs and grits paste. He's not much older than I am. The boy nods as he slops the goop onto my plate. It smells awful. I hope I don't have to eat it.

Servants do not eat well. They deliver food, but do not get to partake of the good portions. The owned ones eat what is left. On the farm, I always had enough to eat. We grew our own food. After that, I was given food as a Sponsored Companion, and then Baako delivered our food. I have never really been hungry or know what it is like to go without food. I never realized just how awful the owned servants were treated. Starvation! No wonder the workers have a hard time and struggle so much. They are malnourished.

Before I consume one bite, Sam, Ned, and John start to argue. It doesn't take long before our table and the rest of the tables join in. They are yelling about the lack of food. The guards come over. I slide under the table during the ruckus and make my way to the serving counter.

"Stay there for a moment." The boy dipping the egg paste slides a gigantic empty pot my way. "Climb in." I hesitate for a moment and he insists, "Now or never, girlie." He points to the melee. "You can stay and take your chances."

I glance over and see the guard slugging a few of the combatants. He's right; I have to trust him. I climb into the pot. It still has remnants of egg paste from this morning. It stinks like vomit, mold, and skunk all rolled into one. I pull out my metal clover from Riley. I hold it, concentrating on how it feels in my hand to take my focus away from the stench. The boy shuts the top. He might be saving me and I don't even know his name. What a strange world we live in. He seals the top and I hear him yell, "This one's ready. Load it on the truck."

I feel my container being shoved. I'm worried because I've only been locked in here a couple of minutes, but I'm already struggling to catch my breath. I shut my eyes and shallow my breathing to compensate. This might be a brief trip. I hold my breath as the container is twirled and then plopped hard on the ground.

Another voice yells, "Need help with this one, it's heavy." A different voice yells, "It's heavy because they didn't want to eat this slop." The first voice says, "It *is* nasty stuff." Laughter follows the comment. I feel myself lifted and slid onto a flat surface, which I assume, is a truck bed. It is hard to catch my breath.

I hear the boy's voice. "I need to check this one." The airtight buckles unclamp allowing air to make its way in. "Good to go!" He yells, and then whispers, "Good luck, girlie." Thank goodness some air! That would have been a short deadly jaunt. It's a few more minutes before I have the sensation of moving. They might be taking me to prison, or worse. I clutch Riley's metal clover tightly in my hand. It might be a long ride. Better save up my energy for whatever awaits me.

Chapter 19

When the truck stops, I hear worker's voices and have the sensation of being lifted. After being slammed around a few times, my large potted prison comes to rest. The room is dark. Must be nighttime. The sliver of light that was getting through is now gone. I sit inside my container of confinement, waiting. I keep hoping that I have a future. Unfortunately, the stench worsens when I wet myself. A girl can hold it just so long. I haven't eaten enough to warrant a need for the other. That would be bad. I'm starving, but it will be better if I wait to eat. Too bad my backpack full of food didn't make the trip with me. I hear rumblings about a journey to another camp after a few hours pass. No idea about the plans for my container.

Obviously, the people in this area are the poorest and have no say about their plight. I can tell by their talk. Conversations about the way the people are being treated run the gamut of livid to benign. I sit quietly, waiting to hear what happens next. Out of all the voices, I haven't heard one female voice and that concerns me. I am supposed to have escaped from an all-male internment to an underground escape of some sort. I have lost track of time although I think two days have passed. I am weak. I'm dehydrated because I don't even have enough in me to wet myself anymore.

Thoughts about Colt and Riley seep into my consciousness. Did my leaving cause them any problems? I steer my mind to focus on the answer to that question or any thought rather than the fact that I'm starving. It's a fleeting lapse at best before my attention reverts to my empty stomach. Fortunately, the egg paste I manage to scrape off the sides has a liquid base and that gives me a small amount of liquid in my system. I'm in trouble, big trouble. I'm going to die in here unless something changes. Soon.

Darkness falls again. I have to attempt to get out of this prison and save myself. It's quiet. I have no idea what I'll be escaping to, but I have to try. The lock is held by one catch of the buckle. I jimmy each latch back and forth until it releases completely. I slide the lid up. I slam my body from side to side until the pot topples. I'm weak and cramped. I crawl out of the pot onto the floor. It's takes a few moments for me to stretch out my legs. I rub them to help the circulation before I pull myself to a standing position and limp a few steps. I'm weary, but steady.

I'm in some sort of a storage closet. Shelves on each side are lined with large cans of beans, vegetables, and condiments. I spy a plastic bag half-opened of apples, grab one, and wolf it down. I eat the whole thing, core, and all. I find a pear and do the same thing. For the next few minutes, I sit on the floor and gorge myself on any food available. A couple of jugs of water rest on the floor and I turn one up, gulping so much that I start coughing. I stop, fearing that I will be heard. After a few moments, I realize no one is here but me so I eat more. I stand up again gingerly, taking baby steps until I can manage a full gait, trying to get my energy back.

I pull the four-leaf clover from around my neck and squeeze it for luck before stuffing it into my pocket. I relieve myself using the container the apples came in and then tie up the sack. After a few more minutes, I start to feel better. I straighten up everything. No way for me to hide the fact that I ate apples and pears and drank the water. I find another carrier to gather the plastic and my other garbage. My only hope is that whoever comes in this area won't remember what was here. There is so much food it would probably be next to impossible to keep a tally. I can't leave any trace. I set the container I was housed in upright and realign the top of the large pot as best I can. I gather the bag of my trash and crack the door to peek out. Black darkness paints my surroundings so I creep out, feeling my way around what seems to be a large storage barn. I deposit my sack of waste in what I hope is a garbage bin. After knocking my way down a couple of corridors, I spy a glimmer of light shining in a window. The small ray of moon light is just enough for me to locate the front door.

Outside, I see nothing but large storage units. No people, good or bad. I am just about to make a break for the woodsy area at the far end of the farm of storage sheds when I hear something.

It's a voice I don't recognize, but it's female. "I can't believe that we just got word about a stowaway from Ned. How long as she been here?"

A male voice answers, "Three days."

"Which shed?" The female asks.

The male answers, "I'm not sure. The note was lost for two days. We just got it."

"She might be dead. Did we get her name?"

The male answers again, "No. The only description we have is that she is wearing a mouse cap."

The woman stops. "She's dead. I just know it."

I have to take the chance. I walk out with my hands up. "It's me. I couldn't wait any longer. I was afraid I was going to starve to death."

He trains a gun on me. "Who are you?"

I pull off the mouse cap and my hair falls out. "Paisley. Ned, Sam, and John said that you could hide me."

The woman pushes his gun down. "We can."

I start to walk to them, but my feet give way and the whole world goes black.

"Paisley." Somebody shakes me. "Paisley, wake up. You're safe now." It was the female voice from the storage-shed area.

I rest on a soft blanket. Warmth surrounds me. I feel for my clothes. I have on a different shirt and pants. I smell a whole lot better. I pat my clothes and around my neck, nothing. "Where's my clover?"

"I'm Via." She lifts my head for me to drink a glass of water. "I tossed your clothes out. I didn't see a clover."

"It was in the pocket of my pants." I sit up and my head spins. "It's important." I drop my head in my hands. "I need it."

"I'll see if I can find it. I know where your clothes are if they haven't been destroyed. I'll be back in a few minutes and let you know what I find." She leaves.

I scan the area. It's dark, but I can see a table and blankets strewn around with people sleeping on them. A couple of maps hang on one wall. They are covered with colored pins and notes. I can't make out what is written on them. In a few minutes, she returns with my dirty slacks. I sift through the pockets.

I sigh, "It's here." I pull the clover out and roll it in my hand before slipping its cord around my neck. It knocks against my chest. "Thanks." I say, "It's from—"

"No need to explain. We all have or want things to remember those that are important to us. Happy you found it." She smiles and pushes my hair back behind my ears. "Glad that Ned and Sam sent you here too."

I look around. "Where's here?"

"Sorry." She stands up and reaches for my hand. "Can you stand?"

"Yes." I come to my feet and steady myself. She holds my arm. I pull at her collar to gain my balance. Above her collar is a red birthmark in an unusual shape, a heart. I have never seen anything like it, yet it seems familiar. We are the same height. She is older, but there is something about her that puts me at ease. Her kind eyes. Her soothing way. It's hard to explain why I feel immediately comfortable with her.

"Via, is that your name?" She nods and I ask again, "Where is here?"

"Underground America." She walks me over to a crate and helps me to sit. "I'll try to explain."

A young boy who looks to be no more than thirteen brings a paper to Via. "Captain, we've found a ship. Our sources say that it is indeed from Germany." She signs the paper and the boy leaves.

I look at Via. "Did he call you Captain? Are you in charge?"

She smiles. "Yes. Women can be in charge too. Although you wouldn't know it from the way the world is now."

I nod. "Definitely." I can't figure out why I trust her, but I do. "So what do you do here and what's your interest in a ship from Germany?"

"Right to the point." She thumps me playfully on the back. "I like that. Maybe one day you'll be Captain and I'll retire."

"I don't understand why we need captains or colonels or lieutenants or anything." I jut out my chin.

"That's what Underground America is all about. We're trying to make a world where there's no need for the military ranks. No human trafficking, no owning of people." She sits on a crate beside mine and sighs. "But especially, we want to make sure there are no more viruses." She cocks her head. "Now I've answered some of your questions. It's your turn. Where are you from?"

"Germany. As a matter of fact, I escaped off that ship that the boy just told you about." No use lying now. I have to get help if I am going to get back to my family.

Her posture straightens. "You're not a spy, are you?"

"No!" I hop off the crate with hands on my hips and glare at her. "Of course not! I want the same as you. No one should be owned by someone else! I was an owned at one time. I served as a living doll."

She pulls me back down on the crate. "I didn't mean to upset you. You never know whom you can trust. We are just starting to make headway." She looks away for a minute then turns back. "Were you a Sponsored Companion?"

I nod.

"I heard about that. You serve as a doll for the wealthy children to play with."

I nod again. "It wasn't that bad. The princess was sweet."

She jumps up and holds both of my shoulders. "You know the royal family?"

"I used to. They tried to have me killed."

Her shocked expression unsettles me, but I continue, "In all fairness, it was the king who wanted me killed. The princess didn't have anything to do with it. She is innocent as is her father, the ambassador. He tried to save me and he did for a while until...never mind, that's a long story."

Her face softens. "You think the ambassador is a good man?"

"The best."

"I've heard that." Her softened features harden and she flusters for a minute looking from side to side. Then she suddenly stands erect and

257

pulls me up. "Let me give you a tour of our facility."

For the next half an hour, she walks me through their command center. "Where we are now is a first station of an extensive underground secret society of supporters who work to end human trafficking and free others owned by the rich."

"Like the underground railroad?" I ask.

"I see you know some of America's history." She explains that they have been underground for quite a while, first taking refuge in the facility that used to house the staff at a deserted theme park. In that underground facility they were able to cook food using the kitchen and house a great many people. "At first, we only brought in those attempting to escape the virus."

"How did you know it wouldn't spread?" I pick up a couple of books on a table. I recognize one, *The Wizard of Oz*. "I know this book."

She takes it from my hand and returns it to the table. "It's a classic. If you were going to stay here, I'd let you keep it."

"Am I going somewhere else?"

"You're being transferred in a few minutes to the next station, the facility in Orlando." She walks me to a door.

I stop just shy of the door. "You never told me how you didn't know the virus wouldn't spread to the underground."

"I wasn't here then. Unfortunately, it did spread. There were lots of deaths, but some survived."

I stare at her. "You were one of the survivors?"

She sighs. "No, I was the doctor relocated here after I was evacuated from my post. I was brought here to figure out why."

"And did you?" I ask.

"Still working on it." She opens the door. "Don't worry. Everyone who was infected died a long time ago. It's safe. Time for you to go."

A couple of young men clad in medical scrubs stand on the other side of the door. A jeep is behind them.

She hugs me. "These doctors will take you to a safe place. Good luck, Paisley."

"Will I see you again?"

She smiles and squeezes me again. "Most likely, no." She lets go and pushes me back, still holding onto my shoulders. "With our world as it is, I find that the truth is always the best. I could lie to you and tell you that I will be checking on you from time to time, but I have no way of knowing that. My place is here, coordinating the resistance and trying to find a way to support the ambassador."

I let out a long breath. "There is something that you might want to know."

"What?"

I purse my lips. I hate to give bad news. "Just before I escaped the ship, the ambassador was arrested and taken away. I saw him being driven off in a car."

She smiles. "Thanks for your honesty. We *did* know that and that's why I cannot go with you. We are in pursuit of that car. We're attempting to free the ambassador. If you'll excuse me, I'd better get back to my job. Take care."

I hug her one last time. "Save him. The ambassador is a good man and very important to me."

"He is important to us all." She closes the door.

I am placed in the back seat of the jeep and wrapped in a sheet. One of the men hooks an oxygen tube around my nose. Another rolls gauze around my head and body. He explains, "We are transporting you through the streets as a medical emergency. You have to look the part."

In a few minutes, I am gauzed up to not only disguise my identity, but to look like I am knocking on death's door.

As we ride through the streets of America, I see that the Mercs are not only policing Germany and Europe; they have a definite presence in America too. It's scary how much power the Mercs have. We are stopped three times. Once for an overturned car that has to be moved out of the way. The other two times for the Mercs to examine the bogus papers about me. I wonder what the papers say. I figure it says that I am contagious because after reading the document, the Mercs back up a little. The two men driving me are wearing protective masks.

It is almost dark. They speed up. The driver says, "We have to make it before curfew."

The other man points to a group of Mercs. "We only have a few minutes. We have to be off this road before curfew. Don't want them to look too closely at our patient."

The driver veers onto a deserted road. "Can't believe they would, with the patient listed as having early virus symptoms, but we can't be too careful."

That answers that question, no wonder not one of the guards or security personnel wants to get near me. The confinement of the gauze makes it impossible for me to move very much. I can only see out the front window of the vehicle and I can only observe what sits up high. I hope our journey is almost at its end.

After a few more turns into alleyways, we enter a long street. The driver says, "It's not too much farther."

I peek through the windshield and cannot believe what I catch sight of, sitting majestically, in front of me. It can't be. It's a miracle.

A big piece of heaven.

Chapter 20

Right in front of me, regally overlooking my little part of the world, is the castle from the postcard my mother keeps in a treasure box.

I murmur, "Orlando, where dreams come true."

The driver pulls up to an alcove. "Yeah, this is Orlando. Have you been to the castle or the park before?"

I shake my head. "Not really. I saw a picture of it once."

The other man gets out of the jeep. He unbuckles me; we both unroll my gauze to release my bondage. When I'm free, he says, "We need to hide the jeep. Grab the other side of the tarp."

In the corner sits a large piece of dark cloth. We pull it over the jeep to camouflage it.

"Covered," The driver says. "Follow me."

In a few minutes, the men duck behind a hedge and descend into a concealed walkway. I trail behind the men down a short flight of stairs and through a hidden door. Behind the door is a corridor. More steps. As we go through an entrance at the end of the hallway, the walkways become illuminated by lanterns and widen into a large room.

"Is there electricity down here?" I ask.

One of the men answers, "This area has its own power source. Don't worry. You're safe here."

We come to a dining area full of tables and chairs and one of the men points to a chair. "Sit, while we find out where we're supposed to take you."

They leave. I watch the scene unfold around me. Men, women, and children scurry about. Some of the children carry food; some of the people haul lumber. Others hammer and nail wood in the midst of completing or starting some sort of construction. Old and young alike engage in various housekeeping duties such as folding clothes. Everyone is busy and smiling. I haven't seen this many happy people together in a long time, maybe never. Some are humming, some are singing. They seem content.

In the middle of the chaotic world and looming virus, I've hit a pocket where everyone is full of joy. Why are they so cheerful? Is it because they are free and safe? Children yell, "Mom! Dad!" Families are together. Smiling men and women, even some disabled people walking with crutches, work at various chores. A few have burn scars and some are disfigured. Is this a refuge for Uncounted and Undesirables?

I smile. For the first time in days, I have a little spot of happiness in my soul.

A man runs up, out of breath. He whispers to me, "Have you heard? It's the worst news ever. How will we ever overcome it?" His face is pale and his mood dire.

My cheerful mood disappears.

He trots off and encounters others. He speaks to them. Their expressions mirror the horror of the news. Smiles disappear. Workers, so happy and carefree just moments ago, turn ashen, their features consumed with fear.

A woman cradles a young girl and rocks her back and forth. She sits at the table beside me. "It's okay. It'll be okay. Don't worry. We will figure this out."

I lean over and ask, "Why is everyone so upset?"

"It's just a rumor." The woman rocks the child more. "It may not be true."

"What may not be true?" I ask.

"The ambassador has been killed."

The world twirls and I feel sick. My father is dead. How can that be? "It can't be true." I drop my head to the table. I cry.

The woman pats my hand trying to comfort me. "It's just a rumor. It'll be okay."

I glance up for a minute. This joyful world has just been covered with a dark fog, one that will suck goodness out of all of us. She is wrong. It will *not* be okay. How can anything ever be okay if my father is dead? And more than that, what will happen to the world if the only hope to end human trafficking and foster democracy has vanished? My father held the key to all of that. Nothing will be fine. It will never be the same. All hope is lost. I let go, crying with the masses.

For the rest of the day, people sport bloodshot eyes as the sobbing continues. I am taken to a holding area without much instruction except to bunk here and wait for directions later. Everything is falling apart, I need to get out of here and make it back to the ship with my family, Riley, and Colt. I have no idea how to go about accomplishing that.

That night, I sit on my bunk, numb. Those around me are distraught and without direction. I am right there with them. **The happiness that permeated this underground city is now gone.** My head falls in my hands as I am hit with the realization that my father, my real father, is dead. It is too much to bear. I cry myself to sleep.

I wake up sadder than I have ever been. I have a hard time moving. I don't have to change clothes because I slept in them. I see a rumpled person when I look in the mirror. I feel on the inside how I look on the outside, discombobulated and without purpose.

"They're serving breakfast now," says a girl on the bunk next to me. "I'm supposed to take you."

"Not hungry."

"I know," she replies. "Me neither, but they didn't give us a choice."

I throw the blanket on the worn cot where I had slumbered the night before and shuffle into the next room. A long table is set up and people are getting their breakfast. Breakfast consists of fresh citrus, oranges and grapefruits, as well as some sort of oatmeal mixture. It's probably good, but I can't taste it. My taste buds must be in shock like the rest of me. I go through the motion of eating. I'm overwhelmed by the news, and the bigness of it all. I feel much older than my fifteen years.

The morning drags, then it is time for another tasteless meal. Groups sit at the tables for lunch.

One girl with red hair asks, "What are we going to do now that the ambassador is dead? How can we expect a win for democracy? We have to free everyone, all of the owned and disenfranchised people of the world."

A dark-skinned young man stomps into the room muttering to himself. He then slams his plate on the table and food flies everywhere. "We can't just give up and we aren't indentured servants. Indentured servants have the chance of being freed. We are *slaves*. When the wealthy own us, there is nothing we can do to free ourselves. That is the difference."

I am reminded of my farm and the army of children training to fight and die if they have to for the cause of freedom. If they didn't give up, then I shouldn't either. There has to be hope. Just has to be. I need to find it. We all need to find it. Now.

I scoot over to the girl with red hair. "There's always hope. *Everyone* is scared. It's okay to be scared. I'm scared too." I squeeze her arm. "What's your name?"

"Julia." She ekes out.

I take in a deep breath. "Julia, we will figure a way out of this. Sometimes when a celebrated leader dies, it makes the cause become greater. Ever heard of martyrs?" She shakes her head meekly and I continue, "I've read about them in books so I can tell you about them. Joan of Arc was a martyr. After her death the cause moved forward using her death to spark their rebellion." I can't believe that I am so calmly able to talk about this. Am I dead inside? How can my father's death mean so little to me? Somehow as I am saying this to her, it makes me feel better. How strange. I continue, "Maybe that will happen here and someone will take the ambassador's place."

The dark-skinned young man sits down beside me. "Like who, you?" He rubs his chin. "Aren't you new? How do we know you're not a spy?" He glares at me. "You might be in with the people who killed the ambassador. We have no way of knowing. Maybe you've been sent here to—I don't know—to discover our secrets."

Julia slams her hand down. "Listen to yourself Eddie. You're not making any sense."

"She's right, you're not making any sense." I hoarsely whisper under my breath. "If you only knew how far off you really are." I stare at Eddie. He's old enough to know better. He should be calming the young ones down, not riling them up. I'm indignant. "I'm not here to spy. I *want* to leave. I need to get back to the ship that docked here a few days ago. I have to try to save my family and friends."

"That ship?" Eddie shakes his head. "Haven't you heard that it's leaving tomorrow? There's no way that you can get back on that ship."

I jump up and put my hands on my hips. "I might not be able to get on *that* ship, but I have to try. And if I don't make it, then I have to find another way to Europe. I *have* to save my family." I slam my fists in the air. "I just have to." I look at them. "I refuse to give up." I take in a deep breath and point my finger first at Julia and then at Eddie. "You, you two! I'm talking to you! Help me figure this out. Any ideas? I am not just going to let this happen to our world." I bang my fists on the table. "You, all of you, should be standing up for what's right too." I point a finger inches from his face.

Julia stands up beside me. "She's right. We need to do something instead of just sitting around crying all day."

A few more stand. In a few minutes, the entire group of adults and children has risen. Eddie lifts me on top of the table. "Do it then. Rally the troops. You're in charge."

This is not what I wanted. I have no idea what to say or how to say it. I rub the bullet clover corded around my neck. What would Riley do? Or Colt? How can I let my father's death be in vain? I can only tell them what I know to be true. I say, "I can tell you stories about what I've seen. I can tell you what I know."

The resistance group contently listens as I regale them of the stories of our farms, farm life, the hidden caves, and the harvest. I also enlighten them about how the Mercs stole the farms from us, the rightful owners, and how the newspapers reported it wrong.

I share more stories about Colt and my escape. About the ship, the princess, the ambassador, the threats, and many failed attempts on the ambassador's life. How through all of this adversity, the ambassador always wanted to forge ahead for democracy.

I enlighten them about my family, the Sponsored Companions Program, the Uncounteds, and the Undesirables. I tell them about the Mercs, their blood lust, and how they kill people for no reason. How Colt and I were to be killed and how the ambassador spared us.

I tantalize them with the luck and the Merc's surprise announcement about our escape back to my farm. I share about the resistance that we encountered and the army of children we were training. I tell them how I came over on the ship and how I came to be here. The longer I talk, the more people gather into the food area. By the time I stop talking, the area is packed.

I pull Julia up on the table beside me. "Tell them your story."

Julia tells about how she was stolen from her family. She wandered the streets until Captain Via took her in. Next, Eddie tells his tale. One by one, each of the group stands and gives an account of how they have been persecuted since the virus outbreak.

A few elderly people paint the picture of what life was like before the virus. They discuss what a democracy is and how everyone in the world cooperates with each other. Americans explain their former political party organizations and an elderly woman from Europe educates us about her country's leadership structure.

Discussions continue for so long that it is time for another meal. As the group sits down to eat, strategies to bring the world together are thrashed out. This talk makes me feel so much better. Nothing could pierce the agony of the loss I feel about my father, but planning some positive actions makes me hopeful that there still might be a chance to defeat the king and the Mercs. The one thing everyone agrees with is that this world *is* worth winning and that our lives, all of our lives, flawed or perfect, are worth saving.

Eddie takes a swig of water. "I can get you on a boat back to Germany."

I drop a fork full of food back to my plate. "You can get me on the ship?"

"No, not that one." He leans in to whisper. "There is a ship that I know of that is leaving soon for Germany transporting a very important person."

"Who?" I ask.

"I'm not sure, but someone who is in danger here. They're trying to hide him." Eddie scoops some beans on his fork.

"Maybe the ambassador isn't really dead," I say.

"I wish." Eddie puts the fork back down on his plate. "But this was set up before your ship came in so it can't be him."

It was too much to ask for. My father is truly dead. My spirit sinks for a moment before I ask, "Why are they going to Germany?"

Eddie takes a bite and chews. "There's a resistance group in Germany."

"I wonder if it is with the same group I was telling you about?"

"This one calls itself PACO."

I shake my head. "Never heard of them, but we need the resistance groups to join together, don't you think?"

"Definitely." He picks up his tray. "Come with me. Let's see when the group is leaving and if we can get you on their ship."

"There is not any *if* to it. I *have* to be on that ship. It's my only hope." I follow him with my tray. We scrape them and give them to the kitchen staff. "Is it a big boat?"

"Big enough." He laughs. "You don't know, do you?"

"Know what?" I ask.

"It's a pirate ship."

Chapter 21

Eddie leads me into another area, full of tables and chairs. He pulls a chair from the stack, points to it, and I sit. He grabs another for himself and sits facing me.

He says, "Groups of resistance fighters from the states, Europe, Asia, the outer islands, and Australia had been trading for about three years when we discovered each other."

I ask, "I don't understand why it's called a pirate ship."

He laughs. "That's the best part. Back when everyone was under quarantine, I escaped on a ship with a group of my friends and family. For a long time, we waited out in the ocean."

I scrunched up my face. "Why?"

"Because if we're out on the ocean and no one is sick then how can diseases find you. Right?"

I nod. It did sound like a foolproof plan. What better quarantine than millions of miles of ocean?

"Anyway while we were out to sea a ship came by so we started talking to them. They told us of other ships. It started with four ships roped together out in the middle of the Atlantic Ocean. We became experienced fishermen and caught rainwater to drink. It was idyllic. We had small boats so we could travel from ship to ship."

"Why did you ever come to shore?" I ask.

"Lots of reasons. We started running out of supplies. We wanted to know what happened with the rest of the world. Plus, our palates were aching for something more than fish. The quarters were so cramped, we began to go stir crazy."

"I understand, but it was very risky coming back to shore." I shake my head. He picks up a packet and nods toward me. I ask, "What is it?"

He unwraps the packet. "Chocolate. You should try it. It's hard to come by. It's more of a luxury. I only get it when someone raids a stockpile somewhere. I remember loving it when I was young. Before the virus."

"I might try a bite." I put the brown substance on my tongue. The sensation of flavor is unbelievable as it melts in my mouth. I wait until the last morsel is gone. "Oh my goodness, this is the best tasting stuff. I can see why it's a luxury. I'm surprised there is any left. But you still haven't answered my question. Why did you ever come back to shore?"

"We ran out of staples: sugar, rice and that sort of thing. In addition, we had a baby born on board and needed different kinds of food. The mother was able to nurse, but we couldn't feed the baby properly. At first, we would send a small boat. We floated the big ship miles from shore then a few of us would travel out. During these excursions, we realized what had happened with our world."

I lean in. "What do you mean?"

He licks his fingers. "It was sad. When we escaped in our ships five years before, our world was a communication empire. We could buy whatever we wanted and the world was at peace. Of course, when we left there was also a virus ravaging everyone. I wasn't sure that anyone had survived. But I wasn't prepared for what I found when I did finally get here." He takes another small piece of the chocolate and hands the rest of the package to me.

I pinch off another piece and place it on my tongue, not talking until it is gone. "What did you find?"

"It's good isn't it?" He smacks his lips for a moment then focuses back on me. "Where was I? Oh, yeah. When we returned, the world was being controlled by the Mercs."

"I know. The Mercs controlled our farms, stole our harvest and then a few months ago, took us out of the picture entirely."

"Same story all over. Same story, different places." He takes the paper from my hand and licks it for the leftover chocolate. "The Mercs re-commissioned the communications devices left by the military when they abandoned their posts after the virus outbreak. For the past year or so, they have been using them to coordinate this take-over."

"Is that when you decided to join the resistance?" I ask.

"Yes. At first, we just bartered for grains and staples. We were happy to just keep it like that. We would stay on the open sea and trade fish for our needs, but then—"

"Something happened to change your mind," I interject.

"Yeah, isn't that how it always happens?"

"What?" I ask.

"We found people in the open waters, floating on a single piece of wood, most likely a left over part of the hull of a ship. Some shared their horrible stories. It seems that a ship had thrown what they considered undesirable people and what they called Uncounteds overboard. Although there were a few dead, most had survived days on that piece of drift wood."

"How old were you when the virus hit?"

"Fifteen."

I smile. "That's how old I am now."

"Hope your next fifteen years are better than this fifteen."

"Me too. What happened to the survivors?"

"They were definitely survivors. They amazed me." He shifts a little in his chair. "They had survived for days with no food. Some were so sick they could hardly walk, but they survived. They flagged us down and we took them in. After hearing their stories, our ships would troll the waters searching for stray people who had been cast overboard. That's how we built up our numbers."

"Are there lots of you?" I ask.

"Yes. Our numbers are many. Our people resist being owned, bought, and sold. They fight against the Mercs and royal's control of the world. We coordinate with every continent. Underground movements exist everywhere, waiting on for the right time to declare ourselves."

I ask, "When do you plan to do that?"

"We thought we wouldn't have to. We thought our fight was about to be over since the ambassador was supposed to make the world a democracy again and the virus was eradicated. But now—"

I choke back a sob. "The ambassador's death has changed all of that."

He nods. "Yes. It is a great blow. We are sending a ship over to Germany to try to make a new plan. That's the ship I need to get you on if you hope to see your family again."

I drop my head. "My family is on a ship too. The "Queen Nalani". I will probably never see them again."

He squeezes my shoulder. "Never give up hope. As long as your family is still alive. As long as we are all alive, there is still hope. Weren't you the one who just gave that speech about hope and never giving up?"

I smile weakly. "I guess."

"*I guess* is not good enough. I'm going to have to move quickly if I want to get you on that ship. I'm risking my life for you. I will most likely have to travel with you, so if *I guess* is all you can muster to say then maybe—"

"I was not giving up hope of winning just getting on that ship." I straighten up. "You don't know me, Eddie, but I will fight until I am no longer breathing. If you think we can catch up with the ship, then count me in."

He stands. "That's what I was hoping to hear you say. No time to waste. We need to leave now."

"How?" I ask.

"Quietly and carefully."

We spend the next few minutes winding our way out of the underground and walk up flights of stairs until we come to a door. Dawn is breaking. For the first time, I look at my surroundings as we come into

269

the brightness. There it stands: the castle from the postcard. It's certainly not as beautiful and picturesque as it obviously once was, but there it is just the same. I am let down – I'm not sure what I was expecting. That my dreams would come true if I found Orlando. That I would somehow come to this beautiful castle and all of my problems would disappear. That most certainly did not happen. Here I am on foreign soil with people I don't know, trusting them to carry me back across an ocean on a pirate ship.

I look around. "What was this place?"

"It used to be a very popular theme park," Eddie whispers as we walk to awaiting trucks. "People from all over the world came here to have fun. It was an escape from the humdrum of daily life."

"The humdrum of daily life, wouldn't we all like to get a taste of a boring life now. I don't know about you, but lately my life is a constant battle to stay alive."

He nods. "Mine too."

I see a few remnants of a Ferris wheel and roller coaster. I recognize them from the pictures that surrounded the castle picture on the postcard. What a wondrous place this must have been! Now look at it: rubble and rust. "Do you think we can ever make the world even close to what it used to be?"

"No, of course not." He guides me around a curve. "We will make it better. Then all of the future generations will marvel. The world will rise again and it will be a more loving place. That is, if I have anything to say about it."

I like this Eddie and his ideals. I can't believe how lucky I've been to escape from that work camp. My luck is continuing as I have now run into Eddie who knows about a pirate ship going back to Germany. It is as if I have a lucky charm. I reach for the four-leaf clover bullet and rub it. A tear runs down my cheek as I realize I now have the lucky charm. What if Riley needs the luck? He has to have been caught by now. What will they do to him? The thought of Riley and Colt and my family still on that ship makes me move a little faster.

He leads me to a clearing where trucks are being loaded for the next shipment to the vessels. "Our ships are not near the "Queen Nalani" liner. It is docked miles from there. We have to hurry. We are going on the truck part of the way, and then we have to ride bikes. You up for it?"

"I am."

We crawl into the front seat of the truck. The driver, a tall man with dark hair, says, "They don't check until we reach the dock. You two can climb out before then. I'll tell you when."

270

Eddie nods and we start on a very quiet trip. No words are exchanged. I scan the countryside. It's flat and devoid of vegetation. What made anyone want to live here? There are remnants of trees. It's not until we get close to the ports that I notice people. We stop and the driver lets us out. Eddie uncovers bicycles from the bed of the truck, pulls one out, points to another, motioning for me to retrieve it. I obey. We duck into the grove, for cover. The driver rides off.

The trek through the grove is bumpy, but nice. The fall weather is crisp, albeit humid. Bavarian air is so light with the altitude. The humidity makes me miss the autumn in Bavaria. I hope that I can find my way back there soon. We travel for a few miles before we come upon a highway. It's a two-lane road with cracked pavement. Probably the hot sun and no upkeep has lent to the wear and tear of this causeway. Even with the cracks in the road, it is an easier bike ride. We are able to coast on the downhill part. We walk alongside our bikes when the climb is steep.

We are riding beside a grove, when Eddie suddenly yells, "Stop! Hide!" He jumps off his bike and pulls it into one of the tree groves.

I follow concealing my bike, just before a large caravan of trucks races by. "Who are they?"

"That's the scout jeep." He points. "Must be some of the Mercs. Don't know why they are coming this way. We'll have to be careful and stay out of their way. We're not on this road much longer."

"Where are they heading?"

He crouches lower. "If I had to guess, it would be to your "Queen Nalani" ship."

"Why?"

"I don't know. Maybe they want more security since the ambassador was killed." He plucks a blade of grass and puts it in his mouth.

I clench the handles on the bicycle. "Why would they need more security? I think it's probably the king who had the ambassador killed?" I hold back a tear.

"Why would you think that?" He glances at me. "You know more than you told us, don't you?"

"Maybe I can tell you more later," I say with a nod. "The one thing I can tell you now is that I thought a lot of the ambassador."

"I can tell," he says, lowering his head. "I hear more trucks, they're close." He pushes the top of my head down. "You'll have to tell me later. We'll need to hurry once this convoy passes." He crouches lower and I follow doing the same. "Wait a minute."

The rest of the trucks pass slower. Perched high atop the middle truck is a man with a black beard and plumed hat. His uniform is adorned with a white satin coat with gold braiding. I assume the rest of his outfit is as costumed although I can't see it since he is seated.

"Who's that?" I ask.

"That's our problem." Eddie grimaces. "Emperor Richard the Great."

"I'm confused."

Eddie throws the blade of grass down. "You probably should be. He used to be just Richard something or another and now he has renamed himself Emperor Richard the Great. Don't know where he got those gaudy clothes. Probably out of a museum. Maybe something of Napoleon's for all I know."

"What does Richard the Great do?"

"He's the blood-thirsty head of the American Mercenaries. He came up with the idea for the identification tattoos and then the rules about limits of people living together. It is because of those limits that we have Uncounteds. All of that led to the human trafficking problems that we now have. He thinks nothing of stealing. His lust for control knows no bounds. He has wealth and power and is very corrupt." Eddie stands his bike up. "It's clear. We can go now."

"Where did he get all of the wealth?" I ask.

"Probably the same place that they get the wealth in Germany. From the hard-working poor, by stealing their lands and harvest. But this Merc got a lot of his power from the king." He pedals back out into the street.

I follow him. "King Ahomana?"

He nods his head. "One and the same. Evil always finds evil." He pedals faster. "We need to hurry. They looked like they were searching for something or somebody. We don't want to get caught." He coasts for a minute. "Must be something or somebody really important to pull the emperor out of his hiding place. He is always in hiding."

I catch up with him. "Do you think they are planning something big?"

"I guess you could say that. A take-over. I think all of this is leading up to the king taking over the world. If that happens, then none of us are safe."

We turn off to another road and wind up and down through barren stretches of road. I have to admit, the trail is confusing. This group is serious about keeping their whereabouts hidden. It reminds me of the maze. Thinking about the maze makes me nostalgic for a minute. I have to find my way home, but more than that, we have to free our world.

"It's right up here," Eddie says. We coast around a long curved downward stretch of highway. When we reach the bottom of the hill, a ship with a large sail comes into view. It looks like a pirate ship or the pictures in a book of what I think a pirate ship should look like. A flag decorated with skull and crossbones adorns one of the masts. People are milling about and loading supplies. We ride up on the bicycles.

"We made it." Eddie smiles back at me and waves to a man in a sailor hat. "This is Paisley. She's going with you as far as Bavaria." Eddie tips his head at the man. "This is Captain Cox."

I reach out my hand while balancing on the bicycle. "Nice to meet you and thanks for letting me tag along."

Captain Cox shakes my hand and winks. "It's not a free ride. You'll have to work for your keep. You're not afraid of work are you?"

I grip his hand tightly. "Been a hard worker all my life."

"We'll start you in the kitchen." He points to our bicycles. "Let's get the bikes stored and Eddie can show you the way to the kitchen and to your quarters." He looks over at Eddie. "It's going to be a full ride this time. We really need you to come with us."

"Sure, if you need me." Eddie gets off his bike. "Expecting any trouble?"

The captain cocks his head toward the people gathered on the road beside the ship. "We have a high priority guest with us. If word leaks out he is onboard, we might be a target."

Eddie rolls his bike up and peers over to get a better look. "Any idea who?"

The captain motions for two workers to take the bikes. The men gather our rides and then the captain motions for us to follow him. "I'll introduce you." The captain pulls out a paper from his pocket. "But first, have you seen this nonsense and rhetoric they are spouting to the people now?" He unfolds the paper and hands it to Eddie.

Eddie stops and reads for a moment. "It says here that the resistance killed the ambassador." Eddie slaps the paper to his leg. "Nothing could be farther from the truth. We were trying to save him. To rescue him!"

The captain shakes his head. "I know that and you know that to be true, but people will read this and believe it. How can we fight this? They control the press."

Eddie folds the page and hands it back to the captain. "It's about time we start controlling the press, or at least get our hands dirty."

"Glad you think that way, old boy. It's wonderful to have you with us on this historic journey." The captain slaps Eddie on his back. "Because that is just what we plan to do and we have just the right genius to start our communication back up."

We walk toward the group. A boy who looks about my age or maybe a little younger than I am steps out. "Hello, Captain. Thanks for having me."

The captain shakes the boy's hand. "Of course, we plan on using all of that technical knowledge. None of us has had the access you have had. We could not have hoped for a better inside man. I have recruited a helper for you. This is Eddie. He used to work with short wave radios and that sort of thing. Thought you could use him. He brought along this girl. If you want, she could work with you too. I was going to have her go to the kitchen, but she could fetch things for you."

The boy scans me up and down. "You're right. We probably need someone to get our food and supplies."

My face flushes with extreme anger so much so that I think I'm going to faint. I clench my fists so hard that my fingernails bring blood to the inside of my hands. I am enraged that they think I am so useless, but I bite my tongue. I'll prove my worth to them. I take in a deep breath to calm my voice. "Since when do you think girls cannot do anything? I'll have you know—"

The captain grabs me around the waist, pulling me away. "Sorry, I guess the kitchen will be a better choice."

The boy grins. "No, she'll do. The last thing I need around me is someone who caters to my every want and need. I've had that way too long. It's time I started going out on my own and use what I've learned to carry on my father's legacy. God rest his soul." With that last statement, the boy bows his head and the others around the ship do too.

"Who was your father?" I ask.

"You don't know who my father was?" The boy gazes into my eyes.

I shake my head.

The boy takes in a deep breath. "Where have you been that you don't know who *I* am?"

Eddie bows. "We just picked her up off the "Queen Nalani." She was sold as a boy into the pits and the men there sent her to our underground. They didn't want her to get hurt. They can't protect a girl in their midst."

The boy nods. "They were probably right. Caged men do crazy things. Good call." He bows back to Eddie and looks at me. "What's your name?"

"Paisley."

"Paisley. I am Oliver. My father was the assassinated Ambassador Grayson." He reaches out to shake my hand, but I feel myself falling.

My brother. He's my brother!

Chapter 22

I see Oliver's face when I open my eyes. He is waving his hands over me and asks, "You okay?"

I sit up. "Sorry, I haven't eaten in a while. It probably caught up with me."

He pulls me up.

I'm touching my brother's hand. I must work with him. I have to get to know him. I gather my senses and explain, "Look, Oliver. I can help you. I'm smart. I'd like to work with you instead of the kitchen. Eddie is the only person I know on this ship."

He shakes my hand. I smile. I know exactly how old he is. Fourteen and I know that he is a genius with communications. I'm so glad that my father was able to share that with me before... I stop with that thought, fearing that I might tear up.

I want to get to know my brother especially since my father is dead. He is the last of my birth family. "I'd work hard and not be any trouble. I promise. You'd be doing me a favor. I'd appreciate it." I hold my breath.

"Sure." He grins. "But you may be in for more than you bargained for. Seems my disappearance has brought out the emperor. He's hot on my trail." He chuckles. "He wants to assassinate me. **He's mad that I sabotaged the communications program I had previously set up for him and the king.**" He smiles a wry grin. "Of course, it could be because I stole vital communication instruments when I escaped so we could set up our own communications system. That loss will cripple his organization." His eyebrow lifts. "You might get caught in the crossfire."

"I'll take my chances."

The captain motions for his men to gather Oliver's belongings. "We have a place set up for you below. You can work and sleep there. There are three bunks, but it's all together." He looks over at me. "Hope you don't mind sleeping in the same room as these two."

"No problem." I pick up one of Oliver's bags. "We're going to be working. I'm sure the sleeping will be just a side note."

Oliver slings the last bag over his shoulder. "We're going to get along fine. Where are you from, Paisley?"

"Bavaria." It slips out, before I can think. Then I question my hesitation, why can't I tell him where I'm from? He would never connect.

"My father used to talk of Bavaria. He and my mother were there before the virus and her death."

"How did she die?" Did he get the same story as me?

"She died after the virus. My sister, Penelope, died too."

I nod. Of course, I know this isn't true since I'm alive. So sad. I will never know the whole truth now since our father has been assassinated.

Eddie, Oliver, and I are led to a large cabin. Housed inside is the ship's main communication, archaic looking with tubes and wires. Can Oliver really make sense out of all of this?

He rushes to the microphones. "It's better than I thought. We have short wave capabilities as well as digital. I can get both kinds of communication. From this ship, we should be able to communicate with the entire PACO society."

I throw my bag down on the floor. "You've heard of the PACO resistance all the way over here?"

He pulls a wire and hooks it to another wire. "How do you think we found out about the resistance? I've been secretly communicating with them for months."

I pull books off a chair and sit down. "Before the ambassador and his wife made it to Germany."

"Back then they didn't have so much organization. They didn't even have a name. The PACO title just started about a month ago."

"What does PACO mean?" I ask.

Oliver lines up wires. "I have no idea. All I know is that when they started calling themselves PACO, they seemed more focused."

"See what I'm doing here?" He places the wires on the desk according to their color. "This is what I need you to do first."

For the next two hours Oliver, Eddie, and I work on dismantling the old communications system. Oliver takes the microphone apart and blows on each of the parts. He asks Eddie to bring him a component from one of his bags. Oliver takes that piece and places it in the microphone.

He clicks it to the "on" position. "This works. Do you hear the hum?" A grin fills his face. "Now on to the motherboard."

Eddie claps his hands. "Well done. Let's take a quick break. We're going to be shoving off soon. Let's go up on deck and watch, and then we can get something to eat. Maybe even some sleep after that."

I nod. "Sleep might make me more alert."

Oliver holds the microphone for a second then places it back down. "Guess we do need to eat. Besides, we're going to be on the open sea for a while. Plenty of time to finish the work. No telling who we might contact." His eyes twinkle as he talks.

My brother really does seem to know a lot about electronics. I haven't seen anyone this excited about anything since I saw Gretel working with the ambassador. Fear shoots through me. If Gretel was the ambassador's right-hand person then what will become of her now that the ambassador is gone? What about Mom, Colt, or Riley? I need to focus. It will be good to help my brother with his project, but my ultimate goal has to be to save my family still captive on the ship. Riley is in this spot because of me. I rub the lucky charm around my neck. I wish I could give this luck to all of them.

I sigh, releasing my thoughts when I arrive on the deck with Eddie and Oliver. Ropes are hoisted and the ship readies for its voyage. It's getting dark. Sun will set soon.

"Do they put on any lights?" I ask as the darkness of the night sets in.

Eddie waves his arms around. "It's the open sea. No lights should be out here unless they are a ship connected to the king. If we put on lights, then we might be discovered."

I widen my eyes. "How will we know where to go?"

"Instruments." He grins back at me. "You don't know anything about ships, do you?"

I crook my head. "I'm a farm girl. Where would I learn about ships?"

He nods. "The king travels in a set path. All we have to do is to avoid that route once we get out to sea. But getting out to sea, we are still visible. We don't want a person walking the beach to see us and report us. Do we?"

I shake my head. "There are people free enough to walk on the beach?"

Oliver laughs. "He just told you about the possibly of getting caught, and all you can think of is how people can walk on the beach?"

"When you've been forced to stay in one place all of your life, it's hard to imagine what it would be like to wake up one day and decide to take a walk. I've had orders to stay on the farm all of my life. Then I escaped to the "Queen Nalani" where I became a Sponsored Companion. Then, I followed more orders."

"What's a Sponsored Companion?" Oliver leans on the rail.

It's hard to be so careful with what I say. I might accidentally clue him in on our real connection. I want him to know that he is my brother, but not just yet. "A Sponsored Companion does not have the freedom to decide to walk on the beach whenever they want. Basically, a Sponsored Companion is an owned person. To do the bidding of those who own them. I was a SC, but I escaped and now I'm here." I take a deep breath. That whole speech didn't make much sense to someone who hadn't lived through it, but maybe my indignation about it all will make him not ask any more questions.

"Sorry, I can tell it's a touchy subject." It worked, he's going to drop it. "If it makes you feel any better, I've been a prisoner my whole life too."

I slide beside him and grab the rail. "How could you have been a prisoner?" I ask. "You were the ambassador's son."

He gazes out onto the shoreline. "There are many different kinds of prisons."

I don't ask any more questions. Eddie finds a chair and we all watch the sun melt into the dark orange horizon. Funny, the sun seems the same no matter where I am in the world. Each day brings hope for something new. A new freedom. Finding my family. Breaking the communication code. Finding out more about my brother. Tomorrow could be the best day ever. I just have to have hope. I have to hold onto it. I'm free now in a sense. If there were a beach around, I could choose to walk on it. There is a certain amount of happiness in just knowing that.

Oliver spends three days redoing all of the wires and completely gutting the motherboard in order to reconstruct it. Being his assistant proves to be a learning experience for me and I enjoy finding out about the inner workings of his contraption. I am filled with great anticipation when he hooks the last wire and says, "We need to try to communicate."

Eddie says, "Should I get the captain?"

Oliver turns the microphone on and off. "Not just yet. Let's make sure that it works." He flicks the microphone on and holds the button down. "This is Ship 0204. Does anybody hear me?"

He repeats the question seven more times. I'm counting.

"Identify your allegiance." A booming voice rips through the speaker in the motherboard.

Oliver holds the button down. "PACO."

The voice asks, "Location?"

Oliver replies, "America, you?"

"Bavaria." The voice sounds again.

"That's where I'm from." I shout and jump up.

"Shush!" Oliver holds up his hand. "We don't know who this is." He pushes the button again. "Code?"

The speaker is silent for a couple of seconds. "I'll name the first part of the code you name the last. Agreed?"

"Agreed." Oliver speaks into the microphone. He presses the button once again. "CO."

The speaker immediately responds. "PA."

Oliver breathes a sigh of relief. "What's the status there?"

The speaker booms. "We are organizing an army. Consisting mostly of children. We number in the thousands. Our base of operation has not been infiltrated. We are joined by a family that has been most helpful."

Oliver presses the button again. "We are on our way to you. I'll bring you more information. The Americans and Europeans need to work together."

"I will send you the coordinates of our rendezvous point." A few beeps follow.

I ask, "Are those the coordinates?"

Oliver nods as he writes down the numbers. "We'll find it on the map." He presses the button again. "Over and out."

"Wait!" The voice booms again. "We need a password for when we meet."

I push the button on the microphone and offer. "What about you say, "Roses are red and violets are blue" and then he says the line, "If you say this line then I'll know it's you." Will that work?"

Laughter seeps out of the airways. "I can do that. Don't know who the girlie is, but she's a keeper."

Oliver presses the button. "Okay, we'll use that line. But about the girl, you might want to meet her before you say that."

I sock him in the arm.

"What is the name of your operation?" The voice booms again. "What do I call you?"

"SONOL," Oliver says and I read what he has written on the paper "SON-OLIVER" with the last four letters marked out. SONOL, clever.

"One more question SONOL. There is an Aunt Sandra here in Bavaria who would like to know if you came across any young people named Colt, Paisley, or Riley. She's worried about them."

I grab the microphone and press the button. "This is Paisley. Tell Aunt Sandra that I am safe, but we will have to rescue Riley and Colt." I take my finger off the button for a second and then press it again. "What about the farm? Did she get the children from the farm?"

The voice booms. "She did. Some are still there, but all are safe." The speaker squawks one last time. "PACO over and out."

Oliver grabs the microphone and sets it down on the desk. "*You're* involved with the resistance."

I frown. "You didn't believe me?"

He sits back in his chair. "Not really. That was a crazy story you told. I thought you might be a spy."

I drag another chair over and take a seat. "If you thought that, then why did you let me work in here with you?"

He shrugs. "There's no escape for you here. I thought you might give us some information. I want to apologize for doubting you."

I smirk and nod. "Apology accepted." A satisfying tingle flows through me.

I could wallow in anger about how he did not believe me, but we have bigger issues. How are we ever going to get our power back when we don't know whom to trust? "We need a patch or tattoo or something that identifies us to each other, but doesn't give us away to the enemy."

Eddie nods. "That's a great idea." He pulls out some paper. "What do you have in mind?"

I think for a moment before an image pops into my mind. I draw the broken egg. "I saw this on a train and also tattooed on a resistance fighter in Bavaria."

"What does it mean?" Oliver asks.

"Below it was scrawled one word—freedom. I guess that's what it means. If we're trapped like yolks inside the egg, we can't do anything. We have to break the shell to be free."

Oliver pulls the paper with the drawing over to illuminate it under the light. "I like it. Let's get this started. We can use this drawing as a guide. Maybe we can make patches for people to put on their shirts or carry. This way we can identify ourselves to each other."

I point to the microphone. "Next time you contact them tell the Bavarian people to find Lieutenant Drake. He'll help them. Last time I saw him was when I was in Hamburg. He offered to help us then. He told us he was with the resistance and had connections to other underground cells."

"Of course I've heard of him," says Eddie, opening the door. "He's one of the leaders. Do you know everybody?"

I smile. "Not quite everybody, but maybe enough to get us started."

For the next four days, we communicate daily with the Bavarian resistance faction. Oliver tries to reach the Americans with no luck. Frustration sets in; we have to be able to connect the continents.

Fortunately, some of the women on board have experience with sewing and they fashion a broken egg patch that we are to carry with us at all times. It is constructed to unravel if we pull on one particular thread of the egg to protect our identity in case we are caught by the enemy. It is a masterful piece of work.

On the ninth day, the sea is rough. Oliver searches me out to inform me that a message has gotten through to the Americans.

"What's the name of the resistance leader in America?" I ask.

"Her name is—"

"Her?" I question.

Oliver laughs. "That's funny coming from you. I remember on the very first day, you told me clearly that women were just as useful as men. You said that you shouldn't be put in the kitchen." He winks at me. "I thought you were speaking the truth, but then again I thought maybe you just didn't know how to cook." He chuckles again.

I feel my cheeks burning. "Of course. I just meant." I pause trying to think of something else to say. When nothing comes to mind, I mumble, "I'm just surprised that's all."

Oliver relishes my discomfort and obviously wants it to continue so he asks, "Okay smarty pants, since you know so much. Tell me the name of the woman leader for the Americans." He leans up against a wall in the room. "If you can name her. I'll give you—"

"Ten free questions to ask you." I pause before adding, "About your past."

He smiles. "If I win, I want the same. Agreed?"

"Sure," I nod reluctantly. No way out of this now. I want to know about my brother. Don't know why my past would be interesting to him though. He probably thinks that I like him or something. Yuck! That's creepy!

"Name?" He pulls Eddie over. "Eddie you're my witness. Right?"

Eddie nods.

I say the name of the only female in charge that I know. "Captain Via."

Oliver slams his fists into the desk. "How do you do that?"

Guess I was right. I win.

We only have one more night before we dock at the designated rendezvous point. It might be my last chance to collect my win. I hunt Oliver down to ask him the questions. We find a quiet place on the deck. The air is cold. Winter is coming and we cautiously travel more north in order to avoid the path of the "Queen Nalani" ship. I am bundled up in a blanket, seated on a chair on the deck. "Did you pick here because you think I'll freeze and give up before I get through all of the questions?"

"No." Oliver buttons up his jacket. "But *will* you?"

I shake my head. "First question. What do you remember about your life before the virus?"

"Not much. I remember that we were all hiding in a small house for a long time."

"Who?" I ask. "Who was hiding?"

"Second question is who was hiding? Well there was my father and me. A woman was with us for a short while. I assume she was my nanny. I

281

don't remember much about her."

"I thought that was a part of the first question, but that's okay. What do you remember about the nanny?" My father never mentioned a nanny, but he did say my mother was with them before I disappeared. I have to believe that there was no nanny, only my mother. That has to be our mother he remembers. I want to know as much as I can about her.

"Why in the world would you want to know about my nanny? That makes no sense whatsoever." He clutches his jacket. He is not invincible. He's cold too.

"My questions and that is number three." I wrap the blanket tighter. "Tell me about the nanny."

"Okay, I'll play along." He shakes his head and sighs. "I haven't thought of her in a long time. She had hair the color of yours. She had a sweet smell."

I prod. "Anything else?"

He retorts. "Is that question four?"

"Yes." I reply.

He sits for a moment as if he is trying hard to remember her. "You know I do remember one thing. She had a heart."

"A heart, everyone has a heart."

"No she actually had a heart." He points to his neck. "She had a heart right here on her neck."

My stomach flutters and I gasp. "What kind of heart? A tattoo?"

"No, I'm not sure what it was, but I don't think it was a tattoo. It was red like a rash."

I hold my breath before letting it out slowly. "Could it have been a birthmark?"

He nods. "Yes, it could have been that. Strange that I remembered that about her."

I can't talk. Could it be? But how could my mother still be alive? It can't be. I need to ask the last six questions carefully. I open my mouth to ask my next question, but I stop. I hear something in the distance. It's faint. "Do you hear that?"

Oliver slaps his leg. "What? The sound of you running out of questions?"

I throw off my blanket and slam my hand over his mouth. "No, listen."

We are silent for a few minutes. The sounds of the waves hitting into the side of the ship come at expected intervals. Oliver becomes as quiet as I am as we stand at the rail leaning over to trying to perk our ears to hear the voice. I don't want to have imagined it.

It's words, someone talking. A distinct voice. I cannot make out what it is saying, but it's definitely a person. "Don't you hear that?"

Oliver leans over the rail as far as he can. "I do." A few seconds later, he runs towards the ship's cabin. I throw off my blanket and dart after him.

Oliver reaches the cabin and slides open the door. "Captain. We heard someone out in the sea."

The captain shakes his head. "Probably Undesirables or Uncounteds thrown overboard." He walks out of the cabin and peers over the side. "I hope we can find them. It's so dark."

I ask, "What about shining a light out there?"

The captain shakes his head. "Not this close to shore."

I look around. "I'll take one of the life boats and go toward the sound."

Oliver frowns at me. "Are you crazy? It's too dangerous. You'll be killed!"

"What kind of people would we be, if we don't at least try?" I take off for the lifeboats before the captain or Oliver can stop me. I noticed the boats when I boarded the ship. I knew right where they were. All I had to do was to unhook the rope. Once that was done, the boat would automatically drop into the ocean. I dodge a couple of mates on the way and when I locate the lifeboat, I jump in and release the lever. The boat slides so quickly down that I fall into the end of the boat. I hear a thud about half way down and the boat rocks. Another person sits on the other side of the lifeboat. It's Oliver.

"You almost made the boat flip!" I yell at him.

He crouches as we splash into the water below. "I can't let you die." The boat heaves a few times before it steadies in the water.

I shake my head. "What about you?"

He grabs an oar and hands me another one. "They have to come after me. Remember I'm the ambassador's son and also I am the only one who can operate the communications."

I start pushing the oar back and forth. "You're risking your life to save me. Am I that good of an assistant?"

"Not at all." He laughs for a minute then stops. "For some reason I think you are worth saving."

"Why?" I ask.

"Because you're willing to jump in this dark water and risk death for people you've never met. I've never had a chance to be heroic. I want to try it, for once. Besides, it's the only way I could think of to make sure you survive."

283

I pull the oar through the water again. "What do you mean?"

He smirks, "They'll come after me, if I don't return. I'm kind of important."

I smile. "It may be the last thing you do."

"Hope not."

We feverishly push the oars through the open sea and the voices get louder.

"Look!" He shouts, "You were right."

In the distance, I spot a piece of wood with three people holding onto it. One of them, a male, yells. "Help!" It's faint, labored cry for help so we quickly steer our lifeboat toward them. We have to be in time to save them, we just have to be.

It's only a couple of moments before our lifeboat is perpendicular to the floating wood. The waves chop into the side of our boat causing it to almost capsize. We struggle to pull in the survivors into our boat. After losing the survivors back into the water a few times, Oliver and I finally manage to drag all three of them into the boat. I take off my jacket and Oliver does too. We try to cover them as much as we can. They are so quiet that I fear we might have been too late.

It takes a few minutes to row back to the ship. We are all lugged back on our pirate ship by our ship's mates and wrapped in blankets. The five of us are carried into the kitchen area. I throw off my blanket as the three survivors from the sea are stretched out on the long tables.

"Are they going to be okay?" I ask.

"Paisley?" The voice saying my name is one I recognize.

Chapter 23

There stretched out on the makeshift medical table in the kitchen is Riley. I can't contain myself. "Riley!" I throw my arms around him.

He groans. "Paisley!"

A woman yanks me off him. "Honey, you need to back off and let this boy breathe." She wipes his face and offers him water. He doesn't move. He stares at me. She hands me the water. "Do you want to see if you can get him to drink?'

I nod, draw him up, and lift the water to his mouth. He drinks a little at first, and then starts to gulp. "Not that fast. There's plenty. You're safe now, Riley."

I pull the necklace over my head and put it around his neck. "I think you need this more than me. You need its luck to make you better."

The woman rubs his hair and feels his forehead. "He needs to sleep. That'll make him better. Tomorrow we will get some food in him as soon as he wakes up. We should be in Bavaria."

I tear up. "Bavaria is our home."

She smiles. "Home always makes everything better."

I nod. Riley settles down holding tightly to my hand. As he drifts off, his grip loosens. I haven't thought to look at the other two people we dragged in. Maybe I know them. I walk slowly over to study their faces. I'm shocked when I realize that I do know one of them.

"Baako." I mutter.

Since Baako is here, does that mean that they caught him? Did he tell them about Colt? Where is Colt? I can't ask either Baako or Riley right now and the older woman is burned too badly to ask. What if Colt, Gretel, or my mother were thrown overboard also, but didn't survive?

At first, I fight sleep. I stare at them both waiting impatiently for either Riley or Baako to wake up and tell me what happened.

After a few hours, I lose the battle and fall asleep. I wake in the morning when I feel a hand brush through my hair. It's Riley. He's awake. He asks, "Have you been here all night?"

"Where is Gretel? What about Mom and Colt?" I rub the sleep out of my eyes. "Where are they?"

"They're all safe." He sits up taller. I let out a relieved sigh and hand him a cup of water.

"Not so fast," I chastise, when he gulps it once again. "You need to remember to take it in slow. I'll get you some food in a minute. Do you know what happened?"

He puts the cup down and looks around. "Did Baako make it?"

I nod and point over to the other table. "He's over there. What about the woman? Who is she?"

"Did she make it?" He shifts around.

"Yes," I answer. "They're taking care of her. Said she should be fine in a few days. Who is she?"

"Her name is Tury. She just ended up with us. I'm glad she made it." He dangles his legs over the side of the table. "When you left, I hid for days. Baako kept coming around looking for me. I finally found Colt and told him that you had run off after the princess recognized you. They looked for me until word came about the ambassador's death."

"What happened when they heard?"

"The queen and the princess went crazy. Colt had to stay with them all the time. He has kind of taken over as a surrogate father to the princess."

I smile. That is so Colt. "Mom and Gretel?"

"He's been looking in on them from time to time. Gretel took the ambassador's death hard. The queen asked Gretel to stay with them since she was so close with the ambassador."

I frown. "So do they not realize that King Ahomana had the ambassador killed?"

"What are you talking about?" He shakes his head. "I don't think the king knew anything about it. From the talk around the ship, the king just wanted the ambassador jailed not killed. Someone else put the kill order on the ambassador. The king is behaving like he's been betrayed. He is *too* distraught that his daughter is so upset. I don't think there is any way he would have done something this diabolical and permanent to hurt his daughter. He loves her. He seems confused and paranoid. He's not doing well at all. He is allowing others to control. He hasn't even recognized Colt. Colt has an inside seat with the royals and he told me that they're all in shock."

I pull myself up and sit with him on the table. "If the king didn't have him killed then who did?"

Riley shakes his head. "I have an idea. It's a scary thought. I think there is a new heinous force to be reckoned with. An American Merc is now running the show. He knows the king is not thinking straight and has swooped in. That's why the queen is so protective of the princess now. This Merc is trying to convince the queen that she needs him to protect them. I heard a rumor that he is trying to marry her while she is in this

286

weakened state. He's pushing hard to make it happen before the baby is born. He's power hungry. He wants to be a royal."

"Is she falling for that?" I scrunch my face up. "That's downright creepy."

He nods. "I'm afraid that she is. The queen wants someone to make sure that her family is safe. I'm worried." He lets out a deep sigh. "The only thing that Gretel and Colt can do is to watch out for the princess. They're doing a good job of that. I guess as soon as the new baby is born they'll take over watching that baby too."

I sigh. "What about Mom?"

He says, "Still in the kitchen. No change."

"What happened?" I look around. "Why did you three get thrown overboard?"

"You don't understand." He shakes his head. "We didn't get *thrown* overboard. We jumped."

I hit the floor and swing around facing him head on. "Why on earth would you jump off the ship?"

Baako lifts up and weakly says, "He did it for me."

"I don't understand." I turn back to Riley.

Riley nods. "He's right. I was hiding with this other woman, Tury. She's an Undesirable and would have been killed. She's been with me for a while now. Baako was bringing us food when a Merc caught him. The Merc was going to turn us all in. Baako would have been executed for treason."

I nod. "So you jumped."

Baako smiles. "We did get the wood we floated on before we jumped over. It was a door that they were replacing."

"I'm glad you made it." I put one arm around Riley's shoulder. "That was a dangerous thing to do. What's Colt going to think?"

Riley drops his head. "He's going to think we are *dead* when he can't find us."

I pull his chin up with my other hand and then hug him close. "Thankfully, you're not dead. Tomorrow we will be in Bavaria. Then we can join up with our army and defeat these Mercs once and for all."

"It'll take an army." Riley squeezes me back. "By the way, what kind of ship is this?"

"A pirate ship."

"Only you would find a pirate ship." He chuckles, pulls the necklace from around his neck, and hands it back to me. "This four-leaf clover is for you. You keep it for luck."

"I do love this necklace." I twirl the necklace in my hand for a second before I pull it back over my head. "It brought you luck. You're going to be okay."

"It'll be a long time before we are all okay, but at least I'm back with you. I was worried sick." He jumps off the table and stutters his stance for a moment before he steadies himself. "Right now, I'll take some food and maybe clean clothes."

I smile. "Right this way." I turn back to Baako. "Baako, you coming?"

Baako slides off the table. He stands over Tury and rubs her brow for a moment. "I'll stay with Tury to make sure she is okay."

"We'll bring food when we come back." I look at the woman taking care of them. "Make sure they're okay." The woman looks over at her patients. "She is sleeping now. He'll be fine. No hurry, take your time. I'll watch over them."

Riley and I walk out the door.

At the kitchen, we run into Oliver. "So you're the reason that Paisley jumped in the water."

Riley looks at me. "You jumped in the water?"

Oliver knocks his shoulder into mine. "She almost killed herself trying to save you."

I stammer, "I didn't know it was you. I just knew that someone was out in the water yelling."

Riley's face drops. "Oh."

I start again. "I didn't mean it like that..." I mumble. "...if I had known it was you...I would have..."

Riley cocks his head.

"I got nothing." I shake my head. "Sorry, but I would have jumped in the water to save whoever was in there. But I *am* glad it was you."

Riley chuckles. "So you're glad that I almost drowned."

I stare at him stone-faced. "I didn't mean that and you know it."

He smiles at me and then turns back to Oliver. "And you are?"

Oliver answers, "Oliver, Paisley has been working with me. We have been trying to reestablish communications with the resistance."

Riley stiffens and curtly asks, "Is that *all* you were working on?"

Oliver nonchalantly nods, oblivious to the tone of the question.

I think Riley is jealous. I like that. Unfortunately, I can't tell him that he has no reason to be jealous since Oliver is my brother because Oliver doesn't know that he is my brother. What a mess!

During dinner, Oliver tells Riley all about the communication system. He explains how we are connecting with all of the resistance factions from all over the world. He shares the plan to get the nations to vote for a democracy and end human trafficking.

Riley eats throughout Oliver's explanation and says, "Well now I know why Paisley is hanging out with you. She does love to get in the middle of the resistance and put herself in danger. She actually tried to take the place of everybody sentenced to die by execution by telling the king to only execute her. I know first-hand what Paisley is capable of."

Oliver leans back in his chair. "So where do you stand on all of this, Riley?"

Riley laughs and pats me on the back. "Right by Paisley. She has not steered me wrong yet. We are in this together." He cocks his head and stares at Oliver. "What's the plan?"

Oliver smiles. "Glad to hear that. I do have an idea and I'm going to need your help. We are going to the maze to recruit people willing to deliver portable communicators to every faction of the rebellion in all of Europe. We need to be able to talk to one another if we are going to organize a coup. I need you and Paisley to help me get in the maze."

Riley nods and I say, "We'll do it. That sounds great."

We spend the last day onboard working on the patches and make enough of them as a guide for others. The plan is to get close enough to the maze for Aunt Sandra's boys to find us. We'll share our ideas and give them the patches and communicators to pass out. Then we will be in touch with everyone so we will be able to coordinate a strike and wipe out the Mercs. It's a good strategy. I hope it works.

Eddie helps us pack up the portable communicators. Fortunately, they are so small we can take many in our backpacks along with the patches. The plan is to wait until nighttime to make our move so we'll be cloaked in darkness. When it's time Oliver, Riley, and I disembark on a lifeboat to shore. We journey through the woods to the designated rendezvous point. Being back on the European continent has its merits. The sights, sounds, tastes, and smells of home fill my soul and calm me.

We sit in the bushes for a couple of hours waiting for contact. I ask, "Oliver, why is it taking so long? Do you think something happened?"

He says, "No. They're being careful. These are the coordinates. Be patient."

Patience is not one of my virtues. I almost fall asleep when I hear rustling in the bushes. It's our contact. A young boy creeps up and says, "Roses are red and violets are blue."

Oliver smiles and says, "If you say this line, then I'll know it is you."

The boy motions to a trail. "I have horses waiting for us. They are only a couple of kilometers."

We all begin our trek down the path.

I catch up with the boy. "What's your name?"

"Josef." The boy slows his pace to match mine.

I ask, "What does PACO stand for?"

He takes in a deep breath. "I love telling this. There was a story about two brave young people who chose to give their lives to save others. Their names started with a pa and a co. Their names are Paisley and Colt."

I gasp.

Chapter 24

Josef turns to face me. "We came for you. We know you are one of the brave ones, Paisley. We know all about you. You are a legend. Everyone talks about you and Colt. We know that you are special."

Oliver leans over to Riley and I hear him whisper, "Is there anything that she is not involved in?"

Riley shakes his head and chuckles under his breath.

PACO, who knew?

Josef leads us down the trail to awaiting horses. I'm thrilled that one of the horses is my old friend, Hershey. I hug her, satisfying a piece of my heart. I am happy to have a few minutes to digest that they used our names for the resistance. We mount the horses, slip our feet into the stirrups, and set off.

It's strange to think of yourself as part of a legend. As we travel through the German terrain, Josef regales us with stories of my and Colt's adventures or misadventures. And as is always the custom, the stories are exaggerated the more they are told. I know some of these are the stories that Colt and I told the other SCs and Aunt Sandra's comrades. They are so altered now, they don't even sound like the same stories.

The story about the train ride has been embellished to include a run across the tracks with us beating up a conductor and saving all of the people on the train. The rescue of the Bavarian farm people at the train station has been inflated to include an all out gun battle with an army of guards and the fib that got us on the ship has been amplified to the point that we invented the Sponsored Companions program to make our way onto the ship.

As Josef is telling us these stories, I try to explain the truth, but he doesn't listen.

Oliver leans over after Josef refuses to listen once again. "People like to have heroes. What's the harm in the stories being more exaggerated than they actually were? You are giving hope to a large contingent of children who are fighting and possibly dying for this cause. Nothing is more inspiring than someone who actually was courageous. You were brave in all of these instances, right?"

I nod. I guess he has a point. How can we convince anyone to take up arms and battle through this fight if they don't believe it can be won? What better way than to have a story about someone or in this case two someones who actually did just that. I guess a little embellishment won't hurt.

"Look!" Josef points out a tree with the letters PACO carved into it. "See I told you, you're famous!"

Riley chuckles, as I turn red. Nothing like a little embarrassment to make the time go faster.

"Where are we going?" I ask as we round a trail high in the hills. We travel most of the day and I still have no idea where we are heading.

Mike rides up. "Always so impatient."

I'm startled for a moment; I haven't seen Mike since we were at the Ferris wheel farm. But the sight of one of our farm children makes my heart sing. I can't help but smile. No bandages or slings this time. I ask, "Your leg is all healed? I guess falling off that Ferris wheel wasn't as bad as we first thought. "

He nods as Thomas rides up behind him and dismounts.

I jump off Hershey. "Thomas, it's great to see you. It seems like being put in charge has agreed with you and Mike." I reach up my hand and touch the top of his head. "You've grown a half a meter."

Thomas stands as tall as he can. I am bursting with pride. I take comfort that we left our children of the farm in good hands.

Hershey nuzzles me. "Hershey, wish I had an apple to give you."

Thomas pulls an apple out of his pack and tosses it to me. "Here, but hurry. The Mercs still patrol here and we have about another hour before we are completely safe."

I feed Hershey quickly and mount again. The hour on the trail is spent filling Thomas and Mike in about how Colt and my family are still on the ship set to dock in a couple of days and how Colt is looking out after the princess and the queen since the ambassador's death. Thomas asks how Colt managed to impersonate a Merc. Riley explains it with the story about the switch and the storeowner.

"There are a lot of people like that storeowner on our side." Mike pats his horse and points to a turn on the trail. "We'll be safe from here. This part of the trail is not marked and is guarded by us all of the time."

"How do you know if people are on your side?" Oliver asks.

"It's guesswork now." Mike sighs.

Oliver lights up. "That's where we can help." He pulls out a patch. "We've made these patches so we can easily identify the resistance and those on our side. We've also developed a portable communicator. We plan to get information to every underground station that we know of. We'll give each of these groups extra communicators and patches so they can pass them out. We want this rebellion to succeed with as little bloodshed as possible."

Mike nods. "I agree there's been enough death." He sighs. "There's something you don't know, Paisley."

Riley crouches on his horse to avoid a tree branch. "Nothing bad, I hope."

"No." Thomas grasps the reins of Hershey, my horse. "Whoa! We're almost there. Maybe Aunt Sandra should tell her." He looks over at Mike.

Mike nods. "Maybe."

I ask, "Tell me what?"

Mike turns and faces me. "They want you to be the new face of the Consortium of the World since the ambassador is dead. We need someone to represent hope."

"Me?" I feel the blood seeping out of my face slithering down to my toes. I'm not a leader. I'm just a farm girl from Bavaria. What would I know about inspiring a movement? I haven't even turned sixteen yet. That doesn't make sense. How would I represent hope?

Mike dismounts. "We're here. We'll talk about it later."

The rest of us dismount and leave the horses in a guard's care. I recognize the beginning of the maze into Aunt Sandra's realm. It takes about half an hour to make our way through the cave, then through the maze before we reach the inner sanctum. I am relieved when I glimpse the top of the castle. Just the sight of the castle gives me a warm feeling all over.

Aunt Sandra, Kelley, and Amanda are there to greet us. We are led to a long table full of food.

"Don't have to ask me to eat. I'm starving." I grab a piece of bread and bite off a corner. "What's this about me being a face for democracy?" I direct my question to Aunt Sandra. "What about you? Why can't you be the face?"

"My place is here." Aunt Sandra picks up a tomato, cuts it in two with a knife, and puts it on a serving plate. "You and Colt are the catalysts that started this whole movement. You need to be the face of freedom."

Oliver picks up the half of tomato and tosses it in his mouth. "I have to agree. Studying history teaches us that we need to have some ideal or someone to follow. The Americans have the ambassador and since everyone thought you were dead, you became the martyr for this side of the world. Everyone over here followed your ideals. We all have to have heroes."

Aunt Sandra pats Oliver's hand. "I was sorry to hear about your father."

Oliver nods for a moment. "Thanks." It's strange how I seem to be more upset about our father's death than he is. I shouldn't judge though, I don't know what he's been through.

After dinner, Oliver shares the portable communicators explaining how they work to Aunt Sandra and to a few of her top allies. He also shows her the broken egg patch. I explain to her how to make it so it can be destroyed in a matter of seconds if the wearer is caught.

"Ingenious." Aunt Sandra announces, "Tomorrow morning, we will begin disseminating the portable communicators and instructions on how to make the patches to the rest of our resistance cells. You should make contact with your shop owner. I'm sure she will know of others."

I light up. "Do you think the "Queen Nalani" ship will be there by then?"

Aunt Sandra nods. "It probably will. But Colt and your family are safe for now. You need to stay on plan and not deviate. Do you understand?"

Riley stands up. "She doesn't understand how to follow the rules, but I do. I'll make sure the plan is carried out."

Riley is always looking out for me whether I want him to or not.

That night, I toss and turn. I'm so restless it's almost impossible to fall asleep. My mind is racing with thoughts about all of the things that can go wrong with our plan. All of the people that can be hurt or killed. I can't stop my mind from running one disastrous scenario after another.

I'm worried about my family. **What will become of them? They don't even know I survived. They must still think I am back in America.** What if they try to go back and find me? I can't possibly know the answer to any of this so I work myself up into a dither, but the good thing about dithers is that you eventually fall asleep.

The next morning we set out to put our plan in action.

The trail is long and arduous, but we finally make it to Hamburg. There sits the "Queen Nalani" ship. It takes everything I have not to run down the street and get on board, screaming at the top of my lungs, "Gretel, Colt and Mom, I'm alive! I'm here!"

Instead, we enter the Sponsored Companions doll shop. The only change in the shop is the addition of a few more posters of new Sponsored Companions. Seeing no living beings in the store to be sold, I can only guess that the living dolls are bought as soon as they arrive. Behind the desk sits a familiar face. Her features are not as chiseled as they were before, her lips are pursed, gray streaks throughout her hair, lines crevasse her face making her look more worn than the last time we saw her.

"Hello, Ms. DeVane," Riley blurts out as we walk in.

Taken by surprise, she gasps and stands. It takes her a moment to gain her composure. Her eyes dart surveying the room. "Follow me."

She leads us to the back where we catch up on what has been going on. She asks about her son and we tell her that we haven't found any information about him yet, but we're still looking.

Oliver props his elbows on the table. "I can find out about your child. Give me his full name and month and day of birth."

Ms. DeVane trembles. "William DeVane. October 26."

Oliver takes out a device. It's not like the communicator; it's smaller with a key pad.

"What's that?" I ask.

"It's a portable computer. I have it hooked up to the mainframe back in America. I'm connected to satellites that have been orbiting our planet since before the virus. As we travelled across the ocean, I re-connected this continent with America." The computer beeps. "Here it is."

Ms. DeVane gasps. "You found him? How?"

Oliver holds up the computer. "I've been collecting information for months. I began this database while I was working on the computer project. I've been inputting the information so we can find our loved ones. I realized early on that most people just want to know where their families are. Once reunited, we can find safe places for them. Many people work with me to help find others and free them."

Ms. DeVane's voice cracks and tears run down her face. "Where's my boy?"

Oliver turns the computer's screen to face Ms. DeVane so she can read it. "He is in a camp in Frankfurt, Germany. He is assigned as a horse trainer." A grin encompasses Oliver's face. "This is the best part of my job. We'll be going through there. We'll find him and see what we can do then." He writes down the information he shared on a piece of paper and hands it to Ms. DeVane.

Ms. DeVane holds the note like a fragile egg. "Thank you. Thank you so much." She throws her arms around Oliver's shoulders.

"This is how we will defeat our enemies by bringing families back together. We'll become strong and democracy will follow." Oliver places his computer back in his bag.

"I had no idea you had something like that." I shake my head at Oliver. "That's amazing."

"Me neither." Riley says. "That device would be very dangerous in the wrong hands. It must be protected."

A voice from the front of the store announces, "That's why we're here."

Chapter 25

It's Lieutenant Drake. He saved Colt and me when we first came to Hamburg. I'm glad to see that he survived and even though he looks like a man not used to physical contact, I hug him. "I was wondering if we would ever see you again."

He hesitates for a moment, but squeezes me back picking me up a little off the floor. "You are quite different now. Back when I first we met you, you had an awful stench about you."

I giggle. "You're being nice, we smelled awful. I never got a chance to thank you."

"Save your thanks," He places me back on the floor and points to the back door. "Because I am going to get you out of a tight spot again."

"What are you talking about?" I regain my footing.

"We were told you were coming here. We came to take you to a safe place. Follow me." He walks toward the back door.

Ms. DeVane clasps my hand. "Take some of the new outfits and put them in your backpacks you might need them later. You know how to pass as a Sponsored Companion."

"Thanks." I embrace her and grab a handful of the new Sponsored Companion outfits as we leave. Fortunately, the hat and clothes are packaged together. I quickly shuffle through the shoeboxes to find our right sizes. I find a copy of the tattoo we need and throw it in the bag too. Could come in handy later.

Riley holds the back door open as we three, along with Lieutenant Drake, exit. Riley asks, "Why the rush? Has something happened?"

"Yes." Lieutenant Drake holds up a newspaper. "The Consortium of the World negotiations have been put on hold and King Ahomana has been put in charge."

I grab the paper and there he is, King Ahomana sitting on the throne in all his glory. "They voted? I didn't hear about a vote."

"No vote, but that doesn't matter now." Lieutenant Drake points to the man beside the king in the picture. "This man is our real problem. The king's second in command is Emperor Richard the Great. He doesn't follow any rules."

Riley asks, "What does this mean?"

"I've heard from a variety of reliable sources that this emperor has his sights set on ruling the world. He doesn't want a vote. He just wants to take over." The lieutenant sighs. "My guess is that the king will be assassinated in the next few weeks and that the emperor will be in charge. Unfortunately if that happens, all this talk about negotiating democracy and the Consortium of the World will be just that—talk."

I question fervently, "What about the queen and the princess? What will happen to them?"

The lieutenant shakes his head. "No idea, but we need to get you to a safe place *immediately*."

We follow the lieutenant through the winding back alleys and streets until we come to a dilapidated clock store. We remove a couple of boards out of the way to enter. Inside the shop, we uncover a hidden door to stairs that lead underground. Once there, lanterns light the way. The corridor of the cavern is about half a kilometer long. At the mouth of the cave is another entrance into another store. We enter it and hide its existence by positioning a crate over it.

Lieutenant Drake opens the inner door. "Stay here for now so we can coordinate our plan."

"We already have a plan. We have orders of what to do." I protest. "We're supposed to go around and pass out these communicators and patches to our allies."

"My men and I will do that. You are much too valuable to be out in the open."

I stand with my hands on my hips. "If I'm that valuable, then what about Colt?"

"I knew you would say that!" Drake smiles. "We are executing a plan right now to free him from the ship."

"No, you can't! He's protecting my mom and Gretel and the princess!" I shriek.

"Quiet! Someone will hear you!" Drake covers my mouth with his hand. "I'm sorry, but Colt's safety takes precedence over your family."

I struggle to free Drake's grip. I mumble through his hand, but my muffled sounds don't make any sense. My eyes search out Riley. I know he reads my desperation. Riley lunges at Drake, but is quickly subdued by others in the store that we now inhabit.

I jerk my head free and furiously spout at Drake. "Are we *your* prisoners now?"

"Sorry. You have to stay put." Drake shakes his head. "There is no other way."

I rock back and forth with my head in my hands. Colt won't go without a fight. He will make them save Gretel. He won't leave her, I just know it.

The night is long. We aren't allowed to move or talk or do anything. Finally, the door opens and there stands Gretel.

"Gretel!" I squeal and run to her.

She yells, "Paisley, you made it! You're alive!"

I hug her tightly. "Where's Mom and Colt?"

She pulls from my grip and motions toward the door. A man carrying Colt walks in the door and says, "He wouldn't leave without her. We had to bring them both."

Drake slams his fist on the table. "Did we lose any?"

The man shakes his head. "No, Colt fought them off. He took a couple of bullets."

Gretel orders them: "Find a flat place, table, floor, anything. I need to get the bullets out now and sew him up before he loses anymore blood."

Drake brushes plates and cups off the table and asks, "Are you a doctor?"

Two of the men hoist Colt onto the table.

"Close as you're going to get. Find alcohol, sewing needle, and knife. If you have it, bring something to dull his pain." She rips Colt's shirt off. "A very sharp razor would be a big help."

Gretel barks more orders. "Bandages or something to use as bandages. Boil some water, a bowl of clean water, and rags. I'm going to need thread and a pair of scissors."

People scurry about finding the items or locating suitable replacements.

Gretel works quickly. "I have to get the bullets out and sanitize the area so it doesn't get infected." She cuts into Colt's midsection. "Looks like the bullets lodged into your muscle. It'll be painful, but you should survive." She digs for the two bullets with the knife. "Sorry Colt, this isn't too pretty and it's going to hurt." She sighs loudly. "A lot."

Colt groans. "Do what you have to. I trust you."

I stand silently, attempting to guess what she will need. I hand her a knife, rags, and water. I try to sop up the blood as the gash widens. As soon as one rag is red with blood, I get another.

Colt moans and grits his teeth the whole time she is prodding. Blood gushes out the deeper she goes. The rags are soaked with his blood by the time she retrieves the bullets. As Gretel jabs, she stops for a moment. "I'm sorry." Tears run down her face and I wipe her cheeks as fast as I can.

Colt manages a meek, "I'm okay."

"Scissors?" Gretel asks me.

I search around and shake my head.

"No scissors, huh?" Gretel looks around the table and picks up the alcohol. "This is going to hurt, but I have to sanitize the wound."

She pours alcohol onto his gash and he yelps in pain.

Gretel swallows a sob, sets the alcohol down, and holds out her hand. "Needle and thread."

I locate the items. She threads the needle and douses the needle and thread with alcohol before starting her work. Colt clenches his fists, groaning the whole time as she sews him up.

When she finishes, Gretel bites the thread with her teeth. "With no scissors, it's the best I could do." She dabs his wound with a clean rag, sopping up the blood.

Colt grabs her hand and whispers, "Thanks. I love you."

She wraps his torso with a bandage and then kisses his forehead. "I couldn't live without you, remember that."

Blood drains from Colt's face and he passes out. Gretel's face is filled with fear until she takes his pulse and breathes a sigh of relief. "Let him rest, he'll be better in the morning." She walks over to the faucet and runs water over her hands, rinsing off blood. She spends a lot of time scrubbing her hands. The blood is gone, but she keeps cleaning them. She's in shock. I know she is used to seeing blood, but this is Colt's. It's different.

I hug her again. "What about Mom?"

Gretel shakes her head. "She was in the kitchen. We couldn't get to her. I am sure they don't know who she is. She should be fine, but we do need to get her off that ship."

I nod. "We'll worry about that later. At least your both alive and here out of harm's way."

She glances towards the table holding Colt. "It's his birthday today. He's eighteen. Happy birthday to him. What away to spend it."

Eighteen. He's a man now. He proved it. The first thing he did as a man was to refuse to leave his love behind even if it meant his own death. I will always love him for that.

Drake looks over Colt and then slides a chair over for Gretel to sit on. "You did a good job on him." He flips a chair around and sits in it backwards. "What's going on with the royals?"

Gretel fills us in. "The new second in command, Emperor Richard, is manipulating the queen. The queen is weak because of the pregnancy. The emperor has been pushing the queen to marry him. He tells her it's because he wants her and her children to be safe, but he wants to make himself a royal by marriage. We can't let that happen."

I agree with Gretel.

It feels good to have Gretel, Colt, and Riley all in one place. Now if we can only get my mom to safety. Not to mention my birth family. Fortunately, my brother Oliver is with me, but the princess and her unborn sibling are on that ship and in the enemy's hands.

It seems so hopeless.

Colt sleeps with Gretel's head resting on his hand. I sit on a chair beside Gretel touching her arm with my finger.

It takes hours for everyone to regain their composure. No one is allowed to leave. I want to go to my mom, but Drake refuses to let me. I am imprisoned for days in the makeshift center of command in Hamburg while Oliver and Drake organize supporters to deliver the communicators and the patch with the guide on how to make it.

Oliver runs diagnostics daily on the communicators. It is through these sessions that we find out our grassroots efforts are making an impact. It only takes a couple of days before we begin to receive messages from cells of resistance all over the globe. I'm angry that I'm not allowed to try to free my mom, but I do see progress every day.

Riley draws a large map of the world and hangs it on the wall. Every time we make contact with a cell, Riley notes it on the map with a colored stickpin. In two weeks, we have most of the map covered. In addition, I have been inventorying the amount of supporters located in each faction. Our numbers grow daily.

With this new information, I am optimistic.

Hope is spreading. The mood is more positive. We gather daily to read the propaganda being disseminated by those who want to remain in control.

The more followers the resistance gains, the more heinous the actions of the Mercs become. Mercs have ruled using fear for so long that they think they can continue to scare everyone into submission. Every day someone is executed for treason. If caught, we will be executed too. Riots break out in the streets. Riley and Oliver try to calm the factions using the communicators. The resistance is told of how many supporters there are and asked to be patient. Our time will come. But it is hard for me to be patient so I know it must be impossible for them. Especially those in the outlying areas. How can they possibly see what we see? All they know is that their food supply is dwindling and there doesn't seem to be anyone to save them from their only two options, a life as a servant or certain death.

Nightly, Colt and I transmit a program called, "Speak to the Troops." It's aimed at keeping morale high. We tell our stories with embellishments that make them so much more interesting. Riley shares his Merc status in an attempt to garner support from disgruntled Mercs. Oliver speaks as the voice of the fallen ambassador. He doesn't identify himself, but only says he served with the ambassador. He fears that if he reveals his true identity, the princess and queen might be in danger. No one wants a little girl or a pregnant mother to die, not even the troops. Drake says scouts report Mercs are scouring the countryside looking for the source of the transmissions.

The goriest is the list of those executed. We received word that there is to be a televised execution, the first ever. Emperor Richard plans to use this spectacle to launch his rhetoric and spread his lies. Our group attempts to shut down the broadcast, but are unsuccessful.

Oliver rigs up a makeshift television so we can capture the signal and view the execution. No one wants to watch it, but we need to keep up to date with what is going on with the Mercs and the emperor.

Gretel and I choose not to observe such a heinous act until I hear Colt. "Don't let the two girls back in here."

It must be someone I know. I bolt through the door and Gretel follows.

On the screen, people are lined up with guns pointed at them. Riley grabs me as I enter the room. "Go back. You don't want to see this."

I recognize almost all of their faces from the ship. They are the Undesirables and Uncounteds. What an atrocious act! I shake my head and bury it into his chest. He's right, I don't want to watch this.

I can hardly hear anything for my own sobbing. One shriek pierces the air loud and clear.

It's my sister. "Not Mom! No!"

Chapter 26

The shots ring out and the thumping sounds of crumpling humans permeate through the television. Gretel and I grab each other and clutch the sides of the small screen screaming together "No!" to no avail. Riley pulls me to him and grips me tightly. I see out of the corner of my eye that Colt has grabbed a sobbing Gretel. My legs give way and Riley holds me up with his arms. I black out for a second. It's too much pain to bear. I can't believe what I just witnessed. Our beautiful mother who never did anything to anyone has been shot for no apparent reason except for the fact that they could shoot her. Painful sensations surge throughout into my body. I force my eyes to watch the television.

My blood boils as I see the Emperor Richard laughing. He addresses the camera and menacingly warns, "This is what happens if you don't obey your king."

My stomach roils. Sickness. I need to vomit, but I control it. Thanks goodness the princess is not on the deck to witness all of this. Her sweet innocent nature could not take it. The king is not even on the deck. How could this be? Has the Emperor Richard taken over completely?

I protect my heart as best I can. My insides are mush. I don't feel like I can go on. My mother is gone and there is nothing I can do to bring her back. I dig deep. I must overcome this. I'll save this horror for a later date. I must resist the temptation to let it seep into my consciousness. I can't let this define me, I have to let it make me stronger. It's what my mother would have wanted. If only—I stop myself. I could go forever with if onlys and none of those if onlys would bring my sweet mother back. The only thing I can do at this point is honor her memory by making sure these tyrants are out of power.

I'm tired of being told what to do. "Drake, it's time we did something about this!"

Drake trembles as a tear rolls down a deep wrinkle on his cheek. He wipes it off with the back of his hand. Visibly shaken by what he saw, he asks, "What do you suggest?"

I shut my eyes to conjure up a viable plan. The few moments of silence allows me to clear my head. I experience a pure moment of clarity, which launches a diabolical thought. I know what exactly what we need to do.

"Hit them where it hurts. We need to cause mayhem and destruction!" I slam my fist on the table.

Drake walks over to me. "I know that you want to kill every last one of them, but some of them can be saved. We can't go blood for blood—"

"You don't know me very well, Lieutenant Drake, but that's not what I have in mind."

He sits at the table. "Then tell me."

"We need to destroy them from within. Make sure they cannot regain power."

He scrunches his eyes. "You've got my attention. I'm listening."

I explain, "I systematically will outline a series of events that will cause their downfall. I'll share my plan to destroy the regime from within. First, you need to understand the idea." I ask, "What do they fear most?"

Somebody yells out, "Loss of power."

I point to the stick pinned map. "More than that, they fear death. What if we start by making them believe the virus has reappeared?"

"Won't work." Riley shakes his head. "They'll know it's not true."

Colt joins in. "We could communicate with the resistance and tell them to bury—"

"Bury anything." Riley turns and faces Colt. "It's the fear. That might work. It doesn't matter what they bury." Riley offers. "Dead horses, farm equipment, whatever. The fear of the outbreak is all we need. We need graves. They can be empty. It's the fear that will push them into hiding."

I add, "They will clump together to ride out the storm. Then we stop their supply runs. We steal what they have. Eventually they will have to come to us. Then, they will die."

"Are you planning on slaughtering them?" Gretel asks, "Aren't we as bad as the Mercs then?"

I let out a long breath. "We're not going to be killing people who don't deserve it."

Gretel swallows a sob, "No one deserves to die. It must be peaceful. When we have them cornered, they must be allowed to surrender. We have to try for a peaceful solution."

I shake my head. "No, we kill them!" I yell, "Kill them all!"

Gretel pulls my face toward her face and stares at me in the eyes. "I'm feeling what you're feeling. I lost what you lost. Remember, we want to change the world. We want to get the bad people out of power. We don't want to become the bad people." A tear rolls down her cheek. "What would Mom want us to do?"

I jerk away. I want them dead. I want them all dead. I want it more than anything. But my sister who has just witnessed our mother's execution doesn't feel the same way. I fight what I feel in every atom in my body, a murderous contempt flowing through my veins. My world moves in slow motion. I curse Gretel under my breath.

I heave with arduous breath. Finally, my harsh and laborious breathing begins to slow. Right this minute, I really want to be a killer, but I know I'm not. I want to hold onto this hate, but I know I can't. I curse Gretel once more before I force my soul to give in to her better judgment. She is always my moral compass.

I take in a last deep breath, calm myself, and embrace my sister. "I hate it. I hate the fact that you're right, Gretel. When that time comes we will allow them to surrender." She is right and I know it. Plus, I know my mother would not want me to turn into a cold-blooded killer. She would have never condoned senseless murder. I need to keep my mother in my mind, not for revenge's sake, but so I will remember the difference between what is right and what is wrong.

We put our plan in motion. We monitor the chatter for days. Rumors of mass graves and return of the virus spread through the regions much like the actual virus. Before long, there is a panic. The roads once peppered by patrolling Mercs are deserted. With the Mercs retreating, we are able to move our rescued people more easily. Our base of operations is the hub for all communications. As fears swell, hopes for a resistance win increases.

Newspapers try their best to squash the dire reports, but it is hard to stop a rumor's momentum once it is started. Paranoia grows. Gretel synthesizes a virus immunization using my blood just in case the Mercs decide to actually reintroduce the real virus. Wins for our side accumulate.

Through the communicators, Riley and Colt locate our original farm group. They are relieved to find out they survived. Riley travels to see them and reunites with his family. Colt is able to talk with his mom and dad through the communicators that Oliver has provided. The farm group has been in the Alps hiding in a series of caves. Fortunately, severe weather kept the Mercs away. The original group hasn't lost too many. The ones who did perish died of old age. The group even boasts three new births.

It is decided that Riley will return to Hamburg along with Colt's mother and father. The rest of the farm group will stay to lead the Alps region of Europe toward democracy. Riley is a renewed and energized person when he returns after seeing his family. If Riley and his family can pick up like the last twelve years never happened, then there is hope for all of the regions. Oliver was right, the key is to put people back with their loved ones. Riley didn't even need to stay with his family, he just needed to know they were alive and that they still loved him.

Hope is a virus that we want to spread.

Another person they add to their number is William, Ms. DeVane's son. Ms. DeVane closes her shop and is smuggled out of the Hamburg to join William's group as it travels to southern Bavaria near the Passau area. All indications are that the group is doing well.

Everything is going our way until one day we get the newspaper and read that the queen has married the **second in command Merc, Emperor Richard, in a secret ceremony**.

Lieutenant Drake shakes his head. "It's only a matter of time before Richard kills the king. We thought the king was bad. If the emperor is in charge, we will *all* be in trouble. Life as we know it will cease to exist."

Chapter 27

It takes a few days to let what happened sink in. Our plans to thwart the regime are still in play, but a maniacal emperor is leading the royals. The emperor has renamed himself King Emperor Richard the Great and has publically professed his undying love and support of the princess and queen. The people don't know any better and follow his lead without question.

News is released that the queen gives birth. She, her new baby, and the princess are kept on the ship "Queen Nalani" as a safety precaution.

No one knows if any of this is true. There are rumors she is dead because no one has seen her in such a long time. It is reported that the new baby is a boy named Ross in honor of the ambassador. That news makes me cringe. I hate the fact that the Mercs are using my family and the love everyone had for the ambassador to further their own agenda.

I find Oliver sitting at the computer one morning looking particularly forlorn. "What are you thinking about?"

He turns away from the monitor to face me. "I know my father is dead. I should hate the queen, but the princess and the new prince are my family. They are my half-brother and my half-sister."

I sit silently by him not knowing what to say. I understand more than he can know. Oliver is my full brother so I feel exactly the same way that he does. I fight the urge to tell him the truth. I tell myself that he has enough on his mind without worrying about a long lost sister that he doesn't remember.

I could turn his world upside down by revealing what I now suspect: our mother is Captain Via of the American resistance. How many people with my same color eyes, same hair color have a heart-shaped birthmark on their neck? Not many. In addition, I do remember her looking at the picture of Oliver and sighing. Plus, she was inconsolable when she found out the ambassador was dead.

My mother. No, she would be my birth mother. My real mother died at the hands of a monster. A monster I plan to stop. It's impossible to keep my mind on the plan when I think about that horrific fiend so I push all of those feelings deep into the crevasses of my thoughts. I will deal with those wounds later after the battle is over and our side is victorious.

It seems that some good is coming out of all this. Colt and Gretel have decided to get married. Colt, Gretel, Riley, and I plan to travel back to the Aunt Sandra's compound. There is a church on the grounds and

Aunt Sandra will perform the ceremony. We have done as much as we can from the city of Hamburg. Oliver will have to finish here and then join us at Aunt Sandra's compound before the wedding.

The next few days we travel back through familiar territory. It's nice to get out from that cramped store and breathe the brisk air of Bavaria. Spring is here and the mountains are green, freshly nourished from the melting snow. It revives me.

I watch Gretel and Colt bask in the love they have for each other. It will be a joyous time and that is exactly what is needed around here.

Colt and Gretel make their announcement on our "Speak to the Troops" nightly program. The happy news revitalizes the resistance and they have been getting all kinds of wedding wishes sent to them via the underground.

The resistance has reached into all of the continents. With the virus scare, we have forced most of the Mercs into hiding.

It is only a matter of time before we defeat them; but for now, I have a wedding to attend.

The weather couldn't be lovelier. The children have decorated the castle with local canola flowers that bloom wild in Germany. Aunt Sandra fashioned a white dress befitting a princess for Gretel to wear.

The ceremony is beautiful. Candles light their way. Gretel's radiant beauty engulfs the room. Love encircles the service. Everyone is here. Riley and I stand up for the bride and groom. I'm dressed in a deep blue dress. Yellow canola flowers are strategically placed throughout my hair.

As I walk down the aisle, I see Riley at the end of the walkway. My brother, Oliver, is sitting in the front row. My heart is full.

I am happy. I follow Amanda and Kelley down the path, a makeshift straw bed with flowers on each side. Colt beams as his parents walk with him. What a wonderful thing for Gretel to be able to gain this entire family all at once. She and Colt deserve to be happy.

I know many of the leaders of the rebellion cells requested a chance to attend, but having us all in one place was too dangerous. Two of our farm's army children, Thomas and Mike, wanted to attend; but it was decided that it was more important for them to head back to the Ferris wheel farm to gather the few residents still in training there. Too bad, more couldn't have been here to watch this profession of love.

My sister glows as she promises to love Colt for the rest of her life. He promises the same back and I believe them. I know Colt has loved my sister since they were children. How many people have a love like that? Over the past year, they have each risked and saved the other's life more times than I can count.

Today in this beautiful place, the world and nature smile upon them as if placing its blessing of their union. The sun shines brighter than it usually does and the sky glows the most beautiful color shining like the blue emerald of the oceans in the picturesque postcards that decorate the kiosks. The weather is cool and crisp without a hint of tension. A perfect day!

Love is truly in the air. The two of them plan to stay at the maze compound for their honeymoon. Colt's dad and mother will travel back to lead the southern German rebellion cell. The lull in Merc activity has allowed the cells to thrive.

The festivities that follow are a part of the biggest party I've ever seen. Dancing and laughter fill the air. The war raging outside these walls is not allowed in. **The invited want change, demand fairness, and hope for the return of democratic rule.** People dancing and singing at this party are the real heroes. Those who sacrifice everything for a better way of life. I stand proud to be counted among them. My pride bursts as I watch my sister and new brother melt into one another on the dance floor.

I'm celebrating too. In a short while, I will return to my Ferris wheel farm for a quick visit. I draw my intensity from the massive giant and the land it inhabits, my farm, my home. If I am to be the positive face of the resistance, I must collect all of the strength I can muster. Colt has his reason for fighting. He has Gretel. I search for my strength. Thomas and Mike left a day ago and I'll travel after the ceremony to join them. Thinking about touching the earth on my farm reenergizes me.

Here at the maze compound, Oliver has used his time wisely, setting up a central communication hub. Colt and I are still the face of the rebellion. We go on the waves nightly for "Speak with the Troops." Fighting is at an all time high, and I want to go home one last time before my job gets even busier. There is no way to know how long the battle will last. Going home was my one request. My request was granted since I have done everything that has been asked of me and have been a good soldier. I am ecstatic to be traveling back to the farm. I wish that Riley could come with me, but he has to stay on the maze compound to train the troops. Oliver is returning to Hamburg.

I smile and pet Hershey. "We're going home, old friend." He tosses his mane. It makes me think he understands me. I squeeze his side, causing him to quicken his pace.

I'm ready to drink in my home.

I can't wait.

Chapter 28

Eddie and Baako accompany me back to the farm. I'm in a hurry. They attempt to trot a slow speed, but end up galloping in sporadic intervals to keep up. The two of them are assigned to take care of me. I roll the four-leaf clover in my hand. What a lucky charm it has turned out to be. On the ride to my farm, I find myself missing Riley. So strange, I've hardly been away from him for a couple of hours, but I miss him so much I ache.

We spend our day traveling through the farmland by horse. I savor every minute of the trip and look for those things I recognize. We even go by the ravine where the Mercs used to dispose of their kills. I place flowers and say a prayer. It's the least that I can do.

My heart skips a beat when we arrive at the outskirts of my farm's land. I don't see the Ferris wheel until we round the corner. There it is—the magnificent metal giant, my Ferris wheel.

A child, Parker, runs out to us as we trot onto my land. "You're back, Paisley!" He is one of the younger ones. He's filled out nicely. His face has a look beyond his years. So sad the children had to grow up so quickly. I dream of a future when children will have time to play and just be children.

Parker pets Hershey as I dismount. He says, "Thomas and Mike said you were coming." He sways back and forth. "I told them I didn't believe them."

"Where are Arlas and the others?" I ask.

"They didn't make it." Another child walks up behind Parker. It's Finn. I didn't recognize him. Finn says, "We buried them in the back. I'll take you."

I walk with Finn and Parker. It's so sad. Would they have survived if I'd stayed? I'll never know. I visit the graves of the Undesirables and the Uncounteds who died on this farm trying to save these children.

It seems weird to be able to travel through our lands unencumbered. The fear about the virus has indeed put the entire world back in quarantine. All except us, that is, since we know the truth.

We still have to overthrow the regime and save the princess and new baby prince from the bloodthirsty King Emperor Merc, Richard the Great. What a joke! He is not great at all. He is pure evil. My fear is that the emperor thinks he is invincible and will stop at nothing to gain complete and total power. It has been discussed that he will kill not only the king and queen, but also the princess and the new little prince.

None of us can let that happen. We must take back the world and make it a place where no one will live in fear. It's a grand goal, but one I plan on achieving. Not on my own, but with help. It's worth the sacrifice. I know it and everyone else on our side does too.

I pull at my four-leaf clover bulleted necklace. I am glad that Eddie and Baako are with me. Gretel and Colt would not have been much company. They went on their honeymoon right after the ceremony.

I wish they could have gotten off the compound, but Aunt Sandra found them a place in the far reaches of her land where they could have some alone time. They have been incommunicado ever since. If they are not careful, we'll be having a little prince or princess of our own. I smile as I think of a little baby running around the maze.

I walk with great anticipation to the Ferris wheel to take my ride. I always wanted to cut my way out of this world. Is the world we've made now any better than the one we came from? Are we better off? We have to be.

It's scary to think about what the world will be like if we allow the Mercs or the emperor to take over. Right now, servants are uprising and leaving their owners. The rich are having a hard time fending for themselves. They don't know how to get their own food or take care of their own needs. They've always had someone doing that for them. It's a change for them and one they're not equipped to handle. It's funny how none of the riches in the world can buy good health. The wealthy are desperately trying to buy a guarantee that they will not contract the virus.

A big secret is that Gretel shared with us is that the ambassador developed the vaccine before his death and gave the formula to Gretel. We are fortunate to have Gretel whose medical expertise allowed her to brew a virus remedy concoction to immunize the masses. That immunization allows those of us who are inoculated to develop a natural immunity to the virus. A major comfort. Gretel thinks her potion might also protect us from any mutations of the virus. Another fear that the ambassador revealed to Gretel shortly before his death.

The wheel is bigger and grander than I remember. Or maybe it's that the farm is so quiet and seems so deserted.

I'm not sure about the future. How long can we hold them off? I fear that the Mercs will hear about our vaccine. I worry about the princess, the new prince, and the queen. I know that I will eventually have to try to save them.

I run my fingers over the rusted prongs of my wheel. I fall into the dilapidated chair. I set the ride on its lowest power. I decide not to think about it right now. For now, for today. I will ride my Ferris wheel basking in the love I witnessed today between my sister and my best friend. I will celebrate their marriage.

The wind blowing through my hair relaxes me. Serenity consumes me. Right this minute, all is right with my world.

Riding the Ferris wheel allows me to look out over the farm. The harvests have been neglected. When this is all over, I'll need help to bring these crops back to life. It excites me to think about working the harvest again. To grow food for consumption by all of the people. How much more worthy of a profession is there than that? Maybe Riley would like to try farm life again after this is all over. A warm sensation tingles my senses.

At the top of this wheel, I spot a group of men riding horses onto the farm. This can't be. Who are they? Are they Mercs? How could the Mercs find us and why would they be out and about? Don't they think the virus is alive and well?

The men on the horses motion to those on the ground to gather. Are they arresting them? If so, I am caught now. I see Eddie and Baako being taken into the farm house. They don't seem to know the strangers. I know they were surprised. The children are huddled together and escorted in the house. The men stand beside their horses outside the house as if they are waiting on me to get off the wheel.

Who are these people? Are they going to kill me now? After all of this, why now? The minute I step off this wheel, I'm their prisoner.

I have no choice, it's not just about me. It's about Eddie, Baako, and the children. It's about all of us. I resign my thoughts. I'll do whatever I have to do to make sure they are all safe.

I grasp the four-leaf clover one last time as I come to the bottom of the Ferris wheel. I step out ready for whatever is coming next. I am willing to take my punishment.

Maybe I can talk myself out of this trouble too. Maybe I can save the others. I might get them to let the children go. All of these thoughts race through my mind all at once. One thing I know for sure, I won't give up. It's not in me. I'm a fighter. I'm a survivor.

I take a deep breath, shut down the wheel, jut my chin out, and walk defiantly to the group standing by their horses. I ready myself.

The leader turns around and faces me.

How can this be and what does this mean?

It is my father—the ambassador. Alive and well.

The big question is—whose side is he on?

Book 3

Battle for the Cure

Chapter 1

After the last few months of being in constant danger, I'm ready to relax.

My self-assigned bodyguards, Eddie and Baako, accompany me back to my Bavarian farm. The rolling hills and green meadows remind me of my childhood. I roll the bullet molded into a four-leaf clover in my hand. I love that Riley gave it to me. I think of him saying, "something bad into something good." What a lucky charm it has turned out to be.

I miss Riley.

If it wasn't for this virus, if it wasn't for the quarantine, if it wasn't for the human trafficking and dictatorship and Merc murders, I might have a chance at a regular life, a relationship with Riley. But not now, I'm fighting a war. A war for democracy, a free way of life.

As we reach the outskirts of my farm, I spot it, the magnificent metal giant, my Ferris wheel. Left over from a long forgotten carnival that blew through town many years ago, the rusty, dilapidated wheel remains workable, albeit tarnished and sluggish. A few of our army of children are still housed here.

Wish I could ride now, but out of respect, I first visit the graves of the Undesirables and the Uncounteds who died on this farm saving these children. It seems weird to be able to travel through our lands unencumbered. Fear of a reoccurrence of the virus has put the entire world back into a self-imposed quarantine. But not us rebels, we know the truth.

Much work still to do. We must overthrow the regime and save the princess and prince from the bloodthirsty King Emperor Merc, Richard the Great. What a joke! He is not great at all. Pure evil. I worry he will murder the queen and her heirs. None of us can let that happen. I pull at my four-leaf clover bulleted necklace.

Eddie shouts to Baako. "Keep up, Baako. Where did you learn to ride a horse?"

"Didn't." Baako shifts on his horse trying to hold on and looking like he might fall off any minute.

Eddie stops beside Baako and shoves him into an upright position. "Sit like this and grab his mane." He takes a handful of the horsehair to show Baako.

Baako grips the mane. "Yeah, that does work better."

Eddie, the consummate frontiersman, and Baako, the servant. They couldn't be any more different, but I like the company.

Hershey is my chocolate colored horse. I love her because when we were quarantined on the farm all of those years, I would sneak out and feed her stolen fruit from our harvest. I claimed her as mine even before I made her mine.

Our dilapidated farmhouse, my home, stands tall and proud. A two-room shack with boards clutching strong to the side of the walls. The paint is peeling. Can't remember what color it's supposed to be. The ripped screen holds on by a hinge that hugs one side of the main door. The inside door is warped and barely shuts.

Are the children still using the raggedy sofa? What changes have they made?

Baako and Eddie herd the children out of the barn. I wave. Time enough for pleasantries later.

Before I enter the main house, I'm on a mission to ride my Ferris wheel. Been too long since I've felt the breeze through my hair. My heart flutters in anticipation as I slowly make my way to the metal giant, memorizing every step to recall later.

Scary to think about what the world will be like if we allow the Mercs to take over. Right now slaves are leaving their owners. The rich are having a hard time fending for themselves. They don't know how to take care of their own needs. Always had someone doing for them. It's a change they are not equipped to handle.

The privileged desperately want to purchase a guarantee to be virus free. But they don't have the cure. We do. The virus remedy administered to me and being distributed to the rest of the resistance is a major comfort.

The Mercs will eventually hear about our vaccine. I worry about my half-siblings, the princess, the new prince, and the queen. Soon, I'll have to go and save them. But for now, I'll ride my Ferris wheel and celebrate love as I think about the wedding between my sister, Gretel, and my best friend, Colt.

The Ferris wheel has been on our farm as long as I can remember. I love it, even though it's rusty, tattered, and the color of a rotten banana peel. I slump into the bottom chair, causing it to sway. I hit the "on" lever and it ascends with creaking movements.

As I fall back in the corroded passenger car, it rocks back and forth like the pendulum on the black forest cuckoo clock that keeps time in our living room. The night fills with rusty scraping sounds; then after a moment or two, nothing but serene silence is left.

Riding the Ferris wheel allows me to look out over the farm. The harvests have been neglected. It will take time to bring these crops back to life. Maybe Riley would like to try farm life again after this is all over. A warm sensation tingles my senses.

From my Ferris wheel perch, I take in hints of grass peeking out of the shimmering snow and watch the hills roll into the evening darkness.

A disturbing scene unfolds as I watch from the top of the wheel. From out of nowhere, four men ride horses onto the farm. Who are they? Mercs? Why are Mercs here? They are supposed to be in hiding, fearful of the virus's return. Something's wrong.

The men approach Eddie and Baako and huddle them and the children together. A surprise attack? Hurriedly one of the men, Eddie, Baako, and the children disappear into the forest's edge. Why are they leaving?

Nothing to do, but watch from my spot in the clouds. My heart sinks. Fearing the worst, I listen for gunshots. No shots. No screams. No sounds. What's going on?

The other three men scan the area. One man goes to the farmhouse door and unbolts it. It swings open. One of the men spies me on the Ferris wheel. He points. They're looking for me. The three of them head over to the wheel. Are they going to kill me now? After all of this, why now?

I grasp the four-leaf clover one last time as I come to the bottom of the Ferris wheel. I reach over and pull the lever to stop it. I step out ready to take my punishment.

Let them come to me. I take a deep breath and wait, readying myself.

The curve of one man's face is familiar to me. So is his gait. Do I know this Merc? I hope not. Mercs are merciless. They kill and ask questions later. I take a deep breath. The man turns and faces me.

How can this be and what does this mean?

It's my father—the ambassador. How can he be alive? Everyone thought he was dead. He was supposed to have died in a car explosion.

One of the other men grabs my arm as I stand on the concrete at the bottom of the wheel. Like a crack of lightning, a loud sound sends a shock

314

through me before I see blood spray on the bottom chair of the Ferris wheel. The man's hand drops from my arm and he falls forward. The force of his head hitting the concrete below the Ferris wheel makes a horrible thudding noise. The sight of the syrupy red puddle turns my stomach.

I gag as the other man lifts me off my feet and runs in a zigzag line behind my father towards the open door of our farmhouse. As my father clears the outside door, another shot rings out. I glance to the side and see a hole in the wall of the house. Only a few inches away from my face. A bullet.

The other man sets me on the floor. No time to wonder about why my father who I thought had perished in a car explosion is now standing beside me out of breath. He yells orders to the other man. "We have to get out of here or we'll all be killed."

My mind immediately visualizes the children. They'll be slaughtered. They have been here for months training for battle. This farm is supposed to be one of the safest place on earth. Why are these people shooting at us? We've been so careful.

"Are they coming for you?" I glare at my father. "Who's shooting at us?"

"Mercs." My father counts the square pieces in the floor. "One, two, three...here. It's under here." He grabs the corner of the huge ornate table that sits in front of the dilapidated sofa. He is careful not to scratch the floor. It's heavy and he struggles to lift it.

The other man yanks at one side and it finally moves. The two of them heave the table, exposing a piece of the plywood floor. The piece has a hole on one side. The other man holds up the table. Blood covers his shirt. Is he hurt?

My father puts his fingers in the hole and lifts the corner of the plywood. As he pulls it up, I peer into the void below. Dark, no source of light. It's a trap door. I've lived here all of my life. I never knew about that trap door.

"What about the children and where are Baako and Eddie?" I can't forget about them. We were supposed to gather the children and go back to Aunt Sandra's compound. Now I don't know where they are and I'm in the middle of gunfire.

The two men ignore my pleas, motioning for me to be quiet. My father slides through the trap door under the floor and disappears into the darkness.

He pulls at my feet and I struggle against him. "I can't just leave the others!"

315

Another bullet pierces the door and hits the sofa right beside where I am standing. Feathers fly.

"Not now." My father tugs hard at my ankle. "Push her." The other man shoves me from behind into the hole in the floor. I'm no match for the two of them. Off balance, I topple into the void. My father cushions my fall as I knock hard into the dirt sides of the opening. I swallow dirt and cough.

The two men work quickly to pull the heavy table over their heads and center it back over the plywood piece disguised as a part of the floor. They snap the plywood back over the opening of the trap door until it drops into place above us just as we hear footsteps.

"Who..." Dirt sprinkles in my face.

My father clamps his hand over my mouth and whispers in my ear. "Guns."

It's dark and I can't see the muddy soil, but I feel it. I know the gun men are walking on the rug above. The sounds of their footsteps echo in the chamber below. We have escaped certain death by seconds.

Muffled voices sound in the living room, soft at first and then loud. No way to know how many. I can't make out what they are saying, but they sound angry. It's dark in the cave area. I touch the sides. More dirt. I reach out my hand and swipe at nothingness. It's void both ways. Hollow. An underground tunnel to where?

It's dark and I try to stand. The tunnel is not high enough to accommodate our height. I get down on all fours. I know my father is crouching also. He reaches back and grabs a wad of my hair before finding my shoulder and pulling me forward behind him.

The other man shoves me from behind. I reach around to feel behind me and touch the man covered in a warm sticky substance. I hope it is not blood. But if it is, I hope that it's not his. I'm wedged in between them. I have no choice but to follow.

My head slams into a hanging part of the cave, which causes a chunk of dirt to fall in my way. I crawl over the mass, smashing it with my knee as I pass, knocking into the sides more than once.

The tunnel is rough and attempting to avoid the protrusions jutting down from the top, sides, and bottom proves difficult. Impossible with the sight factor down to nil. I slam once again into the side of the cave and dirt flies, as we three hurry to make the distance between the trapdoor and wherever we are heading.

The man behind me is moving quickly. Maybe he isn't hurt and the blood on his shirt isn't his. I hope so anyway. I struggle to block all thoughts of the children, Baako, and Eddie and what might be happening to them. I can't think about that right now.

It seems like a long time before we come to a stop. My father opens another plywood door above him. This floor is covered by a rug, which he quickly throws off to the side. A light ray falls into the tunnel. It's my first look at our passage. Exactly what I thought. A crudely dug tunnel. No idea how long it has been here. Could be since the first or second world war for all I know.

My father lifts himself out and then pulls me through. He grips my arms and jerks me up almost wrenching my shoulder out of joint. The other man has a hand on my derrière and shoves me the last bit out of the hole. After he quickly pulls himself up, they replace the door and cover it with the rug.

We are in another farmhouse I don't recognize. It is similar to mine. A threadbare, raggedy sofa sits in the living room. How many of these escape tunnels are there?

An intricate path of trap doors, an underground tunnel escape route between houses. For the twelve years of quarantine, I never knew. This knowledge could have changed everything back then. Why would anyone keep this a secret? It takes a moment, but I process why. We were in quarantine. If we had travelled through the tunnels, the virus could have spread. It was probably safer that we didn't know. I would not have been able to resist the idea of seeing others. I know I would have used the tunnels.

No words have been spoken since we got into the tunnel. Quiet is better right now since all my questions would be about what is happening to the children and the others and I'm not sure I could handle the answer at this moment.

My father opens the outside door of the farmhouse slightly and then motions for the man and me to follow him out. We run through the woods for a long while before we stop. My father removes some brush that turns out to be covering a cave door. This is a cave I know. It's where we keep supplies for Undesirables and Uncounteds to hide out.

As we enter, my father picks up matches by the door, easily lights a kerosene lantern located at the entrance and illuminates the contents of our haven. Huge water jugs rest on the floor. It the first time I've taken a full breath since my ride on the Ferris wheel.

The reality hits me. The children are probably slaughtered. Baako and Eddie are most likely dead. I cradle my head with my arms and sob, loud and sloppy. I can't stop. All of these people are dead and I did nothing to stop it. What kind of monster does that make me?

Chapter 2

"We have to go back!" Each of my words is accentuated by spewing snot and spit.

My father grabs my shoulders and shoves me down on a box.

I lean my head back on the gritty dirt wall. "We can't just leave them there. They don't know about the tunnel. How can they escape?"

"I'm not sure that they can, but we can't go back." My father's face is ashen. "I'm sorry." He turns his attention to the other man. I notice him now. It's the first time I've looked at him since the Ferris wheel. He's covered in blood.

My father asks, "Were you hit?"

The man mumbles and grits his teeth. "Yeah, that last bullet got me in the shoulder." After the man sits, he pulls his shirt off, exposing a large gash. I retch as I look at the blood spurting out of it. It shows no signs of stopping. I'm no doctor, but it looks bad.

My father squats beside him. "Charles, I don't know how you made it this far with this gunshot wound."

"That's what bodyguards do." The man who in essence saved my life a few minutes ago is stretched out on the cavern floor bleeding to death.

Searching around our safe house, I find a rag and stuff it in the wound in an attempt to stop the gushing blood. "We have to help him."

Charles grips my hand, which is still holding the bloody rag. "I appreciate it, but I'm afraid that I'm done for. I knew the risks and I've seen enough wounds to know that I've been hit in a vital place. The blood loss cannot be overcome."

Tears stream down my face. "There has to be something we can do."

Charles reaches for my face and wipes away a tear. "Paisley, I'm glad I got to meet you. I listen to your and Colt's broadcast. It has given me and scores of others hope. You are the face of freedom and I am honored to have helped you escape."

I turn to my father who is sitting silently with a solemn look on his face. I ask, "What does he mean? Wasn't he here to guard you?"

My father doesn't have a chance to answer before Charles emits a low groan. His back arches for a moment before all of the breath in his lungs exhales. He dies staring into my eyes and gripping my hand. As his grip loosens, the life in his eyes evaporates and all that is left is a blank stare. I carefully run my hand over his eyes to close them. Now he looks as if he is sleeping. It gives me comfort. Maybe I want to block out the ugliness. I don't know.

I sit quietly with him for a few moments. His was a quiet death. The look on his face is peaceful. It takes a minute for me to process before my heart breaks. I didn't even know him, but he gave his life to save me.

That is what we Uncounteds and Undesirables do. We sacrifice. My blood boils as I think of the pampered royals and their carefree, sheltered life. Is this what we have to look forward to in this battle for democracy?

We sit silently for a few more minutes. My father finally rises, finds a large piece of fabric, and covers Charles. He takes twine, wraps it around Charles's body, and ties the rags around his feet and at his head. "We will carry him out and try to give him a proper burial when things calm down."

"How many more will we have to bury?" I cover my face with my hands.

My father doesn't answer, but his defeated look gives me all the information I need. It's going to be bad. Faces of the dear children flash in my mind and I take in a deep breath. We have no weapons in here. If the Mercs are storming the farm, we have no chance to fight them off.

"We can't save the children, can we?"

He doesn't answer again, quietly patting Charles as a tear runs down his face. The realization that the smartest move is to stay here and not go back and help the others makes me choke. I succumb to the gagging reflex and vomit in the corner. It takes me a few minutes to recover.

"You okay?" My father asks.

Dipping my head slightly, it's my turn not to answer. My stomach is empty, but the smell of the puke is overwhelming in such close quarters. I have to try to make this right. It's enough to be trapped in a cave with a dead friend. Vomit in the corner is just one too many smells to deal with.

Spying a half-eaten jar of pears, I open it and use another rag to scrape the vomit clinging to the dirt floor into the jar. I choke some more as I am doing this. Fortunately, with an empty stomach, it's just dry heaves. It takes me a while to get the vomit into the jar, between scraping and then heaving when the smell gets the better of me. I finally get all of the vomit and surrounding dirt sealed up. I can only hope that time will mask the smell.

My father takes out a piece of fruit from a fresh jar and waves it around the cavern. "This might help too."

In a few moments, sereneness takes over and I settle. I can't help the children, all I can do is hope that they survive. It's going to be a long night.

Not sure how long we sit there. Finally, my voice pierces the silence. "What did Charles mean he was here to protect me? I thought he came with you." I stop and glare at my father. "What's going on?"

"You need an explanation." My father has no sense of urgency at all in his voice. How could he be some calm? People are dead.

I turn to face him. "An explanation. Yes, an explanation would be nice. While you are at it, how about explain just how are you alive? Everyone was told you were dead."

He lets out a deep breath. "I faked my own death."

"Faked your death?" I clomp around the cave waving my arms. "What about your family? You had just found out that I, your long lost daughter, was still alive. For goodness sakes, your wife was pregnant. You left her and the princess with no protection."

I point my finger at him. "The queen has been suffering a deep depression. Not a good thing for a pregnant woman. The queen really loves you. She's been inconsolable." I glare at him. "Did you even know that the baby was born? How could you leave them?"

The expression on his face gives away his emotions. Guilt. Sadness. Almost to the point of defeat. "I know my son was born." His face contorts again and the tortured look is replaced by a look of anger. He growls. "I also know that she has married the evil Emperor Richard."

His voice is so full of pain. I reach out and grab his hand, but he pulls away. I can't help, but feel sorry for him. I say, "We won't stand for the manipulation and everything it means for the poor. If it's any consolation, I think the queen was pushed into marrying Emperor Richard. We have been trying to organize a revolt of the Undesirables and Uncounteds. The poor."

He takes in a deep breath and as he releases it, his look softens. "I have to control myself if we have any hope of overthrowing the emperor's evil regime." The edges of his mouth turn up slightly. "I've been following your rogue radio broadcasts." He squeezes my hand. "You've made me so proud."

My chest puffs. "I haven't done it alone. You know that Oliver is with us." Oliver, my long lost brother.

He takes in a labored breath. "Did you tell him you are his sister?"

"How could I?" I cross my arms. "What kind of explanation would that have been? Hi, Oliver. It seems that before the virus happened to the world, me, you, our father, and our mother were living on a military base in Germany." I uncross my arms. "After the virus outbreak, you and father escaped to America, leaving my mother to perish, and me to be adopted by a German family who raised me as their own. Yeah, that's what happened. What do you think he would have said?"

Father nodded. "He'd have thought you were crazy. Not telling him was a better choice."

"Thanks." I didn't really know what to call my father. I didn't feel comfortable calling him dad since I didn't really know him. The man who raised me, my real father, had died long ago. It seemed disrespectful to him to call the ambassador "dad."

I cut my eyes over at my father. He wasn't the only one keeping secrets. I certainly couldn't tell him my suspicion that our mother hadn't actually died, but is alive and a leading force in the rebellion. I think his wife being married to the brutal dictator and his new baby and little girl being raised by him might be all the news he could handle right now.

Changing the subject seems like the best course of action. "Why did you come to the farm?"

"We came to save you. We heard that the Mercs were planning to raid on this farm as soon as you or Colt showed up. Our sources alerted us to the fact that you were indeed travelling here. I'm glad we made it to you in time."

"What about the others with you?"

"It's not what you think." He pulls out a jar of pears and opens it. He hands it to me.

I shake my head. "Just puked, remember? Think I should wait a while before eating."

He eats the pear himself and moves the jar away from me. "Probably a good idea."

There is something I'm desperate to know. "Do you know anything about the children and Eddie and Baako?"

"They should be fine. One of our group took them away before the gunfire started. Charles and I weren't alone. But you need to stay hidden for a while." He sits beside me, grabs out a pear, and swallows it whole.

"Why did they attack the farm?" It makes no sense to me. "The children have been safe for months now with no sign of trouble. Why now?"

"The king is dead."

He says it so matter of factly that I lose my breath. The king. I hated the king. He controlled distribution of the root that helps cure the virus. I'd personally witnessed him killing Undesirables, those in our world who are not perfect because of disability or disfigurement, and the Uncounteds, those in our world who have no family and are alone. He was evil. He preyed on those weaker than him. I hate to admit it, but this news makes me happy. I'm happy that the king is dead. "Why is that a bad thing?" I surprise myself with my calmness in speaking of another's demise.

"The evil Emperor Richard is now in control."

Chapter 3

A day passes. I wake to see a dark silhouette hovering over me. The stranger leans down and shakes my father awake. "Ambassador Grayson."

"Yes, I'm here." My father bolts upright, rubbing the sleep out of his eyes. "Hello, Soldier. Glad to see you. Is it safe?"

The soldier shifts his rifle to his shoulder and pulls my father to his feet. "As safe as it's going to be for a while. We need to get you back to base camp."

My father pulls my arm helping me to my feet. "We have to get Paisley to safety first. She is the top priority now."

The soldier dips his head. "Paisley. What an honor." He salutes me.

I raise my hand quickly to my forehead trying to copy his salute. It seems like the right thing to do. "What about the farm children, Baako and Eddie? Did they survive?"

His head drops. "Not sure. We lost a few, but most survived. We did take out that Merc patrol." He pauses.

My father looks at him. "But..."

"We wanted to have you hide here longer, but unfortunately one of the Merc patrol got away. We are afraid he'll report to the others. That's why I am here. It's imperative that we move from this area. It will be crawling with Mercs soon." He looks around. "Where are Charles and Roger?"

My father pats the soldier's shoulder. "Roger died at the farm and..." He points to the canvas. "Charles didn't make it either. We need to bury him."

The soldier's face drops and he turns ashen. "No time."

I step in front of my father. "We can't just leave him here."

The soldier locks his eyes with mine and says, "You're right, I'll carry him. We will bury him when we are safe."

My breath calms and I feel my features soften. "Thanks. What's your name?"

"Donald."

Donald pulls a handgun out of his pocket, gives it to my father, and wastes no time heaving the canvas-covered body over his shoulder. He crouches through the cave door. It's completely dark. He says, "We'll travel at night. It's safer."

I'm glad that Donald is with us because with no source of light we are completely vulnerable to the treacherous hills and cliffs that make up the terrain of this part of Bavaria. He tethers the three of us together and we travel single file. Donald leads, carrying the body, I follow, and my father is behind me. It's unbelievable how far we travel in a short time. We have no chance to slow down with us tied to Donald and following his track speed. It helps that we have no fear of slipping or falling.

Donald stops all at once. "There are signs of Mercs closing in on this area. We need to hurry." He motions to the side. "Be careful. There is a deep ravine over to the left side. Make sure you match my steps. One fall and you're a goner." How he can see this with the darkness is beyond me, but I don't question.

My father asks, "How can we go faster?"

Donald heaves Charles's body down into the ravine. "I know it was a terrible thing to do, but this is the ravine that many bodies are thrown over. It won't be noticed. I'm sorry Paisley. I know you wanted to bury him proper."

A tear escapes my eye and runs down my cheek. "I did, but I believe that Charles would want us to survive." I peer towards the ravine and whisper. "Thank you my sweet Charles for giving your life for me. I won't let your sacrifice be in vain. I will do everything in my power to survive and complete the mission."

Without the added weight, we triple our moving time. I am unable to keep with the gait of the long legged men and Donald finally untethers me and squats down. "On my back," he orders.

I obey. I can't argue. I know I can't keep up. I am jostled as he runs full speed. Jumping over crevasses and climbing hills like a monkey scaling a tree. I hear my father struggling to keep up. His breathing is hard and labored, but he does not complain.

As the sun rises, we arrive at familiar place. It's the entrance to Aunt Sandra's lands. I recognize the bushes and see the back of the cart. It's a proven safe haven. Aunt Sandra has managed to keep the whereabouts secret for years.

"There's our girl." It's Aunt Sandra. Her gray hair flies in every direction and her smile reassures me. She uses her cane to step out of her carriage. "I thought you might like to see a familiar face." I throw myself off the back of Donald and run toward her, encircling her in a big bear hug.

Colt and my sister, Gretel, who were married a few nights ago, appear from behind the bush. My heart dances and I feel a sense of calmness. I'm with my family.

My father bows slightly to Aunt Sandra. "Donald and I are going back to Hamburg. We are needed there."

Aunt Sandra squeezes my father's hand. "Thanks so much for finding Paisley and bringing her back to us. She doesn't realize how important she is to the resistance."

My father smiles at me. "She's important to me too." He winks at me. "More than you know." He hugs my shoulder. "I'm sorry that I can't stay here with you, but I must help my son, Oliver. He is doing dangerous work. Drake has gathered the resistance fighters from around the world. Together they are making up a plan. Lieutenant Drake and an American woman leader, Captain Via."

Captain Via, I met her when I escaped from America. Through talking to Oliver, my brother who doesn't know he's my brother, I have a sneaking suspicion that Captain Via may be mine and Oliver's mother and the ambassador's long lost wife. Of course, I can't tell my father of this because I don't know it for sure. Plus, he's already married the queen. Wait! The queen is now married to Emperor Richard. What a mess! Maybe after this war we can straighten all of this up. I smile a little inside. It's my only salvation; I must find humor in the craziness of it all.

Enough of that mixed-up thinking. I certainly can't fix it all. I direct my attention to my sister, Gretel, and Colt, her new husband (and my best friend). I squeeze them both hard. "Sorry about interrupting the honeymoon." Tears that I can't control run down my face.

Gretel brushes my hair. "It's fine. There is plenty of time for a proper honeymoon after all of this is over. We were so worried when we heard about the king."

Pausing for a moment, I ask, "Does anyone know how he actually died? It seems awfully convenient for the Emperor. He just married the queen and her father, the king and ruler of all, dies."

My father nods. "That is why it is imperative that we get back to Hamburg at once. We must sort out all of this and try to control the misinformation being disseminated daily by the evil emperor. We thought the king was evil. The king is nothing compared to this maniac."

Aunt Sandra extends her hand. "Please sir, let me thank you once again."

My father shakes her hand. "Of course."

She squeezes his elbow with her other hand. "I don't think you realize how important it was that you sent your men to save the children on Paisley's farm. If those children had died..." her voice trails off.

"But they didn't, Aunt Sandra." Gretel smiles at her. "They're safe."

Aunt Sandra points to the hidden corral of horses. "Even your horse, Hershey, made it back. My boys found the group from your farm hiding back a ways and brought them here."

"The children are alive!" My hearts jumps for joy. I walk over and pet Hershey. "I love you, my sweet horsie."

My father turns to me. "You are in good hands now. I will take my leave. I am sure that you and I will run into each other again. When this is all over..."

Deep in my heart, I know what he wants to say. When this is over, we will pick up the pieces of our lives and sort through all of this. But him being my father is still a secret so I simply say, "I know."

Aunt Sandra motions to the horse. "Please ambassador, take two of the horses. It will make your ride a lot easier."

My father nods. "Thank you." He smiles at me. "Don't worry. We won't take your favorite." He and Donald pick two of the horses, leaving Hershey behind.

It's difficult watching my father ride off, but I know that my brother could use his help and I definitely know that the resistance needs him. The Consortium of the World will be convening in a few months to vote on how our world will be run. We want a democracy and the royals and Mercs want a dictatorship. Our side must win.

After my father rides off, I stare at Colt. "I'm so glad the children are safe. What about Eddie and Baako?"

"They're fine." Gretel guides me to the wagon. "One casualty. A child."

It's hard for me to hold back my sorrow. A child who would never see the teenage years. I spit out the words rolling in my head. "What kind of war would prey on innocent children? What kind of monster would order their murder?"

Colt lifts me into the wagon. "An unjust war that we are going to stop. Are we ready to end this thing?"

I stand defiantly and look around. "More than ever. Do we have a plan?"

"Yes." Colt's face is stern and full of hate. "Kill Emperor Richard!'

Chapter 4

Aunt Sandra bounces down the uneven trail in her horse drawn wagon coach as the rest of us trail behind her in the dense wooded area. We tramp deep into the forest until we come upon a vineyard with vines so thick they are almost impassable. The horses are skittish, but allow themselves to be led. At the clearing stands a large concrete barrier fence covered completely with greenery.

"You count it off, Paisley." Aunt Sandra says.

I number the bricks on the wall, one hundred and thirty four, before stopping. Reaching into the mass of vines, I unlock the gate. We carefully conceal Aunt Sandra's buggy and corral the horses in a hidden area before we make our way down the path through the cave. At the threshold, we come upon two sentries guarding the entrance. They bow when they spy Aunt Sandra. About a kilometer ahead beyond the maze, the tops of the tower spikes peek through.

I'm tired and out of breath, but the sight makes me smile. "We're here."

"Almost, dear." Aunt Sandra points to the towers. "You know they're not as close as you think." She winks at me.

Aunt Sandra motions to a few of the boys who have run to greet us and says, "The boys will lead you through the maze." Along the way, I bump into the sides and stumble on the uneven terrain. It's not like when I went through the maze the first time blindfolded. I thought the maze was made out of bristled vines. But it's not, it's a thick hedge.

The hedge grows in so many different ways that it causes prickly points and unevenness. It'd be nice if it were trimmed in a perfect square. But that won't happen anytime soon. We go forward then backwards, and then wade through a stream.

The climb up the ladder is last. Aunt Sandra is carried by one or two boys at all times. Finally, in front of us stands Aunt Sandra's castle. The structure's regal splendor begs respect. I am so happy to be back that I give the magnificent place a little royal-like curtsy.

We follow Aunt Sandra across the open drawbridge of the dried up moat. The inside assembly houses a massive courtyard which is visible when Aunt Sandra opens the outside gate allowing us to pass into the main quarters.

"Paisley!" Riley throws himself onto me with such force that I teeter. "They wouldn't allow me to come."

"Let her breathe." Gretel pulls him off me. "You're going to choke her. Remember, she was almost killed. Give her some room."

Gretel, Colt, Riley, and I make our way to the large dining room table.

"What happened?" Gretel asks.

Slumping in the chair, it's the first time I feel really safe. "We had just gotten to the farm when they started shooting at us. Have you seen Baako and Eddie?"

Gretel shakes her head and motions to Colt to bring a jug of water. She pours me a glass. "Drink some."

"Not thirsty." I push the water away. "I thought that the Mercs believed the virus was back. If that's true, why did they attack us?"

"That's right. You don't know what happened." Riley brushes his hair out of his face and slaps dirt off his knee with his hand. "Some of Emperor Richard's men intercepted a message being sent to the Americas exposing our ruse. They realized that we had been lying all the time and decided to orchestrate a surprise attack and it almost succeeded."

I throw my hands up in disbelief. "How did *we* find out about it?"

Riley explains, "One of the children overheard them planning the strike. Unfortunately, she was captured soon after that. The Mercs thought they had killed her and threw her down a ravine. She managed to crawl out and we found her. She was barely alive. Before she died, she told us about their plans. She gave her life to get that information to us."

Tears well in my eyes, "Who?"

Gretel whispers, "Kelley."

Kelley, the child who had led us to Aunt Sandra's in the first place, was a hero. My mind flashed to an image of Kelley playing with the other children in the courtyard. So innocent, so full of excitement with so much of her life in front of her. Not fair. Not fair at all. My face reddens and I pound my fist in the air. "How can we ask these young children to fight this war?"

Gretel cradles me in her arms. "How can we not?"

Gretel is right. In order to be victorious, we have to enlist everyone available. The Mercs are a formidable foe. Not to be taken lightly. We have to win. No matter the cost. My stomach churns. I vomit for the second time in two days.

"That's enough for today." Gretel rubs my hair. "You need to sleep."

"What about this mess?" I point to the fresh throw up. An older woman comes in with a mop and it is clean almost before I get my question out.

"Time for your own bed." Riley stands up and pulls me to my feet. "I'll walk you."

Riley helps me back to my quarters. He stands at the door and points to my bed. "Get some rest. We can figure this out tomorrow. Today you should take it easy."

Reaching for the four-leaf clover bulleted necklace, I begin to twirl it in my fingers. "This thing always saves me. Every time I think that I'm about to die, it pulls me through. It is such a powerful good luck charm. I *should* give it back to you."

Riley clasps his hands around mine. "No, keep it. If it keeps you safe, it's doing its job. I don't know what I'd do without you. When I heard that your farm had been attacked, I died a little inside. You don't know how much you mean to me." He brushes my hair back with his hand. I like his touch. I like it more than I should.

"You made it!" Eddie rushes through the door knocking Riley away and wraps his arms around me. "I can't believe you survived all those bullets."

"Eddie's right." Baako trots in after him. "It's a miracle you're alive. I thought for sure you were dead."

Baako throws his arms around me and Eddie. "And the ambassador is alive too." I teeter backward from the force of the hugs.

Riley jerks Baako and Eddie away and uprights me. "She's been through enough today. She needs to rest." Riley pushes me through the door and shuts it behind me.

Their voices fade from the door as I plop down on the bed. Riley is right. It's been a long day. I don't realize how tired I am until my head rests on the pillow. My eyes slam shut.

No idea how long I sleep. When I finally come out of the room, the compound is bustling with activity. People are scurrying about carrying supplies and in the courtyard, buggies are being loaded. I see Baako and ask, "What's going on?"

"War."Baako whispers.

Chapter 5

"War?"

"Yes." Baako stops moving for a minute. "Haven't you heard? We just got word that Emperor Richard is telling everyone that we, the resistance, released the virus back into the population on purpose and that we hold a virus inoculation, but we're refusing to give it to anyone." He shifts a large load of wood from one shoulder to the other. He struggles to keep it balanced. "I have to go."

"Wait." I grab his shirtsleeve. "Where's Riley?"

"He left for Hamburg this morning." Baako scurries off, juggling his heavy load.

Riley's gone? Why would Riley leave without telling me? Wait, I'm not the boss of him! Of course, Riley has every right to do whatever he wants. What if I wanted to leave? Would I go and report to Riley? Of course not. I shake my head. Don't think about Riley. Focus!

I have to find Colt, Gretel, or Aunt Sandra. I can't believe I slept so long. Was war declared while I was dreaming?

Everyone must be at central compound. It's a house in the middle of the compound that is used to discuss strategy and give assignments. I enter the sparse room populated with a couple of tables, a few chairs, books, folders, maps, weapons, and various other war paraphernalia. I'm right. Most of the organizers are here and deep in discussion. Colt hovers over a table full of papers with Eddie.

"Colt, what's going on and why did Riley leave?"

Colt motions for me to take a seat beside him. "We need to catch you up. We have to go on the air tonight. This thing has escalated out of control. I don't know if you heard, but the emperor is blaming the resurgence or fake resurgence of the virus on the resistance. We have to get in front of this misinformation."

Pulling out a stool, I pick up a paper to study. "How did we find out about all of this?"

"Oliver." Gretel announces from the back of the room. "Oliver hacked into their transmissions and found out that *they* have a plan to reintroduce the virus back into the poor communities."

Dropping the paper to the table, I slump in my chair. "What do you mean reintroduce *the virus*? The deadly virus? The one that caused a forced 12-year quarantine? That virus?"

Gretel nods her head as she takes a seat. "Yes, the emperor is not only evil and cruel. He's obviously a madman."

"What is the rationale?" I ask. "It could kill him too."

Colt folds up a paper. "That's the horrible part. He knows we have the cure and that we are inoculating people. He is trying to force us to reveal the formula."

"Shouldn't we?" I ask.

Gretel pats my hand. "Of course everyone should have the inoculation, but we can't let him control it. Then it will not get to everyone. It will be saved just for the rich."

"No way!" I shake my head. "Can't we give him the formula and still control our part?"

Gretel takes a deep breath. "What a nice thought. Unfortunately, you need trained scientists to make the formula." Her eyes widen. "We can't give him any of our scientists."

"Do we know how far the emperor is willing to go?"

Colt stands up. "That's the bad part. From our sources, his plan is to inject people with the virus until we surface. Once he gets the inoculations, he will control the world's health. From what I hear, once he is able to make the formula, he will wipe us out so we can't give the cure for free. We can't let that happen."

"Even if..." Can I really ask the question, if I don't want to hear the answer?

Gretel answers, "Even if people die." She swallows hard. "Paisley, you know I'm a nurse for all practical purposes. If you would have told me a year ago I would let anyone die if I had the means to save them, I would have told you that you were crazy, but now..."

"It's not right." I can't believe this. My sister is willing to let innocents die. "Let's give them the cure. We'll keep some for ourselves."

Colt pipes up. "No, not a chance."

I turn to Colt. "Why not?"

"We have to give up something irreplaceable. Because the only way that can happen is if Gretel takes the inoculation to them and shows them how to manufacture it. I'm not going to let her go."

"No one else can go?" I ask.

"One other person could." Gretel answers, "But we are *certainly* not going to let him go there."

"Who?" I ask.

"The ambassador." Colt answers.

There are only two people in the world who can synthesize the inoculations. One is supposed to be dead and the other is my sister. I understand now.

"Show me how to synthesize it." I demand. "I'm smart. I could learn how to do it." I stare at Gretel. "Why are you being so secretive? Why can't everyone learn how to do it?"

"Because." Gretel crosses her arms and grunts. "Why do you have to be so hard-headed, Paisley?"

I lean close to my sister's face, nose to nose. I know she can't stand it when I do this. "I want to know why others can't learn how to make the inoculation. Wouldn't that solve the problem?" I wag my finger in her face. "Then it wouldn't be just you and you wouldn't be in so much danger."

"Whoa!" Colt slams his fist on the table. "Then you would put yourself in danger. You and I are the face of the resistance. We have to stay here and let the people know what is going on. Gretel has to be here to synthesize the inoculation."

"Why is the technique such a secret?" I put up my hand. "I understand about Gretel, but why can't others learn?"

Colt's voice rises. "Gretel is not the only irreplaceable part of this. We only have one machine that synthesizes and replicates the cure. The DNA replicator."

Gretel talks over Colt. "We can't give that to the emperor and without it, I can't show them how to make the cure. If the replicator breaks, I don't know how to repair it. Only the ambassador knows how to fix it and he is not here. So if we want to make sure that we keep manufacturing the vaccine, which we *have* to do, I'm the only one who works the machine." She glares at me.

"Do you think I would tear up such an important piece of equipment?" I get close to her again nose-to-nose, breathing onto her face, just like when we were little.

Colt breaks in. "Sisters, quit bickering. It's perfectly reasonable. Gretel doesn't trust anyone else with the machine. So Gretel and only Gretel will synthesize the cure. We will load her lab with people who can measure or bring her things. But she is the only one handling the one of a kind device." He points at Gretel and me. "You two understand?"

We nod and he turns his attention to the others in the room. "Baako and Eddie will organize a group to deliver the inoculations to our resistance group. We all know where the emperor will introduce the virus. It won't be with his rich royal friends. It will be with the poorest of the poor."

Baako looks at me. "It will be the Undesirables and the Uncounteds. It will be those he considers throw-aways."

Gretel chimes in. "It will also be with the people who are owned. The human trafficking problem is out of control. The royals and rich will use their owned people as guinea pigs. It'll be pandemonium. We have no choice. We have to take care of ours first."

It made sense. It just hurt hearing it. Our world had lost so many. We couldn't afford to lose more. "Have we inoculated all of the people on Aunt Sandra's farm?"

Gretel smiles. "Just about. You can make sure that we have. Why don't you take this list around and see that everyone has been up to the medical center and been given the vial of the cure. When you finish you can help me get stuff in the lab while I synthesize the inoculations. The more hands we have in the lab the quicker we can make the antidote."

For the next two hours, I scour the camp looking for anyone who has not been given the vaccine. I don't find a single person. First good news today.

Entering the lab, I don't see Gretel. She must be on break. I look at the vials filled with hope. Such a simple remedy. Just a swallow and you can't contract the virus ever.

Uneasy questions enter my mind. Have my half-sister, the princess, or my half-brother, the prince been inoculated? Does the emperor have access to any of the antidote at all?

I stuff two vials in my pockets. Wouldn't hurt to have two extras for the princess and the prince? I can't help what I'm thinking even though I know how dangerous it will be. Do I have a death wish? It's not in me to stand idly by while my sister and brother die.

Walking out of the lab, I have a specific purpose in mind. My plan is to sneak off Aunt Sandra's land, find the prince and princess, protect them from the illness, and make it back before supper without being caught.

Sounded possible until I listed all of the steps. Oh well, better get started.

Chapter 6

"Paisley? Where do you think you are going?" Colt catches me by the arm. "I know that determined look on your face. Riley said you would try something."

I jerk my arm from his grip. "What does Riley know about what I will or won't do? I'm just checking on the people to make sure they've all been inoculated."

He reaches his hand in my pocket and produces the two vials. "And what are these?"

"Oh those. Extras. Just in case I need to give someone the cure." I mumble unconvincingly.

"Right." Colt turns me around and guides me back into the lab. No use going anywhere or fighting it. There is absolutely no reason to find my brother and sister unless I have the cure in my hand.

Colt walks me to the table. "Sit down." He continues, "Riley begged me and Gretel not to tell you. He was afraid that you would come after him. You won't will you?" He looks deeply into my eyes.

I spring from my seat, but he quickly pushes me back down.

"What does this have to do with Riley?" I jut out my chin and cross my arms. "I don't know what you're talking about. Why would I follow Riley? I don't care what Riley does. Riley means nothing to me at all."

Colt laughs. "Right. But I can tell you mean something to him because he came to us while you were sleeping and asked to do an errand."

My insolent stare chills the room. "What kind of errand?" I pout like a child. "And by the way, what could Riley possibly do that would make a difference to me?"

Colt thumped my forehead with his thumb and finger. "He took the cure to the princess and the new baby. He knew you wouldn't be able to stand it and would insist on taking the cure to them."

My heart flutters. I'm in shock. Riley does know me. "Who went with him?"

"No one. He went by himself. He plans on meeting up with Oliver. It seems that Tury..."

"Tury?" I interrupt him. "The lady we found floating in the sea with Baako?" Tury, she was fortunate to be alive. She survived being thrown in the icy ocean with Baako. Certain death. She was lucky to have been found by Colt and me.

Colt continues, "Yeah, Tury. She took your..."

What's he trying to say?

I press him. "She took someone's place?"

"Never mind." He says.

"Where is she? Is she on the ship? How can she get close to the princess and prince?" I drop my head. She's on the ship. I know exactly whose place she is taking. My mother. My mother who was killed by the evil king for the entire world to see on live television. Now the king is dead, but the emperor still lives. A rage boils inside of me. My mother's death sears in my mind. "Tury's working in the kitchen." I whisper.

Colt hugs my shoulder. "She wanted to go to keep an eye on the little prince and princess. She's been reporting to us via Oliver for about a month now. Using Tury to get the cure to the little ones is the perfect plan."

"It is." I have to agree. I rub my temples. Quit obsessing about my mother's murder or Riley being in danger. It's exhausting. "I'm going to go to bed." I trudge to my room and fall onto the mattress.

The next day, I find Gretel in the lab. "Any word on Riley and how he is doing with getting the cure to the children?"

"Nothing yet." Gretel dons her lab coat, picks up a beaker, and swishes the liquids in it. "But we didn't expect it would be quick. I'm sure that Oliver will send word as soon as he knows anything."

"I was just hoping to hear from him." I twirl a test tube in my hand. "What exactly do you want me to do?"

As I fumble the test tube out of my hand and it drops, Gretel catches it. "I really think your expertise would be better used somewhere else."

"Like where?"

"Training the army." She sets the tube in its holder on the counter.

What a great idea! Cooped up in a lab all day is not using my strengths. "Where are they training?"

"Colt has the troops in the southwest quadrant. They start early. The children are out there now. He would love the help." She opens the door for me. "You two finish early to be sure that you make it to the radio broadcast on time tonight. We have to debunk the negative chatter going around about the resistance."

"You're right. One step forward. Five back. It isn't fair. How can the emperor have so much power?"

"We'll figure it out. We have to believe we will win. But we won't be victorious without a trained army." She gives me a quick hug.

"See you later." I take off out the door. It's a beautiful crisp morning. If this place wasn't a training camp for a war and a haven for the persecuted, I could take a few minutes to enjoy it.

Our training area is an open space in the middle of a courtyard. A short stone fence surrounds the space, enclosing it entirely. A gate is used to enter. I imagine centuries ago when this castle was first built on these lands, knights joisted with their swords in the very same pasture. Maybe this exact spot is where the knights learned how to wield their swords and win their battles. I hope some of that good karma is still left on this ground as we train our army of children.

Following a loud voice, I spot Colt yelling at the children. Our trainees are haphazardly milling around as Colt barks orders. "Line up! Let's get together and fall in."

A few of the children hover around Thomas, one of our original army from the Ferris wheel farm. It was his close friend, Kelley who had perished. One girl pats his shoulder. "Sorry. Let me know if you need anything."

Another of our army of children, Amanda hugs a dark haired boy, Parker, and says, "Kelley was such a wonderful person."

"She died helping us all." Parker wipes a tear from his eye. "She was a hero."

"She was wonderful." Thomas chokes back the tears. "I miss her."

Mike sums it all up when he says, "Kelley will always be one of our family. We can't forget her sacrifice and that she died for our freedom.

"Kelley was a wonderful soldier." Colt pulls Thomas in line. "We will all miss her terribly. But we must move on. We must make sure that her death is not in vain."

"Gretel sent me." I walk up and stand by Colt. "She thought my time would be better spent helping you train rather than bothering her in the lab."

His face widens into a grin. "I bet she did. She's particular about her lab. She wants it just so. I think she is worried about that replicator. She is so scared that she is going to tear it up. It's made her question everybody."

"What if Gretel gets sick? Did she ever think about that? She could be sick then none of us would know how to run the machine. What a disaster that could be."

"I'm sure she's thought of that." He shakes his head. "But maybe not. You know I can't talk Gretel out of something once she sets her mind to it. It's like talking to a leaf." He pause for a minute, then he slaps me on the back. "Glad to have you. We make a good team, sister-in-law."

We spend the next few minutes organizing the group.

"Do we get to use weapons?" Mike asks.

Colt drops his arms. "Not yet. But soon."

Mike grins. "I like that."

Parker runs around with his arms formed like a pretend gun. "I'm ready to shoot someone."

Amanda yells at Parker. "Stop, Parker. Be serious. We have to learn the right way to do things or we could get killed."

Wrapping my arm in a stronghold around Parker, I momentarily stop his movements. "Calm down." He jerks away from me, but I grab a hunk of his shirt and refuse to let go. "First, we have to train." Finally, Parker quits squirming, gives up, and sits down to listen.

For the next hour, we put the children through a series of drills. They fight hand-to-hand combat. They crawl on their stomachs practicing evasion maneuvers.

Colt barks, "Perfecting how to elude the enemy is one of the best tactics, we will teach you." He drops down and demonstrates how to hide behind structures. "You need to learn how to sneak up on the opposition and subdue them without calling attention to yourself." He slips up behind Thomas and takes him down by pinning Thomas's arms behind his back and says, "See?"

"Most likely, we will be outgunned and outmanned." I chime in. "The only way we are going to win is for us to be smart. We have a limited supply of guns. We must make weapons out of the terrain, bark, sand, boulders, everything and learn how to use those weapons."

I guide the group over to another section of the training area. On the ground is spread a variety of tree limbs, rocks and other items found in nature. "Here we'll show you how to make dirt bombs, slingshots and catapult throws."

Colt stops me for a minute. "If any of you have an idea of how to make weapons with what we can find out here, please share that information with us. We are going to need all of the help we can get if we have any hope against the emperor's weapons."

"The one thing we have that they don't is a desire to change our way of life." I pick up a rock. "These pampered people have been leading a life of luxury. Although they outnumber us…"

"Why does that matter?" Thomas interrupts. "Aren't the rich lazy? Why are we worried about them fighting?"

337

"That's a good question, Thomas." I point my finger around the room. "The rich are lazy. That means they aren't going to fight their own battles. Does anyone know who will fight their battles for them?"

Amanda raises her hand and I motion to her. She answers, "They will hire Mercs."

Obviously, Amanda has been paying attention. I nod. "Amanda is right. The rich have no desire to be in the middle of the fray. In fact, they want to stay as far away from it as possible."

I take a breath. "We need to work that to our advantage. Most of the mercenaries are hired. Some of them are like Riley. They are farm boys forced to serve in the mercenary army. I hope that if we win a couple of battles, we can free them. We need to give them a better choice."

A crowd gathers. The children we are supposed to be training make up the front row of our audience. The crowd obscures the stone fence.

Aunt Sandra uses her cane to hobble through the gate and stand beside me. "Don't stop dear. We all need to hear this. You wonder why we want you and Colt to be our voice to the resistance. This is why. While you have been inspiring your young recruits, others have joined them to hear your message too. It's powerful to hear from people who have been in the middle of the battle." Aunt Sandra looks out at the crowd. "Quiet everyone. Let's hear a story to inspire us."

Shrugging my shoulders, I ask Colt. "What should we tell them?"

"I know." Colt begins. "We were just like you. We worked on a farm and did not even know about each other's existence until the Mercs took over our farms and lied to the people. They published falsehoods reporting the Mercs owned the farms. That wasn't true was it?"

The crowd shouts in unison. "NO!"

I say, "Colt and I escaped from our farm with the sole intention of saving my sister and my mother." I feel myself choking up, but hold back the tears. "We searched everywhere and were told that my mother and sister had boarded an ocean liner."

A person in the crowd shouts out. "Your sister is Gretel and you and Colt saved her."

"We wanted to save all of the farm families," Colt says, "I was lucky and found my father and siblings right off. We sent them and the rest of the families to safety to continue our search for Paisley's mother and sister."

Colt paces. "It was then that Paisley and I happened upon Lieutenant Drake. It was the first time we met him. He told us of the underground resistance movement. We knew that if we could get to safety then we would be able to join up with the resistance and here we are."

338

A shout from the crowd egged us on. "Tell us about the royals."

Another voice asks, "How did you get on that liner?" He looks at the person sitting beside him and whispers, "I love this one. These two are legends."

"One quick story, then we need to get back to work." I continue walking back and forth. Younger children have joined us, some sitting in adult laps. "When we got to Hamburg there was no way to get on the ship. We happened into a doll shop with a kindly owner, Ms. DeVane. We met the princess and her nanny, Miss Brita. Princess Kamea decided that she wanted to add the German dolls to her collection of "Sponsored Companions""

Colt broke in. "And we fit the bill of German dolls. I mean look at me! Don't I look like a living doll?" He puts his hands under his chin, looks up, and smiles. The crowd laughs.

I slap his hands away from his chin. "Ms. DeVane created documents so we could board the ship where we were assigned to play with Princess Kamea. It was fun, but we were owned."

My voice goes solemn. "We are fighting for the Uncounted. The people who are sold to others. We have to stop human trafficking." I look out to the crowd. "How many of you have been owned?" Ninety percent of the hands shoot up.

Colt shouts. "This is unacceptable. How many of you have been deemed Undesirables and slated for annihilation simply because you have a disability or are flawed?"

Many hands shoot up.

"This is not right!" I yell, "Everyone is equal. No person should own other people. Our way of life is broken and we must fix it. We must win this battle. The future is dependent on what we do in the next few months."

I slow my speaking to accentuate every word. I want to be understood. "We have the cure. We control the virus. It can no longer hurt us. The Mercenaries want to take over our world and make it their own. They want us to serve them. Emperor Richard has stolen the throne and is using it for his own agenda."

Colt trots across the front of the crowd his fist raised, as he yells, "We must win. I say this is our time."

The crowd stands and yells. "YES!"

Colt shouts some more. "They feel the only way to defeat us is from within. They want others to think we are the bad guys."

I shoot my own fist in air. "WE MUST WIN! WE MUST WIN!"

Everyone in the crowd is pumping a fist and chanting. "WE MUST WIN! WE MUST WIN!"

The chant eventually morphs into "WE WILL WIN! WE WILL WIN!"

Aunt Sandra leans in, cups my ear, and whispers, "And that is how you fire up the troops."

I whisper back. "No, that is how you start a war."

Chapter 7

For the next few days, the mood of the compound is one of determination. It sweeps through every nook and cranny of the large area, affecting everyone. Spontaneous chants erupt everywhere. This positive energy makes living on the compound wonderful for these three idyllic days.

Training is great. Everyone is focused. The vaccine is being manufactured by Gretel and her crew in record time. Aunt Sandra and her boys make a plan to deliver the cure to the resistance all over the world.

A large map is set up. Through Oliver, reports of struggles to motivate troops in other places surface. It has proved a more difficult task than first realized. The emperor has massive control over the media and is doing everything he can to undermine the resistance.

There are daily bulletins blaming our side for putting the disease back into the mainstream. They use pictures of dead people, reporting they are casualties of the virus.

Oliver works day and night, releasing stories that contradict this negative influx. He hopes that by reporting the truth to resistance, they will remain loyal to our cause.

Colt and I are summoned to the radio room one morning.

Aunt Sandra stands in front of the massive radio. Wires are hooked at various spots and lights flicker on and off. "It's time for you two to start back on your radio messages." She punches a button on the radio and speaks. "SONOL, they are both here." SONOL is the call sign for Oliver at the resistance's communication center in Hamburg.

The radio squawks and Oliver's voice is heard. "We have some good news for you."

Good news? My heart skips. "What news?"

Oliver's voice sounds again. "Your friend has reported that the cure has been delivered to the two packages. There is no chance they will contract the virus."

Reading between the lines I realize Riley was able to get the cure to the prince and princess. I grab the microphone and press the button. "What about my friend? Is he okay? When is he coming home? Any word on the queen?"

"Be careful about names." Aunt Sandra takes the microphone away from me and presses the button.

Oliver's voice comes back on. "This should be a secure line. But it's always better to be careful."

Aunt Sandra speaks in the speaker. "Don't worry about telling us when our friend will return, dear."

I jerk it back. "Yes, SONOL, worry about it now. I want to know when my friend is coming back."

A familiar voice sounds. "So you miss me."

Riley.

The speaking device drops from my hand and Colt catches it mid-air. "Yeah, we *all* miss you. What happened?"

Riley and Oliver report using a code without people's names and the ship's name about how Riley was able to sneak the cure onto the ship via some supplies that were delivered to the kitchen. Tury intercepted them and followed the directions giving the vials not only the prince and princess, but to the rest of the other "Sponsored Companions" who were still captives.

After they finish, Aunt Sandra asks, "Did the main man make it?"

My father's voice comes on next. "Yes. I'm here and we're working on a plan. As soon as it's finalized, we will get together and implement."

Aunt Sandra cocks her head. "Lieutenant, will the plan work?"

Lieutenant Drake's voice sounds. "I hope so. It's the only chance we have."

For the next hour, Colt and I are instructed by Lieutenant Drake, Oliver, and my father regarding exactly what they want us to say on the address to the troops.

As we are leaving, I ask Colt, "How do you think the young ones are progressing in their training?"

Colt shakes his head. "As well as can be expected. The problem is we are expecting young children, children under fifteen, to be in charge of groups of twenty or so. It will be hard for them to make decisions. They're too young. It's too much responsibility. I wish we had more experienced people to be in charge."

"Funny you should say that." I knock into his shoulder. "Did you forget that I'm sixteen and you are eighteen? How are we any more qualified to lead the entire revolution? I think we have to realize the future we are trying to create is the world people like me and you, the young people, will have to live in. We want to be free. We are the ones who will be living in that new world."

Colt kicks a piece of dirt. "You're right. Some of *us* will be in charge."

"Scary thought, huh?" We both chuckle. I love it when something is funny. There is so little in the world that is humorous nowadays.

Throughout the rest of the day, we work on the script for the presentation we are to report to the troops tonight. Many people labor over every word, making sure that we say everything just right to not give away any information about troops, the resistance in general, or anything about the cure and its location.

It's finally time.

"Paisley and Colt with a message for the resistance troops." Aunt Sandra introduces us.

Colt starts. "Fellow resistance fighters, it has been far too long since Paisley and I have addressed you. I know that you are hearing through the media that the resistance has brought back the virus. That is simply not true. We are here to tell you the truth."

"There was a rumor the virus had started back up." I take a deep breath. "That's not true. We, the resistance fighters, did indeed start that rumor. Our purpose was to try to limit the movements of the mercenaries and royals and those opposing democracy, allowing us to move freely. We had hoped to get information to the troops more easily and try to organize our side."

Colt clears his throat. "Unfortunately, our secret plan was intercepted by Emperor Richard and now is being used to undermine our regime."

"We must not let that happen." I interrupt. "It is imperative that we stay the course."

"There is good news." Colt says. "It could very well be the changing point of the entire war."

"Great news." I am hopeful that all is not lost.

Colt points to the paper. He wants me to follow the script. I hate following orders. Colt continues. "We, the resistance, have indeed found a cure. It was developed by a lab assistant in the ambassador's lab."

I interject. "My sister, Gretel."

Colt shoots an aggravated look my way and covers the microphone, "This is not a secure line. This is a message to everyone. We weren't supposed to reveal her identity. Or say her name. That could put her in peril."

"What?" I ask. He points to the microphone. I cover the microphone and whisper, "I thought only the resistance would listen to this."

"Shush." He places a finger over his lips. "Are we telling them that the ambassador lives?"

I shake my head. Aunt Sandra motions to us. "Stay on script."

"Sorry about that, technical difficulties." Colt begins again attempting to explain the dead air. "Like we were saying, the resistance does indeed have a cure. The vaccine is being sent to every person. We will make sure that all of the people fighting for freedom get inoculated first."

"Then we will be sending the cure to everyone." I look at my script now trying to follow every word exactly. "There will be no charge. We don't want to withhold the vaccine from anyone. We want to make sure that the virus is gone forever."

I pass the script back to Colt, who continues, "Make sure those in remote areas make it to your rendezvous points to take the cure. It is nothing more than a vial of medicine. There are no side effects."

Once again, Colt slides the paper back in front of me. "The best part of the vaccine is that after two days it takes effect and you can no longer get the virus. You are immune forever. We plan to make this world ours again. No one will ever be called an Undesirable or an Uncounted. This is our world. We will make sure everyone has a voice."

Aunt Sandra and Colt nod.

Colt and I say at the same time. "Power to the resistance!"

The address ends and the microphone goes silent.

Colt and I hug.

"How did I do?" I ask.

Aunt Sandra says, "You two are strong leaders. I am hopeful. We might just have a chance to win this war."

I roll the four-leaf clover in my hand as I silently make my only wish: that Riley was here.

Chapter 8

Gretel shakes me awake. "Paisley! Wake up!"

"What?" I rub the sleep out of my eyes. "What do you want?"

Gretel sits on the side of my bed. "Colt wants to see you in the radio room. He said to hurry."

Swinging my legs over the side of the bed, I jerk my head. "What time is it? Did something happen?"

"I don't know." Gretel lets out a big breath. "He wouldn't tell me. He said he couldn't talk to me about it." She looks at me, cheeks flushing with urgency. Why is she upset? She throws my jeans at me and says, "You just need to go."

Tugging on my jeans, I fling my sleep shirt off and pull the fleece wear over my head. "I'm sure it's nothing." I knock into her shoulder. "Don't worry, whatever he tells me, I'll tell you. You know that."

She embraces me. "I knew you would say that. I knew you would tell me. Sisters don't keep secrets." She puts her finger on her chin. "Definitely tell me, unless it's a present or something like that. I do like surprises."

I roll my eyes. Why would Colt drag me up at dawn to tell me about a surprise present for my sister? I like that her work as a lab rat has kept her sheltered from a lot of the ugliness of war. Her mind is in the books and science; the death doesn't seem to register with her. Still, she witnessed our mother's public execution on television along with me and about a million other people.

I pull on my boots and follow my sister. She chatters all the way to the radio building about nothing. I barely listen. She drops me off at the door. "I'm not allowed to come in. He actually said that to me. Can you believe it?" I pat her on the back and give her a half-smile. I had to wake up for this drama? Go figure. I open the door and go inside.

Colt is slumped forward. The expression on his face tells me everything I need to know. This is something serious. I ask, "What happened?"

"Gretel is being targeted." His voice is low. Sweat trickles down his cheek.

"Why?"

His glare pierces my soul. It's because of me. My sister is in danger and it's my fault. I was so proud of my sister that I said her name over the airwaves last night.

Tears well. "It's because I gave them her name. I'll never forgive myself if she is hurt because of me."

"Calm down. I'm not going to let her out of my sight." He grabs my hand. "I know you didn't do it on purpose. But I don't want to scare her so I'm not going to tell her and you can't tell her either."

"I can't keep this from her. I appreciate you telling me first. But it's important for her to know the danger she is in." I take a deep breath. "How did you find this out? Tell me everything."

Colt bites his lower lip. "Last night the radio operator woke me up to come and hear the broadcast. When I arrived at the radio building, Oliver told me the chatter was that since Gretel knows how to make the cure that she is the number one "get." She is priority one and they are to make sure that the emperor has her as soon as possible."

"The emperor is in possession of one of the machines. They need the machine to manufacture the cure. He needs her to work it." Colt shakes his head. "It must be a replica of the machine that Gretel clamors on about being delicate and rare. If it's so rare, how did they get ahold of it? When they heard her name, somebody remembered her as being the ambassador's assistant. They put out a description and everything."

"And it's all because I mentioned her on the radio? Go ahead you can say it. I know it already. I've put my sister in danger."

"Forget about fault and focus on their plan." Colt continues, "The plan is that they get her. I know the compound is safe, but what if they follow a courier back here?"

He pauses for a second before continuing, "They hope that without her the resistance can't make more of the cure. They plan to make Gretel work for them." He sighs. "I'm worried. The royals and Mercs are desperate and desperate people do crazy things. We have to protect her."

"The best way to protect her is to let her know what's going on." I shift in my seat. "You said that you are going to make sure that you keep an eye on her all of the time." I turn my head from side to side. "If that is true, where is she?"

"I don't know what I was thinking. I'm her husband and I just want to protect her." He jumps up. "She won't know to be on the lookout for trouble if she doesn't know about it."

"She was going to the lab." I head for the door. "Let's go and tell her together."

As we exit the radio room, people scurry about. This is unusual. At this time of morning, everyone is usually at his or her assigned stations. Amanda crosses in front of us. I ask, "Amanda, what is going on?"

Amanda stops. "They sounded the alarm. Didn't you hear it?"

346

I hear it now. The bells are ringing.

She continues, "Someone has breached the outer realm of the maze. Everyone is scrambling to find out who it is."

"That's impossible. It has to be a hoax." Colt grabs her arm. "Wait. Where's Gretel?"

Amanda looks around. "I haven't seen Gretel." Colt releases his grip and she scampers off.

"This doesn't sound right. There is no way anyone found this compound. Something is very wrong." Colt looks at me. "Let's go to the lab and get Gretel first."

"I agree."

The two of us zigzag in and out of people running all around. The army of children is perched around the compound. A few have guns pointed at the opening of the maze.

"Did you see that the children are armed?" I shriek as we turn the corner toward the lab.

Colt's face is tortured. "Not now. First, Gretel."

I nod. He's right.

In a few minutes, we make it to the lab.

"Gretel!" Colt rushes in the door yelling. "Gretel, where are you?"

A lab worker is measuring some liquid into a vial. "She just left. No one came for the new batch of the cure set to go on a ship to South America. She took a bag of cures to deliver to the new couriers."

I ask, "What new couriers?"

The lab worker pushes his glasses to rest on the bridge of his nose, pulls his latex gloves off his hands with a loud popping sound, and tosses them in the trash. "The message. I thought you sent it. It was here when she got back." The lab worker shifts some papers around.

Colt's eyes get huge. "I didn't send anything. You have to find that note." He grabs the lab worker by his collar and spits as he talks. "Where's my wife?"

"Stop it!" I pull Colt off the bespectacled man.

The man shifts his collar around. It takes him a couple of seconds to compose himself again. "I said I'd find it for you. No reason to manhandle me."

"Sorry." Colt mumbles.

A few minutes later, the lab worker produces a paper. "Here it is."

Colt studies the note. "It did come from our office."

I grab the message. "What does it say?" I flip it over. "And when was it sent? Weren't you at the radio room?"

"I was there all morning." He stops for a moment and puts his hands on his hips. "Wait a minute, I left to tell her to get you. It must have come through then."

I run out the door. "C'mon we need to get up with Oliver. They have to be the ones who sent it."

Colt runs after me. "You go do that. I need to find Gretel." His eyes scan the compound. "I'll be there as soon as I can. Call Oliver and find out what's going on there."

My feet pound the dirt as I run back to the radio room. The operator is still there. I ask, "Did you take this message?"

He reads it aloud: *Virus cure that was on its way to South America has been destroyed. Please send more. I will meet you at Paisley's farm.*

"Yes." He hands the note back to me. "It was received this morning."

"Move over." I grab the microphone. "Oliver, come in." I stop for a moment. I'm not supposed to use his name. I'm supposed to use our code names. PACO. It's a mix of our names, Colt and me. PA for Paisley and CO for Colt. I start again. "PACO calling."

Oliver's voice comes on. "SONOL here." SONOL is Oliver's code. Son-Oliver.

I begin. "We received a message this morning which reads: Virus cure that was on its way to South America has been destroyed. Please send more. I will meet you at Paisley's farm. Did you send that?"

His voice booms into the speaker. "No. Paisley's farm home has been compromised. Make sure that no one goes there. They must have hacked our system. Did they use the SONOL code?"

Looking over at the radio operator, I know the answer before I ask him.

"Can't find her." Colt throws open the door and enters the room out of breath.

The boy in the radio room sinks his head in his hands. "I didn't think anyone else had the capability to use our radio system."

"I didn't think so either, but the message has been delivered." I release the button for a moment and then hold it down again to deliver the bad news. "The message was delivered to the lab."

"Why?" Oliver asks.

"Were you told to deliver it to the lab?" A feeling of despair overcomes me as I look over at the radio operator.

His shoulders droop. "I was told to deliver it to Gretel."

"Oh no." I let go of the microphone.

Colt gasps.

Oliver's voice booms. "We all heard all of that. You are to stay put. We will figure it out from here."

Colt bolts out of the doorway. I press the button again. "Too late. Her husband heard it all and is gone."

Riley's voice sounds. "My friend, you stay. I'll go after him. I promise I'll bring him home okay." Silence. Riley whispers, "I promise to bring them both back home."

Chapter 9

In the next few minutes, the radio operator delivers a message to the compound about Gretel's disappearance and the danger she is in. It doesn't take long for Aunt Sandra to show up. Aunt Sandra talks back and forth on the radio trying to sort the details. Amanda attempts to keep me calm.

Aunt Sandra pats my shoulder, "You and Amanda write everything that has happened this morning word for word. Don't leave anything out."

Write the whole thing up? Is she nuts? It's Aunt Sandra's rule. We don't want to miss anything. We must record all acts, mistakes, and successes. She says knowing our mistakes will help us not repeat them. But now? My initial reaction of rage slowly changes to calm. The writing seems to make me feel better. At least I have something to do. Aunt Sandra is so much wiser than me.

I'm worried about Riley and Colt. But I'm mostly scared for my sister. We can't find her anywhere. Aunt Sandra has scores of people scouring the countryside for her. A group is sent to try to join Colt in his quest to intercept Gretel before she gets to our farm.

Gretel knows all of the back ways to the farm. This is the farm that we grew up on. I wish I could have told her about the tunnels. She might have used them. If I had had time to tell Colt, he definitely could have used them. Everyone is scattered; even Riley is somewhere looking for Colt and my sister. My sister's in trouble because she is a good person trying to save people.

The sitting and waiting is killing me and now Aunt Sandra has insisted that I go on the air to rally the troops. I don't feel like it. Not at all.

After communicating back and forth with Oliver all day, the only thing he can tell me for sure is that Riley has left. There will be no way to reach any of them until they radio us. Most likely that won't happen until they return or find a resistance camp.

I'm so tired I doze off for a minute in the chair in radio room. I dream Gretel is unharmed and in one of the caves. She is eating pears and laughing at us for being so concerned. The next minute I am soaring on my Ferris wheel. I feel the wind in my face. I am peaceful and happy. I wake to see Aunt Sandra's face as she sits quietly beside me.

"This is SONOL. Come in PACO." The noise breaks my serenity.

Grabbing the microphone, I hear Oliver's voice.

I say, "PACO here. Any news."

"No." Another squawking noise. "Are you going on the air tonight?"

"Yes." I pause. "Alone." I place the microphone down.

My father's voice breaks in. "We need you now more than ever. The media blitz is bad. The Mercs think they can find the one they seek. We need to keep morale up. You represent hope. You have to keep the resistance forces in a positive frame of mind. Please. Let's make sure that we do this right."

I push the button again. "I wish I knew Gretel was okay."

My father's voice again. "Don't use her name please. The Mercs have developed a new device that specifically searches for names. Oliver thinks that is how they were able to hack in last night."

My heart sinks. I suspected it, but now I know. I tipped them off about Gretel. It is my fault that my sister might be killed. I have to make this right. I push the button again. "I'll be on at the regular time." I release the button. I can't let everyone down. I will do what a good soldier has to do. I won't be happy about it and my heart won't be into it, but I won't let anyone else know. My shoulders slump and I place my hands on my cheeks.

"We have to believe everything will work out." Aunt Sandra pats the back of my head. "Stay positive."

It's time. I sit in front of the microphone and shift it to "on." The lights flash on and off.

Aunt Sandra introduces me. "Tonight you have a treat. Colt is off on assignment. So we will have our Paisley to talk to us." She looks at me. "Paisley?"

"Hello resistance." I take a breath. "This is Paisley. I know that I'm supposed to tell you a story about Colt and me. About an adventure that we had and how we were able to get out of it. I know those adventure stories are fun and I know how they cheer you up."

I pause. "But tonight I want to talk to you about something real. I want to tell you about just a few of the people who have died trying to fight for our cause, for freedom. These people have given their lives to make sure that the rest of us have a shot at democracy."

Aunt Sandra smiles.

"One of those brave people was someone I met on the ship that Colt and I were on. An Undesirable. This Undesirable was more desirable than anyone I had ever known. He was the leader of the bottom floor of this ship. He made sure everyone had something to eat. He put others before himself and he tried to make everyone smile." A tear rolls down my cheek.

351

"He was a father. He was a brother. He was a husband. He was thrown off the ship because the king thought that he carried the virus. But more than that, he died because he was thought of as a lesser person. A person who could be owned and given orders. He was expendable or so they said. I don't believe this man was expendable. He was needed by his friends and family, but most of all he was needed by his children." I wipe my tear.

"I loved this man and I want to make sure that when we're finally free, we remember each and every one who gave the ultimate sacrifice for all of us."

I take in a labored breath. "Another of those brave people was a child. She was no more than ten years old. She gathered intel for our group. She never did anything wrong." I choke back more tears. "When she learned about the raid on my farm, she tried to make it back with that information. She was found barely alive and held on long enough to get her message to us. I owe her my life. She saved us all. She does not have a family. She was an Uncounted. But I'm here to tell you that the resistance was her family. We were all her brother, sister, aunt, uncle and mother and father. We love her because she was one of us."

"Another brave person was the bodyguard sent to protect me from the raid on the farm. He not only saved me," I clasp my hands together. "He pushed through a fatal injury to make sure that I survived. He said it was an honor to meet me. I say instead that it was an honor to meet him. He gave his life for me. He was my brother and your brother too."

"This is not the kind of uplifting message you were expecting tonight, but this message is real. This threat is real and if we don't do something now to stop this, then more of our brothers and sisters will die."

I puff out my chest and take in a deep breath. "The rest of us will forever live in a world in which we are owned and ordered around. We will be bought and sold like livestock. When we get too old or if we are hurt or if we are deemed by someone in power to be no longer useful we will be killed as if we are insects. We cannot let that happen. We must win. We must be strong. We are stronger together than we will ever be apart."

Alone, I raise my fist, "Power to the Resistance."

After I shut down the microphone, I hear applause. The radio room is filled with the people of the compound.

Aunt Sandra's eyes are brimming. "That was the most loving tribute ever given for the lost ones. You are truly a special person."

Amanda hugs me.

352

It's a struggle to get out of the chair. I'm exhausted. I find my way through all of the well-wishers. They pat me on the back.

"Wonderful." One of the trainees squeezes my hand.

Tears flow down an older lady's cheeks. "She was talking about Kelley."

A man nods his head. "I knew Charles. What a nice tribute."

"We should make a memorial wall or something for the people who have passed away." Aunt Sandra says to a passer-by.

"Everyone is important." A man with a pronounced limp shakes another man's hand who says, "I agree. She's right, we must win this war."

Amanda claps her hands together. "If we don't do something about it now, then the world will be lost forever."

Applause thunders throughout the compound as I make it back to my quarters and crawl into bed fully clothed. I am almost asleep when I hear Amanda. "Paisley, get up. There's news."

On the way to the radio room, I beg under my breath. "Please be good news. Please be good news."

As I enter, I hear my father's voice reporting on the radio. "The emperor has captured Gretel."

Chapter 10

My sister Gretel. I want to scream. I want to climb through the wires and choke the emperor, but I know I can't. I have to remain calm. I sink down in my chair for a moment unable to speak. My sweet sister is in the hands of the monstrous emperor.

I speak softly into the microphone. "How..."

My father's voice booms. "We are monitoring the situation. There are two heading to her location to try to free her. Will let you know as soon as possible what happens."

"Okay." It's all I can manage to get out.

"Your radio message to the troops was wonderful tonight. You should be so proud."

"Thanks." Once again, I can't get any more words out.

His voice softens, "Are you okay?"

Even though I try, I can't stop the tears. I did not notice Aunt Sandra in the back of the room. She comes to the microphone and presses the button. "We'll be okay here. PACO over and out."

She shuts down the microphone and sits beside me. I weep until I can't cry anymore. I don't know what to do. I can't think straight. My mind wanders from fear for my sister to the realization that we have lost our only way to make the cure. What if the emperor sells the cure? I don't think they will kill my sister. She's too important. She is the only person alive who can make the cure. Even the emperor wouldn't risk losing that.

My thoughts go to Riley and Colt. They will certainly make sure that they do everything to save her. What if they are killed trying to rescue her? Why am I only thinking of the most horrible things? I want a positive thought. I search for one, but nothing. I fear all is lost.

I slump in the chair unable to move and I cry myself to sleep.

My eyelids flutter awake. I'm in my bed in my room. I peek under the sheet and I'm fully clothed so someone must have carried me here. I go to the bathroom, wash my face, and brush my teeth. A shower will help. No time to feel sorry for myself; I must formulate a plan to get Gretel back.

After I dress, I go to the laboratory. I want to feel close to my sister. When I walk to the lab, everyone I see gives me the poor pitiful look like I'm an Uncounted with a time set for my execution. I hate that look.

The flurry of activity in the science laboratory surprises me. What's going on? Did Gretel leave instructions so explicit that the technicians are able to copy her work? That fleeting thought makes me happy.

"Hey, want to help?" My father stands in a white coat holding a vial of what I can only assume is the cure.

At this moment, it doesn't matter how many people are in here or how many people see me. I run and hug him. I wonder what the other lab technicians must think of me and why I would be so close to the ambassador. They don't know that he is my father, and to be honest I really don't care what anyone thinks right now.

The action takes him by surprise, but he hugs me back and I cry again.

He strokes my hair. "It'll be all right. I'm sure that Riley and Colt will get Gretel back."

"How can they? They must have her guarded. Why didn't she wait to talk to Colt or me about the problem? Why couldn't Colt or I have gotten to her first before she received the fake message? If only she had stayed here for just a while longer, she would have known about the danger." I bury my head on his shoulder and sob. "She thought everything was fine. She left thinking that she was helping; my heart aches with what ifs. I hate what ifs. If only Colt had told her they were looking for her. She might have been more careful." My voice breaks. "If only I hadn't said her name over the broadcast."

"Don't blame yourself." My father puts his finger to my lips. "No looking back, only looking forward. We must be positive. The best way to keep our minds off it is to stay busy. It's important that we keep busy."

"You're right." I wipe my eyes and take in a calming breath. "What are you doing here and when did you get here?"

"After you went to bed last night, Aunt Sandra and I talked on the radio. We decided it was paramount to keep up our manufacturing of the cure. Lives depend on it. I travelled here last night to keep our manufacturing on track."

I smile. "I'm glad you're here."

Picking up a beaker, he looks around. "I was truly surprised by this place. I had no idea it was here." He picks up a microscope. "They have managed to collect some state of the art equipment for this lab." He places the microscope back down. "Not sure how they collected some of the more modern devices. But I'm not going to question it. Aunt Sandra has done a great job hiding it all of these years. We did decide it's important to make sure that more than just a couple of people know how to make the cure."

"Is that why all of these people are here?" I turn in place looking at the full room. I see Amanda, Thomas, and Mike. "Are you also teaching the children?"

He nods. "I'm instructing anybody who is interested in learning. The more people who know how to manufacture it, the less chance we have of actually having an outbreak."

"Here." He sits in a chair and rolls another toward me motioning for me to sit down.

"What about Lieutenant Drake? I thought you were his right hand man." I take a seat. "What will he do without you and Riley there?"

"He has Oliver." He takes in a deep breath. "Although Oliver is more an intellect, not a fighter. And you are right about Riley. He's great at battle strategy. But it seems that there is another captain coming over from America."

"America?" This perks my interest. "What's his name?"

My father smiles. "Captain Via and he is a she."

Captain Via. I can't contain my reaction as I make a high squeaky noise.

"Do you know her?" My father asks.

I slow my breathing, calming my excitement. What if I'm telling my father about my mother? A few seconds pass before I'm able to speak without giving away my secret thoughts. "Yes, I met her when I was in America. She is the captain who introduced me to Eddie. She helped me return to Bavaria. She's great."

His comments are monotone as if he is talking about nobody special. "I've heard nothing but good things about her. I've never met her. From what I understand, she has a lot of knowledge about the virus and its cure. I am very thankful that she is able to come over to us. Oliver has been communicating with her."

"Ambassador..." One of the lab assistants taps my father on the shoulder. "I don't quite understand this step."

"I'll be there in a minute." My father pats me on the arm. "You sit here as long as you like. I need to show as many as I can about how to manufacture and mix the cure. It's important."

He walks over to the students, patiently explaining each step of how to mix the virus.

How wonderful that Captain Via is coming over from America. I would love to be there when they meet. My brother will be working with her. I could be wrong but I just know that she is my mother, my real mother, my birth mother. The only proof I have is a distinct birthmark on her neck. I can't tell my brother that he is my brother and I can't tell my maybe mother that she could be my mother and I can't tell my father about my maybe mother. It is so mixed up. But for the last few minutes I haven't once thought of Gretel, Riley, or Colt. And maybe just for today, that is a good thing.

Thomas, Amanda, Mike, and I learn how to mix the virus cure. It's not hard provided you know the basics. The cure is synthesized from blood.

My father winks at me when he introduces the blood. "This is your blood that we used to make the DNA strand." Fortunately, my father has invented a replicating machine that strips the DNA out of anyone's blood. The DNA voided blood then passes through his device and replicates another's DNA strand.

For the cure, the machine replicates a synthetic form of my blood which contains the antibodies needed to immunize the populace from the virus. Actually, after seeing this I wonder if Gretel will have any luck at duplicating the cure without all of this equipment or any of my blood.

"How many of these replicators are there?" Mike asks my father as he holds up a vial, swirling its contents.

"A least a hundred," My father answers, "This is what I did for the military. This is the machine I was hired to invent."

Thomas pours a beaker full of fluids and measures it out in a test tube. "Why would the military want this type of machine? What could it be used for?"

Amanda shouts, "The only thing I can think of is for bioterrorism."

My father's face goes ashen. Did he know that this science was slated for use as a bioterrorism weapon? Is that what he had been working on all those many years ago? A weapon? The thought of it turns my stomach.

He completely ignores Amanda's comment and goes back to explaining the steps involved in making the virus cure. I don't press for an answer. Not sure if I want to hear it.

At first, the time ticks off the mounted clock slowly, but as I get better at the procedure, the hours fly by. I see Baako on my way back to the bunking area after the day is over.

Baako kicks some dirt as he walks by. "I think we should go and get Gretel. We've been training for just such a thing."

My heart leaps. Another who wants to *actually* do something? "Sure," I whisper. "But we have to make a plan. We can't just storm out of here, walk onto the ship, and get her."

He smiles. "So you've been thinking about rescuing her."

357

"She's my sister." I sit on a bench near the drawbridge. "Of course I have. I've thought of practically nothing else, but we need a plan."

Baako sits beside me, nudging me with his shoulder. "Luckily, I have a plan."

Chapter 11

I want Gretel back so badly that I don't press Baako for the specifics of his plan. I just follow him. I know it's dangerous to leave the compound, but I have to try to save Gretel.

It doesn't seem right that only the men and boys are expected to go into the dangerous situations. I've been in plenty of difficult situations. I do it because I have to. This is one of those "have to" times. I want my sister back unharmed.

Knowing that sneaking off will not be easy, Baako and I grab some essentials and throw them in a backpack. I grab a scarf of Gretel's and a sock of Colt's from their room before I leave. Might need their scent to track. It is so dark.

Baako says he knows where a couple of sentry uniforms are. The sentries dress differently so they can be identified easily. I follow him to the laundromat. Smart thinking. We find the extra uniforms, change quickly, and throw on our backpacks.

We need weapons. I take Baako to the area where we train our army of children. We gather as many dirt bombs and sling shots as we can carry. We take care not to weigh ourselves down, as that would defeat the purpose of being stealth.

The uniforms get us quickly and invisibly out of the compound and through the maze. The sentries ignore us as we grunt through. They most likely think that we are extra guards as Aunt Sandra made a big announcement about adding more security for the compound.

After passing through the entrance gate without any trouble, we travel to our hidden pasture. Baako picks a horse and Hershey nuzzles me when he sees me. I pull a couple of apples out of my backpack to give to each of our horses. We feed the animals and then we are off.

It will take all night to reach Hamburg.

Baako's plan involves finding Tury. Tury and Baako have a special relationship. They were saved together after being thrown off the ship. Thank goodness Colt and I were able to save them!

A simple plan. We get off the compound. Done! We make our way to Hamburg. On our way! We get on the ship and find Tury. Hopefully that will be as easy to accomplish as the rest. Baako thinks that Tury will know where Gretel is.

It might not be the best or most thought out plan, but I don't have a better one. It's certainly better than just sitting here doing nothing. My father and everybody else on this compound will be very upset in the morning when they find out we're gone. I can't worry about that now. I'm on a mission to save Gretel.

The trail is treacherous at night, full of many places to fall and break our necks. If we happen upon a stray Merc or two, it's certain death. Thank goodness, Hershey knows her way. I give her a smell of Colt's sock, after which she tracks his scent all the way to Hamburg. That book about equine air scenting is paying off.

We hit Hamburg early in the morning just before sunrise. The hills that had been hidden by the navy black now explode with orange hues. We are no longer cloaked by darkness.

Baako pulls at his sentry clothes. "We need a better disguise."

I smile. "Let's hide the horses first. Don't worry, I have an idea."

We leave Hershey and the other horse safely behind in the woods. Far enough away to not be easily found, yet close enough that we can get back to them.

As the morning dawns in Hamburg, I notice a familiar store. It's the "Sponsored Companions" store. Ms. DeVane won't be there. She is off with her son fighting the good fight for the resistance side.

"Where are we going?" Baako asks.

I lead him down barren streets. It's so early that not even the bread stores are open.

Standing in front of the doll store, memories flood my mind and I lose my breath for a moment. This store helped Colt and I gain access to the ship the first time. Could it be lucky for me again? It's been a while; at least it's still in business.

"It's too early. It's not open." Baako says.

He follows as I make my way around back, carefully hiding in the shadows. "We don't want it to be open."

Baako's eyes widen. "Are we going to break in?"

"Sort of."

I walk to the entry door of the adjacent store. "The doll store is actually connected to another store that's not in business anymore. That shop is used as storage. I'm hoping that we can get in that way. Wouldn't that be great?"

"It would be a miracle." Baako's eyes widen in amazement as he watches me jiggle the doorknob.

360

It's old and offers little resistance. I open the unlocked door. "I can't believe it."

"Hurry." I shove him in front of me through the door and pull it closed behind me. "We don't want to be seen."

We climb over the junk and debris and come to another entry. I hold my breath. "The back of the store is through this entrance."

"Can our luck still hold out?" Baako laughs.

I twirl the four-leaf clover and pull on the doorknob. Sure enough, this door opens also. No jiggling needed, it's not even locked. Now safely inside the store, I let out a big breath.

The large storeroom is divided by beams and an archway. The far side of the room is full of hanging clothes, men's and women's of all shapes and sizes, but all basically the same design. A life-size poster reading "Sponsored Companions," stands on the far side of the room. The rest of the room is populated with dolls and doll clothes.

Baako sits on a chair in the store. "What are we looking for and what exactly is the plan?"

"You do remember what my "Sponsored Companion" outfit looked like, don't you?" I flip through the hanging clothes. "I'm looking for the dress that matches the Norwegian doll. See?" I point to a large poster advertising the Norwegian doll as coming soon.

"Oh." Baako smiles with recognition. "Do all Europeans dress alike?"

"Guess so." I pull a Norwegian outfit out to study. The outfit consists of a black skirt, black tights, white apron, finished off with the red bib with the rickrack embellishments of ribbon along the edge. I put on the red hat. Best of all, the shoes are black and flat and look comfortable. I hand Baako the male equivalent. "This is the newest doll's clothes. Let's hope the princess doesn't has them yet."

"I get it now. Where do I change?" Baako asks.

Along the back wall, I open another door. "Here's a bathroom. Put these clothes on. Then I'll do the same. Don't take too long."

Baako reappears in a few minutes, pulling at the white tights and knee length black pants. He also dons a vest and shirt. After he puts on his shoes, his outfit is complete. He admires his reflection in the mirror, posing in the tailored jacket, and cocks his head commenting, "I make this look good."

I slip into the bathroom and change. Unzipping my backpack, I grab my other clothes. "Let's put the sentry outfits into our backpacks in case we need them later." Baako does the same. With the exception of the missing outfits, we leave no trace.

We're ready. We exit the store the same way we came in: through the back entrance, being careful not to disturb anything.

Finding a way onto the ship might prove to be difficult, but walking down the street is easy. The streets are still vacant, no people milling around.

"Are they hiding because they believe the virus is making a comeback?" Baako asks.

I stop walking. "Maybe." I had not thought of that.

He continues, "We might not be able to get on the ship. What are we going to do if we can't?"

"We're going to find a way." I cock my eyebrow. Did he think we would come all of this way and not try anything and everything to get on the ship?

A strong feeling of relief overcomes my senses when the ship comes into view. "Look." I nod my head toward the massive vessel. The original name, "Queen Mary IV," had been written with raised letters that could not be completely erased. It has been consigned to rest as a shadow beneath a new moniker in bolder brighter lettering. A name I know, "Queen Nalani."

People scurry about pulling ropes and polishing railings and banisters, anything tied or not tied down. I twirl the four-leaf clover again. We need all of the luck we can get.

"C'mon Baako." My hand clutches Baako's arm. "And please act like you belong." I strut a couple of steps, pulling him along. "Be confident. They can smell fear every time."

Baako trembles. "But I am scared."

The ship's gangplank is down. No one pays any attention to us. So far so good.

It can't be this easy.

I was right.

The sentry at the gate yells, "Halt! Who goes there?"

Chapter 12

"We are the new Norwegian "Sponsored Companions" sent for Princess Kamea. We just arrived," I rattle on. I squeeze Baako's arm since he is shaking so much. At least he is smart enough to know not to say a word.

The sentry questions my announcement. "I haven't heard about any new dolls. I'm going to need verification."

I open my mouth to protest.

"Silence. I have to call Miss Brita and find out what's going on."

Miss Brita. We might have a chance. I am relieved that Miss Brita is still in service to the queen. She knows me and she knows Baako. She might let us pass. It's a gamble, but one I am willing to take to save my sister.

Baako doesn't move. I know he recognizes the name of Miss Brita too. We wait for our fate.

It seems like an eternity before Miss Brita arrives. A large burly man pushes her in a wheelchair. I had hope that she would make a full recovery from a gunshot wound she'd endured during a botched attempt on the ambassador's life. I remember that scary day. We are all lucky to have survived it. She does not look well.

"What is this about sponsored comp..." She stops mid-sentence when she sees us. "Oh yes, those "Sponsored Companions."" She looks us over. "Remind me, where are you from again?"

I curtsy. "Norwegian "Sponsored Companions." We're new."

Miss Brita motions to the sentry. "Let them pass."

We follow Miss Brita and the man who is pushing her onto the main deck of the all too familiar ship. We're quiet. Can't say anything until we get her alone. Not sure who is friend or foe.

As we make our way onto the main part of the ship, I scan the deck. The emperor has changed a lot of the decor. The old art has been replaced. There is no longer the great oil painting of the king adorning the hallway. Now a sculpture of the emperor riding a horse takes up most of the lobby area. The beautiful paintings of the queen and princess have been removed to make room for two paintings of the emperor. The servants are dressed shabbily, even Miss Brita. She always used to have every hair in place. Now her outfit is worn and frayed.

It seems the emperor is not only evil, he doesn't take care of those in his service. I make a mental note of that fact; it might become useful later as we search for a way to dethrone this self-appointed ruler.

All of these people need rescuing. This is what the resistance is all about. These people need to be able to choose the path of their own lives. The emperor is much worse than the king and the king was a monster. We have to save them all.

My thoughts are interrupted by the sound of Baako's teeth chattering with fear. I tighten my grip on his arm.

We arrive at the elevator and Miss Brita rolls herself in. "John, you can go. I'll take care of this myself."

Baako and I take our place in the elevator. John stands outside the elevator door and keeps it from closing. "Are you sure?"

She nods, he removes his hand, and the door closes.

"Well?" Miss Brita glares at me.

Ignoring the indignant tone in her voice, I release Baako, lean down, and hug her shoulders. "Oh my goodness, it's so good to see you."

Her facial features soften and she reaches an arm up to acknowledge my embrace. "I've missed you too." With her other arm she reaches for Baako. "And you, my dear."

Baako clutches her arm, his muscles relax, and he draws in a deep breath. His trembling subsides.

Miss Brita releases her grip. "What are you two doing here? Everyone is looking for you." She glances at Baako. "Well not you. They all think you're dead. I thought you were dead. Didn't you get thrown into the ocean?"

"Long story." Baako tips his head and doesn't offer an explanation.

Miss Brita turns her attention to me. "Why are you here?"

Without taking a breath, I explain about how Gretel was kidnapped and how we think she is on board the ship. I also share with Miss Brita how the resistance lied about the virus and that it's not out again, but that we do have a cure.

"Miss Brita, we have a vial of the cure, you should take it." Baako pulls a vial from his backpack. "We don't want you to get the virus." He holds the small tube out to her.

She carefully reaches out for the miracle vial. "I didn't really believe that you had found the cure. I heard rumors. But with the ambassador dying. I thought the ability to protect ourselves from the disease went with him." She gazes for a moment at the ceiling. "He was a great man. I miss him so much."

I couldn't tell her that my father, the ambassador, was still alive. That knowledge could get her killed.

She cradles the vial in her hand. "So this is all we needed to stop that horrible disease from ravaging the world."

"You thought of everything, Baako. I had a bunch of those vials sitting in my room and I didn't think once about bringing them." I smile at him.

"I know. I saw them in your room when we packed." Baako shuffles his feet. "I thought, why not? We might need them."

I slap him lightly on the arm. "You got them all?"

Baako nods, with a slight grin.

I smile. "Good thinking."

Miss Brita rocks the vial gently in her hands. "I'm not sure I can accept this. How could I ever repay you?"

I interrupt, "That is what the resistance is all about. It's free. Please take it and then that is one less worry for you."

"Thanks." She gulps it down in one swallow. "Better not leave it out or throw it in the trash. Might cause someone to ask questions." She hides the empty vial in her pocket. "Now tell me what you are doing here."

I'm not able to answer as the elevator reaches its destination and the door opens.

"Come with me." Miss Brita rolls her wheelchair out. "There's a free room at this end of the hall." She wheels herself down to the end of the corridor. "This one."

Baako opens the door. "This takes me back. I remember this room." He playfully knocks into my shoulder. "Some good memories, not all bad."

This is one of the staterooms we stayed in before while we were in service to the queen and the princess as "Sponsored Companions." I take a second to glance around before I flop on the mattress. "We are here to find my sister Gretel." I pat the bed to clue Baako to sit beside me.

Miss Brita locks her wheels in place. "I haven't seen Gretel. Are you sure that she is here?"

"Is the emperor here?" I cock my head.

"Of course." Miss Brita lets out an exasperated breath. "He doesn't let the royals out of his sight. I think he is fearful that it's only their presence that ensures his reign." She shakes her head. "He's probably right."

"Tell us what has been going on." I stare at her. "What happened to the king?"

Miss Brita tightens up for a minute and white knuckles the arms of her chair.

"I don't want to upset you. If you don't want to tell me, it's fine. I'm just worried." I pause for a minute before continuing. "There is no love lost between me and the king. I was surprised when I heard that he was dead."

"Emperor Richard the Great swooped in soon after you left, Paisley." Miss Brita folds her hands in front of her lap. "Right after we heard that the ambassador had been killed."

She pauses for a minute before continuing. "He managed to marry the queen before she gave birth. I don't blame the queen. She was in a weakened state and then the emperor took her father from her."

I grab her folded hands. "Did he actually kill the king?"

She clears her throat. "The only thing I know is one minute the king is vibrant and the next he is sick and the next he is dead." She leans over and whispers, "I think he might have been poisoned."

"That would make sense. Not a quick death or a messy murder. The emperor is smart," I whisper. "He probably used a slow poison."

That would follow the timeline Miss Brita had just explained. If the emperor had indeed poisoned the king, then it would have taken awhile for him to get sick and finally succumb to the deadly drug.

I squeeze her hands for a moment. "I'm sorry for your loss. I know you've been in service with the king and queen for a very long time." I pause another minute. "Go on, Miss Brita, tell us the rest. What is going on now?"

She shakes her head. "I'm worried about the queen and the children. The emperor doesn't need them anymore to gain the power. He never goes and visits them. He ignores them completely. I am in charge of their food intake. We have one cook who brings them their meals and she is the only one who I will allow to give them food." She pauses and looks up as if she is trying to conjure up a memory. "Tury, that's the cook's name."

"Tury, she's one of us." Baako lights up and shifts his whole attention to Miss Brita. "We need to find her. She may be able to tell us if Gretel is here."

Miss Brita's lips purse. "I can do that, but why is Gretel so important?"

Baako starts. "She's the one who makes..."

"She's important because she's my sister." I interrupt. I glare at Baako. No reason to load Miss Brita down with information that could be used against her at some point.

"I didn't realize that. I'll keep a look out for them, but for now if you want to see Tury she will be delivering the food at 0900 to the playground location on the fifteenth floor." Miss Brita rubs her forehead.

"You rest. We can find her. I can see you're tired. You've done more than enough." I squeeze her hand. "Thanks, Miss Brita. We will take it from here."

She clasps my hand and Baako's. "What will you do now?"

I let go of her hand. "It's best that you don't know. If we're caught, we will protect you until our last breath. I promise you that."

Her face contorts. "Goodness, I hope it doesn't come to that."

Baako nods. "Me too."

Miss Brita looks over her shoulder as she wheels herself out. "If I don't see you again...." She pauses. "Good luck and be careful." She pulls the empty vial from her pocket. "Thanks for this. Thanks for the cure. You've probably saved my life." She disappears down the corridor.

Baako and I sit quietly. He rubs his eyes. "We don't have anything to do until 0900. I don't know about you, but I'm tired. We might want to sleep at least an hour. It could be a very long day. Don't know when we'll get to sleep again. Because we might have to travel all night tonight too."

He's right. Fortunately, the bedroom cabin that Miss Brita put us in has a security lock. No one should be coming but if they do, there is another door to the outside hall that we can access by the connecting door. I set the alarm clock in the room for 0830 and we both curl up to sleep.

At 0845, we peek out the door into the corridor. All clear. We are fresh from our short nap and ready to get Gretel and escape before the morning crew awakes. We decide to take the stairs. It is easy to duck and hide while on stairs, but impossible on the elevator.

Trudging down the five flights, we are quiet and my adrenaline is pumping. I notice the elegant carpet on the stairs is more worn as the steps descend. The paintings that decorate the landings also deteriorate in value. The first flights, so embellished and rich looking with gold fluted frames are replaced with decorations, less ornate, until finally the paintings disappear completely. At the fifteenth floor, peeling wallpaper and stained carpet become the norm. I push a piece of wallpaper back in place.

I'm elated when we finally reach our destination. "Here it is. The playroom must be at the end of the corridor."

"Baako." A voice from behind us whispers.

Baako turns and almost knocks the tray out of the woman's hand. She steadies it before it falls. He hugs her, draping his arms over her back. "Tury. We're looking for you."

"Me?" She scrunches her face. "I'm happy here, I don't need to be saved."

"Did you give the children the cure?" Baako pulls out a cure vial and offers it to her. "Did you take it yourself?"

She shakes her head. "There were only two vials left. The "Sponsored Companions" took the rest. I think they were told to take the cure."

She is right. I remember that being the instruction. Of course, Tury would have been unselfish and made sure that everyone else got it before her. "When did the prince and princess get the cure?"

"I gave it to them two days ago." Tury takes the tube from his hand. "Is this extra? Did you come all this way to give me the cure?" Her eyes brim with tears.

Baako nods. "Good about the children because it takes two days for you to have an immunity from the virus." The food tray wobbles and Baako steadies it. "One of the reasons we came was to deliver you the cure. Take it now." He holds the tray while she throws her head backwards and gulps the medicine.

"I can't stay." She steadies the tray. "I have to feed the children. They will be looking for me soon if I don't deliver. I can't risk being late."

"Of course." I say, "Have you seen my sister Gretel?"

Tury leans in and whispers, "I'm not supposed to know she's here. But I accidentally heard talking about opening the ambassador's research laboratory. I saw a young woman with a bag over her head. From what I know about your sister that has to be her. She's a prisoner in the lab. The emperor is personally overseeing her captivity. That is not a good thing. If you want to save her you better hurry." She turns to Baako. "I'm so glad that you are well. Stay well. I have to go. Good luck."

"Thanks for taking care of the children." I say quickly.

She smiles. "Thanks for the cure." She disappears down the hall.

I turn to Baako. "Come on."

We travel the stairs two at a time until we see the big double doors marked "LAB." I put an index finger to my lips. We don't say a word. I lean up to peek through the glass at the top of the doors while Baako keeps a lookout. I don't see her, but I remember the room from the time the Mercs kept me and Colt imprisoned on that floor.

Suddenly I hear footsteps from inside the room near the door. Baako and I slide down the corridor and sink into an alcove.

The door flings open and two men bolt out. "I don't understand why we need all of this security for one little girl. She's so scared she's not going to try anything. It's crazy. Besides what's with all of the hazardous suits? You would think she had the virus."

"I'm just glad to get out of that binding contraption. I hate it." The other man says, "I don't care. I just do what I am told. Especially when they tell me it's important to wear that stuff. I'm going to listen. Where's our relief?"

Two other men enter from the stairs and meet them at the doorway entrance. On man says, "We're here. Any problems."

I whisper to Baako, "Must be their replacements."

One of the first men shakes his head. "Not a peep. If we didn't have to wear the biohazard suits, this job would be a piece of cake."

"Biohazard?" Baako whispers.

"We've been inoculated against the virus so we should be fine." I say softly.

It's not long before the original two disappear up the stairs. When the other two enter, the door swings back and forth. It's our chance– maybe our only chance to enter. We make a run for it.

We carefully slide through the doorway and sit quietly in a corner for a few seconds to see if we've been noticed. Nothing. We're home free.

All we have to do is find Gretel, knock out the guard, and make our way back safely to Aunt Sandra's compound. It's still a lot to accomplish. Never easy.

Scuffling sounds come from inside the room. I look at Baako. "Do you hear that?"

"Sounds like a fist fight," he whispers, "Don't move. Maybe we will be lucky and they'll knock each other out. Goodness knows we need some luck."

I twirl the four-leaf clover in my hand. Instinct to touch it any time luck is mentioned. I whisper, "What about Gretel?"

Baako pats his backpack. "We might be able to trade the cure for her release."

"Good thinking. It's worth a try." I take in a deep breath and we quietly come out from our hiding place to confront the Merc security.

We're right, there was a fight. Two Mercs are slumped over on the floor, unmoving. They are dressed in full body bio-suits. It's confusing. Two other men are standing over them, fists drawn. They wear regular security clothing. No bio-suits. Strange. The only good news is that we will only have to take out two of them. I look at Baako. "Ready?"

We run full force at the two Mercs. Baako locks his arms around one.

Abruptly, I stop. I see a familiar face.

Riley.

Chapter 13

"**P**aisley?" Riley throws his arms around me and squeezes.

I tip backwards before hugging him back. "What…"

"We haven't got time for this." Colt shoves Baako off of him and slaps my shoulder. "You shouldn't be here. We told you that we had it covered. We have to find Gretel." He points to a locked room in the back of the lab. "That has to be where she is." He glances at me quickly. "No time to talk. We'll talk later. Let's find her and get out of here."

"Agreed." I nod, release Riley, and motion toward the lab entrance door. "Baako, keep a lookout."

Riley, Colt, and I quietly sneak toward the locked room.

Colt whispers, "Gretel."

My sister's soft voice makes my heart skip a beat. "Colt?"

Colt's voice cracks. "She's here. Let's break the lock."

Baako steps forward. "Riley, go watch the door."

"What are you doing here?" I grab Baako's arm. "You're supposed to be the lookout."

"I can get in that door. I can break in."

"Let him try." Riley bolts to stand guard.

Baako places his backpack on the floor and pulls out a piece of wire. He puts the end of the wire in the lock and jiggles it. The pin tumblers lock in place and the knob turns.

Colt throws the door open and rushes in to Gretel. She's on the floor, a canvas bag covering her head as she struggles to right herself.

Colt wastes no time reaching his wife, cradling her as he pulls off the bag. "Gretel, I was so worried." He unties her hands and her feet and lifts her in his arms.

Tears run down her cheeks. "I knew you would find me."

I hug them both quickly. "Save this for later. We have to get out of here before we're caught."

"We can't go." Gretel digs her heels in the floor. "*I can't go.*"

Colt presses her head into his shoulder. "You're confused. You'll feel better when we get you back to Aunt Sandra's compound. It's not safe here. We have to go. I just don't know what would have happened…" His voice trails.

"The children." Gretel pushes her husband away. "We have to save the children."

"What children?" I turn Gretel to face me.

Gretel rubs her wrists. "The children, the prince and princess. They gave them the virus."

I cock my head. "What do you mean they gave them the virus?"

Colt pushes me forward toward the door as he guides Gretel through the room with Baako following behind.

Gretel whispers quickly, "What did you think the bio suits were for? They injected me with the virus to test the cure and make sure we weren't lying. Then they injected the queen and the two children. The emperor plans to use their deaths to incite the people against you and the rebels."

"Remind me." I inquire, "How long does it take the virus cure to take effect?"

Gretel trips, but grabs Colt's shoulder. "Twenty-four to forty-eight hours."

"The children will be fine." I put a hand on her arm. "Also, we gave Miss Brita the cure last night and Tury the cure this morning so they will be immune too."

Gretel claps her hands together. "Thank goodness the children will be saved. As long as Tury or Miss Brita weren't infected with the virus last night or this morning, they'll be fine. But the queen..." She wipes a tear from her cheek.

"Will the queen die?" I swallow the lump forming in my throat.

Gretel sniffs. "Yes and the emperor will know the children have been given the cure when they don't develop the virus. Tury and Miss Brita could be in danger too. We have to warn them. They have to come with us."

"We'll get them out." Colt holds his wife close. "Us. Not you." He gestures to Baako. "Take her to the horses."

Colt tugs Gretel's sleeve and motions to me. "Gretel, change clothes with Paisley. You and Baako should be able to slip out as "Sponsored Companions.""

I quickly pull off my skirt. The boys turn around. Really? Like I'm worried about modesty at a time like this.

"I'm not sure," Gretel protests. "I want to stay and help."

"My sweet wife, you have to make it back." Colt gently rubs her cheek. "You've been through enough. We can get them to safety without you. I can't risk losing you again. Besides, I can't think unless I know you are out of danger." He looks deeply into his wife's eyes. "I promise to get the children and the others to safety. I promise. Besides, we stand a better chance with less people. We'll be able to maneuver less conspicuously just a couple at a time. Trust me."

371

Gretel doesn't argue; I know that she knows Colt's right. Gretel and Baako change into the Norwegian "Sponsored Companion's" clothes.

Colt kisses his wife as she and Baako sneak out the door and up the stairs.

He turns to Riley and me. "Plan or any ideas?"

"What if you two, dress as security." I purse my lips. "And walk with me as if I'm a prisoner?"

"Might work." Riley nods. "Let's see if we can get to the fifteenth floor before Tury goes back to the kitchen."

"Wait a minute. I've got a better idea." Colt disappears and returns in a few minutes with a biohazard suit. "I found this one hanging beside the others. "

"I get what you're thinking." Riley snatches the suit and shoves it at me. "You dress in this one. Colt and I will take the other guards' suits. This ought to scare anyone we run into."

"A better plan," I say, "While I change, put one of the guards in Gretel's place." I pull off Gretel's skirt and sweater. "Here!" I throw the clothes at Riley. "Put these on the knocked out guard and cover his head with the sack. Rip them and place them over him. Just make sure that he is knocked out and gagged. Hopefully, no one will think she is gone. Might buy us some time."

Riley grabs the clothing mid-air. "Devious." He smiles. "We'll hide the other guard in a closet or something."

"Make sure the guards are securely tied up and gagged. We can't have them telling anyone about us." Colt puts on the guard's suit. "Let's hurry. Somebody might come in and we could be discovered any minute."

"Definitely." I help Riley pull one guard into a closet to hide and place the other guard in Gretel's place.

The three of us run down the stairs, Colt in front, me center, and Riley bringing up the rear. Two flights down, we see a man. He gasps as we get near. "Don't touch me!" He shouts and slams into the wall trying to avoid us.

"Wow." I laugh as we fly down the stairs. "This might work."

The outside door of the fifteenth floor is guarded by two men in biohazard suits. They must be worried about the contagion. Might should have thought of that before they purposefully started infecting people.

One of the men asks Colt, "Are you here to relieve us?"

Colt grunts, "Yes."

Great! Our plan is working. The men are excited to leave. Standing guard over a potentially contagious person is not a desired job. They waste no time disappearing up the stairs.

"I'll stay here." Riley peers at me through the plastic covering in his hood. "No offense, but you can't stay out here. We can't chance them getting a good look at you."

I pull at the front of my suit. "True."

Colt and I make our way back to the children's room. Tury is holding the little prince and soothing his soft cries while Miss Brita tries to calm down the princess who is sitting in her chair. Their eyes fill with fear when they see us.

Colt pulls off his hood and the children calm down. He says, "We need to get you out of here. The emperor gave the children the virus."

"What kind of a monster is he? How could he do that?" Miss Brita's tear streaked face looks up at Colt. "He said they had tested positive for the virus this morning. When he told me that they had contracted the virus from the resistance, I knew he was lying."

I remove my hood. "The emperor had them checked this morning?"

Miss Brita sobs holding the princess. "Yes, this morning."

"How?"

Miss Brita wipes a tear from her cheek. "A doctor gave them a vitamin shot this morning and then said they had the virus."

"That had to be the virus. Gretel said they were injected this morning. That's what all of the bio suits are for." Looking over at Colt, I say, "The emperor gave them the virus this morning."

A look of horror covers Miss Brita's face. "The vitamin injection was the virus?"

"Yes, but don't worry. I spoke with Gretel. The prince and princess have the immunity because they were given the cure in time. Thank goodness they're immune. You and Tury have been given the antidote so you will be immune in a couple of days."

Miss Brita's face is ashen. "A couple of days?"

"He didn't inject you, did he?" I take the princess from her as Miss Brita's arms go limp.

"This morning." Miss Brita takes in a deep breath. "I had no idea it was the virus. I thought it was a vitamin shot. The emperor's physician said it would help the children fight off diseases. I watched him inject the queen and the children. I thought it was safe. I was happy when he offered to inject me too."

Her eyes brim with tears. "I didn't realize it was actually the virus. I overheard the emperor and the doctor talking. I should have known." She strokes her fingers through the princess' hair. "I'm glad the children will live."

I look to Colt as my eyelids flutter to hold back tears. Too late. I swipe my cheek. "She could still survive."

"No way to defeat the virus once it is in your system." Colt's face loses its color. "The only way is to be immune."

Miss Brita leans down to the chair and kisses the princess's head. "She's fallen asleep. Please save them both. Tury has not been injected with the virus. She can help you get out. She knows the way."

Miss Brita kisses the curls of the prince as he cuddles in Tury's arms. "Tury, take them through the sixteenth floor. Go the back way. When you get there, walk down the gangplank used to bring supplies on." She turns to gaze at us. "Take off your bio suits and smuggle the children off in potato sacks. I'll distract them as long as I can."

"No!" I throw my arms around Miss Brita. "There must be another way."

"There isn't and you know it. Even if I wasn't doomed to die, I would slow you down because of this wheelchair." Miss Brita grips the wheels and smiles. "Paisley, I am proud to have known you. Your mission now is to save the children. The emperor will kill them if he finds out they survived the virus. There is nothing you can do for me. Go! It's my time to die. I know it and you know it."

Colt catches me as I sway, almost falling. She's right, but it's so hard to accept.

Tury stands up holding the prince. "Miss Brita, I promise to protect these children with my life. When they are old enough to understand, I will tell the children of your bravery and sacrifice. I will make sure they know the part you played in their escape."

Colt picks the princess from her chair as she starts to wake up.

I pull her from Colt. "Give her to me." I sit the princess back down on the chair. "Do you want to play a game with Paisley and Colt?"

The princess rubs the sleep out of her eyes and nods. "I missed you."

"We are going to play potato sack. Do you think that you can sit in a potato sack and not make a sound?"

"A game. Yea!" She squeals with delight.

"It's a race," I continue. "Guess who'll be carrying you?"

She looks around and I point to Colt. She squeals again.

Colt pats Miss Brita on the knee. "We have to go."

I hug Miss Brita one last time. Don't cry. Stick to the plan. We take off the top covering of the bio suit. I rip the pants to make them look more like work clothes. Colt tosses me his undershirt. Hope we look like we belong.

Tury carries the little prince and Colt, the princess. We meet Riley at the door and tell him about the plan and Miss Brita. He clenches his teeth as he pulls off his suit. He keeps a belt. We toss the rest of the discarded bio hazard garb into the fifteenth floor corridor maintenance closet.

Miss Brita rolls to the door. "When you leave, I'll bolt it behind you."

Miss Brita hugs Riley and he hands her the belt. "Wrap the belt from the bio suit around the handle. It will make it harder for them to open."

She clutches the belt.

"Sorry, Miss Brita." Riley's eyes fill.

"Don't worry I've seen this virus at work before. It won't be long. Maybe a day then I'll be free of this world." Miss Brita rolls her wheelchair back into the room and locks it in place.

My heart breaks. Tury leads as we travel down the stairs hopefully to find our freedom.

We enter the sixteenth floor and are surprised that there is no one there. Colt grabs up two potato sacks. "The children."

Tury carefully slides the prince into the bag while still carrying him like a baby. Colt grabs the princess and she gleefully lets him put her in the sack. She squeals with delight when he throws her over his shoulder. I spy a rag and tie it around my head similar to Tury's headdress. Not much of a disguise, but better than nothing.

No one stops us as we exit the gangplank; it seems that all of the guards have been dispatched elsewhere. Maybe the guards aren't expecting supplies and assume no one needs to guard the exit. I don't have the energy to figure out why it is not guarded. My heart is happy and sad all at the same time. Happy to be saving my half-brother and sister and sad that we couldn't save Miss Brita.

My mind wanders quickly to the image of the last time I will see or speak to Miss Brita. I glance one last time at the ship. Unfortunately, this escape is not without cost.

Chapter 14

We make our way quickly down the streets of Hamburg and back through the forest to where the horses are hidden.

Gretel and Baako are huddled together under one blanket beside the horses shielded by a low-branched tree. Our movements cause them both to bolt up, throwing off the blanket.

Baako stands, fists drawn at first, before Gretel runs to Colt. She thrusts her legs around his waist and throws her arms around his neck. "I was so worried."

"You were supposed to go back to the compound." Colt peels his wife off of him and kisses her.

Baako shakes his head. "Have you ever tried to make Gretel do something she didn't want to do?"

"I know what you mean." Colt pats Baako's shoulder. "But we need to hurry."

Tury and the prince ride on one horse and Gretel and the princess ride on Hershey.

Along the way, the mood is somber after we share the news about Miss Brita's fate. We travel only at night. It is slow with the children and only two horses. Thank goodness Baako brought enough food.

All that can be heard is the gentle clapping of the hoofs on the path. When we arrive at Dead Man's ravine, I relax. We're close to Aunt Sandra's place.

"Halt, who goes there?" The voice of the sentry guarding Aunt Sandra's property is the best sound that I have ever heard. We've finally made it. It takes a couple of messages before Aunt Sandra gives the okay for us to enter.

When we exit at the end of the maze, I am surprised that my father, the ambassador, is there to meet us. He picks up the princess first and hugs her, tears streaming down his face. "I have missed you, little girl."

Princess Kamea giggles, "Daddy, mommy was wrong. You did come back!" That makes him cry more.

The ambassador holds up the little prince who he has never seen and studies him. "I'm glad to finally meet you, son."

He cuddles his new son and hugs each of us, me, Riley, Colt, and Baako. "I can't thank you enough. You have brought my life back to me."

Word of the rescue spreads through Aunt Sandra's compound. There is a huge banquet thrown midday with plenty of food and drinks. The mood is festive. Lots of laughs and storytelling. The prince and princess smile and giggle along with everyone else.

I sit by Riley. My cheeks flush being this close to him. I haven't had a chance to talk to him alone. I want to tell him what it means to me that he is back at the compound and safe. I can't seem to stay away from him. Maybe he feels the same way. Maybe he knows how I feel. I don't want to let him go. We don't have to say anything. I just need to be near him.

When he was gone a part of me—the part I love the most was missing. But now—now that we're here together, I am whole again. The food tastes sweeter, the sky seems bluer, and the air smells fresher. Hope is alive in me again.

As the festival winds down, Thomas tells me that Aunt Sandra is searching for Colt and me. Colt hasn't left Gretel's side. Guess they'll be on a perpetual honeymoon all their life. I hope so.

Riley is standing by me when Aunt Sandra approaches. "It's imperative that we keep this positive momentum going. We want you and Colt to address the troops tonight. Tell them what happened. Don't hold anything back. They need some good news. There have been attacks all over and some of the resistance groups have suffered a large number of casualties. We are going to lose the war if we can't win some of the battles. We need you. Will you go on the air for the good of all?"

I glance at Riley. I can't explain it, but I want his approval on my choices. He gives a quick nod and I say to Aunt Sandra, "Of course. I think I can give a very uplifting message tonight."

Colt must have thought the same way since he and Gretel join us as we walk to the radio building.

Inside, Colt and I take our place in front of the microphone. Riley and Gretel sit behind us.

Aunt Sandra pushes the microphone's "on" button and the light flashes on and off. Aunt Sandra says, "Troops of the resistance. I give you Paisley and Colt with their uplifting message on what's going with the resistance front." She looks at Colt.

Colt begins. "We are happy to report that our manufacture of the cure is being amped up and we should be able to deliver as many doses of the cure as the resistance needs in the next two weeks. After that, we will be passing the cure out to all of the people. We will eradicate the virus for good."

He turns the microphone toward me. I take in a deep breath. "There have been more sacrifices by good people. All I can tell you is to hold tight. The cure is on the way. Don't be bullied by the emperor or by his mercenary army. If we stand together, we will win this war."

Colt and I smile at each other and say together, "Power to the resistance."

The lights flash and the set goes dark. Everyone hugs. We are almost at the door to retire to our beds for a good night's sleep when we hear the radio charge back up.

Squawk!

"People of the World."

The voice is that of the emperor. How is he broadcasting over our waves?

I gasp. "Can we make it stop?"

Colt shakes his head. "I don't know how. I don't know how he is transmitting over these airways." His eyes glare with hatred.

I feel my blood boil. What could this maniac, this killer of children, say? It can't be anything good. I take in a big breath as I ready myself for the worst.

"People of the world. Paisley and Colt are nothing but liars and outlaws. They have stolen and lied to you. They have single handedly brought back the virus."

I gasp. Colt squeezes my hand.

"They have used the virus to kill those who oppose them. I have been fortunate enough to escape this, but my wife has not. The queen is on her deathbed, her body ravaged by this deadly virus. My doctors have said she does not have more than a day to live."

I want to make the transmission stop, but I can't. I have to endure the emperor's voice pouring out of the radio speakers. It's difficult to hear about the queen.

The emperor continues his broadcast. "My beautiful and sweet wife is dying because these criminals wanted her dead. I ask you, my admiring public, don't you want someone who will control evil like Paisley and Colt? Do you want them using the virus as a weapon to wipe out all who oppose them?"

"Help me deliver these outlaws, Paisley and Colt, to justice. I want them dead or alive. If you bring them to me, you will live in a palace forever. You will never want for anything. You and your family will have all of the servants you could ever want. You will be treated like kings and queens. You will save your people."

"Bring me Paisley and or Colt and all of these things will be yours."

The radio goes silent.

We all sit for a few moments before Riley breaks the silence. "I don't understand, they didn't even mention me."

The room breaks out in nervous laughter.

It begins.

Chapter 15

When we walk out of the radio station room, most of the inhabitants of the compound are milling about discussing the emperor's words. It's obvious that news of the announcement and its contents has spread. Many people pat Colt and me on the back in a show of support. I can't detect one nonbeliever in the crowd. Wish the rest of the world could know what this group understands. The real truth.

Aunt Sandra shakes my hand. "I have to go now. We will have to double or triple the security. Unfortunately, that announcement might make some good people go bad. He virtually put a target on both of your backs."

Riley shoves in beside me. "You don't have to worry about Paisley. I won't let anything happen to her. "

I am terrified about the possibly of becoming a target and excited about Riley's chivalrous comments all at the same time. Why can't my life be normal?

Aunt Sandra pats Riley's hand. "I know you will do whatever it takes to protect Paisley." She turns to Colt and me. "The resistance and all of its resources will protect you both. This is your haven. We will not let anyone get in here. No one will be able to come near you." Aunt Sandra puts an arm around both mine and Colt's shoulders. "I know that you are sorry that the queen is dying. But there is nothing that you could have done about it."

"I'm not worried about me and Colt." I pull away from Aunt Sandra's hug. "Why did he have some of the virus left anyway?" I cross my arms. "If they didn't have the virus, then they couldn't have injected anyone. It was an easy fix. Why didn't someone make sure all of the virus was destroyed?"

"My fault." My father makes his way up to me, Colt, and Aunt Sandra. "I heard the hacked broadcast. I'm the reason that there was some live virus. I gave him the murder weapon to kill my wife. It seems unreal."

I grab my father's arm. "What would possess you to keep something that dangerous?"

"It's the only way to make an antidote. I had to have some of the live virus. It still took many years of trial and error. I perfected it by using a machine I had invented twelve years ago. The only way that I could have enough science and equipment and money to develop the antidote was to give in to the king." My father covers his face with his hands. "What have I done?"

"You saved the world. Don't ever forget that." I hug him. "You can't blame yourself. I shouldn't have faulted you. You had a perfectly good reason to keep the live virus. I shouldn't have questioned you and your honor. We need you. We needed you to find the cure. If you had not found the cure, then we would still be fearful about the virus."

He shakes his head. "But the cost. Was it worth it?" He looks at both Colt and me. "And now there's a price on your heads and many who will stop at nothing to turn you in. The emperor is blaming you." He buries his head in his hands. "You didn't even know about the virus. How can he do that? I hate that people will believe him."

"You couldn't have known." Aunt Sandra releases Colt and walks over to my father. "You are grieving that the mother of two of your children, is going to die. You are guilt ridden that you made the antidote, but was not able to save your wife."

"I did give it to her while she was pregnant but it didn't work because she grew up with the root that was used as part of the formula that slowed the virus down before the cure was discovered. It changed her metabolism. I could have worked with her blood and developed a cure for just her. But I wasn't given the chance. I didn't give myself the chance because I chose to be selfish. I faked my death and left my wife and my children in the hands of a monster and that monster gave his power over to another more powerful monster and now..."

Aunt Sandra motions for Colt to bring my father a chair. "Sit, ambassador. Think of what you do have. You have brought us the cure. You have Oliver and the prince and princess. You saved many. By giving them the antidote, you saved your children's lives."

A tear runs down my father's cheek. It might be a long time before he can think clearly. Right now, he is riding on the guilt ship and he doesn't seem to be coming to shore anytime soon.

Until we are caught or the emperor gives up on his obsession of finding us, Colt and I might as well be prisoners on Aunt Sandra's safe haven. We can't risk being caught. If we're punished for the outbreak of the virus, the rebels could lose faith. It would endanger our hope of a democracy.

It is not long before the emperor announces, "The Queen is dead." There is a great funeral, with lots of pomp and circumstance. The queen's body is cremated. Fears about the virus possibly returning sweep once again throughout wealthy communities. These people are completely dependent on the emperor for their food and to provide the mercenaries who will fight their war. Because of their dependence, the emperor grows very powerful.

Chatter on the radio is monitored all of the time. People ask every once in a while what has happened to the royal children, Princess Kamea and Prince Ross. Rumors that they are dead circulate, but most of the questioners are answered with a quick change of subject or silence.

The emperor doesn't know what happened to the children. He does know that he gave them an injection of the virus. He likes to spread his favorite rumor that he has the prince and princess safely tucked away in a beautiful countryside villa with constant guards. Elaboration of this rumor include that the children play daily and are happier than they have ever been.

I laugh when I hear these stories because they are close to the truth. The children frolic daily in the meadows of Aunt Sandra's compound. They want for nothing. They have plenty of playmates and a father who adores them and is making up for lost time.

Gretel and the ambassador entrust Colt and Riley to build a replica of the machine in which the cure is synthesized. It's a complicated machine that clones DNA. The cloned DNA used for the cure is mine and the machine being replicated is the one the ambassador designed and built when he was in the Army stationed in Germany before the virus outbreak.

Over the next month, the resistance strengthens, not an easy feat with the emperor feeding the paranoia. It helps that the vials of cure are distributed worldwide. Oliver begins to reset worldwide communication. There are a few television stations up and running. Every one of the stations is owned by the emperor and the Mercs.

Since airwaves and bands cannot be controlled, Oliver breaks in and broadcasts on one of the stations for the resistance. He calls it "Rogue."

The television stations send out breaking news. Through these communications I find out my friend Ms. DeVane, the original owner of the doll shop that sold the "Sponsored Companions," has been reunited with her son. Oliver guides families back to each other and to the cure. Lieutenant Drake confiscates weapons to arm the resistance fighters all over the globe.

The emperor's propaganda about the reintroduction of the virus does scare many people. Some of our resistance is afraid. We hear rumors of pockets of rebels fleeing the resistance safe havens and seeking refuge with the emperor's side. The wrong side. The emperor and his goons. We do what we can to stop that bleed by reassuring the resistance that we will win the war.

Colt, Riley, and I train the children daily. Despite the conflicting messages from our side and the emperor's side, our numbers are growing. Every day Aunt Sandra's maze brings in new "strays." These strays are children or grown-ups. Usually Undesirables or Uncounteds, but now even a few disgruntled Mercs make their way into the fold. They take the cure and join in training. Lieutenant Drake along with Captain Via have a plan to make sure democracy wins.

Television stations report a date has been set for a meeting and vote by the Consortium of the World, a federation uniting all of the countries of the world. The vote will decide on how our world should be governed. We begin a strong push for democracy on our station messages.

Oliver is on the verge of starting the World Wide Web again. The emperor has been working on this project for a while with no success.

The meeting of the Consortium of the World is to be held in Hamburg because Hamburg is an international port. Many of the countries of the world are able to send dignitaries by ship. All countries must have representation.

The emperor is unaware that my father, the ambassador and author of the first articles proposed by the Consortium of the World and the new father of democracy, is still alive.

Aunt Sandra, Colt, Oliver, Lieutenant Drake, Captain Via, and I plan to attend the meeting. If things start going awry, the ambassador will step in.

I'm hopeful.

If all goes as planned and democracy wins out, then I'll be back on my Ferris wheel farm and harvesting my own food very soon.

A few nights later, Colt and I are waiting for the radio announcement. I check the door. "Where's Aunt Sandra? She's never late to introduce us."

Colt and I patiently wait. "So how's married life, Colt?" I tease, knocking into his shoulder.

"Why? Are you thinking about getting married yourself?"

My cheeks burn and my stomach churns. I squirm in my chair. "What do you mean? I'm not really the marrying kind. I like my independence." I kick his foot. "Besides, who would I marry?"

"Like you don't know." Colt burst out laughing. "It's so obvious every time you and Riley are together. You know you like him."

A snort escapes my nose. How dignified is that? "I don't know what you're talking about? You know that Riley and I are just friends."

Colt laughs again. "Yeah right, just friends." He leans back in his chair. "So I guess it wouldn't bother you if I told you I saw him talking to that pretty girl Gina."

My face turns hot. My stomach flips a couple of times. "Of course it wouldn't bother me." I don't like Gina. I don't think she's that pretty. How can Colt find her attractive?

The door opens and in walks Gretel. Thank goodness. Gretel is here to stop this ridiculous conversation. Colt doesn't know me at all.

Something's wrong. Gretel's face contorts like she is in pain. I've only seen her like this one other time in my life. It's the same look she made when she saw our mother murdered on live television. I shoot up out of my chair. Something bad has happened. "Gretel, what's wrong?"

"Aunt Sandra just died." Gretel sobs. "Amanda discovered her body." She makes her way to Colt. "Aunt Sandra never woke up from a nap and died peacefully in her sleep."

Gretel cries in Colt's arms as I sit stunned. Aunt Sandra. It can't be.

What will happen to us now?

Chapter 16

The next few days are scattered and unorganized. No one takes charge. Some of the chores get done, while others are neglected. I know that everything will eventually fall apart unless someone takes control. It takes a while for the news to sink in.

Specifics about Aunt Sandra's cause of death are brought to light. Aunt Sandra had been taking medicine to control her diabetes for quite a while. She didn't share her condition with anyone. Why didn't she tell us? We could have been more prepared.

One thing that Aunt Sandra worked out down to the smallest detail is her funeral. Her lists of final wishes keeps everyone busy during a time of great sorrow. I'm happy to have the distraction. The entire compound shuts down for her funeral. Colt and I are to give her eulogy.

In her instructions, Aunt Sandra was very specific that everyone is to gather in the courtyard of the compound. It is a beautiful spot and big enough for all to sit comfortably on the ground or in chairs. The growing flowers and trees will decorate her funeral as they did her life. A fitting setting for her send off. After the funeral, there is to be a great party.

Aunt Sandra left detailed instructions about the food and decorations. A celebration of her life is what she called it. I liked that. Since she lived a large life, it should be celebrated.

That night all of the compound inhabitants pay tribute to Aunt Sandra's life. Because everyone has a part in the celebration, the compound has a purpose and path once again.

A full moon is high in the sky lighting up the night. The air is crisp; not too hot or too cold. It makes me think that Aunt Sandra herself is sitting in heaven directing nature to her specifications. For this one night, there will be no talk of war, democracy, or even viruses. Tonight, we will talk about a great woman. Our Aunt Sandra.

Colt begins the eulogy. "Aunt Sandra chose to live her life to protect others. She gave up her freedom for those quarantined to be free on her farm. Her generosity towards others is legendary. Aunt Sandra will go down in the history books as a friend to the downtrodden and needy." He chokes as he reads his notes.

It's my turn. I take a big breath, determined to get through this with strength. Aunt Sandra would have liked that. "When I first met Aunt Sandra, she could tell that I was telling the truth. She knew my heart. It was a gift and one we will miss terribly. Aunt Sandra fought hard for democracy."

My voice catches for a moment. "She never turned anyone down who needed help. She never recognized a disability; she only saw people's ability. We will miss Aunt Sandra, but we must honor her by carrying on her legacy and fighting for her hope of a new democracy."

I take in another deep breath, fighting the cracking of my voice. "I will fight to my death to make sure that Aunt Sandra's memory lives on. I loved Aunt Sandra."

Tears are shed as others share specific stories. She was such a significant and driving force in the new regime that it's hard to think of going on without her. The children of the compound will especially miss her.

Aunt Sandra was a sounding board for people haunted by problems along with those making hard decisions. But the greatest thing about Aunt Sandra was her ability to tell in a short conversation if a person was good or bad or if his or her intentions were honorable or not. She had become the mother I lost. She took me in when I needed her.

Colt was great at explaining her quirkiness. Her love of that buggy. The way she loved raw potatoes. How she was our best cheerleader on the broadcasts and how she never gave up on freedom.

When the funeral ends, it is time for the dinner. The masses are serene and quiet. I imagine that they are grateful knowing how wonderfully blessed we all were in having Aunt Sandra in our life. Aunt Sandra would be happy to know how much she meant to everyone and how significant her life had been.

Colt announces at the end of the service. "Eat drink and be merry. That was Aunt Sandra's last request for the celebration of her life. It's what she would have wanted."

"That was a nice funeral, Colt. Or I guess I should call it a celebration of life." I touch his arm. "I liked everything you said."

Colt hugs me as Gretel joins him. He and my sister still seem to be one person. I hope they never get over this honeymoon phase. How wonderful to be so much in love. Colt and Gretel join Tury and the little royals, Prince Ross and Princess Kamea.

I am so focused on watching them play a game of stick and ball that I am surprised by Riley when walks up behind me and asks, "What are you doing for the rest of tonight?"

"No plans." I shrug my shoulders. "Not much to do on a night like this. It's time to reflect and think about Aunt Sandra." Thought he would be with Gina tonight. I burn when I think of her. The thought of them together bothers me.

Riley points to the buffet table full of food. "How about we get a plate of food and share more stories about Aunt Sandra?"

The tables are heaped with all different kinds of food. Everyone brings a favorite dish. They raid the food storage to serve a one of a kind meal that will be remembered forever. The aroma of the different food scents is overwhelming in the courtyard. The food looks and smells great. I know that it will most certainly taste as good as it looks.

Colt and Gretel are all curled up with each other and my father is playing with the little royals. Yes, it might be nice to hang out with Riley tonight. It's been forever since we had a real conversation. "Sure. That sounds nice."

Someone has made chicken and dumplings, kielbasa, and a schnitzel. I choose food I don't normally eat.

We take our plates and water over to a nice grassy area. Riley looks at the sky. "Can you believe that moon?"

"Nice spot." I sit down. "I can't believe how full it is." I lean back. "Do you think that Aunt Sandra is smiling down upon us?"

"I'm positive she is." He takes a bite of bread. "Do you remember the first time we met?"

"You mean the first time you tried to turn me in to the Mercs and Hershey knocked you down?" I laugh thinking back to that day. I look at Riley. He has really grown since then. He's taller and more handsome.

Leaning close to me, he touches my neck.

"What are you doing?" I slap at his hand.

He shrinks back. "I just wanted to see if you were still wearing the four-leaf clover?"

"Oh." I pull out the four-leaf clover made from the bullet that was meant to kill Riley. I loved what he said about it. He made something good from something bad. "Yeah, of course I still wear it. You know it's my good luck charm."

"You're my good luck charm." He voice softens and his eyes twinkle in the moonlight.

Riley is the most handsome person I have ever seen. I giggle. "Right. I'm a good luck charm." I twirl the clover in my fingers. "I'm charmed. I've been kidnapped, almost hanged, almost dragged over a ravine, and jumped in a lifeboat..." I stop for a minute.

He leans and nudges my shoulder. "Well if you put it that way."

I wink at him. "I've been on death's bed quite a few times." I toss a grape in my mouth. "I guess none of those times took." I chuckle again.

We burst out laughing. He takes a grape off my plate and throws it at me. "What would the world be like without you in it?"

"Or you." I smile.

Our arms are close, almost touching. He grins. "Do you mean that?"

"Of course I do. I'd miss you if you weren't in my world."

"Good." He lies flat of his back. "I get scared thinking about war. We have to make split second decisions about what we are going to do and when we are going to do it. I don't want to die."

Stretching out on the grass alongside Riley, I prop up on my elbow sideways gazing down at him. "I don't want to die either. I should have died that very first day. If I had been home on the farm and not tried to go and save Colt from the trap then I would have been home when the men raided the farm. They would have discovered that I was there and that I was an Uncounted. What would have happened to me then?"

I suck in air. "Every day since then has been a gift. A beautiful gift where I get to meet people like you and Colt. And Gretel marries my best friend."

"You have a beautiful way of looking at the bright side of life. I love the way you think." He turns his head away for a minute, the back of his neck is beet red.

"I like the way you think too." I slap at his shoulder.

He grabs my wrist to stop me from slapping at him. "And how do I think?"

I rub the four-leaf clover in my fingers. "Take this four-leaf clover for instance. You were almost killed. So what do you do? You make a four-leaf clover. You're an optimist. I like that you can take something bad and make something good out of it."

Smiling, Riley rubs my arm. "How much do you like me?"

"How much do I like you?" Springing upright, I squirm a bit. "I like you just fine." I bump my shoulder into his. "You're one of my best friends."

He sits up for a moment and shoots a wry smile at me. "Best friends huh?" He crosses his arms. "Nothing more?"

"I like you more than other guys." I turn on my side again. "Is it the same as Gretel feels for Colt? I don't know. I don't have time to figure it out. We have the war. To be honest, I don't know how long you or I will survive. Does that answer your question?"

"Yeah it does. I guess I was hoping..." He stops and picks up a blade of grass and throws it.

"Hoping for what?" I stop his arm from leaning over to pick up another piece of grass. "Seriously, hoping for what?"

388

He shakes his head. "It's stupid after what you just said. I can't tell you now."

"Just tell me."

He takes in a deep breath and comes up on his side so we are facing each other resting our heads on our hands and our elbows on the ground. He says, "I always think today I might die and I don't want to die without ever having kissed a girl." His face turns the most interesting color of crimson. "If I'm going to kiss anybody, I want it to be you, Paisley."

Maybe it's the moment. Maybe it's that he seems so vulnerable. Maybe it's that he wants to kiss me and not Gina. I'm not sure what it is. But right in that moment, I want to kiss him too. He's right. We might die tomorrow.

I take the plunge. "I think my first kiss should be with you too." I close my eyes. I push my face and my lips to his face. He softly leans into my lips. His are moist. It's nice. Nicer than I thought it would be. A quick kiss. Our first kiss. It's sweet. More than sweet, it's magic.

He strokes my face. My stomach jumps and my head squeezes. It's like the feeling I get when I'm riding on my Ferris wheel only a hundred times better. Like I'm falling off the top of the Ferris wheel and I know I'll hit the bottom, but I'm not scared. Heat rises like an electric bolt shooting through the top of my head.

He brushes his hand through my hair. "Thanks. Now I won't die never being kissed."

"Me neither." I take his hand in mine. "But let's try not to die."

We talk about other adventures, about Aunt Sandra, Colt, and Gretel. We gab about everything but that kiss. It almost as if conversing about it would make the kiss disappear.

It's late. I notice most of the party goers have gone to bed.

Riley stands, grabs my hand, and pulls me up. "Guess it's time to go to bed."

"Yeah. I guess so." I turn to grab my plate.

He gets both of our plates, walks toward the garbage cans, scrapes them off, and walks back toward me.

I wave at him. "See you tomorrow."

"Wait a minute." He pulls me near and pauses for a minute, his face close to mine. He leans down and I feel his breath on my lips. His warmth makes me feel safe. He says, "Do you think it would be okay if we had two kisses before we die?'

My eyelids flutter slightly, signaling my permission. He presses his lips to mine and his warm touch is exhilarating, exciting, and scary all at the same time. What is he thinking as his lips caress mine? I am in a trance or something because when he finally releases his embrace, I am almost unable to stand. I don't know what has come over me. I stumble for a minute and he catches me.

"Are you all right?"

I catch my breath. "You?"

He puts his arm around my shoulder. "That was some kiss. Thanks. I can die a happy man now."

"No talk about dying. " I snuggle closer to him. "I say we think about living."

"You're right." He squeezes my shoulder. "You've definitely given me something to live for."

He walks me to my door with a big grin on his face. I peek out the door as he leaves. He is dancing and clicking his heels together. He looks like an idiot.

But as he disappears down the street, I know what he is feeling because I feel it too. My heart is singing out loud.

Chapter 17

It is hard to sleep. My room is glowing from the light of the shining moon. I toss and turn replaying the kiss in my mind. Will it be different between us now? Are we together now? It's hard to know.

I need to talk about this whole night, the kiss, the conversation, everything with Gretel. It's hard to wait until morning to go to the research lab. I am supposed to be training the children. Riley and Colt will wonder where I am. Maybe they'll think I am sleeping in. Good thing Gretel never sleeps late.

As I enter the lab, I'm surprised to see people working. Fires are lit and test tubes are bubbling on every counter in the place. Conversations between technicians make my entrance go unnoticed.

Finally, I spy Gretel holding a clipboard and marking off some kind of a checklist. Always perfectly coiffed–even when we were saving her from the emperor and she had to ride from the ship to the woods, she looked flawless. Must be her skin and hair type. Some people look wonderful all of the time.

She doesn't notice me right off, but my father does. He fiddles with the machine. "Good morning, Paisley," my father says cheerfully. "You look different today. Did you change your hair?"

I pull my hair over my eyes, trying to hide my reddening face, and mumble, "No."

Could my father see that I had been kissed last night? I dismiss the crazy thought and focus my attention to Gretel who is working at the counter.

"They're reading Aunt Sandra's last will and testament publically in the compound square." Gretel jiggles a test tube in her hand and the liquid inside swirls. "Today at noon."

A jolt of reality. I let go of my hair and stand erect. "Where did you hear that?"

My father chimes in. "They announced it at the party." He cuts his eyes over to me. "Where did you go? I was looking for you last night and I couldn't find you anywhere."

I shuffle my feet, spy a rolling office chair, and plop in it. The chair rolls across the floor and I slam into a cabinet. Bam! The chair lunges forward and propels me onto the floor.

A small price to pay to not answer that last question.

"Are you okay?" My father rushes to my side and pulls me up off the floor.

Gretel holds her hand to her mouth trying hard not to burst out laughing. No use. Boisterous chuckles slip through her fingers. I begin giggling, and then my father starts chortling. Gretel attempts to go back to work, but she starts snickering again. Then my father tries returning his attention to his work, but is unsuccessful, letting go of boisterous laughter that fills the room. Technicians whisper and point at us. I can guess the content of their conversations.

I tease. "Ambassador, aren't you supposed to be in charge?"

He snorts as he spits out: "I'm sorry. The image of you flying across the floor was funny." He leans over, his hands rest on his knees, and he coughs from laughing so hard.

The laughing is a nice release from all of the stress. Finally, we're able to regain our composure and my father returns to work on the machine and Gretel fiddles with the test tubes on the counter.

Sliding up next to my sister, I watch as she pours something on a slide and looks through a microscope. "What are you doing?"

"Looking for changes in the virus." She rolls the lens adjuster up and down and writes a notation on paper.

I cock my eyebrows. "Does the virus change?"

"Every virus I have studied has mutated. This particular one hasn't changed since it started which is odd because with its longevity, twelve years, it should have adapted. It's almost as if this is a virus that was manufactured. It hasn't naturally evolved in nature." Gretel pulls the slide out and shakes her head as she studies it.

"I'm not going to try to figure that out. You figure it out. You're the scientist." My fingers drum the counter.

"Don't worry. I will." My sister puts her hand on mine. "Did you want something, Paisley?"

"Why would you think that?" I clasp my hands in my lap. "I just wanted to visit."

"You're supposed to be training the children." She puts the slide down and stares at me. "I'm sensing you came here to talk about something."

My flinch lets her know she is right. I hate that about my sister. She knows me too well. "Yeah, I do need to talk."

Gretel scans the room and sees my father still focused on his machine. A few of the lab assistants are filing in. "Let's go for a walk." She pushes some papers next to the slide. "This can wait." She calls back to my father. "Be back in a minute." He grunts our way.

As we exit the lab door, the morning air is crisp. The hills are glistening with new fallen snow. It's always a little winter here at Aunt

Sandra's' place. I miss Aunt Sandra's smiling face. Not many people wandering around. Everyone has a place to be.

Gretel quickens her step. "It's a little colder than I had thought." She pulls the collar of her sweater around her neck. "We must have had a cold front move through last night."

"It was perfect last night." I cross my arms to hug my sweater. I put one arm around my sister's back and rub. "There, better?"

She scrunches in closer to me. "So tell me all about it. I take it this has to do with Riley."

How does she know? Was I that transparent? I mumble a question, "Why would you think that?"

"I saw you two go off together last night and I didn't see you again. That and Riley came by our bungalow this morning to talk to Colt. He dragged him out of bed and everything." She cocks her eyebrow. "What did you do to that boy last night?"

Leaning down and grabbing a bunch of wild flowers, I pluck the petals one at a time. Was Riley upset about last night?

"What did he say?" I toss a petal on the ground.

"I couldn't hear most of it as they went outside, but I heard Paisley this and Paisley that. I think that boy is seriously smitten with you." She places her hands on each of my shoulders. "So spill, what happened?"

"We kissed."

Gretel throws her arms around me. "About time."

I stiffen. "Is that all you have to say?"

"Anything else?" She squeezes me. "Details. Where did it happen?"

Pulling back, I look at her square in the face. "You're not really asking me for details. Are you?"

"Not if you don't want to share." She shrugs her shoulders. "What do you want me to say? Be careful? Wait until you're married? I'm your sister, not your mother. Life is too short. If you have found someone who you like and makes you happy, then I say kiss him some more." She makes a kissing sound smacking her lips. "Kiss him today, kiss him often. Enjoy life. The way things are going, we are not promised tomorrow. Might as well enjoy it while we can." My perfect sister, always knows exactly what to say.

The smile on my face is as big as the smile glowing in my soul. "I will and I might even give you some details at another time when I'm not so embarrassed." I lift my head for a moment and ask, "What time is the reading of Aunt Sandra's will?"

"Noon." My sister hugs me and we stroll back to the lab arm in arm. Usually our talks are of war, human trafficking, slavery, The Undesirables,

The Uncounteds, the royals, and the Mercs. Just for today, a new topic to talk about is nice.

At precisely noon, a member of Aunt Sandra's security detail steps into the middle of the square to read Aunt Sandra's last will and testament.

Children and adults line the area. The man uses a bullhorn because of the sheer numbers of people who have gathered. I haven't realized how many people live here now. I crane my neck trying to spot Riley. It will be hard to concentrate on the reading if he is here. Fortunately for me, Colt and I are led up front. We sit among Aunt Sandra's children. No Riley in sight. Better, at least I will listen.

The bullhorn screeches and people cover their ears. Then the officer reads:

"I, Samuel Atkins, was appointed by Sandra Becker, also known as Aunt Sandra and who will be listed as Aunt Sandra from this point forward, to read her last will and testament."

His head is down. He pauses for a moment, swallows hard, and takes a breath.

"Being of sound mind and body, I do hereby bequeath the following: each of my security detail a plot of land predetermined to call their own. My vast lands have been divided. These small plots together equal to five percent of my land. The deeds are registered in the back of this document."

Aunt Sandra didn't leave anything to chance. No wonder she was a great leader.

Mr. Atkins continues reading Aunt Sandra's' last wishes. "If you were on my security detail, then you get a place to call your own. Take care of your families and work the land. I appreciate your service and I hope this small token will somehow repay you for all of the kindness you showed me. I simply say thank you."

Whispers ripple throughout the crowd. Officers shake hands and hug their loved ones.

Mr. Atkins continues, "My one request is that you will consider staying on to protect the next person who runs this compound."

"Who is going to run the compound?" A man shouts from the back. Voices collide as separate speculations and discussions circulate the group.

A loud voice interrupts, "Aunt Sandra's children and grandchildren will inherit the land, that's for sure, but would they run the place also?"

Too many voices for any answers. Mr. Atkins yells for order. Few listen. This will could change everything. What if Aunt Sandra sees fit to divide the compound? Will we be able to still operate this place, the heart of the resistance, without her?

The bullhorn screeches loudly and quiet follows. Mr. Atkins continues, "To my children, grandchildren and one great grandchild, I leave sixty five percent of the rest of my holdings. The following property..."

I gaze off toward the drawbridge. Aunt Sandra's lands are vast and she is generous in her division and precise in where they are located. Still no mention of the thirty percent of her holdings where most of the compound's inhabitants live.

My brain is like cotton. Mr. Atkins's words drone in my head. "West, acres, my beloved..." I quit listening. Standing next to a large tree is Riley.

He first enters from the left side of the crowd. He stops occasionally for a random hand shake or pat on the back. He scans the crowd as he walks. Is he looking for me? It's a few more moments before he spots me. His face lights up. My heart jumps a beat.

Mr. Atkins's voice dissipates as Riley inches his way towards me.

The crowd erupts with loud cheers. The applause is deafening. The crowd hovers closer around me. I lose sight of Riley. Where did he go? I'm hoisted on someone's shoulders. Why are they picking me up?

At this height, I scan the crowd. I spot Riley and I lift my hand to wave to get his attention. He is staring at me and clapping. Another person from the crowd grabs my hand and shakes it.

Totally confused now, I take my focus off Riley and try to listen to Mr. Atkins's words. He is clapping too. The man who holds me on his shoulders takes me to the stage. He sets me down feet first. I stumble for a moment before I see Colt traveling over the crowd on another's shoulders. When he reaches the stage, he is placed beside Mr. Atkins. Gretel is pushed up beside us.

"Power to the resistance!" The crowd shouts. "Power to the resistance! Power to the resistance!"

Colt and I join hands, raising them together over our head in a sign of unity. He smiles and asks through his teeth like a ventriloquist, "Can you believe it?"

"What?" I shake my head at him. "I couldn't hear above all the shouts. What happened? What does the will say?"

Mr. Atkins holds his hands up and shouts above the crowd. "We need to read this last portion again and the rest of the will. Remember this will is Aunt Sandra's last wish."

The crowd quiets and Mr. Atkins continues. "I, Aunt Sandra, owner and ruler of the lands known as Becker Bavaria, do hereby bequeath the following which is the last thirty percent of my land holdings known as the Becker compound and the last portion of my monies: the castle and the compounds, barracks and surrounding lands and 30% of my fortune."

Mr. Atkins looks up from the document and makes eye contact with the crowd. "And rule of the Becker compound is now passed forward to the new leaders." Mr. Atkins takes in a breath. "They own the compound lands free and clear to house the Uncounteds and Undesirables and to grow their own families. The deeds and specifics are listed on the back of this document. Giving this serves as my commitment to the resistance cause and also to ensure the continuation of my legacy. The compound is given in equal portions to Paisley Mueller and Colt Granger."

Loud cheers erupt.

Mr. Atkins pumps his hands palms down to quiet the crowd. "Be patient. Just a bit more."

"Shhh." The crowd whispers.

"Paisley and Colt have been an inspiration to us all. I ask that you follow their lead as you have always followed mine. To my children and heirs, I have amassed a fortune and have seen fit to break off part of it to continue my legacy. I know this will free you to pursue your own happiness without the burden of continuing my legacy. I love you, all of my heirs."

"Paisley and Colt, I entrust our cause to you along with the future of the world. I have every belief that you two will see it to the end. You have no idea how peaceful my end will be, knowing that my work will be in such loving hands."

"Power to the Resistance. Carry on my family born to me and the family I have chosen and who has chosen me. I love you all."

Mr. Atkins folds the document in his hands.

Aunt Sandra's family joins Colt and me by joining their hands with ours. One of Aunt Sandra's daughters hugs my sister and me and whispers in our ears. "She called all of us in and told us what she had planned. We all agreed with her. It was a family decision to leave you and Colt with the running of the compound. None of us has the inclination, drive, or knowledge and it was so important to her. I know she is smiling down upon us today."

A tear runs down my cheek. I'm overwhelmed. I feel an arm around my waist and I am swooped up into a massive embrace. The smell is familiar and enticing. It's Riley. I whisper to him, my lips almost touching his ear. "I was looking for you."

He breathes into my ear. "Our time will come later. You are one of the leaders of the revolution." He pulls back and gazes into my eyes. "I would follow you anywhere."

Chapter 18

The next few minutes are a blur. It's hard not being able to talk to Riley alone, but I have a feeling that's the way it's going to be for a while.

After the announcement, Mr. Atkins points to a bearded man and says, "Follow him to the house. He will show you around." Colt and I accompany the bearded man to Aunt Sandra's house on the compound. It's located in the main castle.

The bearded man extends his hand to me. "I thought I should formally introduce myself. It was a little crazy this afternoon. I'm Mark. I've overseen Aunt Sandra's properties for years. You own a portion of those properties so I hope you will keep me on, at least through the transition."

I shake his hand. "Transition?"

When I release Mark's hand, Colt grabs it with both of his and gives it a vigorous shake which almost causes Mark to fall down. "Of course you'll stay on. Paisley and I need help. We train children and speak on the radio; we are clueless about all of this. This was a total surprise."

What is Colt saying? He is making us sound like we are total idiots. I know I am not an idiot. "We catch on fast, Mark, but of course we want you to stay on and we would love any help that you have to offer."

Mark opens a door to an outside one-room bungalow that sits adjacent to the castle. I peek in to the sparsely decorated room. A chair and a small bed and a counter are all that are housed in the small abode.

"Since you said you want me to stay on, these are my quarters and if it's okay with both of you, I will stay out here. I can be in the main house in a matter of seconds." Mark bends his head slightly first to me and then to Colt. "It will be an honor to serve the leaders of the revolution."

His room is lovely albeit sparse. It is very utilitarian. I wonder if the castle will be this way.

As Mark walks us toward the castle, I can't contain my excitement at being able to tour Aunt Sandra's house. Sitting down in my dwelling, I often wondered what was inside Aunt Sandra's living quarters. I had never been invited in this inner sanctum.

As I enter the castle, it is just as I expected. Several antiques fill the space. It is ornate, but in a medieval way. The wood mantel above the fireplace is large and imperfect, but fitting for the residence.

Boxes are scattered about with frames and pictures. I assume that the security and family are boxing up Aunt Sandra's personal effects. The walls are stone. Castles back in the day were built to withstand war. A good thing, since our largest battles are still to come.

Mark opens another door. It opens into a large bedroom. "I didn't know which room each of you would want. I guessed Paisley would take Aunt Sandra's old bedroom. We're in the process of packing up her things for her children. We're switching out her furniture to some in storage." He stops for a moment and looks at us. "Aunt Sandra left specific instructions about the items that would go to her children."

"Of course," I stammer. "Whatever she wanted." I freeze for a minute and glance toward Mark. "Wait, are we supposed to move into the castle?"

Mark cocks an eyebrow. "I thought you understood that at the reading of the will."

"Wait a minute." Colt holds up his hands. "I don't know about moving. I mean Paisley can move in here because it's just her, but I want to live with my wife."

"Of course." The corners of Mark's lips turn upward slightly. "No reason to get upset. Calm down."

"What about Gretel?" Colt frowns.

"I'll have a security officer pick up your wife now." Mark leaves for a moment.

After Mark exits, I stare at Colt. "I don't know how to react to all of this. Do you think we can do everything that Aunt Sandra did?"

"Absolutely not!" Colt shakes his head. "But we have to try."

"You're right." I take in a deep breath. "It's what she wanted and she was a wise woman." A tear runs down my cheek.

Mark returns. "Gretel will be here in a moment. I figure she might be the one to pick which area you will live in. There are many choices. Many of them better for a growing family."

Colt's cheeks redden. "Okay, I'll wait on her to decide the room or if we will move in here. I will do whatever she wants."

"The castle is much more convenient. She might want to convert one of the rooms into a personal workshop." Mark guides us deeper into Aunt Sandra's room. "Ultimately, it's your choice, but I think that Paisley should take this room. It has a balcony, the personal radio station..."

"A personal radio station?" I walk over to the table and look over the microphone and the board similar to the one in the radio station. "I didn't realize that Aunt Sandra could communicate on her own."

Mark picks up a microphone and sets it back down. "There are many things that you don't know. That's why I am here. I am going to walk you and Colt and of course Gretel through all of the secrets of the Becker Bavarian Castle."

A knock at the door alerts us to another man. "I have Miss Gretel."

"Mrs." Colt corrects.

The man stammer. "Of course, Mrs. Gretel."

Gretel walks into the room beside Colt. "Well, the missus is here. What's all of this about? They drag me out of my lab right in the middle of an experiment. My work is important too."

Colt holds his finger to his wife's lips. "They want us to live here. They say that you can have your own personal lab. You can conduct all of the experiments you want at all hours of the night without ever leaving home."

"Really? My own personal lab. I like the sound of that." Gretel looks around Aunt Sandra's room. "In here? I don't see any place I could set up a lab in here."

Mark interrupts her. "You arrived quicker than I thought you would. We were just establishing Paisley would be staying in here." Mark looks at me. "Right, Paisley?" I dip my head slightly and he continues, "There is security around the clock, the personal radio, your own bathroom, dressing area, and ..." he opens another door to a sitting room.

Inside is a large conference table with chairs all around. Bookshelves full of books line all three walls. File cabinets take up the back wall. There are no windows. There is a large map spread out on the table with troop's movements and marks indicating resistance group's locations.

I run my fingers across the map. "Is this a war room?"

Mark scans the area. "Aunt Sandra never named it. But war room seems appropriate. Her heirs will not be taking anything out of here. This is all of the information we have gathered about the resistance." He pulls a book off the shelf. "We have a list of all of the people we have identified as resistance fighters." He hands the book over to me.

I open to a page. "There's a lot in here." Written in the ledger complete with headings are names and locations, along with a paragraph or two about each individual's personal journey during the twelve years of quarantine and after. "How did you get all of this information?"

"It took years." Mark takes the book, rubs the cover with reverence, and replaces it back on the shelf. He points to the computer. "We have it all stored on there now."

"Where did you get that?" I run my finger over the keyboard.

"Oliver Grayson." Mark mentions my brother's name without any fanfare. My brother, one of the main reasons we might win this war. My chest juts out slightly. It makes me proud that he's my brother.

"He is on the verge of reestablishing the World Wide Web and through him, we have been able to construct computers from components with his direction." Mark flips to a clipboard page with a diagram. "It's a much more efficient way to communicate and keep data." He sighs. "Although Aunt Sandra's way definitely did have its charm." He murmured Aunt Sandra's name with a respectful tone. We all respected Aunt Sandra. She will be missed.

Colt pipes in. "Yeah, this will be where Paisley stays." He taps my forehead. "Somebody had to make the decision."

I'm sad about the reason, but I have to admit I'm a little excited to have this much power. I had no idea that Aunt Sandra was this involved. Is there more I don't know about?

Mark leads us out. "Paisley, your room will be ready tomorrow night. I'll have one of your security detail come and help you pack tonight."

"That won't be necessary. I don't have much. I can get it all just fine. I might need help tomorrow morning bringing it here. So it will be okay to send someone tomorrow morning."

"Let's go find our new living quarters." Colt tickles Gretel's side and she laughs.

Mark, Gretel, Colt, and I tour the rest of the house. Colt and Gretel decide on three adjoining rooms on the other wing of the castle. As Colt says, "Far enough away from the sister-in-law to have some private time." Gretel and I both turn red.

Their three-room wing will house their bedroom, Gretel's personal lab and a personal communication and war room for Colt.

Gretel asks, "What about the ambassador? Could he move in too?" She looks at me. "It would be so much easier to develop the cure if we were both here."

Colt agrees.

Mark shrugs, "That's entirely up to Paisley and Colt."

"Yes." I feel my face light up. I'm excited to think about my family living under the same roof. "I think that is a great idea and it would be safer for Prince Ross and Princess Kamea with all of this security. We probably need to find a place for Tury too. Tury has been the royal children's babysitter since they escaped the ship."

Gretel weaves her arm through Colt's crooked elbow. "Colt, let's go and get our stuff. I want to set up the lab tonight." She turns to me. "Would you like for us to tell the ambassador?"

"Definitely." I might not be able to control my emotions telling my own father that I want him to move in with me. Gretel could use the lab as the reason. Yes, that would work for me.

"Guess we're not training the children today?" Colt asks as he opens the outside door.

I turn to take a last look at the inside of the castle. Can't believe I'm going to live here. "I'll drop by and put Thomas and Mike in charge. Training needs to continue, but we might not be there as much as we used to be."

Colt waits for Gretel to exit in front of him. "That's true, tell them we'll be available to consult or for emergencies but not much else." Colt turns his attention back to Gretel and slips his arm around her waist and gazes into her eyes. "We going to pack so we can move in tonight."

Dipping my head to indicate my understanding, I rush out in front of Colt and Gretel, looking for the one person I want to talk to. Riley.

Unfortunately, I run into Mike first. "Colt, Gretel and I are moving into the castle to run things. You and Thomas are going to have to continue the training."

"I'll tell Thomas. I think we are ready." Mike puffs his chest out.

"We'll come as much as we can, but it might not be as much as before."

"Thomas and I can handle it." He touches my arm. "You and Colt have trained us well. We're ready to take over. You're needed elsewhere. Aunt Sandra believed in you and Colt and I do too." He leaves, heading to the training area.

As I turn toward the workshop, I see Gretel and Colt exiting the lab with my father trailing behind. He smiles at me and I know that he has been given the news. The prince and princess will be told next since Colt and Gretel are making the move today. Where's Riley? I'm desperate to find him. I want to be the one to tell him.

I dash to his bungalow, but he is nowhere in sight. I check his favorite eating area. He's not here. I look everywhere I can think of, but no Riley. Where is he?

Finally, I walk over to the place on the northwest quadrant where we kissed for the first time and there he sits. Alone, his head rests on his knees. When he hears my movement, he faces me. He's not happy, the corners of his mouth and eyes are curled downward. He looks sad and dejected. Is it because of me?

"You okay?" I slide in beside him and crook my arm in his. He slumps. I can tell by the limpness of his frame that he has heard the news. "I tried to find you. I wanted to tell you first. It came as a complete surprise."

He squeezes my hand. "It's the best choice. I know *that* in my head. I heard you were looking for me. I know you tried to tell me first." His eyes hold a sadness that breaks my heart.

"Who told you?"

"Colt."

That makes me feel better. I'm glad it wasn't some random person. "Then why so sad?"

"He told me about the security." He brushes my hair with his hand. "We won't be able to see each other like this for a long time. Probably not until after the war."

Leaning up close so I can inhale him, I pull his face to mine. "Then we better make the most of it."

He turns his body to face me, places his hand behind my head, and wraps his other arm around my waist. I melt into him and we embrace. I bury my head in his shoulder and he kisses the back of my head. He whispers. "It'll be hard to not be able to hold you this way."

"I'm not in jail."

His lips caress mine ever so lightly. I want to stay like this forever. I want to forget about the war, the Undesirables, and the Uncounteds. I just want to run away with Riley. We could kiss and hold each other until the end of time. I love his kiss, his touch, and the way he holds my head and rubs my back. Time stops when I am in Riley's arms.

My face flushes and I feel faint. "Wait."

"Are you okay?" He immediately stops and faces me. "Do you want me to stop?"

"I'm sorry." I rub my head. "I just got hot all of a sudden. I thought I was going to faint."

He hugs me close. "I feel it too. It's like I have all of these emotions and when I look at you I'm whole, but when I touch you or kiss you all of this passion arises like it's sitting on top of my skin shouting. My heart, so empty before, overflows, erupting each time I'm near you."

"How are you able to verbalize my emotions?" I choke back the tears. "It's amazing. I could never say exactly what I'm feeling."

"We're in harmony." He rubs my hair again ever so lightly. "It's like we're playing the exact same song."

My eyes brim. I can't speak. I'm trembling. "How can you be so perfect?"

"I'm not perfect." He laughs. "Far from it." He kisses the top of my head. "And you. You can say what you feel. You do it every time you speak to the troops. You give me the courage to fight. I'm not afraid. You make us all want to be the very best that we can be. You're wonderful. I'm so happy that you are here and in my life."

He leans in and kisses me again, lightly, and sweetly. "Go live in your castle. I will wait for you forever and a day."

A tear runs down my cheek. I never want to leave.

Hrumph!

A sound comes from behind us. Riley and I release our embrace. I trip trying to stand up. Riley grabs my arm as I straighten my clothes trying to pretend that this stranger didn't see anything embarrassing.

"Hello. I'm Darrell. Your personal bodyguard. Sorry about the intrusion, Miss Paisley. The whole camp has been looking for you. Now that you are our new leader, you must be protected at all times. I pledge that I will give my life for you." He salutes.

I snap my hand to my forehead. "Just Paisley is good enough."

Riley whispers, "Maybe you *are* in jail."

The red in my face begins to subside and I chuckle. This is what my life will be like until the war is over. I am so thankful for my last moments alone with Riley. Now that I have him, my thirst for a normal life is more than it has ever been. I have a taste of freedom. Freedom to kiss, to love, to see who you want. That kind of life is worth fighting for.

We steal a last glance before we separate. Riley leans his lips close to my ear and whispers, "I'm glad to know you will be safe. Until next time."

I touch Riley's hands slightly before leaving him, silently pledging to win this war for me, for Riley, for us all.

Chapter 19

Settling into my role as leader is an easier transition than I thought it would be, possibly because everyone is helping me. There's a revolving door of well-wishers catching me up on how things were done, making suggestions regarding how they think things can improve, and providing nonstop assistance.

Everyone wants me to succeed and they will do just about anything to make that happen. They explain codes, decipher books, suggest varying combat scenarios, or anything else they feel will help. With all of the support, it doesn't take long for me to move into my new room and orient myself to the war room and to the computer.

After a couple of nights, I decide to try the radio. I flip on the switch and lights flash on and off. "PACO here."

The microphone squawks and Oliver's voice rings out. ""This is not PACO. The radio sign and location do not match. Could this be another call sign?"

Is Oliver trying to get me to identify Aunt Sandra's sign? I look around the table and don't see anything that could possibly be a call sign.

I press the button. "I will get back to you on that call sign."

Oliver's voice booms out. "Initials?"

He knows what the call sign is. Why is he making me search for it? I look at the top of the door on the inside. Each door has a big BBF blazoned on the top. Becker Bavarian Farm.

I press the button again. "BBF here."

A noise. A beep, then a voice. "This is SONOL, come in BBF."

"Hey, I guess I figured out what the call sign is. What's going on?"

The light flashes. "We're glad that you are on line again. We're sorry to hear about our loss. We need another broadcast tonight by our two favorite people. A secret message will be coming shortly. It will only be broadcast on this BFF channel, but it needs to be rebroadcast from PACO. You will need to write it down exactly. It's a message for the troops. Do you understand?"

"Yes." I speak into the microphone and hold my breath waiting for the message. It comes too quickly. I don't have a chance to get anything to write on or write with. A voice I don't recognize says: "Emergency message. Please take this down. Joy is imminent in SA number five, C number 3, NA number 10, and E number 3—heads up about that one BBF. We need our two favorite people to tell factions that the only safe food to eat today is the noodle, the egg, spinach and walnuts are not good eating today. Be aware. Don't get compromised."

I beep in again. "What are you saying?"

"BBF, write this down. It's an emergency. Please get the message out immediately."

Grabbing a notebook and picking up a pen. I beep in again. "Okay I have a pen. Please repeat."

"Joy is imminent in SA number five, C number 3, NA number 10, and E number 3—heads up about that one BBF. We need our two favorite people to tell factions that the only safe food to eat today is the noodle. The egg, spinach and walnuts are not good eating today. Be aware. Don't get compromised."

"Emergency message terminated." The lights cease to flash.

A long sigh escapes my lungs, my shoulders droop. "What in the world?"

"Paisley?" A voice startles me.

"Colt." I stand up, fists raised. "Don't sneak up on me. You scared the life out of me." I lower my fists and show him the paper. "Thank goodness you're here. I need help. Colt, Oliver sent us a message. We need to decipher it and send it out."

Colt pulls up a chair and grabs the paper out of my hand "What do the initials mean? A name? A place? Who's in charge?"

I shake my head. "I don't know. Let's look in some of the books. I have no idea how to decode this message. Maybe Aunt Sandra left a clue somewhere."

We flip through pages of different books. I try to see if anything falls out. Colt studies the table of contents. "Nothing here."

Reading the spines of the notebooks is no help. Nothing anywhere near the codes that are on the message. "We have to go on air in less than thirty minutes. How could Aunt Sandra have trusted us? We're messing up already and we haven't even moved in yet. We are going to lose the war and it's going to be our fault." I sit on the floor in the middle of the strewn books and put my face in my hands.

Books clap open and closed as Colt searches through them. Each time he drops one to the floor, he lets out a big sigh signaling growing frustration with each failure. "Maybe if we had a map. Is there a map of where the troops are and the resistance is located?" He rubs the back of his neck as beads of sweat form around his temple.

"Look!" I peek through my fingers at the map sitting on the table. "Initials." I sprint to my feet. The number "3" stares at me. "Wait a minute."

Colt sees it at the same time I do. "The initials are continents. SA is South America."

I point above it. "NA is North America."

He finishes the initials. "C is Canada. E is Europe."

Making my way around to his side of the map, I see it's South America. What does the number "5" have to do with South America? What are these?" A series of stickpins identify various locations.

Colt pulls a set apart. "This one has four. Are there any in South America that have five pins?"

"Five?" I scan the continent. "Yes, this one has five."

Colt is meticulous. He counts the pins two times each making sure that none of the groupings has five. "No, so where are the pins with five? What's that location?"

"Argentina." I point to the numbers. It makes sense now. "Number the countries in South America, one is Columbia, two is Brazil, three is Paraguay, four is Uruguay, and five is Argentina. Argentina is going to be attacked!"

Colt looks at the clock. "We have to hurry. We're now down to twenty minutes until we have to broadcast."

"Quit talking and count." I examine the amount of pins. "Concentrate on Canada. Less pins."

"Only four. So one is British Columbia, two is Manitoba, three is Ontario. So Ontario is the one that we need to worry about," Colt gasps. "They are being attacked tonight."

I scream, "Hurry! Time is running out!"

He moves around the map to North America. "This country has so many."

I say, "Just pick one and count it. Look at Florida. I'm interested in Florida. It's the only place in North America that I've ever been to. I loved it there."

"How did you know? Florida has ten pins." Colt looks up.

"Lucky guess," I say, "So Florida is being attacked tonight. Only one left. Europe."

Colt looks at the left side. "Fewer pins on the left side. Start counting."

Our home has to be counted. I shake my head. "Count Germany."

"Three." Colt turns ashen. "It's us."

Colt flashes a side view to the clock. "Ten minutes! What's the rest of the message?"

Picking up the note, I read. "Eggs, noodles, spinach and walnuts. What could that possibly mean?"

Colt shakes his head. "I have no idea. Five minutes left."

"Get to the radio." I take a deep breath. "Start the broadcast and give them the first part of the message and I'll try to figure out what the end means. Maybe they'll understand. I hope so."

Jerking up the paper, Colt bolts out the door. "I hope I make it in time. Come as soon as you can."

I start pulling books off the shelf, looking at spines. No book on cooking or foods or anything like that. Eggs, Noodles, Spinach and Walnuts. I keep repeating the same four words. What does it mean? I'm breathing hard. I shut my eyes trying to calm my heart down. It's beating out of my chest. I jerk a piece of paper in front of me, grab a pen, and write the words down

Eggs

Noodles

Spinach

Walnuts

Try first letters, maybe they mean something. Maybe that is the clue.

Eggs

Noodles

Spinach

Walnuts

E,N,S,W. "OooHHH!" East, North, South, and West. I look at the supply areas for each faction. There is an east, a south, a north, and a west distribution center. This is where they will stock up on guns, weapons, everything they need. Oh no, they must be watching all of the supply areas except noodle or the north. My feet clomp on the hardwood floors as I dash out of the house, almost knocking a vase off a table at the front door. My poor bodyguard goes crazy when I sprint out toward the radio building. "Sorry, Darrell. I have to hurry."

He yells back, "Right behind you."

Slinging the door open, I pant for air as I hear Colt giving the directions. He has just finished. "...aware. Don't get compromised."

"Wait." I jump in. "Important. JOY is coming to SA number five, C number 3, NA number 10, and E number 3—heads up about that one BBF. The egg, spinach, and walnuts are no good today only thing safe to eat is the noodles. Make sure you eat the noodles."

I grab Colt's arm and raise both of our hands in the air. "Power to the resistance. Over and Out."

The power shuts down and the lights go dark.

Colt shakes his head. "You realize that they can't see us holding up our hands. We just do that when they see us."

"I like doing it." I turn my chair to face him. "I found out what the message meant."

"No kidding." Colt crosses his arms. "I'm not sure what gave it away. That you ran in here like a crazy person or that you emphasized everything in the message. I think they got it Paisley. So fill me in. What does it mean?"

"We were right about the continents and everything but the eggs, noodle, and all of that is directions." I pull out the paper. "Noodle is north so the supply station to the north is the only safe one in which to get guns and replenish supplies. I take it the others have been compromised or raided or are being watched. Either way, it is not safe for them to go. Joy is a military term for snipers. No joy means it is not clear and joy means there is a clear shot. So in this case joy means that these resistance stations are going to be hit tonight."

Colt takes a deep breath. "What can we do?"

"I don't know. Should we call Oliver and contact Lieutenant Drake or Captain Via and see if we can offer any help from here?"

Colt swings his arms around to the microphone. "It couldn't hurt." The radio hums. "PACO to SONOL."

"SONOL here. That was quite a message tonight."

Pressing the button again, I speak. "Sorry. My fault I got a little carried away."

SONOL comes back. "Yes. E three had already sent a convoy to get the package of spinach. They may be in trouble."

Southern Germany is close to us. "Near here." I speak into the microphone.

"Be careful. Radio silence until tomorrow 1530. Good luck SONOL over and out."

My eyes lock with Colt's. "The ravine and the cave. It's right on top of my farm. We have to go help them."

Colt's eyes look up to the ceiling. "We can't send out the children. They're not ready. We could deploy a small convoy to intercept. Wouldn't need more than four."

As I spring to my feet, heat rises in my face. "I know what you are thinking—you and three more. You're taking me. I'm coming. You are not leaving me behind."

Colt grabs my shoulders. "We can't risk us both."

I grasp his hand. "We know that area the best. The back roads—we can find them when no one else can. You know the caves." I raise our arms over our head. "Together we stand."

"You're right." Colt drops his arm, releasing mine. "We can go and get back before anyone misses us. You and me. Who else?"

"My bodyguard. I won't be able to get away from him anyway."

"There is one other person who knows the lay of the land." Colt pulls on his backpack. "Riley."

Chapter 20

Colt opens the door. Rain pelts down and he pulls his jacket over his head. "I'll find Riley. You tell your bodyguard. We'll meet you at the maze."

I step outside, holding my arm over my eyes to shield the raindrops. "Do we need weapons?"

"Not you." He bops me on the head. "Riley, Darrell, and I will be packing. Not you."

He's probably right. I don't know if I could shoot anyone. I am excited to be able to spend time with Riley and ride my horse, Hershey. Now if we can just make sure we save the group before they are in danger. This rain and a muddy trail will slow us down.

Bodyguards are not allowed to question orders so Darrell is easy. Colt and I made our own choice to go on this mission. No one has jurisdiction over us to talk us out of it or tell us we can't leave. It's a lot of power and responsibility.

Darrell and I enter the maze. We are saluted at each sentry post, but not questioned. At the end of the maze, Riley and Colt stand ready.

Riley holds onto Hershey's reins. "Wasn't a question about which horse you would ride."

Smiling as he gives me a leg up to mount my horse, I enjoy Riley's warm touch. I murmur, "Thanks." My clothes, wet from the rain, adhere to my body. It takes a moment to shift my shirt into the right place.

"Stick by me." Riley mounts his horse and shakes his head, spraying raindrops everywhere.

I flick Hershey's reins and the horse canters to the front through the drizzling rain. "I'm now the boss."

Riley rides next to me. "I told Colt I didn't think you should come, but he reminded me that you two are in charge. It's not that I don't think you can do it. It's that I don't want you to get hurt."

"I understand." I pull out the four-leaf clover. "That's what this is for."

Staring at the necklace, he grins. Darrell and Colt hang back. It is not lost on me that Riley talked to Colt so he knows about us. Darrell caught us kissing so in reality this is a trip where Riley and I don't have to pretend. That makes it nice. I reach over and clasp his hand. I'm glad we can have this time.

Riley squeezes my hand. No looking back at the others. He never pretends. What you see is what you get. It's one of the things I love about Riley. Do I love Riley? What a time to wonder about that. We're on our way to confront a Merc posse.

Muddy trails and the pelting rain slow us, but also hide our movements. We follow the familiar path using short cuts here and there and before long, we hear talking.

"Shush!" Colt whispers. We communicate through hand signals. First, we slip off the horses and each one hands me their horse's reins. I hold the horses to free the guys to cock and ready their weapons. They move forward toward the voices.

Don't panic, I remind myself as I nuzzle Hershey, running my fingers over his wet coat. I try not to imagine what is happening with Riley, Colt, and Darrell.

Waiting is horrible. I squat beside Hershey. What are they doing?

"Paisley? Paisley?" Riley's voice sounds through the rain. "Where are you?"

I lead Hershey toward Riley's voice and see the others. "What happened? Did you find them? Did you warn them?"

"Yes." Colt takes off his jacket and wrings it out before he pulls it back on. "We sent them home, but something seems off. There was no sign of an invasion. I have a bad feeling. We need to get back to the compound."

Riley grabs me around the waist and lifts me on Hershey. "Colt's right. This could be a set up."

"I agree." I squeeze my legs into Hershey's sides and turn toward home. The four of us waste no time trotting back. The rain has slowed, but the terrain is muddy. The sun is coming up as we see the edge of our haven. We tie the horses up and rush back through the maze.

At the end of the maze, we are saluted by the guards. I quickly return the salute. "Let's go to the radio house and see what if anything happened last night."

We pass muddy paths in between the various stone living quarters. The weather keeps the inhabitants inside and off of the streets. I'm happy there is no one to stop us or slow us down. Inside the radio room, Thomas is acting as a radio operator with a long pad full of writing.

"That's a lot of notes." I observe. "What happened?"

"Got word there is supposed to be another announcement." Thomas hands me the list with messages scrawled in the margins. "I looked all over for you. I didn't know what to do so I decided to stay and transcribe the chatter. Where were you?"

412

"What does it say?" Colt takes the list from my hand. "How about Gretel? Did Gretel realize you couldn't find me?"

"Yes." Thomas stares at him. "She was crying."

"I need to find her." Colt hands the list back to me. "She's probably out of her mind with worry. Let me know what you find out."

"Go." I shove my hand toward him. "Riley and I will figure this out and stay for the message." I look back at Riley, who nods. I knew I could count on him.

Colt bolts out the door.

Darrell walks toward the exit. "Don't leave this room. I'll wait for you outside." He looks at Riley. "I'll be right outside the door. She is not allowed to walk without escort."

Riley nods. "Don't worry she's not going anywhere without you." Darrell's chest puffs out as he closes the outside door behind him.

Thomas stands and pulls on his jacket. "Let me know if you need me to man the radio again. I'm heading home to get some sleep."

"Thanks for staying." I follow him to the door. "When is the announcement supposed to come?"

"It won't be long now." Thomas disappears out of the door.

It isn't two minutes before the lights flash on the radio.

No introduction of the SONOL or PACO. I don't recognize any call signs and the setup is all wrong.

The voice. It's the emperor. "This is your emperor speaking. You have been listening to this fanatical radio broadcast for months. I am here to tell you that the radical radio station has finally been found in a suburb in Hamburg. The culprits were arrested. Lieutenant Drake is in custody. He's been a menace to the government, fraudulently calling himself a lieutenant."

I spring up and fall into Riley's arms. "They've hacked our radio broadcast. Was this all a ruse to get us to be off guard? Or what?"

Riley sets me down gently into the chair. "We need to listen."

Sniffing as I wipe tears from my cheek, I sit up. "You're right."

"Captain Via has also been captured."

I gasp.

"Captain Via saw fit to travel from America to Europe to go against the Consortium of the World. The last arrest is a very upsetting one to tell you about, my fellow world inhabitants. I know that you all loved Ambassador Grayson. He and my wife, the late queen, and her father the great King Ahomana, saved us during the terrible virus outbreak. None of us will ever forget the day the king brought the root to us that staved off the virus. And all of the years our beloved ambassador worked on the cure. "

I'm going to vomit! What a liar! My blood boils. I am enraged. The emperor killed the king and conspired to kill the ambassador. Would people believe him? I don't want to, but I know I have to focus and listen to this evil. I squeeze Riley's hand.

"People of the world, the last of the leaders of this heinous group is none other than Oliver Grayson, son of our beloved ambassador. It seems that he has been rebelling against the government, the mercenary army put in place to keep order, and the royals themselves. The royals are his family. Oliver is a royal. Lieutenant Drake and Captain Via will be tried for their crimes of treason and treachery. If found guilty, they will be put to death."

"Our sweet Oliver, who has been led astray by these hooligans, will not be harmed in any way. We will keep him in the bosom of our government and make sure that he is rehabilitated. We want what is best for the citizens. We will stick together and drive out this underground force. Emperor Richard signing off."

The microphone squawks one last time and the light on the board flashes off.

Colt rushes in with Gretel. It takes Riley and me a few minutes to fill them in.

"What are we going to do?" I ask, hugging my sister.

Colt sits in one of the straight back chairs. "We'll think of something. We always do."

Just then, there is another squawk from the radio. A menacingly evil, familiar voice is speaking. "Paisley and Colt, I know you can hear me."

I drop into a chair beside Colt.

"I know that you monitor this channel and that you are behind the resistance. I am a peaceful man looking for peaceful solutions. Turn yourselves in."

Colt whispers under his breath. "Never."

"Trade yourselves and I will let all traitors go. Lieutenant Drake, Captain Via, and all of these little Undesirable and Uncounted children you love so much. You will get a fair trial in front of the Consortium of the World. It meets in one week. Please come and be heard, and let others ask you questions. Answer for the crimes which you are accused of. The whole world is listening. I'm calling you out. Come and face your judge and jury. If you are found not guilty, all will be released."

"Liar." Gretel murmurs.

"If you are found guilty, you two will be the only ones put to death. You can save all of your people. You have until next Sunday at 1200. We will all be at the Consortium of the World in Hamburg. Save your people. Face your peers. Signing off, Emperor Richard"

My eyes look deeply into Colt's.

His sweaty hand squeezes mine.

We know what we must do.

Make sure both of us, Colt and I, are in Hamburg in a week.

We have to try to save them.

Chapter 21

"No! I know what you're thinking." Gretel swings her arms around Colt. "You can't leave me. I love you. Don't listen to him. Find another way."

Colt embraces his sobbing wife. "I'm not going anywhere tonight." He looks back at me. "We'll talk tomorrow. I'm going to take Gretel home." He picks her up and carries her out the door.

Riley and I sit quietly alone. I don't want to leave. I place my hand on Riley's cheek. "I have no choice. I have to try. You do know that, don't you?"

His eyes fall. "I don't know anything of the sort. We'll find something else to trade. Anything else." He leans in, holds the back of my head, and presses his cheek to mine. "I would give my life for yours without hesitation." He whispers. "You know that."

I grab both sides of his head. "And that is exactly why you must understand why I'm willing to give my life for so many. It's a fair trade."

He pulls my lips to within an inch of his. "There is nothing fair about it."

Darrell peeks in. "Miss Paisley."

Riley lets go of my head.

"I'm right out here if you need me."

"Thanks Darrell. Everything is fine. I'll be out in a minute." I cock an eyebrow at Riley.

"Don't go." Riley leans back in his chair. "Stay. It makes me crazy to think about losing you. I can't imagine life without you."

I stand up, walk over, sit in his lap, and cuddle with him, my head on his shoulder. "I'll have to present and defend my side of the story before the Consortium of the World. I have to answer for how I have conducted myself. If we produce enough evidence, we can end the emperor's tyrannical reign and stop this war. We can bring democracy back. Isn't that worth the risk?"

"Maybe I'm being selfish, but no it's not." His lips caress mine. He rubs my back and my arms. He takes in a deep breath. "I love the way you smell." He leans over and rubs his lips along the nape of my neck. "I love the way you feel." He grabs the small of my back, presses me up close to him, and kisses me again. "I love the way you taste. I can't lose you. I won't lose you. You're what I live for."

We don't say a word. I am glad that we have this time, but now I have to be the leader that I'm supposed to be.

I can't stay here any longer. It would be too tempting to forget my duty. "I have to go to bed." I crawl off his lap. "I need rest. I need to be able to think clearly tomorrow."

He stands up, still holding onto the fingers of my hand. "We'll figure this out. See you tomorrow." He pulls me close for one last kiss and then he walks out ahead of me. "Night, Darrell."

Darrell is obviously startled when Riley walks off. Darrell says, "I wouldn't say anything if you two spent the night together."

I pat Darrell's shoulder as I watch Riley disappear into the night. "Darrell, I can't deal with that right now. I have a week to save the world."

The next morning, Gretel and Colt busy themselves making breakfast in the kitchen. Moving together as they make coffee and pull croissants out of the oven, they are never more than an arm's length from each other. Gretel eyes are swollen as if she might have been crying most of the night. She and Colt have bags under their eyes. I don't think they got much sleep. I know that my face probably mirrors theirs.

Princess Kamea bounces in. She is as carefree as an autumn leaf skipping its way off a tree and down the rolling hills. I feel a touch of jealousy about her carefree nature. She is in the middle of a worldwide war, but because of her royal status, she is completely sheltered from its horrors. Soon after, Tury arrives carrying Prince Ross.

Gretel and I help Tury fix the two royals a bit of breakfast. When the young ones finally settle, Gretel takes a sip of coffee. "Where's the ambassador?"

Tury fusses with the bib around the prince's neck. "He left out last night. Said he was going to find Paisley and Colt." She takes the bib off the boy, straightens it, and reties it. "He never came back."

"What do you mean he never came back? He's been gone all night?" I swallow a bite of toast.

Tury nods as she pushes Princess Kamea up to the table and places a plate of breakfast in front of her.

"Where could he be?" Colt puts his coffee cup down on the table.

"I'm not sure, but we need to find out." I scan the room. "Darrell can't be far away. I'll head over the radio building. Colt, check with the rest of our security detail. Gretel, check the lab and see if he possibly went there to work for the night."

Gretel smiles a half grin. "Look at you barking orders. You would think that you ran the place." We share a nervous laugh, and then we both abruptly stop. No time for brevity in this horrible situation.

Our half-eaten breakfast is tossed in the garbage while cups and plates are placed in the sink. The children giggle and squeal the entire time watching us run around. Tury attempts to quiet them to no avail.

Gretel and Colt take off in different directions, and I head over to the radio room with my shadow, Darrell, in hot pursuit.

Riley trots along beside us and snuggles my scarf tighter around my neck. "It's cold out here."

"Have you been here all night?" I ask.

He nods. "I know I can't come in, but I ran home and got a change of clothes. Darrell let me share his room. A blanket on the floor is all I need. I wanted to make sure that you were protected."

Darrell moves quickly to my other side. "Right now, two bodyguards can't hurt."

I have to agree with them and am very happy to see Riley. We three make haste to our destination. I walk in with Riley. Darrell stays outside. The room is empty except for the lone operator, Thomas, monitoring the radio.

"Hope you got a little sleep." I pull off my scarf, not waiting for a comment. "Any more news or broadcasts?"

Thomas flips a few pages on a notepad that sits on the table beside him. "A lot of chatter." He flips through his notes and then he sighs. "Do you really want to hear this?"

"Probably not." I plop down in the chair. "But lay it on me anyway."

Riley pulls up a few chairs in anticipation of Gretel, Colt, and others who will be joining us.

The messages center around the demand for my and Colt's immediate surrender. The quotes range from simple requests for us to turn ourselves in to demands that we be locked up for our atrocities committed toward humankind with the re-release of the virus. There is not one message in our support. Riley sits silent, occasionally reaching out to rub my shoulder.

A tear escapes my eye. I'm hated. What would I do without Riley?

Thomas reaches out and pats my hand. "I warned you, the opinions are brutal."

"What about you, Thomas?" I wipe my cheek. "How do you feel about us?"

"I'm just the radio operator." He shifts uncomfortably in the chair. "I'm not qualified to comment."

Riley stands and stretches. "Don't make him answer that, Paisley. He's right, he's not qualified."

"You're wrong, Riley." I slap the notebook. "Thomas is more qualified than the rest of them. He knows me."

Thomas blurts out. "I think you and Colt should turn yourselves in and prove your innocence."

Riley cringes. But Thomas is right, there really is no other choice.

Gretel and Colt come through the door and bring with them a blast of cold air that flutters the pages on Thomas's notebook. Gretel shivers and then pushes the door against the wind. She claps her palms together and blows in them for warmth. "The ambassador's not in the lab."

Chair legs scrape against the floor as Colt scoots one out for Gretel to sit in and slides into another. "I asked all around. Or at least to the people who are awake. Not one person has seen him since last night."

"The ambassador?" Thomas flips a couple of pages back on the notebook. "He was here earlier. Wait a minute." He turns two more pages and then holds a piece of paper out to me. "Yes here it is. He sent a message out."

Colt leans forward. "What did it say?"

I read aloud: "This is Ambassador Grayson. The emperor is a liar. I am proof of that. I plan to travel to Hamburg and negotiate the release of my son Oliver as well as the other two leaders, Captain Via and Lieutenant Drake. There is no need to involve Paisley and Colt. I am the true leader of the resistance. They are innocent and this has all been a ploy to find me." I read the words in disbelief. What has my father done?

"Why would he do that?" Gretel shakes her head. "His job here is so important. I need him. The world needs him to keep developing the antidote." She holds her hands up and shakes her head. "I don't understand."

Colt hugs his wife's shoulders. "I'm sure he didn't think it through. He was just trying to save Paisley and me. Don't worry. We'll make it right."

"We have to go to Hamburg now." I slam down the notebook. "We must save them."

The lights on the radio board start flashing. Thomas perks up and scoots into the table pen in hand, ready to take notation. "Another message is coming through."

It is the emperor's voice. "Ambassador, if you are listening we will await your arrival."

Thomas drops his pen. We sit silently as the emperor continues spewing his lies. "We're so relieved to hear that the ambassador is alive.

How wonderful! We look forward to reuniting him with his son. The resistance's efforts to quiet this man were unsuccessful. I know what the ambassador said. I have followed the chatter and the resistance is trying to use him to confuse you."

More of the emperor's lies follow. "Good citizens, you know what the truth is and the truth is that Paisley and Colt are the number one enemies of the world. If any of you know where they are, please let any Merc know. You will be rewarded with treasures and your station in life will be elevated to a level that your heart cannot imagine. Help us take back our world from these monsters. We will report as soon as our beloved ambassador is safely back in our hands. Power to the world. Stomp out the resistance. Signing off Emperor Richard."

"What now?" Riley places his hand on mine. "I don't see how this is not going to be a bloodbath."

Thomas hands me his notebook. He says, "I hate to be the bearer of bad news. But even if we wanted to fight the emperor's regime and obliterate the Mercs, we are losing support everywhere."

I flip through the pages of comments Thomas has written since last night.

Thomas says, "I count at least three strong holds in three different parts of the world that have fallen. There have been reports of resistance supporters putting down their arms and returning to their villages."

"If it keeps going this way," Colt cuts his eyes over to Gretel, "there will be no resistance to fight for."

"We have no choice." I stand and square my shoulders. "We must go and turn ourselves in, and hope that the emperor will release everyone else." I pat Gretel on the shoulder. "I see no other way."

Riley jumps up and embraces me. "There has to be something else we can do." My cheeks flush as he hugs me in front of everyone. I am surprised by the open show of affection. I wrap my arms around his waist and bury my head in his shoulder for a moment.

"You're right, Paisley." Colt slams his fists on the table. "We must turn ourselves in. Let's log all of the information about the resistance. We need to make note of where the troops are and where the weapons are stashed. We have to find out what pockets of the resistance have fallen because of Merc intervention or because they have given up. We must know what we're up against before going to Hamburg."

"Wait a minute, Colt." Riley releases his embrace of me. "I'm not going to fight you or Paisley about turning yourselves in anymore. But give yourselves every chance to come out of this unscathed. Please be smart about it. You need to wait until all of the leaders of the world get to

Hamburg. If you go too soon, then the emperor can murder you and blame it on the resistance or an accident."

"But what will happen to the ambassador, Oliver, Lieutenant Drake, and Captain Via while we wait to turn ourselves in?" I shake my head. "No, the safest thing for us to do for them is to go now."

Colt places a hand on each of my arms and turns me to face him. "Riley is right. We have to make it a public spectacle. It's the only way to have any chance at a fair trial."

"None of this is fair. Do you really think any of this is fair?" I jerk out of his grasp. "All of these lies. The emperor's evil deeds turned back on us as if we were the ones who committed those heinous crimes. How is any of this possibly fair? Why would anyone think the emperor would be fair now?"

Gretel drapes her arm around my shoulder. "You're right Paisley. The emperor is a liar and a cheat, but that is even more of a reason to make sure there is a public trial. The eyes of the world *must* be watching. It's the only chance you and Colt have. It's the only chance for the truth to come out. Don't you see that?"

Gretel squeezes me again. "I know you, sister. I know you want to march head on and take on the emperor. But not this time. You need to pause, take a breath. Rest and make a plan. Please."

"She's right. Listen to her." Riley clasps my hand. "We'll help you and Colt make a plan. It's the right way, the only way."

Darrell joins us now and holds out his palm. One by one, I along with Thomas, Gretel, Colt, and Riley join hands. We whisper. "Power to the resistance." We say it, but the fire is not there. If we hope to defeat the emperor, we must get our passion and determination back. We will definitely need luck to make it happen. I pull out the four-leaf clover and twirl it in my fingers.

Colt and I spend the day updating the map. It doesn't look good. Our forces are dwindling. Winning seems impossible. With the ambassador heading back into enemy hands, the emperor will now have a monopoly on manufacturing the cure. My father's brain wasn't thinking about the cure. He's my dad. He did it for me, Oliver, the little prince, and the princess. He did it for his family. An unselfish act. A reckless act, but an understandable one. My father unconditionally loves his family. Of that, I have no doubt.

That night we gather for the broadcast once again. Gretel and Colt sit close to each other. Darrell stands in the back of the room. Riley slides a chair near me. Thomas mans the radio board. I dread the news. It will be bad, I'm sure of it.

We don't have to wait long. Lights flash and the emperor's voice sounds. "Good evening fellow citizens. Tonight, I share wonderful news. The ambassador has come back to us."

The sound of clapping hands in the background of the transmission is followed by more of the emperor's voice. "He is standing here with me and will be given an opportunity to speak in a few minutes. The ambassador and his long lost son have been reunited. It is a great day for the right side, our side. Those evil resistance fighters have lost many of their strong holds in the countries of South America..."

Thomas flips a page and starts writing.

The emperor continues, "We have taken control of the camps in Canada and half of the resistance bases in the United States, all in Asia and one in Europe. Don't worry my friends there will be no place for the heathens to hide. Paisley and Colt still cower like the cowards that they are, and I have faith that they will be caught and brought to justice very soon."

The emperor clears his throat. "Our government, the one and only true government, sanctioned by the Consortium and led by me, your emperor, will now begin the manufacture and distribution of the cure. For those who have not had an opportunity to be inoculated, no fear, this small vial represents life and peace of mind, and will be available to you by the week's end. Go to any local stores backed by the Consortium of the World and you will receive the cure. There is a small service charge to pay for our costs. If you have no money, we will take food or other valuables as trade. We have implemented the barter system and all of you will be able to get the boosters that are required to keep the immunity..."

Leaning in close to Gretel, I whisper, "Booster, do you need boosters?"

"No. He must be working on lessening the dosage to force the need for the booster." She shakes her head. "He's trying to control the people forever."

We listen to the vile emperor's lies. "Boosters need to be taken monthly. If you have no means by which to pay, we will provide opportunities to earn small stipends. Contracts for service will be available for you to sign. You will be able to work off your debt."

Legally binding human trafficking, complete with a signed contract. How horrible! Uncounteds and Undesirables will sign their freedom away in order to obtain an immunity from the virus. It's a guarantee that should be given for free, no strings attached. Emperor Richard must be stopped. My face reddens as heat surges through my body. I force myself to remain calm.

The emperor continues, "We must have Paisley and Colt in custody before the cure will be available."

I can't believe it. It takes all of my self-control not to scream. He's holding the cure from everyone to try to force us to turn ourselves in. He wouldn't have the cure if it wasn't for my father. How could my father been manipulated by this maniac? I put my hand over my heart trying to calm its increasing beats. "Keep yourself together," I tell myself.

The evil man spews more lies. "More good news. Our Oliver has agreed to repair the World Wide Web. Please go and find any old television or computer because communication will soon be restored. Our Oliver is one of a kind. We appreciate him and are so happy he is back on our side."

A few claps are heard over the broadcast before the emperor continues. "We plan to have everything up and running by next Sunday, the first day of the rule of the new Consortium of the World. This is a great day and I am proud to be your leader. I know the people are behind me and that I will be voted to carry on as your leader. Fear not fellow people of the world. Our side, the right side, will win." He takes a breath. "And now for a message from Ambassador Grayson."

My heart leaps when I hear my father's name. He is alive. Of course he is alive, the emperor needs him. He needs him to make the cure. I am sure he is using Oliver to control him and obviously, the emperor is using the ambassador's arrest to control Oliver. How can I hold onto hope?

"I'm here with the emperor, which is true." My father's voice increases my faith. "I have found a cure, which is also correct. My son, Oliver, is here with me, another truth. There is one thing that you don't know. If you and the emperor want me to live because of my connection to the royal family…"

The emperor's voice cuts in. "Stay on script Mr. Ambassador."

My father interrupts, "Oliver and I are alive because we are royals. Isn't that correct, Emperor Richard?"

Colt moves closer to the speaker. "What's he doing?"

Gretel scrunches in close to Colt. "He never does anything without a plan."

Emperor Richard clears his throat. "Of course Ambassador Grayson. The world wants you to live. Royals have immunity from prosecution. No harm will come to you and your son. You are a royal. I, Emperor Richard, and the government promise on the public radio that no harm will come to you or your family."

Unintelligible mumblings follow. The emperor coughs. "There is one piece of disturbing information that I have chosen not to share with the people, but I want to tell you now. Our little prince and princess are missing. In fact, I promise safety for Prince Ross and Princess Kamea if whoever is holding them will release them. I suspect as I have for a while and especially since Ambassador Grayson is alive and does not have them, that a faction of the resistance, maybe Paisley and Colt themselves, are holding our precious young and vulnerable prince and princess."

Emperor Richard spews more evil. "I shudder to think what will happen to them. Please return them unharmed or give us information regarding our young royals' whereabouts. Per usual if you give any information to my government or any of the Mercs, the sanctioned security of this government, you will be amply rewarded."

Riley scratches his head. "This is making no sense. It's as if the ambassador has cut a deal with the emperor. It sounds as if he really is on his side. What does all of this mean?"

"No way." I say aloud. "He would never sell us out."

"Shush!" Gretel hisses.

"I have your promise." My father comes back on the radio. "No harm will come to any of member of my family."

A pause is followed by the emperor's voice. "I give you my word and my word is witnessed by this national audience. No harm will come to any member of your family."

My father comes back on. "Well then I ask for safety for my daughter."

The emperor says, "Of course. I have already told you that. Princess Kamea will always be safe."

"Oh no." I mumble to myself. I know what's coming.

"No." My father says, "My other daughter. I ask for safety for my oldest daughter. The one you seek, Paisley, is my daughter and I can prove it."

The lights blink on and off and the radio goes silent.

Chapter 22

All eyes in the radio room train in on me. I shoot up out of my chair.

"Paisley?" Gretel walks over and stands by me. "I knew you weren't ours, but I didn't realize that the ambassador was your father. When did you find out?"

Colt interrupts, "Wait a minute. Is this true?"

I nod.

Riley slides over close to me. "You could have told me."

"I know." I touch his arm. "I should have told you." I scan the room. "I guess I should have told all of you."

"It's fine. No one is angry. Tell us now." Riley guides me back to my chair. "You're among friends."

Darrell peeks in. "You should probably tell everyone. It seems that the emperor's announcement has been broadcast to the compound via loudspeaker and the message has been heard by all. Rumors are flying. I think maybe you should tell everyone at one time."

"Didn't realize you were doing that, Thomas." Colt glances at Thomas, who is sitting quietly in front of the microphone. "Don't worry. I'm not mad, it's fine. Everyone should know. No secrets."

Colt stands up and taps Thomas's shoulder. "Thomas, go out and pass the message that in thirty minutes Paisley and I will address the troops. Make sure that everyone knows. All should attend."

I put my hands on my hips. "I probably should go talk to Tury and the prince and princess right now. I'll bring them with me."

"Paisley?" Gretel holds her hands on each side of my face. "You want me to go with you?"

"Not right now." I pat her hands. "But I appreciate the gesture." Squeezing her hands, I assure her. "This doesn't change anything. You're still my sister." We hug tightly.

Gretel says, "I know. Sisters now and forever. Sisters always." She releases the hug.

Before I leave her, I glance at Darrell. "We need to go the castle." Darrell opens the door wide.

I get to the exit and turn around. "Riley, would you mind going with me? I'd like to have you there when I tell the children."

Riley beams. "Of course, whatever you want." As soon as he reaches me, he kisses me. It's a small kiss, but a kiss just the same.

Riley pulls back and says, "No more secrets."

The public kiss announces to the people in the room that we are together. It's liberating.

Telling the children is easier than I think. Not sure if they understand, they don't ask many questions, but I feel better. Having Riley there helps. If I could only figure out a way to win this war while rescuing the prisoners held by the emperor, including my father and brother, all would be right with the world.

Did Oliver listen to the broadcast? What did he think of my father's confession? Did he ever consider the possibility I was his sister? My questions will have to wait. I must address my compound now.

As I arrive, I hear whispers from faceless mouths in the front of the crowd. I have lied to them. How will I ever be able to get them to trust me again?

Colt introduces me. "Here is Paisley to explain the ambassador's message."

I fold my hands in front of me trying to look as demure and honest as I can. "I want to tell you the truth about what is going on. I know that I have not always been honest. For those who do not know, this morning the ambassador revealed that I am indeed his daughter."

Gasps from the crowd cause me to pause a few seconds before continuing. "Oliver and I are the ambassador's children from his first marriage. First me, a few years before, and Oliver after the virus broke out. Through a series of unfortunate circumstances, my family was separated. I was lucky enough to have been rescued and cared for by Gretel..." My eyes lock with Gretel's. "...and her family for the years following the virus quarantine. I never questioned that I was a member of that family."

Gretel pipes in. "You *are* a member of my family."

I smile. "Of course I am. When Colt and I stowed away on the ship in an attempt to rescue Gretel and my mom we ran into the ambassador. During a routine blood check, he discovered it was my blood that provided the key for the cure..."

"Your blood is the blood we use for the cure?" Someone in the back shouts.

"Yes, good citizen. It's my blood. This is when the ambassador realized who I was and revealed himself to me. He told me that he was my father. He begged me to keep it a secret for fear that the king would have me killed."

Most heads nod in the crowd signaling that they were in agreement with Ambassador Grayson's choice to keep me a secret.

I continue, "My father explained that the virus was discovered many years ago. He made a serum that would provide an immunity for the disease. He saw no need to advise the distribution of the cure to everyone because the virus was just an idea. A couple of cells in the Petri dish. There was no need for a mass inoculation and it was deemed inappropriate to scare the world by forcing injections on the masses. He knew the inoculation was safe so he gave himself the cure and he injected me and my mother who was pregnant with my brother."

Colt moves a little closer to me to show support.

"After the virus infected the world my father lost me and my mother." I take a breath. "While searching for us, he found my infant brother, but was told his wife was lost. He couldn't find me. When he went back to the lab, the cure and all of the machines had been moved."

"I know about the machines," Colt interjects. "The ambassador told me it was unclear where those machines were moved. Years later he found a working machine during his travels to Africa."

Colt motions to his wife. "Gretel, why don't you explain about the DNA since you are the scientist?"

Gretel jumps up on the platform beside us and addresses the crowd. "After he travelled to Africa, he needed the perfect DNA. His DNA contained a flaw and he would not be able to manufacture the cure from his own blood. He discovered the same problem with all of the donors. He found out that he had to have a female donor. That perfect donor turned out to be my sister, Paisley. That is all I can report about the DNA. Now my sister, Paisley, will tell you anything else she thinks she needs to share."

"Thanks for filling that in. See there are things that I did not know. We are not the bad people the emperor is making us out to be. But I am indeed the daughter of the ambassador, the sister of Oliver, and the half-sister of the young royals, Prince Ross and Princess Kamea. I am sorry that I have kept you in the dark but I promise not to do that anymore."

I glance at Riley. "In keeping with wanting to tell you everything, I need Riley to come to the front."

Riley slowly rises and joins me. "What are you doing?"

"In the spirit of not hiding anything. I need to tell you one more thing." I hook my arm through Riley's. "Riley and I are together. So for those of you who might see us holding hands, I mean we are..."

"Okay, Paisley." Colt pops up in front. "You are entitled to a private life. Who you choose to spend your time with is entirely up to you. I am sure that this is more information than this group needs to know. You do have some privacy." He scans the group. "Questions?"

A voice from the back yells, "Yeah, how long have Riley and Paisley been a couple?"

Colt claps his hands together. "Any question about the virus or Paisley being the ambassador's daughter." He swings his finger as if he is polling the crowd. "Seeing no hands, let's move along with the problem at hand. Paisley and I are going to be turning ourselves in to the authorities of the Consortium of the World on Sunday."

Gasps break the silence. A few loud "no's" are heard throughout the crowd.

"Colt and I have to turn ourselves in. We have to trust the system." I yell, "Truth will win out. We have no other choice."

The crowd quiets and Colt continues, "We need to figure out some contingency plans for the compound."

Leaning close to Colt's ear, I whisper, "I know my emergency plans for my half. What I want to do. Do you?"

"Obviously." Colt points to Gretel.

Looking out at the group, I announce, "If Colt and I are found guilty and sentenced to death we want to continue Aunt Sandra's refuge for those downtrodden and for the Undesirables and Uncounteds."

I motion for Riley. "Riley will be in charge of my half of Aunt Sandra's farm. He will hold it for Prince Ross and Princess Kamea who will each own half as soon as they come of age. There will be a provision for Tury and Riley to have their own piece of land."

The crowd groans.

"Might not work." Riley leans over and whispers in my ear. "I'll be going with you, I might not make it back."

What a horrible thought! I hate to think about it, but I can't let the children be without a guardian. So I continue, "If something happens to Riley, Tury is in charge and then Thomas."

"Don't go!" A soldier yells.

"Finished?" Colt joins me. I nod and he walks in front of the group. "My half will be in the hands of my wife, Gretel. She will complete the ambassador's work."

A young mother cries, "What will we do without you?"

"You can't leave us." A teenage boy hollers.

The crowd drowns us out now with their objections.

"Quiet!" Colt and I yell in unison and the crowd goes silent.

"Look, people," I say. "We don't plan to die. This isn't a suicide mission. We plan to win this thing. We want to come back." I grab Colt's wrist and raise our arms up in the air. "Power to the resistance!" I yell, emphasizing each word. "We must not let Aunt Sandra's legacy die. Aunt

Sandra's legacy must live on. No matter what. Accept our decisions. Do it for Aunt Sandra."

A young boy stands up and claps. One by one, the crowd claps. I am moved by the ovation of reverence. I choke back the tears.

The great Aunt Sandra is truly a hard act to follow.

Chapter 23

Only a few days remain before we must depart for Hamburg. Lots of work to complete and plans to make. Colt and I work feverishly sending couriers to each of the standing factions of resistance to update them on our plan.

We urgently ask them to make sure to get the cure to all and to watch out for the weak in case Colt and I are killed. We encourage the troops to remain diligent in their fight for freedom with or without us.

I try to spend as much time as I can with Riley and the prince and princess. This may be the last time I see them. I want to make happy memories. The thought of not being with Riley makes me full of empty. I spend my nights in the children's room and Riley stays there with me. I'm cuddled with a blanket on the floor and he is draped over a chair. It fills my heart with joy to see him when I fall asleep and when I wake up.

Gretel and Colt spend all of their time together and are not apart for a minute. I can't tell where one starts and the other begins. I'm not sure if my sister will survive if something happens to Colt. But that is something I don't have the luxury of time to worry about now in the middle of this fight for our lives and democracy.

We make no formal announcement of our exact time for departure. It'll be better that way. No pomp and circumstance. We need to be mission ready, heart, soul, and mind. No distractions. In the wee hours of Saturday morning, we make our move. The darkness of the night will hide us from the enemy.

Colt struggles at the thought of leaving Gretel behind. At least Riley will be with me should Colt and I get the death penalty. Is my father still alive? Oliver? The World Wide Web is running, a sure clue that Oliver is still alive. I hold onto hope that I will see my father and brother again.

What about Lieutenant Drake and Captain Via? Could Captain Via really be my birth mother? What if I'm right and she has already been executed? Sadness enters my soul and tears well. Stop thinking that way, I tell myself. I must be sharp if I'm to answer questions from the tribunal of the Consortium of the World and convince them of my truthfulness in order to save mine and Colt's life as well as the scores of innocents caught in the middle of this battle.

The night travel leading up to the Sunday morning is foggy. I'm scared. More afraid than I've ever been. So many people are depending on me. I must keep my mind on other things, so I concentrate on Riley, the best thing that has ever happened to me.

Sunday at noon, Colt, Riley, Darrell and I ride down the streets of Hamburg amid scores of people lining the streets.

At the end of the street, Emperor Richard is perched upon a makeshift throne on a second story balcony of the tallest building. "Paisley and Colt, are you here to turn yourselves in?"

Colt and I step in front of Darrell and Riley. Riley holds tight to my hand. I let my arm stretch behind me, afraid to let go of him. I squeeze his hand for strength. I shout to the emperor and to the masses. "Emperor Richard, please keep your promise and let the prisoners go."

The emperor stands and glances from side to side. "I'll keep my promise." Guards open a gate. A flood of people move out. I recognize some. Some hobble, all are dirty. They are afraid, but free.

Colt commands to the recently released. "Leave this place quickly." He looks at the emperor. "We would like your solemn oath that you will not harm or capture these people again."

The emperor lowers his head in a slight bow. "I promise."

We watch the parade of people pass us. The group mainly consists of children with a few crippled adults guiding them along. They mouth "thank you" and cry, while smiling and holding onto each other. It is a few minutes before they disappear at the end of the street, scattering everywhere. I hold onto Riley.

Not seeing the captives I expected to see, I inquire to the emperor. "What about Lieutenant Drake and Captain Via?"

The emperor glances at a Merc guarding another gate. The gate clangs as it slowly rises and guards pull out a blindfolded Captain Via and Lieutenant Drake. They stumble as they are led out.

I yell, "Captain, Lieutenant are you okay?"

Lieutenant Drake calls out, "Paisley, is that you?"

"Yes. You are to be set free."

The captain shouts out, "What did you have to trade for us?"

Colt sums it up. "A chance to tell the truth in front of the world."

Lieutenant Drake yells. "Sounds like a good trade."

A Merc slams Captain Via and Lieutenant Drake to the dirt on their knees and their blindfolds are removed.

"Wait!" I shout. "You promised they would be set free."

The emperor gives a sly grin. "If you can prove your innocence, all will be set free."

He will always be a liar. We sacrificed ourselves on the promise of a liar.

Is hope for peace and freedom for our world lost forever?

Chapter 24

"**W**here are my father and brother?"

The emperor shouts. "Who are you to ask questions? You are a secret daughter. He didn't know about you until a few months ago. I will not listen to you." He stands and raises his arms outward to the masses. "Citizens, I submit to you that Paisley is not a true royal. She committed treason. She is a traitor. She should be reviled, not saved. She is the scum of the earth."

A few "boos" escape the mouths of the audience. I do have some who are on my side, some support. But not enough, I fear.

"Citizens! Citizens!" Emperor Richard adjusts his crown. "I know who the real royals are and you do too. I will keep our true royals safe. For you, my people, I will show you that the ambassador and his son are not harmed."

There is a large screen set up to the side of the emperor. It turns to black and beeps. The images of my father and brother come into view.

"See, Citizens. I have kept my promise. The ambassador and his son are completely unharmed. The members of the Consortium of the World will view these proceedings via the television." The emperor points to various cameras mounted around the balcony and aimed toward the street where we are being held captive.

"This is a public trial. We will begin." The emperor grasps both sides of the collars of his robe and paces back and forth across his stage bellowing to the cameras. "People and members of the Consortium of the World, I have spent the last two weeks gathering evidence about these four conspirators. Paisley, Colt, Lieutenant Drake, and Captain Via."

The emperor nods slightly to the Merc holding the lieutenant and the captain. The Merc jerks them to their feet and pushes them next to Colt and me. Another Merc pulls Riley back and our hands are forced apart. Riley and Darrell are held at gunpoint by Mercs behind Colt and me.

The emperor continues, "I sent packets to the members of the consortium two days ago. They took their time and painstakingly read over the evidence. This morning, I visited and gathered votes from each member of the Consortium of the World and have personally counted those votes."

"After tallying those votes, I have a verdict." He rolls out a parchment. "I will read the verdict. It is the consensus of this panel of the

Consortium of the World that these four: Paisley, Colt, Lieutenant Drake, and Captain Via be sentenced to immediate death for the charge of treason. I have also attained the signature of the ambassador that he too agrees that his own daughter be sentenced to death because of her traitorous nature and her continued threat to our way of life."

My vision blurs. Everything spins. Colt and the Lieutenant catch me before I fall. The other three stand steadfast. Colt shouts, "Don't we get to defend?"

What am I going to do? I've let everyone down. Our world will never be free. My heart sinks as I stare at the screen with the image of my father. I cannot believe that my father would ever betray me.

Wait, something is wrong with the feed on the monitor. Why is my father repeating the same movement on the television screen? Neither he nor Oliver has changed actions since they came on the screen. I focus for a minute before I realize it's on a loop. It's the same each time. What does that mean?

Have they already been killed?

If they have, then all hope is lost.

"No!" My father's voice pierces through the speakers. The screen above the emperor morphs into a different picture. Every one quiets.

The image is that of Oliver, my father, and the leaders of the Consortium of the World.

"Emperor Richard is lying!" My father addresses the crowd through the mounted monitors. "He did not meet with any of the members of the Consortium of the World. No votes were gathered. They have been held captive just as I was held captive. We managed to break free."

My father takes in a big breath. "We managed to keep our escape secret from the emperor using the expertise of my son, Oliver, through fake images displayed on the security monitors. We also have found help through resistance sympathizers who have helped us keep up this ruse."

My father speaks quickly. "I know that you thought you were going to witness a public execution of traitors, but I have been meeting with the leaders of the world and we have come up with a better solution for our world. Hijacking this media blitz is the only way I knew to deliver this message. I represent not only myself, but the leaders of the world. Every region is represented. I am here to shed light on what is really going on. Please listen to these leaders."

One by one the elders of each country tell of the atrocities that have happened because of the virus and subsequent quarantine. Each horrible account of the atrocities committed in their respective countries is followed by gasps from the crowd. After sharing, each leader publically endorses the new democratic constitution.

The emperor enlists help from the Mercs by his side and scrambles the whole time the leaders are speaking, trying to no avail to find the cut off for the feed. His desperation grows with each failure to shut off the broadcast.

The ambassador says, "We have spent our time huddled together hashing out the fine print. Even though it is a document, it is an ever-changing one. We need to reestablish communication, stabilize the farms, distribute the food, and make sure everyone is given the cure. If the correct dosage is given, there is no need for a booster. The need for a booster is another lie spread by Emperor Richard."

Our captive group watches along with everyone else. My hope increases with each word. Finally giving up on shutting off the broadcast from his perch, the emperor disappears from the balcony. What can he do now? Everyone knows about his treachery. Maybe the emperor will run away. I hope he leaves and is never seen again.

"Fellow citizens, no one from the resistance was trying to reintroduce the virus." My father drops his head. "Since you must know the truth and the whole truth, I have a confession to make. When I was working for the military, I was contracted to develop a machine that would take the DNA out of blood and then be able to replace it with another DNA."

My father stares intently into the monitor. "Unfortunately, I was paired with other scientists who were contracted to make a virus. The virus was to be a bioterrorist weapon that would be used on parts of the world considered enemies. That virus caused the first outbreak. The bioterrorist weapon that should have never been developed in the first place almost wiped out the entire population. Because I was involved in that horrible mistake from the very beginning stages, I have made it my life's work to find and develop a cure. I succeeded thanks entirely to the DNA of my daughter, Paisley. "

"I propose," he begins, spreading his arms wide, "we stop this war and get behind this democratic process..."

A deafening, loud bang resonates from the television and I watch in horror as my father slumps over. The crowd screams as blood pours from his head. Oliver cradles my father. The emperor, his face mad with rage, is wrestled to the ground by the Consortium of the World's new security team. A gun is wrenched out of his hand.

The emperor screams. "Take them men."

More men with guns rush the room and surround the Mercs.

One of the Consortium of the World representatives announces, "The Mercs now are under arrest by the Consortium of the World security. They no longer work for you." He says to the emperor. "You have just been ousted and stripped of power."

The new security personnel quickly lead the handcuffed emperor and his Mercs out of the building.

The crowd cheers. The Mercs responsible for us release their hold, fling off their caps and jackets, and attempt to escape by blending in with the crowd. They are quickly rounded up by the new security. Riley wastes no time getting to my side, pulling me close.

The screen goes black. I look at Riley. "I need to find my father."

"Does anyone know where the ambassador is?" Colt yells to the new security men now surrounding us.

"I do." A security man standing by Riley holds out his hand. "I'm John. At your service. Follow me."

Riley shakes John's hand. The lieutenant, the captain, Riley, Colt, Darrell and I all follow John. He leads us into the building. We make our way quickly to the room that was showing on the screen earlier. The room where my father is. Inside, sobs echo throughout the room. Members of the Consortium of the World and the new security surround my father.

Forcing my way to my father's side. I drop to my knees. "Father?" I take his hand.

He is bleeding and Oliver shakes his head. I realize that my father doesn't have long. His eyes brim with tears when he spies me. He reaches up. "My sweet girl." Then the look in his eyes changes as he looks over my shoulder and his face lights up. "Oh, Olivia. My beautiful Olivia."

"Why is he calling me Olivia?" I squeeze his hand and turn around. Captain Via and Lieutenant Drake stand behind us.

"Yes, Ross, it's me." Captain Via squats down beside my father and grasps his other hand. "I'm sorry. I thought you were dead at first. I didn't realize you and Oliver were still alive until you had already married the queen. I thought you were better off not knowing I was still alive."

A tear runs down my mother's cheek. "I thought you and Oliver were better off where you were." She sniffs in another tear. "I'm sorry I should have told you."

"Don't cry, my wife." My father wipes a tear from my mother's cheek and reaches his hand toward Oliver. Struggling to make a sound, he finally grunts out. "Oliver, this is your mother. This is my family. We all made it. We're here together. I'm so happy."

Tears stream down my face. My father is dying. We finally find each other and now my father is going to die.

"Olivia." My father whispers as my mother leans in. "I always loved you. I always will."

My mother nods. "I know, me too, my love." She leans down and kisses his forehead. His grip loosens from my hand.

My father is gone.

Chapter 25

Everything that is me hurts. My heart, my soul, my body. I miss my father so much I can't function for a few weeks. I am taken to the infirmary and while I recuperate all of the specifics of the new world order are voted on.

A new constitution is drafted. Lots of compromises. The whole world will be ruled by a democratic vote. A first. A great start for world peace. In a way, I'm glad to have missed it all.

Riley never leaves my side although he and I don't speak much at first. I'm not strong enough. As time passes, a numbness takes over and I don't hurt as much. After a few weeks, all that is left is a hole in my being that my father once occupied.

I am glad to have Captain Via, my mother, and Oliver, my new found brother. The two of them are great, visiting many times. We share stories and with the connection of my father to link our past and the young prince and princess to connect our future, we are well on our way to building a long-lasting relationship. I love my newly found family. I guess in a way it's poetic that on the day I lost one loved one, I gained so many more.

My mother, Captain Via, agrees to work with Lieutenant Drake to travel to each of the countries to set up communication and democratic rule. A United Nations is established and the governments become part of one entity, living in peace. Worldwide distribution of food is established and volunteer fire and police departments are set up in each country. Locals make the specific rules about their products. Barter systems are in place. The virus cure is free. The outlook for total and complete peace is positive.

My brother, Oliver, begins his job to train others in the technology. Even though we had a twelve-year hiatus from technology and communications, the world quickly catches up. Oliver plans to travel the globe.

It is a joyful day when I return to the compound. Tury and my half-brother and half-sister are living happily with me in the castle. It is amazing how resilient children are.

Gretel is busy in the lab and making the Becker Bavarian a home. She surprises Colt and the rest of us with the news that he will be a father come next summer. She'll be a natural mother. I can't wait to spoil my new niece or nephew. Very exciting!

Riley becomes instrumental and an intricate part of running the day to day operations of Aunt Sandra's lands. Riley and I are still dating. When we get older we may marry, but for now, we are taking it one day at a time.

In late spring, I decide to visit my Ferris wheel farm. It's been a long time.

Riding through the countryside, I realize that I'm no longer an "Uncounted."

This moonlit evening, the giant Ferris wheel casts an ominous shadow beckoning to me. Left over from a long forgotten carnival, the rusty, dilapidated wheel remains workable.

The Ferris wheel has been on our farm as long as I can remember. I love it, even though it's rusty, tattered, and the color of a rotten banana peel. Its uniqueness makes it special. I climb into the bottom chair and hit the lever to take my ride. The brisk Bavarian air pricks my face like a hundred needles.

From my perch, I see hints of grass peeking out of the shimmering snow and watch the hills roll into the evening darkness. I'm overcome by a tranquil sense of freedom. My thrilled heart beats and my face flushes.

The creaking interrupts my thoughts as the Ferris wheel slowly begins its ascent. Complete joy surges through me. I spread my arms. I'm finally free. I am a person. I'm not an Uncounted.

I matter.

The End

ZUGSPITZE GERMANY

ABOUT THE AUTHOR

Susan Womble is an award-winning author. Her first novel "Newt's World: Beginnings" won the 2008 Gold Medal Florida Book Award. "Newt's World: Beginnings" is also on the 2009-2013 Just Read Florida Recommended Reading List. Her writing credits also include "Newt's World Beginnings Workbook" (teacher's and student's editions), the second in the series entitled, "Newt's World: Internal Byte" and accompanying workbook. Susan Womble lives in Tallahassee, Florida with her family. She is a National Board Certified teacher with a career of teaching grades K-12th in the areas of reading, special education, language arts, math, social studies, and the profoundly handicapped. While teaching overseas in Hohenfels, Germany, she travelled extensively throughout Europe. Visit www.susanwomble.com for more information. Contact her at susan.womble@gmail.com.

www.ingramcontent.com/pod-product-compliance
Lightning Source LLC
Chambersburg PA
CBHW071002280626
47160CB00014B/12